Old Wounds

GIACOMO GIAMMATTEO

Also by Giacomo Giammatteo:

Fiction:
Friendship & Honor Series:
MURDER TAKES TIME: Friendship & Honor: Book I
MURDER HAS CONSEQUENCES: Friendship & Honor: Book II
MURDER TAKES PATIENCE: Friendship & Honor Book III

Blood Flows South Series:
A BULLET FOR CARLOS: Blood Flows South: Book I
FINDING FAMILY: Blood Flows South: the Beginning (A Novella)
A BULLET FROM DOMINIC: Blood Flows South: Book II

Redemption Series:
Necessary Decisions
Old Wounds

Non-Fiction:
No Mistakes Careers
NO MISTAKES RESUMES: Book One of No Mistakes Careers
NO MISTAKES INTERVIEWS: Book Two of No Mistakes Careers

Sanctuary Tales (True Stories From An Animal Sanctuary)
WHISKERS & BEAR (Coming soon)

Old Wounds

A REDEMPTION NOVEL

GIACOMO GIAMMATTEO

INFERNO PUBLISHING COMPANY

OLD WOUNDS
by Giacomo Giammatteo

INFERNO PUBLISHING COMPANY

For more information about this book, visit
www.giacomogiammatteo.com

ISBN: 978-1-940313-10-8 (ebook)
ISBN: 978-1-940313-11-5 (print)

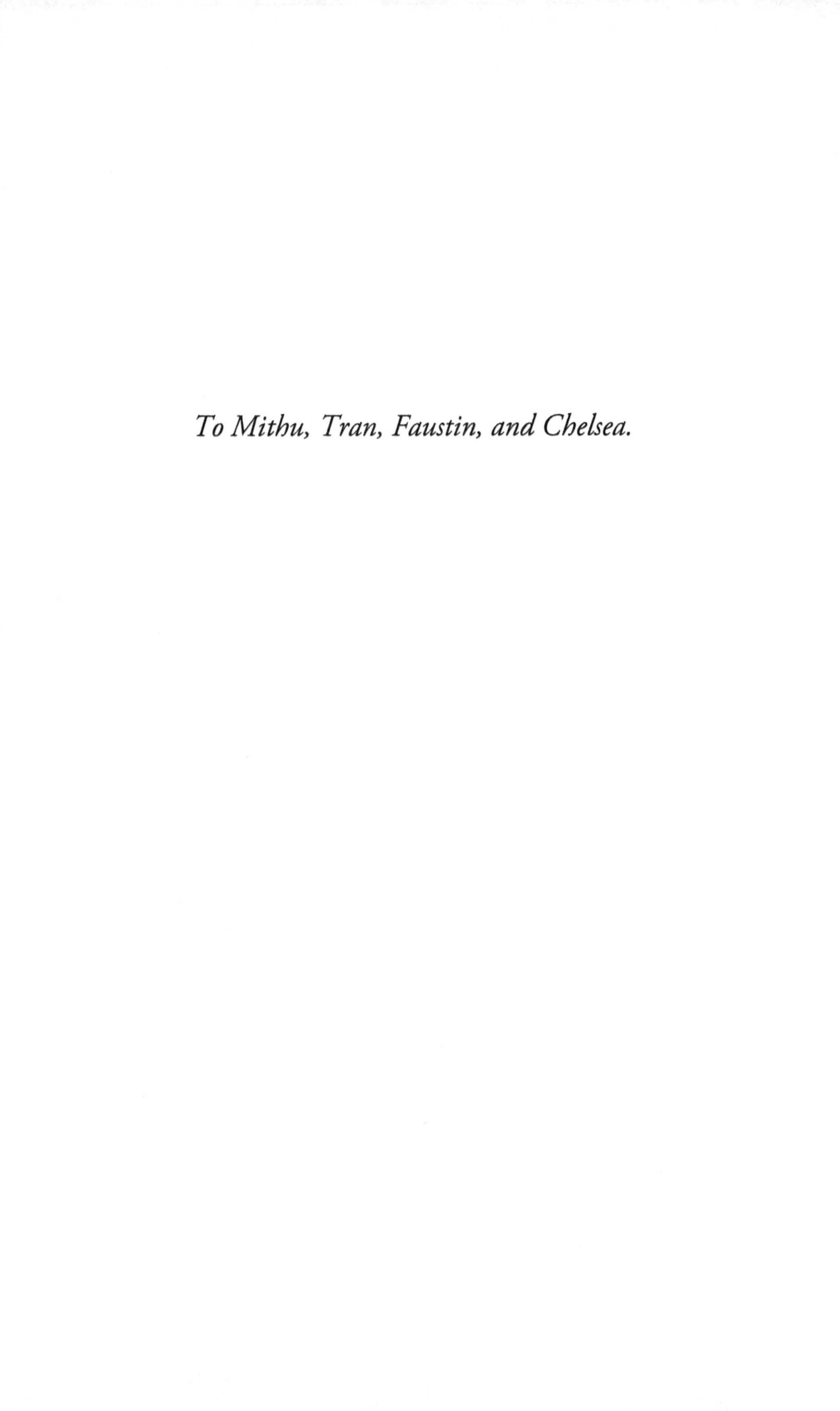

To Mithu, Tran, Faustin, and Chelsea.

Lines are meant to be crossed. Laws are meant to be broken.

Gino Cataldi

CHAPTER 1

A SURREPTITIOUS MEETING

Houston, Texas

Barbara stared into the mirror and practiced her line. She wanted the recording to be just right—after all, it would be the last time anyone heard her, if things didn't go well.

She pursed her lips and said, "My name is Barbara Camwyck. If you're watching this video, I'm dead."

Barbara rehearsed it a few more times, then thought about how her life was about to change. All the shit she'd been through would finally pay off.

She slipped on a comfortable pair of jeans, turned sideways to admire herself in the mirror, and then stepped into the closet to select a top. Something light, as it promised to be another unusually warm day for January. She decided on a cream-colored wrap top, one of her more expensive casual blouses. Sometimes subtlety worked best, but this top would work better today, especially with the sliver of skin peeking out at her waist.

Barbara reached up and pulled a pair of Giuseppe Zanotti Crystal-Embellished sandals from the shelf in her closet. They would be the perfect complement. She slipped them on, stepped back, and smiled.

She then went to the kitchen. As she brewed tea she thought about her life. It wasn't as if she hadn't done well for herself, but doing well and 7 million dollars was different; in fact, doing well and 7 million dollars was another stratosphere. And if her blackmail scheme went as planned 7 million was exactly what she'd have.

She poured the tea, and then made a call, careful to use the burner she had purchased for just such an occasion. It had gotten to the point where a disposable phone was almost a necessity—nothing more than another monthly expense—at least in her current line of work.

A woman with a smoky voice answered the phone. "Hello?"

Barbara kicked her open-toe sandals up on the coffee table and said, "It's Barbara. I'll be ready in a few minutes. How long will this take?"

"Stop by on your way. It won't take me more than a few minutes."

"And you're sure it will work. I can't afford to have this fucked up."

"It'll work. Don't worry."

A half hour later, Barbara exited the 610 Loop and found her way to the dingy barbecue place where she had arranged the meeting. It was not a place she would frequent, but for today it worked perfectly; neither one of them would be recognized.

She leaned forward and adjusted the rearview mirror so she could fix her hair. Afterward, she applied lipstick, looked in the mirror again, cleared her throat, and then started the video.

"My name is Barbara Camwyck," she said. "If you're watching this video, I'm dead."

Barbara finished recording, straightened her blouse, then spoke into her mic and said, "Okay, I'm going in now."

She opened the car door, got out, and walked into the restaurant, thankful it at least had air conditioning. From the looks of the outside she had wondered. Half a dozen people stood in front of her, a sign that maybe the food was good. *Or maybe it's just cheap.*

Camwyck craned her neck, scanning the place until she found the person she was searching for, sitting at a table near the back, in the corner. *At least they followed directions. Camwyck needed that table so the mic didn't pick up unnecessary sounds.*

She weaved her way through a mob of sweaty construction workers, careful not to touch them, and not daring to inhale the odors until she passed them. She pulled a chair out and set her purse in the seat next to it. "It's been a long time," Camwyck said.

"Not long enough."

Camwyck smiled. "Not interested in pleasantries? Good. Let's get right to business."

"Business? That's what you call this?"

The comment drew another smile from Camwyck. "I guess in your world they call it leverage, but I see little difference. Blackmail or leverage. It's all the same in the end."

"Let's discuss *leverage* then."

Camwyck pushed a thumbnail drive across the table. "You know the terms. I have all the proof I need. After you pay, you'll never hear from me again."

"Remind me of the amount."

"I'm surprised you've forgotten. It's an easy number to remember. Seven million."

Camwyck ignored the scoffing sound prior to them speaking. "Easy to remember doesn't mean easy to arrange—especially in cash."

"I'm certain you'll think of something," Camwyck said. "You've always been creative."

"It will take me a while."

"That's fine," Camwyck said, "But if we don't do this within the next month, I may have to resort to other means."

A waitress walked by and stopped at their table. "Ya'll need to place an order at the counter. Then they'll get you a number."

"Thank you," Camwyck said, and stood. She tossed two twenties on the table. "Order what you want. And you can keep the drive to inspect. I have the original."

"One more thing," the guest said, scooting the chair closer to the table. "If you try to come back on me, I'll make sure it's the last thing you do." A pause preceded a glare. "You understand that, don't you?"

"I understand," Barbara said, "but you don't have to worry. Seven million is enough for me. Once we conclude our business, you'll never hear from me again."

"If you try—"

"I won't," Barbara said, and she exited the restaurant.

As she walked across the parking lot, Barbara punched a number from the recently dialed list on her phone. She'd have to remember to delete that when she was done. "Did you get it?"

"Perfectly. Good sound and good video."

"Good. I need a copy, but I want the original hidden where it won't be found."

"Not a problem. I'll call when it's done."

"No. I can't know either. If I don't know, I can't tell anyone."

"However you want it," the man said.

"Good. I'm throwing this phone away now. In the future, if anyone calls you from this number, or from my regular number, ignore it. In fact, run! If I need you I'll make contact the same way as the first time."

"Good luck."

"Thanks," Barbara said. "I'll need it."

CHAPTER 2

DRUGS AND LIES

Houston, Texas

I wiped sweat from my brow and moved a cardboard box from the fake homeless shelter, leaving just enough room to see. I checked my gun—safety was off. I didn't like killing people to start the day, but I would gladly make an exception for Rico.

Two years ago, I collared Rico on a routine drug bust but his high-priced lawyers got him off. Since then, he'd probably been responsible for the death of half a dozen kids.

Should have killed him when I had the chance.

A beige Mazda pulled into the parking lot and nestled beside a light pole. Dave, my partner, got out and walked around, lighting a smoke as he kicked at loose gravel with his brown Lucchese boots. He pretended to stare at the ground but his eyes shifted left and right. He was ready.

Four unmarked cars were positioned within a few hundred yards. I was stationed as close-in back-up, ready to go in at the first sign of trouble.

Halfway through Dave's second smoke, the dealers pulled up in a black Lexus. Three guys got out. One of them checked Dave's car, the other two kept their eyes on Dave. A fourth guy stayed in the driver's seat. I squinted, trying to make them out. I expected Rico to be here, but it looked as if he wasn't, and if he wasn't here now, he wouldn't show at all.

The no-show pissed me off, but busting these guys would hurt Rico, and that would be better than nothing.

I leaned forward so the wind didn't make noise, and whispered into the mic. "Three outside, one in."

"Got it," came the reply.

Dave was talking to one of the dealers. The other two had their hands on guns. I prayed there'd be no trouble. If they started something, it would be tough to contain from here. A dealer frisked Dave, who then opened the trunk and handed a gym bag to him. *I* knew there was $130 grand in there, but this guy just looked inside then closed it up, didn't even count it. The hairs on the back of my neck bristled. I got on the horn.

"Something might be up," I said. "The guy didn't even count the money. Be ready."

The lead dealer turned, or at least I presumed he was the honcho from the fine leather jacket and the shades he wore. He said something to one of his men—the one wearing a dark blue hoodie over a T-shirt—then headed toward the Lexus. The guy wearing the hoodie drew his gun and fired, one shot into Dave's head.

"Officer down! Goddamnit, Dave's down!"

I raced from my hiding place, gun in hand, dodging bullets. When I got close enough to matter, meaning fire a shot, I opened up, taking down the hoodie on the second shot. *At least the prick that shot Dave got his.* Another one fell after two or three more shots. The lead dealer and another one—I think the one who drove—were in the car taking off. I knelt, fired until I was empty.

Two of the backup vehicles cut them off, and a third one pulled next to their car. The backup team opened fire, taking out the driver with the first volley. The leader got out of the passenger side, firing. I ducked behind the Lexus, popped in another clip, then crouched and made my way to the driver's side. I took a couple of deep breaths, and wondered for the first time in years if I should say a prayer; instead, I took two more breaths to calm my nerves, then peeked from behind the bumper. The leader had gotten out and was facing the back of the car. He fired once. I pulled the trigger twice, hitting him in the chest. When he fell, I emptied my gun.

I ran back to check Dave. Blood pooled on the asphalt parking lot under him, and there was a gaping hole under his left eye, where his left cheek used to be. The back side of his head was almost missing.

"Goddamn." I kicked the car, then kicked it again. "Goddamnit."

I knelt next to Dave, holding him. Inside I was crying but I managed to keep it there; I wasn't much the crying type. The last time I cried in public was when my wife died.

"Anybody call a bus?" one of the other officers yelled.

"No need to rush," I said.

I felt a hand on my shoulder and looked up at Bobby Lynch, an old timer from the department.

"Gino, I'm sorry, man. I know what it's like to lose a partner."

"I can't believe those fuckers killed him like that," I said, but what I thought was—*I should have been there for him. I was supposed to protect him.*

Bobby helped me up and held onto me afterward. "It's the drugs. They turn everybody into an animal."

All I could do was nod. We waited around until they finished processing the scene, then Bobby said, "You got a ride?"

"I rode with Dave."

He grabbed my arm and started toward his car. "C'mon, I'll drive you back to the station."

As I followed Bobby to his car, the smell of fajitas from a restaurant drifted across the parking lot. Dave loved fajitas. Wherever he went, I hoped they had an endless supply.

Bobby dropped me off at the door, and I went inside. Captain Gladys Cooper had left orders at the desk for me to see her as soon as I arrived. Why she hadn't called me I'll never know, but that was how Gladys worked.

She also hated it when I called her Gladys. Most of the guys called her Coop. She had taken a liking to that and wore it like a badge of honor, like she was really one of the guys. Rumor had it that she played for the other side as far as sexual preferences go. The fact that she arm-wrestled the guys and won about half her matches didn't provide much of a defense—if she wanted it. Either way, it didn't matter to me. I had a lot more to worry about than who my captain might be sharing her bed with.

Cindy met me in the hall with a cup of black coffee. "I heard about Dave. I'm sorry."

"Yeah."

After an awkward moment of silence, Cindy walked toward Coop's office.

"She's waiting for you."

I went into the office wearing a frown, a little agitated that I had to be here. But things had to be done when an officer was shot, things had to be done, and preparing for the press was of paramount importance. "Hey, Gladys. Nasty stuff, huh?"

She got up from a reading chair and gave me a big hug. "More than nasty. It plain sucks. These drugs will kill us all if we don't watch out."

She offered me a seat and punched a button on the intercom. "Cindy, will you please get me more tea? And bring your recorder."

I sat on the edge of my seat, feet planted on the floor. "I know we need to get a statement out, but let's do it quick, I need to tell Mindy first, before she hears it on her own."

"Mindy's already being notified. And by the way, I don't mind you not calling me captain, but I wish you'd stop with Gladys. I've always hated that name; besides, that's what Cybil calls me."

I nodded. Now I knew why she hated the name. Cybil was the mayor's wife, and could be more than a bitch when she wanted. "What do you need?"

"Wait until Cindy gets here. She's bringing a recorder. We need this to be official."

Cindy arrived a moment later and sat next to me, but not before handing Coop her cup of tea.

"Whenever you're ready, Gino," Coop said.

Cindy turned the recorder to on.

I took a deep breath, cleared my head, and related the events leading up to Dave getting shot and the subsequent shootout.

"And we're clean on this?" Gladys asked.

"We're clean. There's video to back it up."

The captain shifted in her seat and gestured to Cindy. "Turn that damn thing off," she said, then looked at me. When she had witnessed Cindy turn off the recorder, she said, "I'm not trying to rub salt in the wound, Gino, but how *the hell* did this go wrong?"

I shook my head. "Dave gave them the money. They didn't even count it, just looked inside the bag then shot him. From my position nothing seemed out of order. I think the bastards just wanted the money." Silence followed for a moment while I thought. "I should have been there with him. If there were two of us…"

"Then we'd have two dead cops."

I heard what Coop said, and in some remote corner of my mind I agreed, but I didn't say anything. I couldn't. After a brief moment, I stood. "If that's all you've got…"

"Whoa, Cataldi. Not so fast."

I turned to see Coop with her hand outstretched. "Sidearm, please."

I handed her my gun. I didn't like it, but I knew it was coming. It happened with any shooting. "I know, psych in the morning, right?"

"You know the drill," she said as I headed out.

All the way home, images of the day haunted me—the dealer with the hoodie shooting Dave, his blood on the pavement, the chunk of his face missing…him lying there with blank eyes staring at the sky. I punched the steering wheel two or three times, cursing everyone I could think of, including God and all of his angels. Why the hell didn't He take care of the good people? First my wife, Mary, and now Dave. As I drove, I thought of a few more people I wanted to curse, but most of all I cursed myself.

I should have been there with him.

It had turned dark on my way home. I flipped on the headlights as I exited the freeway toward my house, and soon found myself parked in the driveway next to my son's car. I gathered my thoughts one more time, and then made a vow to get justice for Dave.

It's time for Rico Moreno to die.

CHAPTER 3

RICO SHOWS UP

Houston, Texas

I kicked leaves out of the way as I walked up the sidewalk. A fat squirrel chittered when I passed by. Sooner or later I'd have to take a broom to those leaves, but I couldn't think about that now. I had to focus on working myself into a good mood for Ron. He'd had a tough go of it since his mother died, and our relationship had deteriorated. I grabbed the door handle and forced a smile and hoped my voice might reflect it. He was sitting at the kitchen table and looked to be sulking.

"How's it going, Ron?"

"It's not."

It was definitely a sulk, and I wasn't in the mood for it. "What's the matter?"

He stared at me with a hurt look in his eyes, although it was bordering anger. "You forgot, didn't you?"

"Forgot what?" As soon as I said it, I felt like an ass. "Shit. I'm sorry I screwed up your birthday. Jesus Christ, how could I forget your birthday?"

"Same way you did last year, on my *sixteenth*. It must be getting easier." Ron got up and left the room. I think there were tears in his eyes. I know there were in his voice.

I went after him. "Hang on. I'm sorry, I had a tough day."

He spun around and glared. "Mom had *lots* of tough days, and she *never* forgot. Not even when she was dying."

I grabbed his arm but he tore away from me and raced up the steps to his room. By the time I hit the fourth step I realized the futility of going after him. No way he was listening to anything I said right now. Maybe ever.

I grabbed a bottle of water and went to the family room to watch the news. Before half an hour was up, Ron came down the steps. He grabbed a baseball cap from the rack on the wall and started for the door.

"Ron, wait a minute. I want to talk."

"Nothing to talk about," he said, but didn't look at me, just reached for his hat.

I quickly got out of the chair, and grabbed his arm.

He shook it off, and screamed, "Let *go* of me."

I stared. His eyes were glazed. The kind of glaze I hated more than anything—drugs. Ron had already had one run in with drugs—one that I knew about, but it was likely more than that. I'm sure he was more experienced than I'd like to admit.

I waited a moment too long then ran after him. He was already in his truck, heading out. Tempted to let the situation go, I followed instead, slowing as I neared the bend. A couple of miles later he pulled into the parking lot of a corner store, choosing a spot off to the side near the dumpster. I passed the store, turned left down a small street with a row of older houses, and parked in the driveway of one that looked as if no one was home.

I got out of the car, took my spare gun with me, and shoved it into my coat pocket. I moved to a spot where I could see him. There was no way in hell he could see me. Spying on him stirred a sick feeling in my gut. I grew up thinking parents were supposed to *trust* their kids. for a long time, I did trust him. Now…now I was following him and hiding behind trees.

As those thoughts roiled in my gut, a blue van pulled alongside Ron. Three guys got out. They looked to be teenagers, Ron's age or a little older. It didn't take long to confirm my worst fears. After a few surreptitious glances, Ron gave one of the kids what looked like a small wad of cash. He received a bag of something—drugs, I presumed—in return.

Motherfucker! I'm gonna kill them.

Any guilty feelings I'd had about following him disappeared.

Ron got in his truck and headed north. The blue van headed south. I was torn between who to follow but decided on them. I knew where Ron would be later.

I raced to my car, backed out, and quickly caught up to them. I stayed two cars behind them, close enough to keep a watch but not be noticed. After a few miles they turned into a What-a-Burger, pulled into an empty spot and went inside. I parked on the other side of the lot, walked to their car and opened up the driver's-side to get in. I damn near gagged with the first breath—beer, weed, and stale cigarettes. After composing myself, I climbed in, getting behind the back seat. *They better not be long.*

They returned in ten minutes. The driver got in first then the passenger and the one in the back. As soon as the doors closed, I moved, shoving my gun under the chin of the guy in front of me, the kid in the back seat. "Nobody move or I'll blow this fucker's head off."

The driver turned. I reached up and smacked the side of his head with the gun, then jammed it back into the guy's throat. Blood spurted from the driver's scalp wound.

"You fucking cut me, dude."

"Move again and I'll kill you."

I must have put the right amount of tone in that threat because they shut up. "Driver, put your hands on the dashboard, palms down." I stared at the passenger. "Face me, and wrap your arms around the seat. Keep your hands locked."

I turned to the guy in the back seat and cocked the hammer.

"Whoa! Whoa, man. You don't want to do this."

"Shut the fuck up," I said through gritted teeth. "I ought to kill you fuckers."

"Give him the drugs!" The guy next to me said. When the passenger didn't respond fast enough, Back-Seat screamed louder. "Give him the *fucking* drugs."

I yanked on back-seat's hair and held him, then shoved the gun in the passenger's face. "The drugs, *now.*"

He shoved a few bags of pills in my direction. I pressed the barrel of the gun into his cheek. "*All* the drugs."

With that he reached around to the floor.

"Come up with anything but drugs in that hand, and you won't see tomorrow."

He lifted a backpack from the floor. When he turned to me, I saw the sweat beading on his forehead. "It's all here. I swear."

I believed him this time. "All right, here's what we're going to do—"

My phone rang, and though tempted to ignore it, I knew it was Chicky by the 'Love in This Club' ringtone. Chicky Ramirez was my best informant. I had told him to be on the lookout for Rico.

Keeping the gun trained on the guy next to me, I answered the phone. "Yeah."

"I found him."

Goddamnit. "Where?"

"A new club down on Richmond—Sueños. Better hurry. Don't know how long the dude will stay put."

"On my way."

I had the plate number for these kids and felt certain they weren't skipping town. I could get them anytime. Rico was another story. "You fuckers are lucky," I said to the kid next to me. "But if you ever come back to this area again, anywhere near it, I'll kill *every* fuckin' one of you, and then I'll dump your bodies in the swamps." I gave each one a glare. "Clear?"

"We won't," Back-Seat said, and the others chimed in.

I walked to the dumpster and emptied the backpack. They couldn't see me from where they were, and I was willing to bet they wouldn't go dumpster diving with people around. I got in my car and raced toward town.

It took me almost thirty minutes to get to Richmond. I found Chicky parked with a good view of the front door. I pulled up next to him.

"He's still inside," Chicky said.

"I'll be in the back of the lot. Call me when he comes out."

"I'll call, but I ain't coming with you, man."

"I don't want you with me."

I tried calling Ron while I searched for a place to sit. The call went to voice mail, which meant that either he was still out or he was home and afraid I'd recognize his "high voice." He knew I could tell when he was on something by the difference in his voice. Fifteen minutes later, I tried calling again, and then twenty minutes after that. Frustration was setting in. I still hadn't heard from Chicky, and Ron not answering pissed me off, but the longer it went on, the "pissed off" grew into worry.

Suppose he wrapped his truck around a tree, or some druggie stabbed him?

With drugs involved who the hell knew. I thought back to a saying my mother said whenever she wanted to make me feel bad. She said,

A parent never stops worrying from the time their first child is born.

I thought she might have been exaggerating, which she did at times, playing the martyr. But not on this one. This one she got right.

As I brooded over my horrible day, Chicky called.

"Yeah."

"It's on, dude. He's coming out. Got two of his *guns* with him."

"Thanks. I owe you."

"Careful, Gino. This fucker will take you out."

"I know."

"Good luck, man."

I waited for Rico's Escalade to roll out of the lot. I pulled in tight behind it, damn near hugging the bumper. Rico was in the back. His driver shared the front with another *gun*. A couple of times they switched lanes. By the third time, they knew they had a tail. I could tell by the way they continually switched lanes and checked the rearview mirror immediately afterward.

They turned left on Fondren then left again on Westheimer, the cruising street. Half a block later they settled into an empty parking lot. When I pulled in behind them, their doors opened. Rico's two guns stepped out.

I got out, my Beretta within easy reach. *"Buenas noches, señores."*

The back door opened. Rico stepped out, dressed to the nines in silk, gold dripping off him. "Don't try your cowboy Spanish on me, Gino. I know who the fuck you are."

"Just so that you are fully educated," I said, "I'm from South Philadelphia. I'm not a cowboy."

"You got a warrant, *Philadelphia* cowboy?"

"No."

Rico looked to his right. "Did my driver do something wrong? Forget a turn signal? Go too fast?"

"No."

"So what the fuck do you want? I'm a busy man."

"I came to kill you."

Rico's eyes narrowed for a second, but then he laughed. "Kill me? Just like that? Gino the cop is going to kill me for nothing?" He looked at me for a long time, then he took a step forward, and eyed me up and down. "Or is it for old Dave Skelton?"

I scanned the area. No one was around. His men were at ease. The events of the day came to a head. I expected to have to beat a confession out of him, but he spilled it right out. Waved what he'd done to Dave in my face. Proud of it.

Something inside of me snapped. I pulled my gun, stepped toward his men, and…*almost* pulled the trigger. I was holding the gun pointed at the driver's face and shaking as if I had the chills.

I was still shaking when one of Rico's men went for his piece. That sent me over the edge. I aimed my gun at him and squeezed the trigger. The bullet hit him in the chest. Rico's second man moved, so I put a bullet his head. Then I turned to Rico. Fear shone in his eyes. Hard core fear.

"This is for Dave. And all the other people you killed." I put the gun close to his cheek and squeezed three times. After one more in each of his men, I got in the car and drove home, stopping at Cypress Creek to get rid of the gun.

By the time I hit the street leading to my house, my head was spinning, and pounding. It felt as if I were ready to explode.

What the hell have I done?

CHAPTER 4

SURPRISE MEETING

Houston, Texas

Ron's car was parked in the driveway, which was the first good news I'd had all day. I calmed myself before going in, determined to make things work, maybe even mend the rift between us. The lights were off upstairs. He might be asleep, but more likely pretending. I began to climb the steps, then stopped. I was tired and didn't want to risk another fight. Or was it cowardice causing me to rationalize? Afraid to face the drug problem? Not convinced Ron was doing drugs, but knowing in my heart he was.

A bottle of Cannonau di Sardegna called to me from the wine cooler. As much as I wanted to open it, I didn't. I took a shower instead, trying to wash the filth off. I felt slimy, like the scum I arrested. My hands and arms shook, and my gut churned. I turned the faucet to make the water hotter, hoping the shock would stop the shaking. It didn't work.

After a few minutes I got out, dried off and dressed. I put on a sweater to stop the shivering. I still felt dirty, so I opened the wine, sat in the dark and drank. A couple of hours later I dropped the bottle in the trashcan and went to bed.

Dreams haunted me—the shocked expression on the faces of Rico's men, the smell of fear on the kids in the van. Worst of all was the terror in Rico's eyes when he knew he was about to die. By five A.M. I concluded there was no sense lying in bed awake. I got up, showered again and got coffee. I left Ron a note, which took me damn near twenty minutes to write, then I worried all the way in to work whether I'd said the right things. Twice I almost turned around to go rip it up, but laziness disguised as common sense got the better of me.

My body screamed for more coffee but I figured I'd get more once I got to the station. I called the department shrink and left him a message, requesting an appointment at eight o'clock. I guessed I was fortunate it was a department shrink, as a real one might take a month or two to get an appointment.

As fate would have it, an accident on the freeway caused traffic to come to a standstill. About every three minutes I found myself looking at my watch. I chose the watch even though there was a dashboard clock because Mary had given me this watch the Christmas before she died, and I wanted to make use of it, didn't want it to become just another watch.

I had a thing about not wanting to be late, even though it was the shrink and my inclination was to not care. I should have stuck to the dashboard clock or the one on my iPhone, because every time I glanced at the watch on my wrist, I got depressed. The watch held a special place in my heart. In the past, I counted on Mary for advice. She always had great suggestions on how to handle Ron, and how to deal with neighbors. When we were browsing at the book store, she'd suggest what books I should read, and she was usually right. She even recommended movies to watch. Now I had no one to talk to about anything. If I didn't watch out, I'd be seeing a shrink about that, too.

I blamed a lot of things on the church. The paranoia about being late was one of them. Those damned nuns used to position themselves by the doors with a yardstick or pointer in their hands, waiting to whack anyone who was late—and them, with their internal "nun-clocks" set to know what time classes started down to a millisecond.

When I was in second grade I began wondering if they had invisible watches so I put it to the test. At recess I asked Sister Frances what time it was. She said 'you have thirty seconds left.' I grabbed her wrist to see if I could feel the watch. The next thing I remembered was two sharp whacks to the back of my head.

I learned two things that day: Nuns really *did* have a "nun-clock," and you should *never* grab a nun by the wrist. My head hurt for a week. By the time I got out of third grade I was never late for anything again.

I did a little bobbing and weaving to skirt the traffic, and soon found myself inching through the skyscrapers, the sun shining off the mirrored glass blinding me. I'd been a lot of places, but Houston might have been the cleanest, neatest city I'd ever been to. That thought brought Philadelphia to mind, with its narrow streets littered with cheesesteak wrappers, hawkers on the corners selling pretzels and hot dogs, and an inner city that bustled with people of all ethnic groups. The memories made me realize that comparing Philly and Houston wasn't fair—one was old and blue-collar tough, and the other built brand-spanking new from oil money.

My ruminations ended as I pulled into the station parking lot. I was half an hour early; Sister Frances would have been proud. I checked my messages when I got in. The shrink had called and postponed my appointment, so I got to work reviewing case files.

Halfway through the stack on my desk, Cindy called.

"Hey, darlin'." I tried my best Texas accent, which wasn't very good.

"You still don't say it right, Gino. It's haaaay darlin, with the *hey* drawn out."

"Okay, so what do you want?"

"Now that's the South Philly detective I've grown to love." She paused. "Coop wants to see you in thirty minutes, and you know she's as particular as you about being late."

I took Cindy's advice and, at 8:45, I started for Coop's office. I stopped by Karl's desk and handed him a piece of paper with the plate number from last night written on it. "Run this for me, will you, Karl?"

"I'll have it for you later."

I arrived at Coop's office ten minutes early and, as I approached the last thirty feet of hallway, her door opened. Coop stepped out with a young man who looked vaguely familiar. I was almost ready to say something, but fortunately didn't, because it struck me where I'd seen him—he was the kid from last night, the one in the back seat of the van.

Fuck! I turned, desperate for a place to hide. I ducked into the men's room a half dozen steps away. *What's he doing here? How did he know I was a cop?*

Footsteps sounded in the hall. I sweated it out in a stall and listened for the sound of footsteps to fade. Then, I waited another full minute at least, then opened the door and peeked both ways. When I felt safe, I turned toward Coop's office. Cindy was at her desk, typing.

"She in there?"

Cindy looked at her watch. "She's waiting. You're just in time—one minute and counting."

I reached for the doorknob, then turned back to Cindy. "By the way, who was that kid who just left?"

"Some undercover cop from Montgomery County. Why?"

I almost swallowed my tongue. *Undercover cop. What the fuck.* I managed to compose myself. "No reason. He just looked familiar."

I opened the door to the captain's office, a lump in my throat as big as a peach. "Coop, how's it going?"

She didn't smile, just held me with her beady eyes. "So on the day when I'm gonna kick your ass you coincidentally decide to call me Coop. Very convenient, Cataldi."

I mustered all the bravado I could. "Kick my ass for what? I already called psych. I already have an appointment."

"You know why you're here, and it has nothing to do with psych."

I was about to say something when she threw the paper on the desk. I picked it up to read. The headlines blared at me as loud as her voice.

'Eight dead in one day.'

I read the article without saying a word. It went on to describe the unfortunate death of Officer Dave Skelton, and then listed the seven suspected drug dealers who died, and three of them were *not* as a result of the unfortunate sting operation. The author of the article posed the question as to whether this was retaliation.

"Well?" Coop asked.

"Well what?"

Coop pushed the paper aside. "Where were you last night?"

"Home, with my kid."

"Mayor Johnson called the Chief, and he's all over my ass. That's one cop and *seven* dead drug dealers in one day. The national news is going to have a field day with this. We'll look like the Old West."

I knew when she said the mayor called that it was really his throat-cutting, back-stabbing wife Cybil. At this time of day, old Rusty Johnson was either asleep or on the golf course, and in either case he wouldn't have disturbed his pleasure long enough to call the Chief.

"Captain, I'm not sorry Rico's dead, but what do you want me to do about it?"

She walked around her desk and got within inches of my face. "I'll tell you what I think. I think you went home, maybe tied one on, then got feeling bad about your partner. Maybe you drank some more, then you grabbed one of your spare guns and went out and killed Rico Moreno and his men."

"You're a—"

She held up her hand. "*Don't*. I'd rather you not lie to me, so please don't speak."

I remained silent while she paced.

"Is your boy having drug problems again?"

I almost fell over with that one. *How did she know?* I waited, probably too long. "A little."

She slammed her hand on the desk and shoved a pen holder aside. "He either *is* or he isn't."

I swallowed pride, a lot of it. I hated sharing personal information, especially with my boss. "He is."

"I'm taking you off Narcotics."

I almost went to my knees. "Don't do it, Coop. Please?"

She sat behind her desk, fiddled with a folder, then looked at me with those probing eyes. "We had *another* incident last night. A couple of kids were robbed of drugs and they swear it was a cop who did it."

I swallowed too hard. The kid must have made me. "That's a new one— kids report cops for stealing their drugs? Come on, Captain, if you're looking for a reason to move me out of Narcotics, charge me with something and get it over with."

She stared for a moment longer, then lowered her head to focus on work that lay on her desk. "Get out of here. Go see your psych. I'll let you know what I decide."

"Yes, Captain," I said, and left the office.

I almost ran to Karl's desk, relieved when I saw him there. I managed to speak with a calm, easy voice. "Karl, that plate I asked you to run, forget about it."

"I already got it going. I'll have it back in a few minutes."

"Okay. Thanks." I walked away hiding my anxiety with a smile. I should have just run them myself and figured out a reason why if they ever asked. Now there'd be a record of me asking to have them run, and there was no way to explain that. *It might come back to haunt me.*

Shit!

CHAPTER 5

TRAPPED

Houston, Texas

Coop always got in early to enjoy her tea and the morning paper in privacy. Everyone knew her idiosyncrasies and no one dared to bother her before the "official" time. That time varied depending on how many cups of tea she had.

Today started out as a two-cup day, but that was *before* she read the paper, and *before* that undercover cop came in. Cindy brought her a third cup after Gino left, just as her phone rang. Coop closed her eyes and gritted her teeth. "Cooper."

"Have you seen the damn papers?" the voice on the other end was loud and demanding.

Coop made certain to keep her voice sickeningly sweet. "Is this you, Cybil?"

"You know damn right well who this is."

Coop reverted to her normal voice. "I'm having my tea right now and your screeching voice is annoying. Either calm down or call back."

Coop sipped her tea as she listened to the silence.

"All right, Gladys, but you must know how upset I am. With the change at the White House—meaning with Tom now in there—Houston has a chance to shine. We could be one of the focal points for the drug war. It would mean a *lot* of money, and a *lot* of national coverage." Cybil paused. "It could be a chance for you to shine too. Don't let your cowboy cops spoil it."

"I don't have any cowboy cops."

"You've got at least two, and you let them run wild."

"You told me to clean up the city," Coop said.

"I told you to clean it up, not turn it into Tombstone. Get a leash on that man."

"Who?"

"Gladys, you know who I'm talking about—Cataldi."

"We have no idea if he was involved."

"He was definitely involved when his partner got killed, and I'd bet money he was involved in the others."

The hair on the back of Coop's neck rose. "You think one of my officers is a murderer?"

"Don't take that high tone with me. It hasn't been that long ago that some of *your officers* handcuffed a suspect and threw him off the bridge into the bayou. We can't afford that kind of scandal. Houston has to *appear* civilized."

"Did you call to vent, or do you want something?"

"This is not about venting. I want you to put him where he can't cause trouble."

"I'll think about it."

"Think hard, Gladys. Remember who put you in that big plush chair and that pretty little office."

You fucking whore. "I remember, and as I said, I'll think about it."

"Get back to me, and don't forget we have a meeting coming up."

***

I met with the psychologist, listening to his questions and suggestions, then thanked him for his wise counsel. I knew the asshole wouldn't survive one night on the street, but then again, I'd probably be worse as a psychologist. I guess that made us even.

The good doctor straightened his wire-rimmed glasses and extended his hand. "We'll plan on seeing you next week, Detective."

"No need for me to come back; I'm fine."

He nodded. "I know you *think* you're fine, but there are issues that must be dealt with. The mind is fragile and this is a serious matter." He sat on the arm of a chair and looked up at me. "I'm not saying you *have to* come back, but if you can spare a few minutes, you should. I'll even come in early. Hell, I'll even meet you for coffee."

He had a warm smile, and he seemed like a genuinely nice guy, but I didn't have time for this in my life. "Doctor, I don't know how many men you've killed, but I'd bet it's less than one. You seem like a great guy, and I appreciate your help, but when it comes to dealing with *issues* like this, I believe I'm a better judge of what I need than you are."

He stood and shook my hand again. This time he gave me his card. "My home number is on there," he said. "My cell also. Call if you need to."

"Thanks," I said and headed out. I was dialing Chicky's number before the door shut. Chicky answered in three rings.

"Ramirez."

"It's Gino."

"Hey, dude, what the—"

"Not now. Listen, I'm calling to say we *did not* see each other last night. Understand?"

"You got it. I ain't seen you in a long time."

"Great. Thanks."

My phone rang as soon as I hung up. "Yeah, Chick."

"This isn't Chick, Detective."

I didn't recognize the voice, and when I looked at caller ID it showed unknown. It was then I realized Chicky's ringtone—Love in This Club—hadn't played. "Who is this?"

"Let's meet and we'll discuss it."

"Discuss what? I don't know what the hell you're talking about."

"Really?"

"Pal, I don't know who you are or what your game is, but I don't have time for bullshit."

"Say hi to Ron for me, will you?"

Ron? My gut tightened, and I wanted to reach through the phone and *kill* him, just like I had Rico. I fought for control, and said, "Ron who?"

"We both know who I mean—Ron, your son, the one who takes drugs."

"Who the *fuck* is this?"

"Meet me at the Starbucks on Louetta and 45."

"How will I know you?"

"Be there in twenty minutes. I'll call your cell."

"It'll take me longer to get there."

"I'll wait."

On the drive to Starbucks, I realized I'd been an ass with the psychologist; he was just trying to do his job. I made a mental note to apologize and left it at that. Then I thought—what the hell am I doing thinking about the psychologist; I should be thinking about Ron. Should be worried about him and who this asshole calling me was.

I pulled off the freeway, made the loop back over, and turned into Starbuck's lot. Nobody was waiting inside, so either he wasn't there yet or he was parked outside. I casually 'searched' the cars in the lot, looking to see if I recognized the kid from that night. Nothing.

I went inside, got a coffee, black, and took it outside to the table farthest from the door. Before I sat down, the phone rang.

"Glad to see you came alone."

I looked around. "Where are you?"

"Tan pickup to your left."

Son of a bitch. How did I miss that? I recognized who it was immediately— the guy from the van, the one who came out of Coop's office, the one Cindy said was undercover.

I got up from the table and walked to the passenger side and got in, opting to play it cool. "Do I know you?"

As I looked him over, I realized what an ass I was. Sure he had stringy hair and dressed like the kids, but now—looking at his face—it was plain to see he was older and far from an innocent kid. He had that hard look about him that undercovers get after only a short time on the job. Even his voice sounded aged.

"When you stick a gun in somebody's face you ought to at least remember what they look like."

"How'd you make me?"

The undercover laughed. "You need to get rid of your *cop talk* if you don't want to get made. As soon as you said, 'Driver, put your hands on the dashboard, palms down.' And then, 'Face me and wrap your arms around the seat. Keep your hands locked.' Let's just say it didn't take much to figure out you were a badge."

I almost laughed. "Yeah, guess so. By the way, I'm sorry about the gun thing; it was a bad night."

"Bad night? I thought you were going to shoot me, you crazy fuck."

"I *really* am sorry about that. It was my kid, he—"

"He's why I'm here."

I perked up, nerves on edge. "What? Something happen?"

"Nothing happened, but he's into some heavy shit."

"What kind of heavy?"

"Oxy, benzos, all of it. He's dealing too."

I punched the dashboard—hard—then hit it again.

"Whoa. Go easy on the truck."

"Sorry again. Hey listen, thanks for the heads up. I'm going to talk to him."

"You'll need to do more than talk to him. We're getting ready to bust the whole lot. Your boy needs to be in a program or he's going down with the rest of them."

"In a program?"

"That's right, and not some bullshit go to a psychiatrist once a week thing. I'm talking a full-blown rehab, twelve-step deal."

"I'll get on him."

He reached over, grabbed hold of my arm lightly, and pulled me to face him. "This is no shit. If he doesn't go, I can't cover for you. Put him in a program and I can leave him out of the mix, if not..."

"I understand." I started to get out of the car, then turned back. "I don't even know your name."

"We're better off that way."

I stood with the door open, not knowing how to ask the next question, but he did it for me.

"If you want to know if I told your captain, the answer is no. I saw you heading into the men's room; that's how I made you."

"Why are you helping us?"

The guy shrugged. "I had a brother who overdosed, and I saw what that did to my dad. I don't blame you for wanting to kill those kids, but remember, they're somebody's kids too. They might be one step away from redemption, just like Ron."

I gripped the door harder, squeezed, then asked, "When's it going down?"

"Next week. Not sure which day yet."

"He'll be in a program by Monday. And thanks again. I owe you big time." I closed the door and walked back to my car. I had my work cut out for me.

I stopped at Walgreen's on my way home and bought a piss test, the kind that does twelve different drugs—opiates, benzos, marijuana, cocaine, and others. I knew this wasn't going to be easy, but the first thing I had to do was catch Ron in a lie. That part should be easy—druggies always lied. It was their way of life.

As I thought about it, I realized that while it might be easy to catch him in a lie, it would be a lot tougher to face the truth—that he lied to me.

I decided to wait until morning to do the test. My nerves were shot, not wanting to do this, not wanting to *really* know the extent he was into drugs. But it had to be done, and that knowledge, along with the impending bust, kept me strong. I was eating breakfast when he came down. He seemed in a good mood and that made what I had to do worse.

"Morning, Dad," Ron said, as he poured a bowl of cereal.

I didn't trust myself to talk, not yet, so I set the vial on the table in front of him.

"What's this?"

I swallowed hard, and found my voice. "A drug test."

Ron fake laughed. "I'm not doing drugs." He was into automatic-defensive-reaction mode.

"Then you have nothing to worry about." I stood and put my hand on his shoulder, which he immediately shrugged off.

"I can't believe you don't trust me."

"It has nothing to do with trust. This is responsible parenting. You should understand."

"I *don't* understand, and I'm not taking any test."

He started to leave, but I grabbed his arm. When he tried tearing away, I yanked him back. "Ron!"

He stopped at the sound of my voice. I seldom raised it in anger. "You're taking the test. *Now.*"

"Fuck your test," he said, and moved for the door.

I grabbed his arm. He pulled away and took a swing at me.

He missed, but the fact that he tried broke my heart. More than that, though, it pissed me off, and my training kicked in. He became just another drug dealer, junkie, prick that I hated. I lunged for him, got him in a choke hold and squeezed. "You fuckin' little prick. After all I've done for you."

Ron gasped for breath, bringing me to my senses. I let go of him and spun him around to face me. "I'm sorry. I didn't mean to hurt you, but—"

"Fuck you," he screamed.

I thought he was going to try for the door again. He didn't. Just sat in the chair and cried.

I wanted to hug him. Tell him how sorry I was. Instead, I mustered up the guts and set the vial on the table in front of him. "I still need you to do this."

He grabbed the plastic container and headed toward the bathroom.

I followed, jamming my foot in the door when he tried slamming it shut. "You can turn your back, but I'm watching to make sure it's a clean test. No dilution or additives."

"You don't trust me at all, do you?"

Again, he almost had me feeling sorry for him, but there'd be plenty of time for sorry if he passed the test.

When he was done he handed me the sample, now covered, and washed his hands. "I gotta go. I'm late."

I grabbed him as he tried squeezing by me. "You're going nowhere until I do this test."

Ron yanked away again. "What's the big deal? So I smoked a little weed."

I led him back to the kitchen. In a couple of minutes, I had all I needed. "A little weed?"

"Yeah," he said, but his eyes were burning holes in the table. He wouldn't look at me.

"This test says a little weed, a few opiates, and some benzos."

"Bullshit."

"Are you saying the test is wrong, because we can do it again."

"I didn't take any of that."

I stared at him, *knowing* as both a cop and his father that he was lying, but desperately wanting to—or needing to—believe him. Now I understood all of the parents I had doubted when they did the same thing. "You swear?"

"I already told you."

"You swear on your mother's grave?"

"I can't believe you'd use Mom like that."

"Swear to me on your mother's grave that this test is lying and you didn't take any of these drugs?"

He started crying again, his head buried in his arms. "I'm screwed up, Dad. I'm really screwed up."

I walked over and put my arms around him. "It's okay. Everybody makes mistakes. We're going to get you help."

I let him cry for a minute. When the tears stopped, I helped him up. "Come on, it's late and we need to get going."

"You're driving me to school?"

"Yeah, I'll drive you."

He rode with his head leaning against the window, not moving until we passed his school.

"Where are you going?"

"We're going to get you help. Remember?"

"What are you talking about?"

"I'm checking you into a rehab."

"*No way* I'm going to any rehab." He reached for the door handle but I pressed the locks.

His defiance was good for me. Gave me the strength I needed. "You'll go to rehab or you'll go to jail. You choose."

He laughed, a shitty, taunting laugh. "You wouldn't send me to jail."

"Not the Ron Cataldi I raised, but this one, the drug addict…I would in a heartbeat."

"Come on, Dad. I won't do it again. I swear."

I said nothing.

"Dad, did you hear me? I *said* I won't do it again. What do you want? Blood?"

Still I said nothing.

"You wouldn't do this if Mom were alive. She wouldn't *let* you." The tears came again. I almost turned the car around…but then I remembered what the druggies I dealt with sounded like. The pleading and begging and promising to change. It was all the same, only this was my son. Other than that, there was no difference.

Ron put his hand on my shoulder. His voice reflected a plea for mercy. "Dad, for Mom's sake, for mine, you *have got* to let me fix it on my own. I won't let you down, I promise. I just screwed up a little. I can fix it. You can help me. I know I can do it if you help me." Ron was pulling out all the stops

Jesus Christ. I felt like Ulysses when the Sirens called him, and I wished for some of the wax he put in his men's ears. "You're *going* in," I said. "Don't say another word."

After that the ride was silent. He didn't even try to persuade me anymore, which told me that the entire effort had been fake to begin with. I felt better knowing that. Knowing that I hadn't given in to my feelings being manipulated.

It took a while to get him checked in, going through insurance and signing papers. He put me through hell before I got out of there. By the time I left, Ron had cursed me for everything bad that happened to him since he was born. That was after he tried crying and begging again. He should have stuck with that; it almost worked. And who knows, maybe he had it right. Maybe I *was* to blame for the whole mess—all of it. God only knows I fucked up my own life.

By noon I was out of there and on my way to work. A note from Coop lay on my desk. She wanted to see me.

I shook my head as I picked it up and headed for her office, expecting the worst. Cindy barely said hello, another bad sign, and I was too tired to try and get insight from her into what was going on. I walked into Coop's office ready for anything.

"Sit down, Gino. Do you want coffee?"

Steam rose from her teacup; Cindy must have just delivered it. If Coop needed another cup of tea to have her chat with me, it couldn't be good. "I'm fine. What did you want to see me about?"

"I'm taking you out of Narcotics and putting—"

I jumped up from my chair. "You can't do that."

"*Sit down*, Cataldi."

Her voice carried that stern warning that everyone knew. I sat.

"You're going to be assigned to training recruits for six months."

"Six—" I stopped myself before saying something I'd regret.

"I don't like this, but…never mind, let's leave it at that. I don't like it. You've got six months to show me you can act civil. If all goes well, you'll be back to Narcotics."

"May I ask why, Captain?"

Coop lifted her right hand and took off her glasses. She set them on the desk. Her eyes looked meaner without glasses. "For the record, because the psychologist believes you need a rest. Off the record, because I *know* you had something to do with Rico Moreno's death."

She got even closer to me. Her face scrunched up.

"And I don't like it one bit. Not one *fucking* bit. I don't know how you did things in Philadelphia, but down here we don't condone vigilantes."

"I'm taking the day off," I said. I let some attitude go with that statement, maybe hoping she got offended. Maybe looking for an argument.

"Good, you need it. Take tomorrow off, too, then report to Bill Mercer in training. He'll be expecting you."

On the way home I listened to the radio, trying to find something to lift my spirits. Music usually did that. The DJ was talking about how nice a day it was.

"What do you think of this day, folks. Seventy degrees, sun shining, low humidity—you have got to love life on a day like this."

I laughed. Not really, I almost cried. I was trying my best to love life, but life wasn't loving me back.

I decided to visit Mary's grave. Those occasions were normally reserved for Christmas, our anniversary, and her birthday in October, but today I needed help. I checked the rearview and side mirrors then pulled across a couple of lanes and got ready to exit. About ten minutes later I entered the cemetery and parked a short walk from where she lay. I bent down and straightened a rope necklace draped over the headstone. I had made it myself shortly after she died. It had our names formed from knots—Gino, Mary, Ron. It was simple, but Mary always liked simple things, and anything made out of rope she had a special fondness for.

Despite my disgust for the church, I'd do anything for Mary, so I knelt and blessed myself, saying a prayer as I did. God bless her, she had kept her faith through the last breath, never once blaming God, even while I cursed Him. There had been no reason for God to take her. Not when He let scum like Rico run the streets.

I took a deep breath and held it, then mustered up the courage to speak. "I know it's not my time to visit, Mary, so you're probably wondering why I'm here. I don't even know myself. I guess I felt I had to."

Tears welled in my eyes. I lowered my head. My voice turned into a whisper. "My life's falling apart. I don't know what's going on. And I'm having *so many* problems with Ron." That whisper turned quickly into a voice that reflected my tears. "My God, I wish you were here. You always knew what to do when things went wrong with Ron. You were the voice of reason, when I yelled. Calm when I grew frustrated. Remaining calm seemed so easy for you." I tugged my handkerchief out of my pocket, tried to stop crying, but couldn't.

"I miss you, baby. I miss the time we should've had together, the places I should've taken you. And I miss seeing your face when I did one of the few good things and surprised you on our anniversary. I hope you're doing well. I hope even more that you can't see what's happening to Ron—that would break your heart."

I leaned in close and kissed the part of the necklace with her name. "I'll *never* love anyone like I loved you."

CHAPTER 6

GOOD OLD GIRLS

Houston, Texas

Cybil read the letter for the third time, not quite believing what it said. *That son of a bitch isn't coming. And after all we did for him.*

She clutched the letter with both hands, and, for a moment, thought of tearing it up. But it *was* a personal letter from the president. There was no sense in tearing the letter up, despite the content. She tucked it into a drawer of her private desk then prepared for the meeting with the girls.

***

Coop pulled her car into an empty space in the garage and walked across the bridge to the building, taking time to evaluate what might be discussed or proposed for the meeting. Cybil had told her about Tom not attending the celebration, which meant she would be in a tizzy and likely unpredictable. That wasn't good. But RB Ingle would be there, with all the power and influence money can buy—and he had enough to buy a lot.

Cybil might have been the most ambitious woman ever born in East Texas. If she'd been born a minnow, she would have aspired to be a whale—that, or a great white shark. At age seventeen she decided to leave East Texas, not unusual by itself, but her determination was so great that by the time she turned eighteen, she taught herself to speak without her native accent. Two weeks after her birthday she ran away to Houston, leaving family behind. Whispers from the envious ones say she got her start at a strip club, where she met Rusty Johnson, a man she later married and whipped into becoming mayor.

She was the one who took Coop under her wing and supported her—drove her actually—to become captain. If her after-meeting comments were taken seriously, Cybil now had her sights set for Coop to become Houston's next chief of police. It was a fine line Coop walked between dealing with Cybil to get the support and putting up with her demands.

The captain walked through the big double doors, nodded to the receptionist, and turned left toward Cybil's office. When she entered, Cybil already had a drink in her hand. *Not a good sign.*

"Captain Cooper, you're punctual, as always."

"I live to serve, Your Grace."

"Shut the hell up and tell me what's new in my city."

Coop raised her brows. "Your city? I didn't know Rusty bequeathed it to you."

"Rusty's not dead yet, but it won't be long." Cybil lit a cigarette, blew out a long thin stream of smoke, then laughed. "Whenever I suffer through one of his lovemaking sessions, I extract something else from him—information, a promise, a new connection, something. Pretty soon he'll have nothing left but his baggy boxers." Cybil stood in front of a wide floor-to-ceiling window overlooking the city and sat on her desk. "Speaking of sex, how will you answer if someone asks your preferences?"

"This is the twenty-first century. They can't ask questions like that. And besides, where the hell did that question even come from?"

Cybil swirled her gin and tonic, letting the ice cubes rattle in an annoying rhythm. "They can't but they will, and I'd like to know how the woman I'm going to make my new chief of police will answer the question."

The captain raised her eyebrows. "Is this question personal, philosophical, or political?"

"A mixture."

She nodded but never let her gaze leave Cybil's face. "When you narrow it down, let me know. I'll see what kind of answer I have then."

A devious smile appeared, and Cybil's eyes hardened. "I'm the one who made you. Don't forget that."

Coop took a step closer to her. "If you want to think you had something to do with me getting my job, fine. But don't *ever* get the idea that you own me, *Mrs.* Mayor."

Before Cybil could respond the intercom blared.

"Janice and Millie are here."

"Show them in," Cybil said, then turned to Coop. "We'll finish this later."

People always talked about the "good old boys" network in Texas, but nobody realized there was another network that was more powerful and got more done. Cybil headed up that network, and it included half of the wives from the "boys" side, plus Captain Gladys 'Coop' Cooper, and a few other singles.

"Good afternoon, ladies," Janice said as she entered. "Did you hear the news?"

Cybil stared from her perch on the desk. "What news?"

"Tom Marsen assigned the First Lady to head up his new fight against drugs. I'm sure she'll be coming to Houston before long.

Cybil almost spilled her drink. "I can't believe he appointed *her*."

Janice made her way to the bar and grabbed the gin. "Now that Tom is in the White House maybe we can get things done and bring some civilization to the city."

Millie snorted, trying to control her laughter. Allergies played hell with her breathing. "Tom might have been born in Texas, but that only goes so far. He seems to be firmly entrenched in Washington with his new friends." She took a slug of gin and tonic. "And I don't know if any of you have looked lately, but none of us are invited."

"We'll make our own party," Janice said. "Besides, we don't need Tom as long as we've got RB Ingle."

Another snort from Millie. "RB might be rich, but he's not president."

"You're right," Cybil said. "He's not president. But I'd bet three dead armadillos he's got more than a couple of hands in Tom's pockets."

Coop closed her eyes and shook her head. "Where the *hell* do you come up with those sayings?"

The door to Cybil's office opened. "Anne is here," her admin said, and a tall, slim brunette walked in.

"Well if it isn't Mrs. RB Ingle," Cybil said.

Anne bristled.

"How *is* Mr. RB?" Janice asked.

Anne smiled. "He's fine."

"Fine my ass," Cybil said, and took a swig of her drink. "I happen to know he was getting a lap dance last night. I know this because he was with my husband."

Everyone laughed, and Anne moved over and gave Cybil a hug. "It's better if he gets what he needs outside. I sure don't want him coming to my bed."

"You never know what he might find," Millie said, and everyone laughed again.

The incessant rattling of ice in a tumbler brought everyone's attention to Cybil. "Back to business, ladies. It's true that Tom hasn't been good to those that worked so hard to support him, but everyone has a few skeletons in their closet. I grew up with that son of a bitch, and I know *exactly* what drives his desires." A smile popped onto Cybil's face. "And if I have to bring a few of those skeletons out to wring a little more cooperation out of that dishrag, trust me…I can do it."

"We might even convince RB to help," Anne said. "He's not happy about Tom shunning this celebration."

Coop sat in one of Cybil's plush chairs, legs crossed. "We've got more pressing things to discuss than Tom Marsen's plans for Houston."

"Like what?" Janice said.

"Have you forgotten Rusty was re-elected? You remember him Cybil— your husband. And despite the president not attending the event, RB's celebration will draw a lot of big names. That might not mean much to those of you who only have to worry about cocktail dresses and gowns, but I need to think of event security."

Cybil narrowed her eyes and kept her gaze locked on Coop. "I would have thought you'd have things like security figured out by now, Captain."

"I learned long ago that anytime you think you've got it figured out— that's when the shit hits the fan." Coop stood and set her drink on the bar. "I think we're done, Cybil. I believe you said you had to look for skeletons, and I've got my own work to do."

Coop exited the building, and slowly made her way to the car. She had a headache that wouldn't quit, and she felt sure Cybil had been the cause of it. *Her or Cataldi.*

That thought reminded her of something she had to do, as if she didn't have enough already, Rusty Johnson's celebrations, and the possibility—no matter how remote—that the First Lady might come to town…Coop pulled the remote from her purse and clicked it, unlocking the car door. She started the engine and blasted the air conditioner on. It was on days like this that she wished the A/C had an 'Arctic Blast' setting. She stood outside while the car cooled, especially the seats. Coop dialed a number from memory. She didn't have it on speed dial and she had erased it from the 'recents' list.

"Yes, Captain?"

"Do you have any news?" Coop asked.

"I told you I'd let you know when I did."

Silence, then, "Are you still watching him?"

"I don't go in for this shit. I don't like it one damn bit."

"I didn't ask for you to like it," Coop snapped." It's not my cup of tea either, but I've got to find out what happened."

"You need to find out your own damn self. I've got better things to do."

"Getting a bad cop off the street is a priority."

"He's not a bad cop."

"We'll see," Coop said.

CHAPTER 7

AN UNSCHEDULED VISIT

Houston, Texas

I spent most nights worrying about one thing or another, and I had plenty to worry about. Ron's drug problem was a continuous concern, and what I'd done that night with the undercover cop bothered me. But the big one, the one I couldn't shake off, was Rico. The look in his eyes when I shot him. Even worse than that was seeing his wife and kids at the funeral.

I had gone to the cemetery that day and pretended to be visiting another grave while I watched them bury Rico. I went to gloat at the big bad drug dealer being put six feet under. But then I saw his wife, looking so pitiful in her black dress with the black veil across her face. Her hands rested on the shoulders of two young boys, maybe 8 or 10 years old. I couldn't see their tears, or hear them cry, but I could see the grief in their posture, in the shaking of their heads, the denials—refusing to believe their father was gone. I could imagine them wishing for someone to play ball with or watch a movie late at night when they were supposed to be in bed. And at that moment, I *felt* their aching hearts. Just like mine ached the day I put Mary in the ground. Thank God her plot wasn't in this same cemetery. It would have been too much for me to bear.

A horn beep warned me that I'd drifted into the next lane on the freeway. A sharp pain pinched the left side of my chest. It tightened. I let off the gas, took a deep breath. It was anxiety, I knew, but when the pain started, It made me worry it was something with my heart. God's final punishment for my sins. I had been getting chest pains ever since the day I saw Rico's kids at the funeral.

Maybe if I go there…

I exited the freeway, made a U-turn, and headed south. I hated cemeteries, and yet I seemed to spend a lot of time there.

I drove past the entrance twice—afraid to enter, but I didn't know why. What could hurt me? My conscience? On the third pass, I turned and drove slowly down the narrow road, parking on the side, past the spot where they buried him. I sat in the car, asking myself why I was here, but then I got out and walked to his grave. There was a picture—sitting on an easel—of what his marker was going to look like—a huge stone marker with a big cross. It must have been placed there by his wife.

For a second or two, I got angry, wishing Mary had such a nice tribute, but then I cleared my thoughts. I didn't hate Rico for the monument. I felt sure he didn't pick out his own gravestone. Rico was the kind who thought he would live forever.

I stood for what seemed like a long time, staring. And as I wondered again what I was doing there, words came from my mouth.

"I'm sorry," I said.

I heard myself say it, but almost didn't believe it was me. What was I sorry for? I wasn't sorry for Rico. In a different life, under the same circumstances, I'd do what I did again. I guess I felt bad for his kids.

A few beads of sweat rolled down my neck. I took a deep breath and turned my head, checking to see if I was alone. It was then I realized I was done. I walked back to the car, not feeling any better than when I came. It made me wonder if I'd done any good or if I'd simply humiliated myself.

As I drove home I gave a lot of thought to death, and for the first time I realized I wasn't afraid of death; I was afraid of going to hell and never seeing Mary again.

***

Sitting in his truck, across the street from the cemetery, Officer Christopher Frueh put down his binoculars, picked up his phone, and dialed a number.

"Cooper."

"He's gone."

"Tell me about it."

"Like I said, he went to the cemetery. Now he's gone."

"Which cemetery?"

"The one inside the loop."

"I asked which one, Frueh. Don't make me treat you like a hostile witness. You don't want that."

"Glenwood."

"Whose grave did he visit?"

"You gonna make me walk all the way over there?"

"Unless you can fly, yeah."

"I'll call back." Officer Frueh got out of the truck and walked to where Gino stood. His head was shaking even before the words came out of his mouth. "Son of a bitch."

He dialed Captain Cooper's number.

She answered right away. "What?"

"Rico Moreno."

"That's what I thought."

"What the hell's goin' on?" Frueh asked.

"I don't know yet, but don't say a *goddamn* word to anyone."

"I won't," Frueh said. "But this settles the score between us. I'm through following cops."

"I hope I am too."

CHAPTER 8

NEW DREAMS

Houston, Texas

Barbara Camwyck sat naked on the sofa, hands tucked between her legs and a smile on her face. Last night had been magnificent—almost perfect. There was something magical about their relationship—even at this age—and every time they got together it seemed even better. It wasn't just the lovemaking either. She could tell by his smile, and the feeling she got when their eyes met. Maybe tonight would be a repeat performance. If he could get together.

Nothing had ever been so good in Barbara's life. So...*perfect.* Goosebumps ran up her arms, chased away by a shiver. She picked up the disposable cell phone and walked to the bathroom to run a hot tub. There were few things in life as relaxing as a hot tub—a good meal; a good book; sex; that first cigarette in the morning, accompanied by that first cup of coffee. She gave the list more thought then shook her head. That was about it. She placed the phone on the sink and stepped into the water, swishing it around with her left foot.

The water swirled around her legs. She let herself down slowly, until the warmth wrapped around her bottom. It rushed up her legs, caressed her genitals. She closed her eyes as she slipped into deeper water, head cushioned by a plush towel at the back of the tub. She let her fingers dip down, tickling the sides of her thighs. Barbara shivered, then splashed herself and rolled her knees.

The ring of the phone startled her upright. Smile vanishing, she groped for a towel, which had fallen to the floor, then stepped out of the tub, dried her hands and grabbed for the phone.

"Hello?"

A familiar voice said, "Barbara?"

"This is she."

"It's on for tonight."

Her heart raced, a combination of panic and excitement. "Where?"

"I'll provide directions later. Instructions come first."

Barbara couldn't help the sigh that escaped her. She understood precautions, but this bordered on paranoia. "I remember: Talk to no one; wear a hat and sunglasses; use the back stairs, not the elevator; drive slowly." She waited through a long silence. *I must have forgotten something.*

"Leave *nothing* in the room."

Barbara trembled. "I'll make sure."

"And you remember, of course, that *no one* is to know about this."

"No need to worry."

"I'll see you at nine o'clock. Here are the directions."

Barbara finished writing the notes, then she hung up the phone, her smile returning. Another night with the best lover in the world. Since her rendezvous were always in different locations, she wondered what surprises this one held.

She finished drying, all the while examining herself in the mirror. What had once been a proud, taut, stomach showed signs of movement, and her pert little butt was not quite as pert and not nearly as little as it once had been. Anxiety crept through her. She'd have to start exercising.

For almost two hours, Barbara walked around the room naked. It made her feel sexy, prepped her for the night to come. She situated herself in front of the mirror, one leg resting on the vanity while she applied her eyeliner.

Lace underpants, not much more than a thong, tickled her legs as she slipped them on, followed by a matching bra. No nylons, though she seldom wore them anymore. The blue dress—a gift from Damian's Fine Fashions— and brown Ferragamo low-heel pumps finalized the outfit.

She stuffed the extra clothes into her bag, flushed the cigarette butts down the toilet, slipped on her sunglasses and hat, then left, checking first to ensure the corridor was empty. Quick steps carried her past the elevators into the stairwell.

Only two flights to go, she thought, breaths coming in anxious gasps. It was ridiculous to have to go through this ritual, but she did it so they could be together. She'd do anything for that.

Barbara took a deep breath, held it, and opened the door into the side of the lobby, her head held low, eyes fixed on the floor. She tried to wish her heels to be quiet, but they wouldn't heed her. She prayed she wasn't attracting attention.

She pushed the exterior door open with a bang, and hurried across the parking lot to the blue Ford sedan parked in the center aisle. As the car door slammed shut, she exhaled a huge sigh and locked the door, her head resting against the seat. She lingered a moment, started the engine, then slowly drove off, following the signs to I-45 N. With her head turned to the left, she made her way onto the freeway entrance ramp and gunned it to merge with the traffic. A familiar looking car followed and pulled into the same lane, maybe two cars back. Barbara panicked.

Suppose someone knew?

She pulled into the left lane then slowed down, and all the while she checked the mirror to see what the car behind her did. When it passed her, she relaxed. A few miles later she thought another car was tailing her, but it passed by her also. Paranoia was setting in and she didn't like it.

Convinced that no one was following her, she drove the rest of the way in quiet anticipation. The only time she checked the mirror was to make sure her eye liner hadn't smudged or her lipstick hadn't bled. Forty minutes later she turned down a narrow, dark road and followed it for several miles, relieved when she finally saw the lights of the house through the trees. A long concrete driveway took her under a canopy of old oaks flanked by tall East Texas pines and eventually led to a sprawling two-story house nestled on the north shore of Lake Conroe.

She got out of the car and made her way up a brick sidewalk— herringbone design—that led her to massive double doors with ovals of stained glass in the center. She rang the doorbell, waited as footsteps crossed the marble entry. She put on a wide smile to light her face, tense as the door opened.

"What are *you* doing here?" she asked, smile disappearing.

CHAPTER 9

AN UNEXPECTED MEETING

Houston, Texas

Barbara stared. "Where's—"

"Never mind where he is. I was sent to greet you. And by the way, I made you a drink when I saw you pull up. Gin and tonic with a twist of lime?"

She nodded and accepted the drink, looking around as she walked through the foyer toward the kitchen. It was a grand entry, with a sweeping staircase, two-story ceiling, and alcoves adorned with statues.

She was confused but decided to see what was going on. "Gorgeous house," Barbara said, and took a few sips of the drink. Maybe it would help calm her.

Her heels clicked loudly on the tile as she followed her host into the kitchen. A sheet covered with a plastic tarp lay across the floor ahead of her. Something didn't seem right. "Where is—"

"Let's say I came to negotiate."

"What's that supposed to mean?" She hoped her voice didn't betray her fear.

"It means you should have been satisfied with your normal blackmailing; this time you took things too far."

She lowered her head, shaking it. "I should have known. Was it money or sex?"

"Both."

Barbara took a moment to compose herself then raised her head and pushed back her shoulders, putting as much confidence as she could into her voice. "What are you here for? I haven't changed my mind."

A smile greeted her last statement. "I realized that before I came. But did you forget we knew where you lived?"

Barbara frowned.

"It didn't take me long to find the DVD. How clever of you to keep it with your other movies, hiding in plain sight. Watched a lot of detective shows have you?"

"The DVD will do you no good," Barbara said, but her confidence was waning.

"Follow me," the host said, "And step over the sheet."

Barbara looked down at the floor. She felt dizzy. "What's the sheet for?"

"To cover the blood." The killer reached for a knife sitting on the counter, and with the other hand grabbed an ice pick.

Barbara heard the words, but they didn't register. Even when she saw the knife in one hand and an ice pick in the other, it didn't sink in. Everything moved in slow motion, as if the world had slipped to one-quarter speed. A scream built in her, started in her stomach and roared up through her chest. She felt it tearing at her throat, pushing through that narrow channel toward her mouth.

"I would have killed you quickly if you hadn't tried the blackmail."

Then the ice pick plunged into her throat. It severed the larynx, cutting her scream off before it began. Her muscles spasmed. She tried to force a scream out, but the only thing she heard was the gurgling of blood coming from the hole in her neck.

The knife raced toward her. Cold steel punctured her left side, tearing through flesh, breaking a rib, then rupturing the lining of her lung.

Pain infused her body. It wasn't as bad as she imagined. She felt numb. Her left side collapsed. Air rushed out.

The ice pick continued through her lung, and up, lodging in the cavity beneath her heart. Blood oozed into her lung.

Coughing blood, she fixed her eyes on the killer, pleading for an answer. The killer had cold eyes, as cold as the steel ravaging her body.

Barbara's knees hit the ground first. She fell forward, but got kicked back. Her head cracked when it hit the floor. She felt the warmth spreading under her—blood pooling.

Please, God, let me die quickly.

The ice pick plummeted toward her left eye, but she couldn't turn away. She screamed again but nothing came out, like dry heaves only worse.

The ice pick struck, sinking into her eye as if it were going through jello. Blood filled the socket. She could no longer see, but she still felt a dull, throbbing pain.

The killer grabbed the ice pick with both hands, pulled it out, then slammed it back in. One final surge of excruciating pain. The last plunge stopped the pain. She could see nothing. Feel nothing. Thoughts of her dog, Sacco, came to her. She wondered who would take care of him, or if anyone would even find him. Then Barbara Camwyck drifted away.

***

The killer hacked at her, cutting off part of her breasts, an ear, a piece from her genitals. Sliced pieces of flesh from various spots on her body and stuffed them into her mouth. A piece of her nose was inserted into her vagina. Other things went other places, and when finished, the killer filled plastic bags with what was left, positioned the body on the tarp, then rolled everything up into a sleeping bag that had been under the sheet and the tarp.

Clean-up took a long time, especially the dismemberment of the body, but there was plenty of time. When the killer finished, the bags were deposited in the trunk of Barbara's car then driven to the parking lot of an apartment complex where the truck had been left.

After transferring the body parts, the killer put them in two dumpsters, one in Houston behind a mall, the other behind a Starbucks, north of town. The head and clothes were another matter. Those bags got buried in the woods, not far from a creek. That proved to be a difficult and trying expedition.

The killer knew the bags in the dumpsters would be discovered, fitting into perfectly laid plans. In retrospect, it had been a productive night.

CHAPTER 10

A ROUND OF GOLF

Some people prepared for emergencies by keeping first-aid kits in the kitchen and the glove compartment, having a can of "Fix-A-Flat" in each car, and keeping extra keys hidden under doormats.

Tip Denton was like that too, but in a different way. He never went anywhere without a set of golf clubs in the trunk and a spare gun in his leg holster. He never knew when the opportunity to catch a "quick nine" might pop up—or the need to shoot someone. Today was the *quick nine* type of opportunity.

Tip rode in the passenger seat, half asleep. He didn't like to get up before the sun, but he did it twice a year for a special golf outing with a few of his buddies. The crazy bastards dragged him halfway across Texas to a place where deer outnumbered the golfers.

"Hurry up, Joe," Tip said. "I need some time on the putting green before we start."

"We have time. It's still dark."

"You think that matters?" Tip said, and then his phone rang.

"Tip Denton."

"It's Cindy. We have a body in a dumpster."

"I know a body in a dumpster seems important to you, darlin', but I'm on my way to play golf."

"It's still dark. Are you up."

"I'm going to make it a lot clearer for you. This isn't any old round of golf. I'm going to *The Falls*."

Cindy didn't laugh. "And this isn't any old body in a dumpster; this body was found in *two* dumpsters."

"What's that supposed to mean?"

"Legs in one can, torso in the other."

When she didn't finish, Tip felt a twist in his gut. An instinctive suspicion. "And the head?"

"Nothing."

"Goddamnit."

"Set your GPS for Greenspoint Mall. You have a pair of legs waiting for you."

Tip hung up and looked at Joe. "Got a body."

"You want me to take you home?"

"Drive me to the mall."

"To a murder scene? Hell yeah."

"I'm not deputizing you, asshole. You're just driving me."

Joe mumbled a response as he turned the car around. Half an hour later he pulled up to the back of the mall, close to three patrol cars circling a dumpster.

Tip opened the door. "If you hurry you can still make it, but I'm not fixing any tickets."

"See you next time," Joe said.

Tip Denton wasn't born a cowboy; in fact, he didn't know much about his birth. Not where he was born or even when, not to the day. His mama told him it was sometime in late March and said she was too tired and sick to take note of the exact day. Growing up it got embarrassing not to know, so he kept asking her. About the third or fourth time he asked, she said she thought it was a Friday, and he better stop asking because that's all he was gonna get. That suited Tip fine; he liked Fridays.

From then on, Tip celebrated his birthday on the last Friday in March, no matter the date. He figured if they could reserve a special day for Thanksgiving, he could do it for his birthday.

Tip approached the officers on the scene and waved.

"Hey, Barney, what have ya'll got for me?"

"She might have been pretty once, but somebody took care of that.

Nothing but legs and ass." Barney couldn't hold it together with his last line. He and the other cops cracked up.

Tip laughed too, a little at first, then when they continued, he joined in. "All right, I like that. Good humor, boys."

Tip pried open the bag with a gloved-hand and took a quick peek. "Who found it?"

"Some kids, probably junkies looking for something in the trash."

"She smells fresh," Tip said. "M.E. on the way?"

"Should be here in a few minutes."

Ben Marsh, the Harris County medical examiner, got to the scene about fifteen minutes later, and his crew methodically processed the body, the bag, and the dumpster.

Tip hovered over his shoulder. "What do you think?"

"I think I'll have nothing for you if you don't let me get my work done," Ben said.

"And if I do?"

"I'll have very little. Maybe TOD, some DNA later, but unless she's in the system it'll do you no good."

"Time of death will help. Or could." Tip turned to Barney. "I need ya'll to canvass the neighborhood. See if anyone saw anything. It had to be last night."

"We'll get right on it. Is that all you need us for?"

"Leave one guy here to question people, see when the last trash was taken out and if they remember what was in the bags. Then we can determine where this fell in the mix, whether it was on top of it, or buried under it."

"You got it, Tip. I'll call you."

Tip went back to Ben. "Looks like you drew the short straw. You get to give me a ride home."

"Home? Isn't there a secondary scene, something about a torso?"

"There is, but it's close to my house and I need to get my car."

"Better get this killer fast," Ben said.

"I hear you. I hate to see shit like this, because when you get some crazy fuck cutting people up, they usually...well, they usually don't stop."

CHAPTER 11

CALL TO DUTY

Houston, Texas

I rolled over in bed and tried forcing myself to sleep. Since I left Narcotics I hadn't gotten more than a few good nights of sleep. I wondered again if this was God punishing me for all the wrongs I'd done. He had a big enough list to work with. It's not that I was against punishment or meting out justice, I just wished He'd get it over with in one shot instead of dishing it out a little at a time. I finally went to sleep dreaming of what it would be like to feel normal again—like I felt when Mary was alive.

I got a call early in the morning, before the alarm went off. I jumped out of bed and lunged for the phone. In the old days I'd have let it ring, figuring I'd call whoever it was later, or they'd call me. But ever since Ron got involved with drugs it changed.

With every call I worried. Was something wrong with him? Was he in a car wreck? Did he OD, and someone found him lying in the street? Did an ambulance admit him to a hospital? I never ran out of scenarios to worry over.

I grabbed the phone, and didn't even try to get the sleep out of my voice. "Hello?"

"It's Coop. Training's over. See me when you get in."

Holy shit! I was excited as hell. "On my way, Captain."

✳✳✳

Coop called Cindy on the intercom. "I need the open case files when you get a minute."

Cindy came into Coop's office moments later with the files and a cup of tea. "I figured you'd need another one by now."

"You're the best," Coop said, shuffling through the stack of folders on her desk. "Who caught the dumpster lady?"

"Tip Denton."

Coop slapped her hand on the desk. "Shit!"

"What's wrong? You have a problem with Tip?"

"I need a place to put Gino, but Tip *is not* the best one for him."

Coop shuffled through more papers. "How about that double murder on Memorial Drive?"

"Lambert and Graves got that, and it looks like it'll wrap up quickly."

"Does Denton have anyone working this with him?"

"You know he doesn't, Captain. He hasn't taken a steady partner since he transferred from County."

"That's because he gets away with it, and that's because of Chief Renkin." Coop shook her head. "Denton gives me a pain in the ass." She got up and stretched. "Much as I don't want to put Gino and Tip together, I need this case solved before the national media picks it up." She sighed. "Let me know when Gino gets here. I'll figure something out."

***

I got to the station in record time and ran up the steps toward Coop's office. "Good morning, Cindy. Fine damn day, isn't it."

"A fine day, Gino. Go right on in."

I opened the door and smiled at Coop. "Captain, I could kiss you."

"I prefer you sit. And before you get excited, you're *not* going back to Narcotics. Are you good with that?"

"You didn't call me back to ask where I wanted to work. Just tell me what you have in mind."

"It's a homicide."

"I've got no problem with homicide."

"I'm putting you with Tip Denton."

I sat up a little straighter. "Denton? The one who came over from the Sheriff's Department?"

"That's him. He was Chief Renkin's top dog." Coop sneered. "And he walks around here as if he still pisses in the tall grass."

From what I'd heard about Denton, I didn't much care for him, but I wasn't going to argue. "I can work with anybody."

She had a strange look on her face. "I'm sure Denton will put that statement to the test. He doesn't even know his own birthday, so he made one up, and—are you ready for this—he made it on the last Friday of March. Not a date, but a *day*. What kind of lunatic does that?"

"And you put *me* on training duty?" I got up from the chair. "Either way, I'm happy to be back."

Coop raised her brows. "Okay. I'll tell Tip you'll meet him at the scene. Cindy has the specifics."

CHAPTER 12

NEW PARTNERS

Houston, Texas

Before heading to the scene, I did some research on Tip. I knew him by reputation, but I needed more than that. I made a few quick calls and did some personnel file searching, but I got most of the information from a few informants. Seems like Tip and I knew a lot of the same people.

The cops thought he was great—crazy, but great—and they mentioned the old bare-knuckle jail fights with inmates as proof of what a solid citizen he was. He sounded like a fucking caveman to me, but…to each his own, as they say. The personnel files weren't quite so flattering, questioning his mental stability and even his ethics. There were three instances where they recommended pulling him inside.

But the street talk was the most interesting. Depending on who I talked to, Tip was either their best friend or worst enemy, and he had a reputation for being tough on druggies and gang members. It was even rumored that he'd done away with some of them. Other whispers toyed with him taking money from drug deals, and they mentioned his nickname—Tip—as the proof, claiming he had more money to pass around for information than any ten cops combined. No matter who I believed, working with Tip Denton was sure to be interesting.

I had read a report on the case—a body dumped at different sites. Legs were at the mall, and the torso was in another dumpster, behind a Starbucks off Louetta Road, right next to the freeway. I pulled into the parking lot, already with bad memories. This is where I'd met the undercover cop. I shook that off and got out of the car, moving to the rear of the building, where the action was. It looked as if the place had been gone over pretty good already, with three patrol cars and an unmarked car, along with the M.E.'s.

I approached an officer I didn't know and showed him my badge. "Gino Cataldi. I'm supposed to meet Detective Denton."

He nodded toward a tall guy standing to the side. A scar ran across the left side of his face from ear to mouth. Nasty looking. Made him look mean. I waited for him to finish up a phone call then reached out my hand.

"Gino Cataldi." I offered my best smile in hopes of starting this off right.

He looked me up and down then frowned. The way that frown twisted on his face created a dangerous look. "I'm not that fond of partners, but we'll see how it goes. My last partner changed my mind. Maybe you will too."

"That's all right, I'm not fond of Texans, but we'll see how it goes."

Tip cracked a smile. "Well all right then. Seems like we have an understanding."

He filled me in on the previous scene and the little that they'd found out since he arrived at this one.

"So far we don't have much. We can hope for a fingerprint match on her clothing, but that's probably a long shot since whoever did this cut the tips of her fingers off. That tells me the son of a bitch knew what he was doing, so he probably wiped her prints away."

"Maybe we'll find her fingers somewhere," I said. "Or something."

"That's a thought," Tip said. "In the meantime, we might be able to get an idea of when he dumped her. The coffee shop opens at 4:30 in the morning and it doesn't close until one. Give half an hour on either side for open and close and that leaves less than a three-hour window for somebody to dump the body."

"That's still a lot of time."

"Yeah, but we have a lot of night activity at that motel behind us, if you know what I mean. If we're lucky, real lucky, we might get a witness."

"You mean a John's going to step forward and say, hey, while I was screwing this hooker, I happened to see…"

"Like I said, we'd have to get real lucky."

"We got anything else?"

He looked at me and nodded toward his car. "Let's sit inside for a minute."

"What's up?"

The car was only about fifty feet away. "Get in," Tip said, then waited until we were alone. "The word on the street says you killed Rico Moreno.

"Did you?"

A shiver ran up my spine. "I barely knew the guy."

"I didn't ask if you dated him. Did you kill him?"

"Am I here to work a homicide? Or are you with IA?"

"Rico worked for a guy named Carlos Cortes, a big—"

"I know Carlos. I *did* work Narcotics."

Tip's scar twisted and he got a mean look in his eyes. "Carlos killed my dogs. I'd like to kill him back for that."

"I don't much like dogs, but if they were mine, I guess I'd feel the same way."

Tip looked back at me kind of funny. "You don't like dogs? What the hell kind of statement is that?"

"Tell you what, Tip. How about you don't ask about Rico and I won't ask about all the rumors surrounding you."

Tip laughed, a down-home country-hick laugh. "Guess I deserved that. Let's solve us a murder." He started the car, flipped on the air conditioner so we didn't fry, then turned and looked at me with a hard glare.

"I know you said you don't like dogs, but you *do* like women, don't you?"

I laughed, and then we chatted a few more minutes, exploring options on how to proceed with this case before getting back out of the car. After the M.E. finished, Tip assigned some of the uniforms the task of interviewing the "girls" at the motel, and any employees who had been on duty.

"Come on, Gino. I'll take you to the other site, then we'll see if anything interesting came in from the canvassing.

We checked out the first dump site, mulled over why he chose that particular spot, and then headed back to the station in separate cars.

For the next two days we followed up on interviews and witness reports, but none of it led to anything. Ben called on day three and told us the victim had been alive when most of the wounds were made, but dead before the killer cut her up. I was thinking of the pain the victim must have gone through when Tip's phone rang.

"Tip Denton."

"What? I know exactly where that is."

Tip listened for a moment, then said, "No shit? All right, darlin'. I'll be there."

He turned to me. "We've got the head."

"Where?"

"Cypress Creek. Rains washed up a bag that must've been buried there. Some kids found it."

"I'll bet those kids almost lost it when they looked inside."

"Let's go find out," Tip said.

CHAPTER 13

PICTURES IN THE PAPER

Houston, Texas

We pulled onto Louetta Road and Tip punched the gas, getting up to seventy before we hit the traffic light. He looked at me with those hard eyes of his, and the scar on his face bunched up.

"Think you can go any faster, Denton?"

He ran the red light and dodged a slow car in the left lane. "It's the heat that makes me drive fast," Tip said. "In January and February I drive like an old lady."

"Then I wish this were Valentine's Day," I said, and wiped sweat from my forehead. "Crank that a/c up while you're letting off the gas.."

"Roll the window down."

"Damn, you're an ass."

"Speaking of asses," Tip said. "Have you seen the ass on the First Lady? Damn, it's sweet."

I looked over at Denton. "People don't talk like that about the First Lady."

"Only because we've never had one with a nice ass."

I was starting to see why Coop warned me about him. "All the cops in Houston, and I had to get paired with a degenerate."

Tip hit the brakes and made a hard turn into a parking lot of a closed-down restaurant. "This is it. We're on foot from here."

I got out and headed toward the creek, dreading the trip through a short section of woods. After a rain, and in weather like this, the mosquitoes formed assault teams, just waiting for any sucker to enter their territory. We followed a path from the back of the restaurant through the woods, damn near jogging by the time we got a hundred feet. The mosquitoes bit me five or six times and I killed at least a dozen more of them before we got to a clearing by the creek.

"Damn that was bad."

Tip smacked another one from his arm. "Sons of bitches got no respect for the law."

An officer walked up to greet us, hand extended. "Don Brakker." After we introduced ourselves, he said, "This is a nasty one."

I looked at Don and nodded. The head was sitting in a black garbage bag. Brakker, or someone, had rolled the sides down for easier inspection. "Looks like the third piece of the puzzle. The legs and torso were dumped separately."

"People are getting sicker all the time," he said, then took a few steps to stand beside the bag.

I leaned over and peeked inside, not wanting to get too close. The head was mutilated, especially the face. One of the woman's ears was stuffed in her mouth, and her nose was missing. From Ben's early report, the nose had been inserted into her vagina. Both of her eyes were gouged out, and her cheek had a long vertical slit with another one crisscrossing it in the shape of a cross. Whoever did this must have hated this woman something awful.

I looked around. Didn't see what I was looking for, so asked. "No clothes?"

"None of the other sites had clothes," Tip said, then he looked to the officer on the scene. "Who was the lucky one who found the head?"

Don pointed to the left. About 200 feet away, two boys sat on a raft. "Couple of kids ventured out on the flooded creek. They saw this on the bank, dug up from the waters."

"Get anything out of them?" I asked.

"Nothing. They just happened to find it."

Tip leaned in and got real close to the dead woman's ear, the one that remained.

"I'd bet this is a real diamond earring."

I processed what Tip was saying. "If it's really a rich-girl killing, that makes motive the main issue."

Tip stood. "All the more reason why we need an ID. And we've still got no fingers."

"I don't know that we'll need the fingerprints. There's bound to be a missing person's report, and if we get that, we can surely get DNA."

Tip shot me a look and a scowl to go with it. "When you've been working homicide longer, you'll know not to count on anything. Chances are you're right, but chances are just as good, you're not. The bottom line is, don't count on anything going your way, because it usually doesn't."

I looked down at the head one more time. "Goddamn mess."

"Do you think they can do anything with facial restructuring?" Tip asked.

"I'd be surprised. From what I know it's not accurate enough, but maybe technology's changed."

"We need to make identification a priority," Tip said, and I agreed.

I looked over at Don. "Did you see any tracks?"

"We checked for footprints and also for cars. It was dry before last night, so my guess is whoever did it came in under the bridge in a car, buried it, and got out. The rain would have washed away any tracks."

I nodded. "The ground was rock hard before this. I know because I tried planting some flowers last weekend. Might be why he didn't dig too deep."

"Planting flowers?" Tip said.

"It was my wife's garden. I maintain it. Is that all right, asshole?"

"Guess so," Tip said. By the way, what time did the rain start?"

"It was after midnight," I said. "Maybe one or two."

"One or two sounds right," Tip said. "I'm guessing he buried the head, then hit the dumpsters."

We checked the area for about 15 or 20 minutes, then Tip opened his notepad, wrote a few things and flipped it closed.

"Not much here, Gino. Let's go back to the station and review what we've got. After Ben gets through processing we can regroup. We might even get some real leads."

I tapped Don on the arm. "Let us know if you get anything." I handed him a card. "Here's my cell number. Call anytime."

Tip dropped me off to get my car, then we went to the station. We didn't have much yet, but what we had told us a few things.

Tip had photos of the legs. She looked tall. I hadn't thought about that, but I guessed Ben would have to put her back together to get statistics and do the autopsy. I shivered. No way I'd want his job. Looking at dead bodies didn't bother me much, but I sure as hell wouldn't want it for a job.

"Me neither," I said. "Not to mention cutting the bodies up, inspecting stomach contents, measuring body parts. You name it."

The picture of the torso showed a couple of deep punctures in it, both by the left lung, and they were round. "Could have been a screwdriver," I said.

"Or an icepick, or one of those construction tools…I forget what they're called. Ben should be able to get us something on that."

The most disturbing part of this was the mutilation. Killing someone was one thing, but to cut them up and disrespect the body was something else entirely. "Why cut off the nose and ear?" I asked.

Tip shook his head. "We'll find out when we get this son of a bitch in a room by ourselves."

"That would be fun, wouldn't it? Just us and the killer. No restrictions." I smiled. "Maybe in the next life." I looked through the notes on what we had and jotted down a few questions. "Everything was found on the north side of the city. Did he kill her up there? Or did he dump up there to make us think so?"

"Why did he kill her? And why hide the head?" Tip asked. "You know, this looks like a sex crime, but it doesn't follow the regular pattern for one. It's almost as if the killer wants us to think it's a sex crime."

"Maybe it's a woman," I said.

"Women don't usually get that violent."

"Maybe it's a pissed-off woman."

"You mean a jealous one?"

"That's what I said."

Tip tapped his fingers on the desk. "I can't get away from why he dumped her head, and why at the creek? Convenience, or to throw us off?"

I stopped chewing on my pen and looked at Tip. "Because he didn't want us to know who she was."

Tip nodded. "As we talked about before, identifying her has got to be our priority. If the killer thought that was so important, it's where we'll find the clues."

I stood and shoved some papers into the folder. "Let's get a few pictures in the paper. Maybe we'll stir something up."

"I'll tell you what you'll stir up," Tip said. "Coop's temper. Besides, they're not going to print pictures like that."

"If the pictures are cleaned up they will. As for Coop, we'll have to keep it to ourselves. We can't let her know the pictures leaked from us."

"She'll know where the leak came from."

I looked at Tip. "Do you give a shit?"

He laughed, that same way he had earlier.

"Let's get some pictures in the paper."

"You got anybody in mind to call about it? It will take a reporter with balls, and one we can trust. We don't want the whole thing, but a controlled picture. Maybe with the eyes covered up."

"I know one with balls as big as mine." Tip put his phone on speaker and dialed. It was answered on the second ring.

"Samantha Roberts."

"Hello, darlin'."

A long pause was followed by a huge sigh. "Hello, Tip."

"Damn, I'm glad to hear your voice, too."

"Did you need something?" She put a lot of irritation in that question.

"Stop pretending you don't love me. And besides, I've got a scoop for you."

"The dumpster girl?" Excitement replaced the irritation.

"That's the one."

"Where do you want to meet?"

Tip thought for a moment. "I don't want to meet, but if you were to find yourself wandering around Kuykendahl Road by Cypress Creek, you *might* find something you'd want pictures of."

"I'll be there in thirty minutes."

"The officer on the scene is Don Brakker. Tell him to call me if he has questions. And Roberts, you're gonna have to clean the picture up. It's a mess."

"I've got somebody with software that's amazing. Leave it to me."

Tip was about to hang up when he thought about the most important part. "Roberts, this is not official. You *did not* get this from me."

"I know how to handle it. Thanks."

"Sounds good," Tip said. He looked over at me, and winked. "Now we wait and see what happens."

***

Tip waited until Gino went home, then he headed out, trolling the streets west of downtown looking for Chicky Ramirez. He already called Chicky twice and got no answer, so more than likely he was floating in the clouds or doing something illegal. Chicky was one of Tip's best informants, but his unreliable state of mind was always a factor. After two more calls, Tip got an answer while he was sitting at a traffic light.

"If it ain't the Tipster. What's up, my man?"

"Where are you?"

"'Bout fifty feet from your sorry ass, and walkin' that way."

Tip looked to the side and pulled up to the curb. Chicky opened the door and got in. "I saw you been callin' me, Tipster."

"Have you been helping Gino out on anything?"

Chicky looked at him with a raised brow. "Sure, I mean, you know I help out Gino. Help out lots of dudes."

"Think back in time, Chicky. Did you help him out with Rico?"

Chicky raised his hands. "Don't know what you're talking 'bout there."

"I think you do. I think you fingered Rico for him."

Chicky's expression went from suspicion to one tainted with fear. "Gino's a good guy."

"I know he is. Maybe you're slipping, not up on things anymore. Gino's my partner now." Tip flashed that half-mean look with his scar. "You know how it goes. Whether you're on the street or a cop, a man's got to know who he's rolling with."

Chicky shrugged. "Mind's not sharp like it used to be. Rico's been in the ground a long time."

Tip handed Chicky a hundred-dollar bill.

He started to hand it back, but Tip shoved another one into Chicky's hand. "If I can count right, I gave you two Franklin's. Think hard before you say no."

Chicky didn't say anything for a few seconds. His hands shook. When he began talking he looked out the side window, his voice a whisper. "Might be I helped Gino some. Might have told him where Rico was one night."

"Speak up," Tip said.

He turned to face Tip. "Said I might have helped him one night."

"Which night? The night Rico died?"

"Might've been. Maybe."

Tip reached for the bills, but Chicky pulled away. "Yeah, come to think of it. Was that night."

"Thanks," Tip said.

"This stayin' between us? Can't have Gino—"

Tip pulled another hundred-dollar bill out of his pocket. "Nobody but us and Ben Franklin will know, unless you tell somebody."

He smiled. "You're still the man. Still the Tipster."

"One more thing. You ever hear anything about—"

Chicky was shaking his head before Tip finished. "Man, if you're talking about your mom, got nothing for you. Give up on it. That shit will eat you up."

"Tell me about it," Tip said, and started the engine as Chicky opened the door.

On the way home, Tip thought about what he'd learned. Nothing concrete, but the information from Chicky told him what he needed to know; besides, he felt certain that if he needed more details he could squeeze them out of Chicky. The problem was what to do with the information. He knew what he *should* do—tell Coop, or Renkin—but as he made the turn onto the freeway ramp he decided he'd wait and see how Gino played out as a partner.

He already knew one thing about Gino; he must be a stupid fuck for trusting a guy like Chicky.

CHAPTER 14

RECOGNITION

Houston, Texas

Coop got in extra early, knowing she'd have an enormous amount of work to do, with all the pampering that Mayor Rusty Johnson and his rich friends would need. Coop wasn't handling security but many of her officers had been assigned to help, and she was going to make damn sure nothing happened on her watch.

"Good morning, Cindy," she said as she rounded the corner.

"I'll have tea ready in a minute, Captain. Your paper's on the desk."

Coop went into her office, flicked on the light and took a seat behind her desk, opening the paper as she woke the computer to check emails.

"How *the hell* did this happen?" She grabbed the phone and dialed Gino's number.

"Cataldi."

"Have you seen the paper?"

"No. Why?"

"The dumpster girl is splashed all over the front page." There was a momentary pause, then. "Did you and Tip have anything to do with this?"

"Hell no. We made sure to keep reporters out of it."

"Get in here. *Now.*"

She pushed the button to dial Tip's number.

"Good morning, Gladys."

"Screw you, Denton. Tell me about these pictures."

"I wish I could, but I don't know a damn thing. All I can tell you is that bitch is haunting me."

"What bitch?"

"Samantha Roberts, the reporter who wrote the story about those pictures."

"I don't understand," Coop said.

"She's the son of a bitch who filed charges against me for sexual harassment when I was with the Sheriff's Department. Ask John, he'll tell you about it."

"That's her?"

"One and the same."

Coop settled down a bit. "All right, get in here as soon as you can. Gino's on his way." She paused. "Damn it, I'm going to need help. Cybil and Rusty are going to—"

"I'm on my way," Tip said. "And don't worry, Gino and I will take care of it."

"I *am* worried. That's all I do is worry. And stop referring to the Chief as *John*."

"That's his name."

"I know it's his name, but show respect for his position. And…never mind. Just don't forget there's a big event tomorrow."

"I thought that was last night."

"It was. There's another one tomorrow."

"Good luck, Cap. I'm just glad I don't have to be there."

Coop set the phone on her desk and stared at the picture in the paper. At least the damn snake of a reporter had the decency to touch up the photos. They didn't show the eyes, but the…"

Coop called Cindy over the intercom. "Get the medical examiner's office and have them send an original picture of the dumpster lady's head. I need it now."

Half an hour later, as Coop stared in a trancelike state at the picture, the intercom rang.

"Cybil is on line one," Cindy said.

"I'll call her back."

"She seemed upset. She said to get you no matter where you were."

Coop waited a few seconds, then, "All right, I'll take it."

She picked up the line. "I know—"

"Gladys, what's going on in your department? How did we end up with *this* on the front page while my event is going on?"

Coop let Cybil rant for a while then said, "Did you look at the pictures?"

"That's why I called."

"Did you take a *good* look?"

"I didn't use a magnifying glass; they were disgusting."

"It's Barbara."

After a moment of silence, Cybil said, "What?"

"Barbara," Coop said. "That's our Barbara."

"Oh my God! Are you sure?"

"I'm looking at the pictures on my computer," Coop said.

"Who would…did you tell your detectives you knew her?"

"Not yet."

"Don't say anything."

"We can't hold back evidence. That would make us—"

"Wait until this is all over, then we'll decide what to do. You could say you didn't recognize her. I didn't, and I've known her longer than you."

"They need to know, Cybil."

"You can't let them find out," Cybil said. "Not yet anyway. She might have kept recordings."

"That's not my concern," Coop said, and then, "Wait. Recordings of what?"

"Of things you don't want to know about. Your boss, and his boss, and lots of others."

Coop closed the file on the pictures she'd been looking at. "Shit."

"Shit is right, Captain Cooper. And you'll be knee-deep in it if you let those detectives search Barbara's condo before we find her files."

"This is treading on dangerous ground," Coop said.

"That's nothing new to us."

Coop sighed. "I'll give it a few days and see where it leads."

***

Cybil made sure the phone was hung up, then dialed another number, tapping her foot while she waited. After three rings it was answered.

"Hello, Cybil."

"How did she end up dead?"

"What? Who?"

"Barbara's dead! Chopped into pieces and spread all over town. What in God's name did you people do?"

"Barbara's dead?" A long silence followed, then, "How? What happened?"

"I already told you. Somebody chopped her up into pieces. Butchered her."

"And you think *I* had something to do with this?"

"Did you?"

"Of course not. My God. I can't believe she's dead."

"Damn it," Cybil said. "I don't know what's going on but it's not going to look good. Watch your back."

Coop hung up and leaned back in her chair. Cybil's concern at the end had seemed genuine. Now, it was Gladys's turn to be puzzled.

CHAPTER 15

POLITICIANS AND QUESTIONS

Houston, Texas

Coop thought the event for Mayor Rusty Johnson went as good as could be expected. As good as it could without the president being there. She had done her duty and made the rounds, letting everyone see that Captain Gladys Cooper was there to support the mayor.

Now it's time to go home.

The elevator doors opened. Coop exited and walked across the lobby, heading for her car.

"Cooper, over here."

Coop turned to see Cybil heading her way, weaving through a crowd of people who hadn't left yet, or were waiting for valet parking to get their cars. *For God's sake, will it ever end?*

"Hello, Cybil. I was just leaving."

"After a night like this. It was disastrous!" Cybil grabbed her arm and almost dragged her to the side of the room, away from eavesdroppers. "Where have you been? I've been looking everywhere."

"I've been locked in a room with the president. I thought you knew."

"You son of a bitch. Don't even joke about it."

Coop fought to restrain a laugh. "Did you need something? Or are you just trying to find company for your misery?"

Cybil waved to someone passing by, then looked at Coop. "The first thing I'm going to do is get even with that asshole."

"Do you mean President Marsen?"

"Of course, I mean Marsen, and you knew who I meant. It was bad enough he didn't show up for Rusty, but he didn't even call in. He could have at least placed a video call."

"Cybil, I know you don't give a damn about Rusty, so what are you upset about? You've got a hell of a lot, girl. You're the mayor's wife, for God's sake."

Cybil's eyes flashed murderously. She looked around to make sure no one was listening, then leaned close. "You think I went through all I did to end up some redneck mayor's wife? That could have been me in the White House."

"Get over it," Coop said. "That's long gone and you can't get it back."

"No, I can't get it back, but…"

"Let go of it, Cybil. For your own sake."

Cybil nodded, reluctantly. "I'll let it go, but there's a lot more in store for this country girl."

Coop looked Cybil in the eyes. "While you were dreaming, did you forget Barbara's dead? Don't you think we should be worrying about that?"

"You already said it—she's dead. There's nothing we can do for her."

Coop shook her head as she walked away. "Goodnight, Cybil. I've got a busy day tomorrow."

Coop smiled at everyone as she left, though it took every ounce of will power. What she wanted to do was smack Cybil in the face.

No way I'm taking shit from that bitch. Not anymore.

CHAPTER 16

SUBTERFUGE

Houston, Texas

Cybil shuffled around the kitchen still dressed in her robe and slippers. She brewed more coffee while she finished giving Rusty his instructions for the day.

"Talk to as few people as possible and make sure that none of them are reporters. The papers have already made sure we look like fools."

She rinsed her cup, dried it, and tore open the top of a packet of sweetener. "And whatever you do, stay out of the strip clubs. They'll be watching you."

Rusty didn't even deny it, just nodded his head and took the admonishments as if he were a schoolboy being reprimanded by the teacher.

Cybil tapped a long fingernail on the countertop as the coffee dripped, and all the while she shook her head. "I can't believe Tom did that to us," she said, then slammed a frying pan on the counter. "The least he could have done was give us more notice."

Rusty got up and rubbed her shoulders. "I wouldn't worry too much about it."

She shook her shoulders and moved away to get Rusty to stop. "Don't worry? You can't announce that the president will be at a party, then have him not show. And that fake excuse he gave for not coming down…"

Rusty turned her toward him. "For your own sake, girl, give it up. It's done with. Like my daddy used to say—once the chicken's dead you might as well eat it."

She shot Rusty a nasty look, snatched the coffee pot from the burner and poured herself another cup. "You worry about your business and I'll worry about the rest. You got that, *boy?*"

Rusty grabbed his hat—a Stetson—like any real Texan would wear—and headed for the door. "You know where to reach me."

I know all right. You'll probably be fucking a chicken.

After Rusty left, Cybil sat alone at the kitchen table, reading the morning paper, including the latest news on the 'dumpster murder' as they were calling it, and eating the last of a piece of cantaloupe. When the home phone rang, she grabbed it with a vengeance, but then calmed and spoke in her sweet morning voice. "Good morning, this is Cybil."

"This is RB."

She sat straight up. "I didn't expect to hear from you."

"I wanted to apologize about Tom. He isn't normally—"

Cybil stood and paced the kitchen. "Did *you* know about this?"

"I had no idea."

"Right. I'm sure you didn't."

Cybil made a few noises that could have been interpreted in a half a dozen ways. "I wouldn't be surprised if you two were in this together."

"I can assure you—"

"Forget about that. We have bigger problems."

"What?"

"For the life of Christ, don't you pay attention to anything I say? Barbara is *dead.*" Cybil's voice rose again, tainted with suspicion. "Did Tom do it?"

"Don't be ridiculous. He hasn't seen her in years."

"Now who's being ridiculous? Besides, if it wasn't Tom, then who?"

"I have no idea, but you better get things under control before some kind of evidence turns up. None of us can afford to be embarrassed."

"Don't worry about my end. And if you find out anything, I better be the first one to hear."

"You will. I swear."

"All right. Goodbye."

"Bye."

CHAPTER 17

A LATE NIGHT CALL

I kicked my feet up on the desk and stared out the window. The traffic was already backed up and it wasn't even close to rush hour. As I watched the cars inch along, I focused on how to kick-start this case. The trouble was we had nothing to go on. No fingers for prints, no witnesses, and no match from missing persons. Tip had been right about that.

All we had were pieces of a woman's body with no clue as to where she'd been killed, or why. The *when* part had been answered by the autopsy; she'd been killed sometime the night the killer dumped her.

"Where do we go now, Tip?"

"Maybe we'll get something from the pictures," Tip said.

I turned around, shaking my head. "That'll be a long shot."

"You're right, but it's all we've got right now."

I made a few follow-up calls to potential leads, and then we worked the rest of the day interviewing people who might have seen something at the dump sites. When it came time to go home we still had nothing but the photos and they hadn't produced any results.

"I'm calling it quits for the night," I said.

"You have a date?"

"Yeah, me and a bottle of Chianti. We're going to share a movie."

Tip lost his smile. "Calling it quits tonight is okay, but starting tomorrow, we're on this until it's done."

I headed home, took a shower and got into some comfortable shorts. After cooking pasta, I heated the last of a mushroom medley I'd cooked a few nights before, and scooped it onto a few slices of garlic bread. I took my time eating, something I'd never done in all the years I was married. And I thought about how much I missed Mary.

Dishes only took a minute, then I retired to the sofa to watch a movie—*Predator*—one I could never pass up. It might go down in trivia history as the only movie to star two future governors. I was at the part where Jesse Ventura was about to get killed when the phone rang. I got up before I realized it was the home phone. Nobody had that number, so I sat back down. The alien was in the trees, camouflaged. But that phone kept ringing.

Shit, it might be about Ron.

I rushed to the kitchen, where I still had a phone connected to the cradle. *Ancient*, Ron called it. This phone was so old it didn't even have a screen to view caller ID.

I tried to keep the panic from my voice. "This is Gino."

"I saw those pictures in the paper."

It was a woman's voice, but it sounded strange. A distant, hollow sound. "What pictures?"

"The pictures of the dead woman."

I went from pissed and disinterested to alert, searching for something to write with. "Who is this?"

"I don't think who I am matters. I have a few questions, though."

I found a pen in the second drawer and a small notepad next to it. I pulled it out and sat at the table, writing—woman, called at 9:27. Sounds…funny.

"What kind of questions?"

"Do you know when she died? *Exactly?*"

"Are you a reporter?" I was going to be pissed if this was some goddamn reporter trying to get a scoop.

"How about if I ask the questions and you answer."

It *had* to be a reporter. "I'm not in the mood for games. And my house is off limits. Goodnight." I almost hung up, but she said something just as I reached to place the phone back on the cradle.

"Do you know she had blue eyes?"

I yanked the phone back to my ear.

"What?"

"I thought that would get your attention. Yes, her eyes were blue. I'm certain that the medical examiner has told you that by now."

I wrote on the pad 'knew eye color' while

I thought of what to say. "How do you know she had blue eyes?"

"Ready to answer some questions now?"

Her voice seemed…sullen, and at the same time…concerned. If she was a reporter she had good connections, if not…she had information about the murder that we needed. Which meant she was connected to it somehow.

"What do you need to know?"

"The same thing I asked earlier. Do you know when she died? *Exactly.*"

She said it the same way as before, with the emphasis on the word *exactly.* It must have been important for her to ask it twice.

I wrote it down, then said, "I don't know for sure."

She didn't say anything so I thought I better throw out a small bone. "Not yet, I don't. We haven't gotten the full report from the M.E."

"I find that difficult to believe, Detective. Time of death is typically one of the first things determined by the medical examiner."

I took another note. *Knows about police procedure.*

"We were more focused on the victim's identity, but time of death is coming. I'll have that by tomorrow. Why the questions? Did you know her?"

"What time tomorrow do you anticipate an answer?"

"I'm not sure. Why don't you give me your number? I'll call when I get it."

A throaty laugh answered me. "Pretty stupid, Detective. I'm disappointed more than impressed. Perhaps even insulted."

"Sorry. I thought—"

"You didn't think anything. Goodnight."

"No, wait!"

The line went dead.

I sat stunned for a minute, then dialed Tip. He picked up on the first ring.

"Denton."

"It's Gino. I just had a weird call."

I filled him in on the details and we brainstormed but couldn't figure out who it might have been. He thought it could have been Samantha Roberts, the reporter. He said he'd check on that in the morning.

"All right, I'm going to sleep. See you first thing."

CHAPTER 18

WAITING FOR THE PHONE TO RING

Houston, Texas

I met Tip at the station, then we headed out for another day of interviews. With any luck this would be the last of them. "Did you check with Roberts?"

"The call didn't come from her," Tip said. "At least that's what she said, and I believe her."

"Who has my private number? It's unlisted. You're not supposed to be able to get a damn unlisted number." I kept one hand on the wheel but turned some to look at Tip. "And remember, the caller knew the victim had blue eyes. She *knew.*"

"How the fuck did she know that? You sure you didn't let it slip?"

"Of course I didn't let it slip. I thought she was a reporter, and I was about to hang up when she sprung that on me."

"What did she want?"

"We went through this last night. She wanted to know TOD—exactly. It meant something to her."

"And you have no idea who this was?"

"Not a fucking clue."

What did caller ID say?"

"Unknown. I don't mean it said 'unknown'. I meant I don't have a phone that reads caller ID."

"Jesus Christ," Tip said. Then he calmed down. "Probably doesn't matter. I doubt if we'd have seen who was calling anyway."

Tip stared out the side window for a moment. "You sure it wasn't a reporter?"

"I thought she was at first but…I don't know. The more I talked to her, the more I realized she didn't *sound* like a reporter. Something about her voice…" I thought some more on it, then made up my mind.

"No, I'm convinced. But somebody gave her information on the case, or she knew the victim. One or the other."

"Maybe she'll call back. If she doesn't, we'll get the phone company involved."

"It could just be some wacko who got lucky with the blue-eyes guess."

Tip laughed. "My ass."

We finished up the day, once again with no progress. On most murders if leads didn't come to fruition in the first couple of days the case started going stale. We couldn't afford to let that happen. Coop was already on our ass about finding this killer, and I'm sure the chief was on hers and the mayor on his.

If she called again tonight, I'd be ready with questions. If she didn't, I'd have a glass of wine, a good book, and some of the old crooners playing in the background.

I sat in my favorite chair and, for a moment, relaxed, closing my eyes to enjoy the comfort and serenity. Then thoughts of Ron rushed in and I wondered how he was and what he was doing?

Did he run away today? Was he still sober? Would he be able to stay clean? Does he still hate me?

The questions were the same every day, and, of all of them, the last one was probably the least important as far as his future was concerned but the most important for me. I was forty-two years old, with a dead wife, and a kid in rehab who hated me. And no bridge nearby to jump from.

Where's a fucking gun when you need it?

The trouble was, I *did* have a gun, several of them, and too often I'd been tempted to use them. The irony was that the main reason I didn't was because of Ron, and the main reason I thought of it was because of Ron. I should have been there for him after Mary died. Instead I wallowed in self-pity and left him to his own devices. I took *my* anger and frustration out on drug dealers; he dealt with his anger by turning to drugs.

Somewhere between "woe is me" and "God help me" the phone rang. I nearly jumped from my seat. I let it ring a few more times, then picked it up. "Hello?"

"I tried to call earlier. Where were you?" It was her again. No doubt. I looked at the clock—it was only eight.

"Who are you?"

"No need to go into that again. Names are unimportant. Did you find out about the eyes? They were blue, weren't they?"

I checked the caller ID (I had bought a new phone at Tip's insistence.), but it read *unknown*. That made me think of the grave in the cemetery of the Clint Eastwood movie, *The Good, The Bad, and The Ugly*. Where was Eli Wallach when he was needed?

"I guess you already know the eyes were blue. I have two questions regarding that. *How* did you know? And how did *you* know? And one is as important as the other."

She laughed, another one of those throaty laughs she was so good at. And as I listened to her I felt positive that she was disguising her voice; in fact, it sounded familiar.

"I thought we had an agreement that *I* would ask the questions. Besides, you didn't expect me to answer, did you?"

"Maybe we better tape these conversations so we both know what was said, because I remember it differently."

"Detective, I'm surprised at you. I'm sure you're already taping this call, and tomorrow you'll have it analyzed and traced and followed up on in a hundred ways." She laughed again, and while she was laughing I scrambled for my cell phone so I *could* tape the call, even if I had to use the cell held up to the earpiece. "That won't matter though." A pause, then, "Did you get the time of death? What time did she die—exactly?"

"This should be a two-way street. What do I get?"

"I could promise a lot, but suppose I told you that…let's see…I could tell you what the victim was wearing *before* the body was dumped."

What the hell is going on? Did this woman kill her? "How would you know that?"

"Let's say I've seen pictures."

"There are no pictures."

"Oh my, Detective, you surprise me. How do you know there aren't pictures? How do you know the killer didn't take photos as keepsakes?"

Holy shit! "Do you have pictures?"

I could hear what sounded like her fingers tapping on a tabletop, or something.

"Time of death? I seem to recall that issue still hanging out there."

I didn't figure it would hurt to tell her this, and it might even get us something in return. "Three days ago."

"More specifically?"

One tough bitch. "Sometime from early evening up to maybe ten at night."

"Thank you, Detective. I didn't expect you to be honest. It's refreshing. Perhaps we'll talk again."

"Hang on a minute. You've got to give me something."

A long silence followed.

I thought I heard her breathing, but wasn't sure. "Are you still there?"

"I'm here, and I'm trying my best to help you." More silence, then, "Did you find a dress? Assuming you did, I'll bet if you traced it you'd get clues. Follow that lead and I'm certain you'll have this solved in no time. In fact, if it's the one I'm thinking of, it should be easy to trace."

"And which dress would that be?" I asked, while furiously jotting down notes.

"A blue dress. Very expensive."

CHAPTER 19

TRACE THE CALL

Houston, Texas

I didn't want to bother Tip again at home, but I knew he'd want to hear about this immediately. He answered on the first ring. It made me wonder just where he kept his cell phone, as every time I called, he answered on the first or second ring.

"She called again," I said.

"I assume no caller ID."

"Unknown."

"Anything new?"

"I told her the time of death and when I did, she *knew* it was right, like she was testing me. And oh, yeah, the best part is, she said the blue dress is a clue. That if we follow the—"

"We don't have a blue dress."

"I know we don't. And get this. She implied that she'd seen pictures of the crime scene."

"What the fuck!"

"Exactly what I thought.."

"Who could have pictures of the scene other than the murderer?" Tip pondered his statement for a moment. "Do you think a woman could have done it?"

"Keep in mind, Tip, she didn't say for sure that she'd seen pictures, but she implied it." I wished I had the damn call taped from the beginning, but I have a bad recording of the end."

"Did you get anything?" Tip asked.

"Nothing I could tell. I'll let you listen tomorrow, although I think I recognized something about the voice. And she's definitely disguising it. Which makes me more convinced that we need to find out where she's calling from, but I'll bet it's a disposable cell."

"We'll fill Coop in tomorrow," Tip said.

"All right, see you in the morning."

As I got ready for bed, my cell phone rang. It was the ring tone I used for Chicky.

What the hell does he want?

I grabbed the phone. "What's up, Chick?"

"Not much of nothin', Gino. You good to talk?"

Alarms went off in my head. "Yeah, I'm good."

"People askin' round 'bout you. Thought I'd let you know."

"Asking about what?"

"You know."

"Chicky, I don't play games. About what?"

"That night. 'Bout that night at Sueños."

My heart raced. A pain shot through my chest. "Who's asking?"

"Can't say."

"What the fuck do you mean; you can't say?"

"Can't. You know how it works. I go talkin' on who tells what, sure as shit, I'm outta business. A man's gotta live, Gino."

"I'm asking one last time. If you don't tell me something, I'm coming down."

I waited through a long silence, then Chicky said, "The ones askin' are your people. And that's all I'm sayin'."

I took a few deep breaths to calm myself. "What did you tell them?"

"Ain't said shit. Just figured you'd want to know."

"All right. Thanks. I owe you."

"Everybody owes the Chick. Be careful, my man. Don't trust *nobody*."

"You got that."

I hung up the phone and felt like crawling under the bed. With everything going on, this was the last thing I needed to hear.

What the fuck.

It took me two hours to get to sleep, but it happened. I faded in and out, brushing past a few dream scenarios that had me in prison, but eventually I settled in to some decent sleep. When the morning came—far too early—I polished off three cups of coffee before heading to the station.

Captain Cooper listened to me recount the past few phone calls from the mystery lady, and she even let me finish with no interruptions, though her pacing annoyed the shit out of me. I then let her and Tip listen to the little piece of the conversation I had taped. After three replays, neither one recognized the voice or determined anything. I stared at her when I was done. "That's all we've got, Coop. Until she calls again."

"And you think she'll call again?"

"I don't see why not," Tip said. "She seems to have locked onto Gino."

"But why is she calling Gino? You're the lead on the case." Coop stopped pacing and cracked her knuckles, an annoying habit of hers. "If this woman knows enough to get Gino's private number, she should know who the lead is."

"Gino thought the voice sounded familiar. Maybe she didn't want me to hear her," Tip said.

Coop shook her head. "She has to know Gino would tape it."

"Voices are different on recorders."

"We need a good recorder. Something professional." Coop slammed her fist on the desk. "Make sure you get something. Have the tech guys send you home with a set-up." She mumbled something about stone age, then said, "Now think. What do you believe about the voice sounded familiar?"

I thought about it for a moment before shaking my head. "I'm not sure, I think she's trying to cover up a Texas accent."

"But... I heard a 'but' in that statement."

"But now and then I'll hear a word or two that has that twang to it. It comes out almost as an accident, which is why I'm guessing she's from Texas." I thought some more, closing my eyes to focus. "She seems...concerned, in one way."

"You think she's the killer?" Coop asked.

I shook my head. "I don't know why, but...no. I don't."

Coop nodded. "I don't think so either. I can't see a woman doing this."

"I've seen some jealous women who could do a hell of a lot," Tip said. "And she knows things she shouldn't. She even told Gino there were pictures."

"I heard that part, but until we see them I won't necessarily believe it. And I can't get over the brutality part. Women who kill do it mostly to men," Coop said. "They might blame another woman for breaking up a marriage or luring their husband away, but if it gets violent, it's taken out on the man."

"What's your opinion, Captain? Have you got any idea who this might be?"

"I think this woman is powerful enough to get access to one of my detective's private home number, or…"

I suddenly felt pressured. "Or what?" I'm sure I didn't manage to keep the irritation from my voice.

She glared at me. A warning. "Or you've been careless."

"I don't give out my home phone number. I don't even use it." I gave her a glare right back. "So you think this woman is a suspect?"

"I didn't say that but if she has pictures she might have been there. Maybe she was with a guy who did it? Maybe another woman did it? Hell, I don't know. That's what you two have to find out. And you better do it quickly. I'm catching a lot of heat."

Tip stood. He'd been unusually quiet—for him— since we got here. But I'd noticed since we'd been interviewing that sometimes he did that, sat back and evaluated.

"How about you get us some information on phone records, Captain, and we'll find the dress, since that seems to be a clue."

"I'll look into it, but I doubt if we're busting this case open with phone records. Get out there and do your jobs."

We went back to our desks, stopping on the way to get coffee. Then we went over what we had.

"What exactly did she say about the dress?" Tip asked for the tenth time.

"I already told you. She asked, 'Did you find a dress?' And then later she said, 'A blue dress. Very expensive."

"So, she knew it wasn't with the body."

As soon as Tip said it, I knew we had something. "You're right. That means we missed the dress. The killer dumped it somewhere else."

Tip kicked his feet up on the desk and leaned back, resting his head on his clasped hands. "There's another option. If this lady caller is the killer, maybe she buried the head so we didn't find it. If we assume she didn't want us finding the clothes, maybe she buried them too."

I jumped up. "They could still be at the creek. Let's go."

Tip swung his feet off and followed me, hollering at Fat Charlie—another ex-deputy that Renkin brought with him. "Charlie, get us some shovels up at the Cy Creek scene. We're on our way."

"Some shovels?"

"And some people to work them," Tip said. "Unless you want to do it."

Tip drove, which I didn't like. I didn't mind him driving fast, but the combination of fast and not paying attention was a killer. When he hit ninety, bobbing and weaving between cars, I panicked, one hand on the door edge of the seat and the other on the door grip.

"Hey, Denton, those clothes aren't going anywhere and I don't want to end up in a hospital or morgue."

"Why's that? Underwear not clean?"

"They're clean now, but if we get hit I'm sure I'll shit myself. And *that* would be embarrassing."

He managed to keep it to eighty or less the rest of the way but every now and then he'd punch it to see my reaction. I vowed right then that I'd drive from now on.

A few minutes later we pulled into the abandoned restaurant parking lot and got out, walking down the now familiar path to where the head was found.

"The killer could have buried separate bags," Tip said. "If she did, or he did, the one with clothes could still be here."

"You know, Tip, if it was her, and she didn't want us finding the clues, why did she tell me about the dress?"

"Damned if I know, but now I'm thinking that maybe that's why the hole she buried the head in was shallow."

"Why?"

"Because she's a woman."

"Don't even try to convince me that a woman couldn't dig a hole as deep as a man. If a woman did this to a body, she could sure as shit dig a hole."

"Maybe," Tip said. "We'll see."

We looked around to see if we could spot any differences in the ground, signs of recent digging, and such, but the flooding from the creek would've wiped any of that away. We couldn't tell anything. Soon afterwards, the cavalry arrived complete with shovels. Tip showed them where to dig.

"Start from here and dig until you find it."

"Find what?"

"Probably another bag. We expect this one to have clothes in it."

Two hours later, they found it.

"Got something."

"It's a garbage bag."

I ran over, Tip by my side. "Bring it up," he said. "Careful with it."

We both leaned down and he opened the bag. The stench that came out knocked us back. "Whew!" Tip said. "Goddamn but I hate bad smells." He stood and walked around a bit, gagging, but left the bag on the ground. "How the hell can you stay there?"

"The same way you can drive two hundred miles an hour and not freak out."

I opened the bag wider and looked inside. "Blue dress, I said. It's got a lot of blood on it, but it's blue as the fucking ocean."

Tip came back, his mouth covered with a handkerchief. "I'll be damned."

I looked up at Tip and, when our eyes met, we both seemed to know. "She did it," I said, and something inside of me felt sick. It's not what I wanted to believe.

"What else is in there?"

I didn't touch anything, but looked. "Shoes, dress, maybe panties." I closed it up again. "We'll see when Ben gets done with it." I handed the bag to Tip, who shied away from it. "Get one of Ben's people out here. They'll process it."

All the way back to the station I made small talk, discussed the case, talked about the First Lady and her drug program, anything to keep my mind from my "night caller." Something about this woman was getting to me and for the life of me I didn't know what.

On top of that, I kept looking for signs that it might be Tip who was asking Chicky about me. I knew Tip had the connections, and I wouldn't blame him for checking out a partner. Still. It didn't sit right. Made me nervous.

CHAPTER 20

CLOTHES MAKE THE WOMAN

Houston, Texas

I got home, fixed a salad with some cheese, not in the mood for a big meal. After eating I grabbed the phone and brought it into the family room with me, setting it on the coffee table within easy reach. All night I found myself looking at the clock and wondering when the phone would ring.

Why hasn't she called?

I fidgeted, kept shifting in my seat, reading the same page of the novel over and over. Soon after that I fell asleep on the sofa, the book I was reading still in my hand.

The ring of the phone jarred me awake. I grabbed for it, clearing my throat and doing my best to sound alert. It was midnight. "Hello."

"I hope I didn't wake you."

It was her. "No, you didn't."

She must have heard the sleepiness in my voice, that unmistakable sound that anyone can detect.

"Why do people lie about things like that?"

"Things like what?"

"About being awakened. You were sleeping. Why didn't you just say so?" She sighed. "Why do men *always* lie?"

She said it so low I almost didn't hear her, as if she whispered it to herself. I reached for a notepad.

She thinks men lie to her. Why?

"What are you writing down?"

"Noth—" I was going to lie and thought better of it. "I was wondering why you think men always lie to you, but since I was about to do the same thing, perhaps now I know."

A short chuckle followed, more like a polite laugh, as if she knew it was expected. "A little lie like that I can take, Detective. It's the bigger ones that bother me."

I perked up. "Like what?"

She paused. "Like…'I wasn't with anyone, dear. I swear.' Or, 'That lipstick on my private parts—I don't know how it got there.' Those are the lies that bother me."

I made another note, careful not to let her know I was writing by pushing the notepad further away from the mouthpiece.

Husband cheats on her and she knows it.

Then below it,

Could be motive?

"Not all men do those things."

I thought she was going to comment, but cynical laughter was her answer.

I didn't know where to try and steer this conversation, so thought I'd go straight for it. "Why did you call me?"

Silence.

I was going to ask how she got my number, but thought that would put her on the defensive. *Think, asshole.* I had to get her talking. Had to get her to open up.

"We found the dress."

"I never doubted you, Detective. You're well on your way now."

I shook my head, a stupid thing to do when I knew she couldn't see it. "It doesn't look like it'll give us much. The killer made sure of that…but you knew that didn't you?"

I worried about pushing it that far, but she ignored me, moving on as if I hadn't asked the question. Just then I remembered the tape recording equipment that Coop had me set up, and rushed to the kitchen to turn it on. While I was halfway there she began talking, but I interrupted. I wanted to start the tape first.

"What can you tell me about the shoes?" It was time to see if she knew more.

"Detective, I know you're not stupid. One look at the shoes she wore and you would have known they were important."

It was my turn to play the game. I remained silent, pouring a glass of water from the fridge. When she started up again, I covered my opposite ear so I could listen.

"The first time I saw her she wore Ferragamo shoes. A beautiful pair of suede slingback pumps with leather trim around the toe. I remember that because in high school, Ferragamo shoes were what I wanted most."

A slight pause followed and I let it linger.

"Say what you want about this woman, Detective, but she had good taste."

"Shoes must be important for you to remember so much about them."

A light-hearted laugh followed. "*All* women love shoes. They are what defines you, what makes you shine."

"And you're a Ferragamo lady?" I tried my best to keep her talking; she seemed to be in a talkative mood tonight, but she wasn't giving me much to work with discussing shoes. I'd heard of Ferragamo, and knew they were expensive, but that's all I knew.

"Not necessarily, but shoes have always been important. I remember one of my earliest pair…"

Another silence, and for a moment I thought she'd hung up, but I heard her breathing, so I kept listening.

"There was a fire. Everyone was running and screaming, trying to get out, but all I could think about were my shoes. I had just acquired a pair of new shoes—I say acquired as that's what it feels like, something to be sought after—and they were important to me, they were my life, my existence. At least, they seemed like it at the time. I ran up the steps to get them despite Ginger hollering at me to leave.

"Fire shot out of the door next to mine. I ran toward it, determined to get those shoes, but then I remembered Fluffy. He was stuck in the room at the other end of the hall. I had no choice; I had to get Fluffy."

I heard a sigh, then she started again. "I didn't get those shoes that day, and I didn't get another pair for a week, forced to go barefoot. It was embarrassing."

I took notes as fast as I could write.

Lived in 2-story house. Other kids. Poor, or it wouldn't have taken a week to get new shoes. Had sister = Ginger and a dog = Fluffy.

I suddenly realized she was speaking again. "What? I'm sorry, I didn't hear you."

"Too busy writing down notes? Shame on you. I opened up to you and you're still being a detective. Goodnight."

The line disconnected. I should have been more careful. What the hell was I thinking? I had the tape running. Why was I taking notes?

I sat at the table and transcribed the recorder. After reviewing the notes, I realized she hadn't said Ginger was her sister, and she didn't say Fluffy was a dog. I put question marks next to them. Before I knew it the grandfather's clock I bought with poker winnings chimed twice. I looked at it to make sure I heard right.

Two o'clock. Jesus Christ, I have to get to bed.

***

Ben Marsh called us the next day with information. The victim had been stabbed 71 times. Ben pegged the weapons as an ice pick or something similar, and a knife. The stabbing was done while she was alive, but the cutting had been done after she had died, and she'd been dressed when the killing happened. Many of the stab wounds, with both knife and other instrument, had torn through the dress.

"The killer took great pains to render both the victim and the dress unrecognizable. The victim's eyes had been gouged out and her face cut badly, not to mention the ear and nose being cut off. He went to the trouble of removing the dress, perhaps figuring it might be a clue. The rest of her items seem intact."

"What about rape?" Tip asked.

"Not the normal signs of rape, no tearing or bruising, but there was semen. That could have been consensual, though."

"I'm assuming you've sent the semen for a DNA match."

"We did, for all of the good it will do. When someone is as careful as this killer, I doubt if there's going to be a DNA slip. But you never can tell."

Tip thanked Ben and then we pulled into a breakfast joint to review what we had. "So this guy was afraid to let us know who she was," Tip said. "That's why he mauled her face so bad, and why he buried the head, probably hoping it wouldn't be found."

"And he was obviously worried about prints."

"So who the fuck was she? Somebody important?" Tip got up and walked around.

I thought about what he said, about her being important. "If so, don't you think we'd have a report by now? Missing persons, worried family…something."

"Unless they did it?" Tip looked off to the side, out into the parking lot. "Maybe it's a husband who wanted to get rid of his wife, or mistress."

"Could be, but let's focus on the dress. Our mystery caller said we'd find some clues if we followed the dress."

Tip nodded. "We'll see if Ben can give us anything, but then I'm calling someone who can probably give us more."

"Who?"

"Elena, my girlfriend. She owns an upscale dress shop. She'll know about the dress, presuming it's expensive."

"Take the shoes, too." I lowered my voice when I said it, knowing he was going to be pissed I hadn't told him yet.

Tip looked at me, probing. "You talked to her again, didn't you?"

"Last night."

"And when the fuck was I going to hear about this?"

"It was late. I planned on telling you."

"You should have called right away. We're partners." Tip leaned over the booth, got right in my face. "I don't know if you're falling for this woman and you won't admit it, or if you're the kind of cop that likes to keep shit to yourself. Either way, you need to fix it or get off the case. If you don't take care of it yourself, I'll ask Coop."

"You try to get me off this case, Denton, and I'll make sure you pay for it."

Tip stared at me but this time there was no smile. "I call things the way I see them, and I see a cop who can't control himself. Maybe it's your kid affecting your judgment, maybe it's not having a wife around. I can't let it affect my investigation. I'm sorry, Gino, that's the way I am." He got up, tossed a ten onto the table, then headed out to the car.

I pounded my fist into the cushion. No way I was losing this case. *No way.*

CHAPTER 21

A NEW VICTIM

Dallas, Texas

Patti Richards had spread her legs for a lot of men over the years. Women too. But she still remembered that first one, the fucker who'd forced himself on her in high school. She'd gotten even with him for that. It took years, but she waited for him to get married, followed him to a bar one night and arranged for him to take her home.

It was easy to lure him inside. All men were easy. A little sexy look, a flash of skin here and there, and all of it wrapped up with a soft cooing plea to walk her to the door. Once she had him on her turf, it was impossible for him to resist.

She got pictures that night of the two of them in bed, and those pictures soon found their way into the hands of his wife. It was devastating for him since his wife was the one with the money.

After college, Patti tried a few regular jobs: sales, marketing, administration, but none of them appealed to her, and besides, none of them paid the kind of money that dancing did. The dancing soon led to other things which led to sex—for money—and for the first time in her life sex meant something.

She built a thriving business, and learned soon enough that the real money was in the high-end clients, the ones with more money than sense. The funny thing was, they were the easiest to deal with. Even better, they always told their friends about her.

That's what the one tonight was—a person referred to as Magic, which she assumed wasn't a real name. Magic was a referral from a good client who had already mentioned to Magic that Patti's price was even higher than she normally charged. He probably did that hoping to get a freebie now and then as a thank you. If Magic turned out to be a regular she didn't mind. What the hell was one more fuck. From the way her client described Magic, she might not even mind doing the job.

The odd thing was Magic had asked for her specifically. Not one of her girls, but her. If he was a referral, he had to know she wasn't a spring chicken, and yet, he wanted her.

Patti applied her lipstick, the lightest touch, just enough to color it. A smidgeon of make-up followed. She still looked good, but her skin wasn't smooth like it used to be. It seemed that the older men got the more they craved smooth skin. And dirty talk.

Patti's laugh echoed in the small bathroom. She could *definitely* talk dirty.

She jumped when the phone rang, the sudden disturbance startling her even though she'd been expecting the call. Her nerves twitched as she rushed to pick it up. "Hello?"

"Do you know who this is?" The voice didn't match the image she had. Her tone changed.

"I assume this is Magic."

"Go to the Lincoln Hotel. Be there at 9:30. Take your own car and park it in front. *Do not* use valet. Go into the lobby, up the elevator to the second floor, then down the stairs and leave the hotel by the back exit." A pause followed. "Will that be a problem?"

The impatience was pronounced now.

"No, but—"

"I will see you then," Magic said, and then the line went dead.

The nervous energy she'd struggled to control unfolded all at once, boiling its way up through her stomach, her body twitching. For some reason the call unnerved her. Why, she didn't know. She'd done a hundred high-enders, male and female. Why should this one be different?

Patti shook it off, and finished preparing for the night. It proved to be no decision regarding her attire; Magic's voice seemed to say 'I want a woman in a black dress' and she imagined it as a tight-fitting, sleek, silky black dress, with high heels that exposed her perfect feet and made her toned legs glisten.

Patti smiled, then pulled the dress out of her closet and slipped it on. Magic might even tip her on top of the five thousand she'd been promised.

She slipped on her coat, quietly closed the door, and made her way to the stairs. Patti drove a three-year-old, dark green Ford Escort, an ordinary car to fit her ordinary lifestyle. The only thing extraordinary was her job and the clothes she wore to perform her job.

She popped the key to open the door, sliding behind the wheel with the ease of a ballerina. Not many men would have called her ordinary. Men craved a woman with a perfect body. And her body could lure a priest to the bed—hell, a saint.

She backed up, pulled onto the main drive, and soon found herself driving down the center lane of the freeway, a throng of headlights from the cars and pickups moving along with her. It took her twenty minutes to reach the Lincoln. She parked and followed the ridiculous directions, almost laughing at the paranoia her clients displayed. If they were so afraid of being found out, why did they hire her?

When she exited the back of the hotel she stood on the sidewalk waiting. Within seconds a car pulled up, and the window rolled down.

"Ms. Richards?"

She leaned forward, peering inside. "I'm Patti. Are you…" She stopped. "I was expecting Magic?"

"I *am* Magic. Please get in. You're welcome to use the front seat."

Welcome to use the front? What kind of ass was this? Maybe five grand was too little.

"Thank you." She held her hand to shake, but the gesture was ignored.

"Please buckle up." Magic said, and pulled out of the lot onto the freeway.

"Where are we going?"

"I have a place not far from here. It's private."

Patti nodded. *The privacy thing again.* "Do you live in Dallas?" She knew she shouldn't have asked as soon as the words left her mouth. What was wrong with her tonight?

"I feel it's better if we don't know so much about each other, Ms. Richards."

"I understand. But you can call me Patti…that is, if you want." She was beginning to get a bad feeling about this client.

"Will…anyone else be joining us?"

The driver ignored her again. The traffic thinned to a trickle and soon after that the road turned dark for long periods between cars. They turned into a long driveway and parked in front of a sprawling ranch house.

"This is nice," Patti said.

"We can go inside now." Magic got out and walked to her door, opened it, and led her to the front porch. A light shone on them from above. "Come here. Let me look at you."

Patti went closer but she was feeling less and less comfortable.

"I thought you might have worn something more…revealing." The reprimand in the voice stung. It rankled her.

Patti lifted her head and stared defiantly into the eyes that inspected her so thoroughly. It was then she realized what a mistake she'd made.

The look in her eyes must have given her away. "Yes, you're right to be afraid. Unfortunately, you drew the short straw. I am *so* sorry for this."

Magic shoved her against the stone wall, then wrapped hands around her throat. When she looked up she realized she was staring into the eyes of a killer.

Magic covered her mouth with a cloth. She held her breath against the chemicals on it and struggled to break free.

"As much as I hate to mar your beautiful, albeit, slutty body, I must."

He shoved a cold piece of steel into her stomach. It felt as if it glanced off a rib, then it pierced her lung. She breathed in through the cloth, felt faint, and then, nothing.

***

Blood oozed out of her. In her last moments, she clutched at her wound, trying to stop the blood from escaping. When Magic let go of her she collapsed to the porch floor.

"I'm sorry," Magic said. "It's not you."

Magic waited a few minutes, then checked until there was no pulse. After that, Magic shoved the ice pick in her eyes, then started the cutting. It wouldn't take long.

CHAPTER 22

A RIFT IN THE PARTNERSHIP

Houston, Texas

Tip made his way downtown, still pissed off at Gino for holding back on him, but more importantly for being so stupid as to fall for a potential suspect. Even the damn rookie cops knew that rule. Pinch your dick, squeeze it, take it out and smack it, but *don't* fall for the suspect, no matter how good she looks. And Gino hadn't even *seen* her. How could he fall for someone over the phone?

Tip walked into the station, ignoring, or perfunctorily responding to, the morning well-wishers, the ones who always had a smile on their face and never forgot to wave and greet a person coming in the door. Taking the steps two at a time he was soon heading down the hall toward Coop's office. Cindy sat at her desk, busy at work.

"Coop back from Dallas yet?"

"She flew in this morning with Mrs. Johnson, but she's not in a good mood."

"That's not new," he said, and opened the door.

"Good morning, Captain. How was Dallas?"

"Same as last time I was there, but tenfold the traffic. What's on your mind?"

The tone she used and the way she said it negated the need to say "I'm busy," but Tip got the point. "Listen, Captain, about this case…"

She threw her hands up in the air, and slapped the desk. "I know. I know. The mystery caller. I had the phone company look into it and you were right; it was a disposable cell, so get off my ass about it. You'll have to find the killer the hard way."

Tip hadn't come to ask about that, even though it was on his list to cover with her soon. But now that she'd said it—and he saw what a pissy mood she was in—he decided he'd wait to discuss the Gino situation.

He started for the door. "Let me know when you've settled down. Maybe we can talk."

"Hold on, cowboy. You're not going anywhere yet."

Tip turned back. "What?"

Coop walked behind him and shut the door. "Have a seat. We need to talk."

Tip sat back down. "About what?"

"Have you heard anything about Gino?"

The side of Tip's face twisted, bunching up his scar. "Heard anything? Like what?"

"I know you've heard the rumors, so you know what I'm asking about—Rico Moreno."

Tip shook his head. "I've got nothing."

"Nothing? Even with your famed network of contacts?"

"Let's get something straight," Tip said. "I don't work for IA and I don't bust cops. My job is to find killers and get them off the streets."

"I have news for you, Denton. Somebody *killed* Rico Moreno and his two men. Find out who did it and get them off the street."

Tip's jaw clamped down tight. "Get somebody else to do your shit work."

She leaned forward, almost like she was coming after him. "You son of a bitch."

"I might be a son of a bitch, but I'm not doing your shit work." Tip stood. "If that's all."

Coop closed her eyes, got her composure back. "I know you don't like doing this, and I wouldn't ordinarily ask, but I can't have one of my officers running wild."

"Gino's not like that. He—"

She waved her finger at Tip. "I'll tell you what he's like." She pulled a piece of paper from a folder on her desk. "He asked Karl to run these plates a few months ago."

"I ask people to run plates all the time," Tip said. "It's probably nothing. Did you ask Gino about it?"

"I've been waiting to get more ammunition, but it just so happens these plates belong to a van that was robbed of drugs the night before Gino asked Karl to run them. The guys in that van swear that the man who robbed them was a cop."

"Bullshit!"

Coop shook her head again. "One of those people was an undercover cop."

"Aw shit."

"Yeah, aw shit." She poked her finger into Tip's chest. "Now get the hell back out there and find what I need."

"I'll think about it," Tip said, and let the door slam shut. He walked down the hall wondering what he should do. He took out his cell phone and called Gino. It was time to have a meeting.

***

I drank two more cups of coffee and ate a huge breakfast, an attempt to cover my miserable morning. After a shit assignment in training, I finally got a break and now I was about to blow that. Tip was on his way to see the captain, probably to ask for a new partner. If lucky, I'd get another homicide case, but more than likely I'd get another shit detail.

While wallowing in misery, I decided to go see Ron. Nothing like piling more shit on top of an already bad day.

I didn't like going to the rehab, even to see Ron. Even though he was my son, it made me face things I didn't want to. His rebellious nature, his drug use, his addiction. All of them my failures. And while I didn't *want* to go see him, I knew I had to. If he was ever going to have a normal life, he needed support. I didn't give enough support when he started rehab—just threw him in there and left him to sink or swim. I needed to be more thoughtful, spend more time. This was his last hope, and I was his only support. I had to make this work for him. And me.

I pulled off the freeway, drove to the rehab. I took a minute or so to compose myself, then made my way inside.

Ron met me out back in a courtyard setting with palm trees embracing a small fountain. Small tables flanked by benches dotted the neatly trimmed grass, hedges and bushes strategically planted to afford privacy for family visits. A crazy yellow lab they called Cornbread ran around greeting each new person to come in, nibbling on their hands and stealing anything they were foolish enough to leave behind—cigarettes, lighters, wallets. He even took my car keys for a swim in the fountain. Luckily, they didn't get wet, or at least not wet enough to ruin the battery. After I got the keys from the dog, I came back and sat with Ron.

"How's it going?"

A fake smile popped onto his face. "Great! Got my two-month chip this week." He reached into his pocket and produced a simulated gold coin with "sixty days" stamped on it. "Keep it. It's yours."

I resisted the urge to say, *again*, and instead said, "For me? Thanks, Ron. I appreciate it."

He shrugged. "Not like there's anyone else who cares."

I lowered my head. "Your mother would have been proud."

He shook his. "No she wouldn't. She'd have been mortified that I was in here and worried about what the neighbors would think."

"Nobody's perfect."

"I know."

I stayed silent for a while, not knowing what to say, then he started talking.

"I'm not blaming you, Dad. Things just turned bad after Mom died. We used to have so much fun, then…" He turned his head, and I think he wiped tears away.

When he turned around his eyes locked onto mine and I felt his pain. It hurt. "What happened? It was like you stopped loving me? Like…" he shook his head. "I didn't die you know. I'm still here. But all you do is think about her. Sometimes I think that you've forgotten me or…that you wished I died instead of her."

Tears formed in my eyes. I hugged him.

"Don't ever say that. You know I love you."

He hugged me too, then pulled back, wiped his eyes. "You haven't said that to me since the funeral."

Goddamn, had it come to this…where he knew to the day when the last time

I said I love you to him. What the fuck happened to me? I could barely hold his gaze, but I managed. "I'm *so* sorry. Things are going to be different when you come home. I promise."

He was silent for a long time. When he spoke I heard the old Ron in him, the one from before Mary's death. "You sound like you mean it. That makes me feel good."

He smiled. "I'll tell you what, you work on your part, keep catching bad guys, and be there when I need it, and I'll get my ass clean. Maybe we can go play paintball or catch some movies."

"I'm getting too old for the paintball, but the movies sound good."

His smile grew bigger. "Movies it is. As soon as I get out."

We chatted for a few more minutes, both of us more relaxed. When I left I had a new purpose in life. One I'd lost for a long time.

Thanks, God, for giving me another chance.

I got in the car and headed toward the office. Might as well face the music. Coop would likely be calling any minute to summon me anyway. I hadn't gone five miles before the phone rang.

"Gino Cataldi."

"We need to talk."

I paused, surprised that it was Tip, but half knowing what to expect. Tip was a lot of things but he wasn't the type to tell me bad news over the phone. He'd want to meet in person.

"Did you see Coop?"

"Yeah, and we have nothing on the phone calls."

I breathed to take it in. "We? So we're still best buddies and partners?"

"Yeah, *we* asshole. Meet me at the coffee shop."

"So you still love me then?"

"Fuck you. I'll be there in twenty minutes."

"See you then," I said, and laughed like hell. My day had taken a major turn for the better. First Ron, now this.

Tip was already at the coffee shop when I arrived. He couldn't have been there long because I could see the steam still rising from his coffee cup. I went inside, ordered an espresso, and then joined him at the table.

My ass had barely touched the seat of the chair when Tip started in on me.

"I think you shot Rico and his men," Tip said.

I stared, not knowing what to think or how much he knew. "If you think that you should turn me in," I said.

Tip shot me a look, that said he wanted to hit someone. "Is that what you want?" he said. "You really want me to tell Coop or John what I think?"

I took a sip of espresso, looked him in the eyes, and said, "No."

"Then shut the fuck up and listen." He shook his head, looked around a bit, then back at me. "Part of me wants to turn your ass in. And part of me wants to kick your ass. But another part of me wants to pat you on the back for getting rid of that scum-sucking drug dealer."

I mustered up all the courage I could, and said, "Given those options, I'll take the pat on the back."

Tip didn't laugh, but he seemed to calm down. "I'm gonna hold off, but in the meantime, get your head out of your ass and on this case. I know your kid's in rehab and your wife passed away, but we've got a case to solve and people are counting on us to figure out who did it." He leaned forward, and said, "So, are you in or out?"

"I'm in," I said, and a smile chased my tension away.

CHAPTER 23

WOMEN LOVE SHOES

Houston, Texas

The next morning, I met Tip for breakfast at Cracker Barrel. While we ate, we went over the case, trying to think of anything we missed. "It still bugs me how this damn caller knows so much about the case," I said. "And about me."

Tip shook his head. "People can find out anything nowadays. Suppose the caller has a contact with the insurance company—they've got your life history."

"You're right, not difficult *if* she has access to personnel files or insurance records."

Tip looked at me. "Are you trying to say this is a cop?"

"I don't know what I'm saying, but something's not right. This lady knows too much about me *and* about police procedure."

Tip stared off to the side, quiet. "I don't know what's going on either, but something's screwy. We've got to think differently on this case."

"What about the shoes?" I asked.

He signaled our waitress for more coffee, then told me about the talk he had with Elena. "She said a lot of places carry Ferragamo shoes, but we should check the Ferragamo store first because they have the biggest selection. She said if it was a woman who liked their shoes she'd probably go there."

"Looks like we're going shoe shopping."

"I guess so," Tip said as the waitress poured his coffee. "Hey, darlin', could you get me another order of that turkey sausage. Damn that's good."

"Sure thing, Tip. You want more toast, too?"

"No, just the sausage."

He watched her wiggle her way to the kitchen, then went back to sipping on his coffee. "We need this shoe thing to pay off. Gotta catch a break."

"All we need to do is get an ID on her. As soon as we know who she is, we'll find the killer."

The waitress returned with the sausage, leaving the check on the table. "See ya'll later," she said. "Have a nice day."

"I'll get this," Tip said, and grabbed the check. He finished his sausage with a few hurried bites, gulped the last of his coffee, including grounds, then tossed two twenties on the table.

"You expecting to get something more than free coffee next time we come?"

"She's a single mom with a boy who needs special attention. I try to help her out a little."

"You're a damn good man, Tip Denton."

"You tell anybody and I'll shoot you."

I grabbed a couple of mints as we left, then we got in Tip's car and headed to the Ferragamo store. The manager looked at the shoes and said she'd be back with names in a few minutes. True to her word she returned with two papers in her hand. *They must have better records than the FBI.*

"In that style and size we only sold two pair of those shoes in the past year to local people—Sahrina Mekkin and Barbara Camwyck. I printed the information. It comes from our frequent shopper program. If you want the purchases from out of town clients—"

"How often do you have to purchase something here to be a frequent shopper?" I asked.

She smiled. "Just once—*everyone* is a frequent shopper."

I nodded. "As far as the out-of-towners, we don't need them yet. If we don't have luck with these, we'll come back."

"What other stores would carry these shoes?" Tip asked.

Silvia seemed to give it thought, then said, "Donna, who else in town carries the suede slingbacks?"

A good-looking, middle-aged woman turned to us. "Nordstrom, Neiman Marcus, The Proper Lady, A Taste of Barcelona…I'd have to check and see if there are any others."

"Thank you, Donna." Silvia turned back to us. "Anything else, gentlemen?"

"Not for now, thanks," I said, and Tip and I left the store.

"I didn't expect to get help that fast," Tip said.

I looked at the information on the printouts as we got in the car. "Look at this. Name, address, home phone, cell phone, work phone, email address." I voiced aloud what I'd thought before. "These people collect more data than the FBI."

"Where do you want to start?" Tip asked.

"Let's start with Mekkin."

"Mekkin it is."

We called Sahrina and got an answer on the first ring. She was alive. "That narrows it down," I said.

"We called, but got no answer at Camwyck's. About half an hour later, we tried again, but still no response. "Let's go over there and knock on the door," Tip said.

"Not far from here," I said.

Barbara Camwyck lived in the Four Leaf Towers on San Felipe, the high-rent district. She wasn't in the penthouse, but her place had to go for somewhere between one and two million. After a third phone call didn't produce an answer, and after the manager wouldn't let us in, we called for a warrant. We could have gone in for a welfare check, but if she wasn't there, or we found her dead, we'd want the warrant for a full search.

While we waited I got Julie to get us info on the victim.

"Julie, it's Gino. We need everything you can find on a Barbara Camwyck, spelled with a *Y,* not an *I.*"

"I'll see what I have on her."

I hung up and got with Tip.

"Julie's getting us the rundown on Camwyck," I said. "If there's anything of interest, she'll find it."

"You have a warrant coming?"

"It shouldn't be long. Let's grab coffee while we wait." I said.

Tip killed the engine and got out of the car. "You realize Camwyck could be out of town, or safe at work, or in the damn shower."

"I know, but I'm betting she's dead."

"I hope so," Tip said, and then he laughed. "Nothing against Ms. Camwyck, but we need a victim. At least this will give us DNA to check against the body, assuming she's not lying on the floor."

***

Cindy knocked on Coop's door before going in. "Have you got a minute, Captain?"

"What is it?"

"You told me to keep you informed on this case. Gino called to get a warrant."

Coop set her pen on the desk and sat up straight. "What's the warrant for?"

Cindy looked at her notes. "A lady named Barbara Camwyck. She lives—"

"I know where she lives."

Cindy waited until the silence forced her to speak. "What should I do?"

"Get the process rolling. Keep me informed on anything else."

"I will," Cindy said.

When she left, Coop picked up the phone. Three rings later, Cybil answered.

"The shit is hitting the fan *right now*."

"What are you talking about?"

"Gino and Tip just called for a warrant on Barbara's place."

"You shouldn't have given this case to them," Cybil said.

"Don't try your haughty tone on me. It was Tip's turn in the rotation and if I hadn't assigned it to him it would have raised questions. I know how to run my department, Cybil. Besides, this whole goddamn mess was going to come out sooner or later."

"You better figure out how to cover our asses, Gladys. This one's on you."

"I've got *nothing* to do with this. You know damn right well where the blame falls."

"What else do they know?"

"How the hell do I know, but between Denton and Cataldi they'll soon find out everything. You can bet your East Texas ass on that."

"This could ruin everything. We've got to do something."

Coop shook her head, even though Cybil couldn't see. "It's your problem. Not mine."

CHAPTER 24

EVEN THE DEAD CAN TALK

Houston, Texas

The warrant took longer to arrive than we expected, but we finally got inside her condo. Lying on the floor was a dog that appeared to be starving. It greeted us with a sad look and a wag of the tail from a spot on the living room floor. It didn't even get up or bark.

Tip ran over and knelt next to it, carefully petting its head. "Get some water." He turned to the uniform with us. "Nester, get somebody to take this dog to a vet. He needs attention."

"Sir, I—"

"Goddamnit, Nester, just do it. I don't want any shit."

I brought the dog's water bowl to Tip and set it on the floor next to the dog. "He looks pretty bad. Probably been here a while."

"At least since she died. It's a wonder he made it."

"That's a big bowl. The water could have lasted a few days."

Tip nodded, then stood and looked around. "All right, let's *carefully* and I mean carefully, check for bodies, and get the crime scene unit down here. We don't want to contaminate the place until after they're done."

An hour later, we were still waiting for them to process the scene. In the meantime, we took that time to canvass the neighbors, the manager, and even units across the street. If we got no answer we left cards. As soon as the crime scene unit finished, we started our work of processing the remainder of the data, looking for clues—first to determine if this was the woman, then to determine why someone would want to kill her, and finally try to figure out *who* killed her.

Ben gathered enough DNA to compare against our victim, but Tip and I were operating as if she were dead. We were fairly certain she was.

An area in the living room appeared to be set aside for work, a desk and file cabinet positioned against the wall off to the side. "There's a cord for charging a laptop," I said, "but no computer. I'd bet my ass the killer took it."

"Keep looking, I'm going to the bedroom."

While Tip checked the closets and drawers in her bedroom, I went through the files.

"These files look like they've been gone through."

"How so?"

"Get your ass over here and take a look."

Tip came down the hall and stood next to me. "Check it out. There's plenty of room in this drawer for more files, so why does she put more in the next one. Someone took files out of here."

"It does *appear* that way."

"Appear my ass, the killer did this as sure as he took the rest of her stuff."

Tip pointed to a file in the drawer. "Hand me that one, the one that says *Murphy*."

I gave him the folder, '*Murphy, TP*' and continued looking through the files.

"Son of a bitch," Tip said. "She's got enough information in this file to hang TP."

"Who's TP Murphy?" I said.

"TP is a good friend of Rusty's. Or *was* a good friend. They had a falling out a few years ago."

"What's in there?"

"Besides pictures of TP and Ms. Camwyck in a variety of positions, it looks like business documents that TP would probably want kept quiet." Tip handed me the folder. "You have a file on Andrick Boudin in there?"

I scanned the 'B' section and pulled it out.

Tip thumbed through it. A smile popped on his face. "Same thing, Gino. And I'll bet everything Charlie can eat that all the files are the same."

I flipped through the files quickly, just to confirm what Tip thought.

After looking at more than a few dozen pics of Ms. Camwyck and her clients, I ran across a 1099 form. I handed it to Tip. "You know anything about Eastex Enterprises? This is a 1099 from last year."

He grabbed the paper from me and looked. "I'll be a horse's ass. This is Rusty Johnson's company."

"The mayor?"

"The one and only," Tip said. He handed me back the form. "And if she worked for Rusty, then Cybil knew her." He stared at me, a funny look in his eyes.

I could see the wheels spinning.

Tip said, "And if Cybil knew her, then Coop probably knew her."

"Hold on, Tip. We can't go making that leap."

"I'm not leaping yet, but we'll find out soon enough."

He took out his cell and dialed a number, but I could only hear his side of the conversation.

"Julie, it's Tip.

"I'm fine, darlin', but listen, I need a big favor.

"Yeah, that means nobody can know about this. It stays between you and me. He looked over to me, then said, "And Gino."

"Gino already told you about Camwyck. Besides the normal stuff, I need all financials, phone records, employment, tax. All of it.

Tip listened to Julie, nodding when she spoke. "Okay," he said, "and while you're at it, find out all you can about Eastex Enterprises. But this one you'll have to keep *real* quiet. And one more thing, see if Camwyck had a car registered in her name.

"Okay, thanks. I owe you for this."

Tip hung up from Julie, then signaled me closer. "We need to keep this quiet. I'd bet ten dollars to a doughnut that Coop knew Camwyck, and either Coop or Cybil must have recognized her from the picture in the paper."

"But neither one of them said anything." I looked at Tip, knowing that Coop or Cybil—either one—had the juice to take our badges. "You realize we could be in deep shit."

Tip stared around the room and said, "I don't think there's any question about it. I feel it creeping up around my knees already, so we'll have to watch our asses."

"With all that we found in that file cabinet, it makes me wonder what was in the files that are missing," I said.

"A lot of powerful people are in those files, Gino. I think I'm beginning to see why she might have been killed."

We finished up at Barbara's place then headed out to grab a bite to eat and digest what we learned. Before the day was over we had more questions than we had at the beginning of the day, but at least we had a path to follow, and it started with the victim.

I spent a quiet evening at home, with no calls from the mystery woman. I arrived at the station early in the morning, hoping that Julie had something for us. Tip was already there.

"Coffee?" He signaled me toward the break room—which might as well have been named the coffee room—and I followed.

"You got something?"

He closed the door and grabbed a chair, pulling it next to mine. "Julie gave me this when I got in." He passed me a folder.

As I scanned through it, I shook my head.

"Our victim had a checkered past."

"Yeah," Tip said, "and the most interesting part of that past is that it started in East Texas, the same town where Cybil came from, and, not coincidentally, the same town that our president and his chief of staff came from."

I looked closer at the file. "Says here that Barbara came to Houston 20 years ago, and was arrested for prostitution, but charges were dropped."

"Now that's pretty interesting," Tip said.

"And did you notice where she worked—Baby Dolls."

"What's the significance?"

"Baby Dolls is Rusty Johnson's favorite hangout."

I set the folder down and stared at Tip.

"Son of a bitch! So the victim grew up with Cybil, then came to Houston and worked at a club that Rusty frequents, and then happened to end up as a "consultant" for Rusty's company."

Tip stood and paced.

"And now she's dead," I said.

Tip picked up his cup from the table and sipped his coffee while he continued to pace. "According to Julie, there was a connection between almost all of her "clients" and our mayor. And there's no way a stripper goes from dancing at clubs to entrepreneur with all of these connections without help."

"Possibly even mayoral help." I looked at Tip. "How well do you know Cybil?"

He poured more coffee. "Some. More by reputation than anything. She can be tough."

"So what do you suppose she might do if she found out that one of Rusty's old stripper friends was now a *consultant* for his company, and making damn good money doing it?"

"I think we better find out," Tip said.

"Talk to her or Rusty?"

"Both of them. Somebody has to know something."

I dumped my cup in the trash and headed for the door. "Let's go."

"You care much about your badge? I mean whether you keep it or not?"

"Nah. Not me."

"Good, because we might both lose it today."

CHAPTER 25

AN INTERESTING INTERVIEW

Houston, Texas

Tip called Rusty's admin and set up an appointment. At first there were no openings, but when he explained it had to do with Barbara Camwyck's murder, Rusty's calendar freed up, although his admin said Rusty would be at Eastex Enterprises for the rest of the day. On the way over to Eastex, Coop called us. It made me wonder if this was a response to us having called Rusty.

"Denton, where are you?"

Tip tapped my arm and put it on speakerphone. "Doing interviews on the case. What's up?"

"I just saw the search warrant. I knew her. I knew the woman who lived there—Barbara Camwyck."

There was a long silence, or at least what seemed like a long one, then Coop spoke again.

"I can't believe it's her."

"Didn't you recognize her picture from the paper?" Tip asked.

"Good Lord, no. I could barely look at that picture. Perhaps if I had…Anyway, when you get back in, see me and I'll tell you what little I can about Barbara."

"Okay, Captain, will do."

He hung up and looked at me. "What do you think?"

"I think it was damn convenient that she called right after we called and made an appointment with Rusty."

"Must have been a coincidence," Tip said. "If you believe in that."

"It'll be interesting to see what information we get from good old Gladys."

"I'd bet my last dick that it matches what we get from Rusty and Cybil."

"Your last dick, huh? How many dicks do you have?"

"That's an old Texas expression."

"What does it mean?"

"I'm not rightly sure, but it sounds good."

"Never mind," I said, and shook my head. There was no point in going down that road, but Tip wouldn't let it rest.

"When a man tells you he's willing to bet his last dick on something, that's strong," Tip said. "That's more than a hundred dollars I can tell you that much."

"I'm through with talking about your last dick."

"Well all right then. I'm through with it too."

Fifteen minutes later we pulled into the parking garage for Rusty's building and made our way to the 20th floor. We stepped out of the elevator and went through a set of double doors featuring his company's name. A receptionist sat at the front, painting her nails.

"Tip Denton and Gino Cataldi here to see Rusty."

She gave Tip a sideways glance as if he'd committed a sin by leaving off the honorific—or by interrupting her nails—then she got on the phone, speaking through her headset.

"Nancy, it's Jeanine. I have a Mr. Denton and Mr. Cataldi here to see Mayor Johnson."

She smiled at Tip. "Have a seat, please. Someone will be out shortly."

She didn't bother offering us coffee, and I wondered if that was the norm, or if we were *personae non gratae* due to Tip's transgression.

Twice in the next 20 minutes Tip reminded the receptionist we were still waiting. The second time he didn't bother using his pleasant voice. The stern voice must have worked because a few minutes later they came for us. '*They*' being a tall, slender brunette with a skirt so tight I'd have taken odds on it splitting before we got to Rusty's office. The sight of her wiggling down the hall made the walk nice, though, so nice that I think an elephant could have passed us in the hall and I wouldn't have noticed.

The slender escort showed us into the office and disappeared, once again without so much as a "good day" or an offer for refreshments. Word must have spread of our status. As the door closed, Rusty got up from behind a desk too big for two people, and moved to greet us. He was a large man, tall and thick like an old tree, and his hands were big and meaty.

I took the offered handshake and smiled at him. "Gino Cataldi," I said. "Nice to meet you, Mayor Johnson."

"Call me Rusty, son. None of that mayor nonsense."

He then shifted to Tip. "I know you," he said. "Tip Denton, the terror of the city's criminals."

Tip shook his hand and looked him in the eye, but he didn't smile. He had that mean look on his face, the kind I heard that he normally reserved for the criminals.

"Rusty, I'm glad you made time to see us."

Rusty squinted his eyes, and I thought he shot Tip a glare, but I couldn't be sure. Either way, I sensed tension between them.

"We're here to ask a few questions about a case we're working, Mayor Johnson."

Tip leaned forward in his chair. "It's Barbara Camwyck."

The mayor squinted, and I thought he shot Tip another look, but I wasn't sure. Despite, that something was causing tension in the air. There must have been bad blood in the past.

"What can I do to help?" the mayor asked.

"Did you know her?"

He sat back in his chair and folded his hands in front of him. "What was the name again?"

Tip said her name loud, as if the mayor were hard of hearing. "Barbara Camwyck."

Rusty nodded. "Camwyck. Yes, I knew her. She did some work for my company."

I pulled out my notepad. "Sir, it looks as if she did a lot of work. Our records show that Eastex Enterprises paid her consulting company $145,000 last year."

He wrinkled his brow. "That much…I didn't realize."

"Exactly *what* did she do for you?" Tip asked.

"Consulting."

"Exactly what type of consulting?"

Rusty smiled and leaned forward. "I don't really see where that's any of your business, Detective."

"Considering this is a murder investigation, Mayor, it *is* our business."

"Investigation? Surely you don't suspect—"

"Right now, we suspect everyone."

Rusty snorted, and tilted his head back. "Ms. Camwyck did business development for us. She researched markets and suggested tactics for our sales force."

Tip leaned forward and locked his gaze on the mayor. "Ms. Camwyck? Did you call her that when she worked at Baby Dolls?"

The tension ratcheted up a few notches with that question—Rusty leaned forward, expressing everything but a growl, and I noticed Tip had balled his fists. I tried to intervene. "What time did you get home the night of the murder, Mayor Johnson?"

Rusty stood and walked to the door, opening it. "I think we're done here, Detectives. If you have other questions, call my attorney."

"You can bet I have more questions," Tip said. "You better get your attorney prepared."

As we waited for the elevator, I heard Rusty's door slam, then I patted Tip on the back. "What do you think—was it the Baby Dolls' comment or the alibi question that ended that interview?"

"I think it was Baby Dolls."

"Yeah, me too. By the way, good diplomacy."

"It wouldn't have mattered much what I said. It's well known that Rusty hates me. I didn't see any reason to fake it."

"Him hating you might make it difficult when we talk to Cybil."

"You need to brush up on your political gossip, Gino. As much as Rusty hates me, Cybil hates him more. I can't wait to talk with her."

Cybil greeted us with a smile and a swagger to her walk that hinted at a "nothing to hide" attitude. We entered her private office and took a seat in plush chairs with a view of the entire north end of the city.

"Would either of you detectives care for a drink?"

"No thanks," I said. "And we won't take up much of your time. We only have a few questions."

She mixed herself a drink, then leaned against the bar in a sexy pose. Blonde hair was cropped short, and radiant blue eyes drew attention to the sharp features on her face—thin nose, high cheekbones. She was in damn good shape, and she sported a skirt with a generous slit up the side. I found it difficult not to stare.

"What kind of questions?" she asked.

Tip stared straight at her as if she were no better than a street junkie. "Did you know the victim—her name was Barbara Camwyck. I mentioned that in case you were going to try and deny it like your husband.?"

Cybil took a sip of her drink and smiled. She didn't seem fazed in the least by Tip's comment. "As you probably already know, I grew up in the same town in East Texas. It was the kind of town where everyone knew each other."

"And how about after that, here in Houston? Did you keep up with her?"

She hesitated, swirling the ice in her glass.

"I saw Barbara about once a month."

"Under what circumstances?" Tip asked.

"I don't know what you mean."

"Why did you see her once a month?"

"Business reasons," Cybil said, and gave Tip a pointed look over the rim of her glass. "She worked for one of my husband's companies."

"What did she do for him?"

"I believe she was in business development, something like that." Cybil brushed her hand in the air, as if to say, 'I don't know much about business,' but I could tell that was a crock of shit.

Tip said, "Did your husband know her beforehand—like maybe from a strip club?"

"I don't quite know what you are implying, Detective."

I sat up straight, and thought for a moment that something sounded…familiar. When she said *detective*, her accent came out strong.

Tip didn't let his eyes off her. "I mean that Barbara used to work at Baby

Dolls, a strip club frequented by your husband. Did you know that, Mrs. Johnson?"

Once again she brushed her hand in the air. The diamonds on her bracelet could have probably paid off my mortgage. "Is that all? Of course I knew that. Rusty has known a lot of women in his day. But he knows who to come home to at night."

"And it doesn't bother you that he has "known" all of these women?"

She poured herself another drink and straightened up. When she did she seemed six feet tall, though I doubted she was any more than five and a half. I imagined a scenario where Cybil was thrown in a tank with a shark. I wondered which one would survive.

"Detective Denton, it makes no difference to me what my husband does with his spare time. Or where he puts his dick. I have my own...*hobbies* and he doesn't interfere."

"When was the last time you saw Ms. Camwyck?"

"About three weeks ago. And, no, I haven't spoken to her since."

"Do you know anyone who might want to harm her, or have reason to kill her?"

"You already know that she worked at Baby Dolls. That tells you what kind of woman she was. I have no delusions that what she described as *business development* was little more than lying on her back or other compromising positions, and I'm certain she did it with more than one man." She swished the drink in her glass and fixed on Tip, then me. "You're the detectives. Figure it out."

I thought of that scenario again, the one with Cybil and the shark—she would definitely be the one coming out of the tank.

Tip met her look, but said nothing.

I stood. "I guess that's all we have for now, Mrs. Johnson. If we think of anything else we'll call."

"I'm sure you will." She smiled and walked to the door. "It was so nice to meet you. Please call me anytime."

We walked out in silence but when we got in the car Tip said, "Poor Rusty."

And I said, "Yeah."

CHAPTER 26

RECAP

Houston, Texas

Tip drove back to the station. We reviewed what we knew on the way.

"We need to think about what we learned from the victim's apartment."

"All right," I said. "Let's start with how she afforded it. And then her age. She's too old to be a working girl."

"I think we know *how* she afforded it. What we need to do is go through the clients in her files and see who had alibis. If we talk to enough of them, we'll figure out what role Camwyck had in all this."

"My guess is whoever took her computer and address book was smart enough to take incriminating names out of the files."

Tip turned onto the freeway and punched it. "You know, Gino, that's good. We need to focus on what we *didn't* find. That might tell us something about what was left."

I took out my notebook and looked at what I'd written. "No computer. No address book. No calendar or date book—"

"Which she would absolutely have to have in her profession. She could have it on her phone, but my experience is women like her always have a back-up and it's usually old-fashioned paper."

"No question," I said. "And there was no cell phone, which is another necessity."

Tip slowed down and fell in line with traffic. "Okay so if we look at all of that together—missing phone, computer, and tablet (if she had one). When you add it up, it points to someone hiding her identity, or, the identity of a client."

"Or both," I said.

He nodded. "Yeah, or both. We need to talk to more clients and we need to find her friends."

Tip's phone rang and he answered. "Tip Denton, best damn detective in Texas."

I could hear Julie's sigh through the speaker. She must have heard that line a thousand times. "I've got some information on Eastex Enterprises for you." She said it loud enough that I could hear.

"I'm giving the phone to Gino, tell him."

I grabbed his cell. "What have you got?"

"The biggest news is that Eastex Enterprises might technically be Rusty's company, but it's run by his wife. She's the indisputable king, or should I say queen, of that little kingdom."

"Explain."

"The people I spoke to, on condition of anonymity of course, said Rusty is the chairman but no decisions are made without her blessing."

"You're sure about this?"

"It was confirmed by two sources. Unrelated sources."

"Okay good. How about the phone? Did you get a record of Camwyck's calls yet? I mean land line calls. And what about her cell phone?"

"I'll have the list of calls from her home phone tomorrow, but no record of a cell."

"She had to have one."

"If she did it was in another name."

"All right, thanks, Julie."

I turned to Tip. "No cell phone. You buy that?"

He looked at me sideways. "No way."

"You think she used burners?"

"Maybe. I hope not, but maybe."

"It would be the smart thing to do, and a woman living in a million-dollar condo has something on the ball."

"Maybe Camwyck remembered what it was like to be at the bottom," Tip said, then, "That reminds me. I need to listen to the tape of your caller."

"Come by tonight. I'll cook something and we can have a few beers."

"Is this a date?"

"Fuck you, Denton."

"Not on the first date."

Tip's phone rang again and saved his ass. I answered since I still held it in my hand.

"Tip Denton."

"This sure as hell isn't Tip," a sexy voice said.

I presumed this was Elena. "He never sounded this good did he?"

"Not one day in his life," she said.

"Hang on a minute." I handed him the phone. "It must be Elena."

"Hello, beautiful. What's up? Couldn't wait for me to get home?"

"I wanted to see if that lead on the shoes panned out."

"It did. Thanks. We have an ID on the woman based on what you gave us."

"You did? Great."

"Don't go thinking you're a detective now, or I won't be able to impress you."

"Go to hell. I was calling to tell you I'll be out of town for a few days."

"That's all right. I'm going to be pulling some late-nighters trying to close this case.

In fact, I'm going over to Gino's tonight to listen to a tape we have."

"I'll call when I get back."

Tip pressed the button to hang up, then turned to me. "Elena said—"

"I heard. She's not as loud as you, but I heard."

Tip pulled into the garage and parked. We walked into the station ready to hit the files again. Today's work had provided a lot more information, but we had to figure out what it meant.

Julie came by with a million-dollar grin on her face. "Are ya'll ready for this?"

"Shoot," Tip said.

"Rusty Johnson co-signed for Camwyck's condo. All $1.65 million of it."

Tip whistled. "That could be motive for Cybil."

"Would she care?" I said.

"She wouldn't give a fiddler's dick about him screwing around, but paying for the condo…*that's* a different story. I suspect there's nothing Cybil likes more than money, unless it's power."

I digested what Tip said and, as I thought it over, I had to agree. She would probably be more than a little pissed about Rusty spending the money on Camwyck. "And the way the victim was cut up makes it look like someone hated her."

"About $1.65 million worth?"

"Maybe."

Tip was writing on a notepad. "So we've got Rusty running around on Cybil, which we don't put much weight on, but…it's something. Then we have Rusty co-signing the condo—"

"And remember, the market is horrible now, so the condo is likely underwater," I said.

"Okay, but does Cybil go out and kill her for Rusty's indiscretion? Or does she kill Rusty?"

"What does she gain by killing Camwyck? The condo won't sell for a profit. Rusty will just find another stripper…"

"I'd kill Rusty if I were her."

"If not her, then who killed the victim?" I wondered aloud.

"Why are you asking me? You're supposed to be the smart one."

"We're going to have to get an alibi for Cybil."

Tip laughed. "She'll raise holy hell."

"I guess Coop will have to earn her pay, because we need that alibi for Cybil."

"You want to go back to talk to Cybil now?"

"No, let's give her a chance to talk to people and come up with a plan."

"Smart ass."

I dialed the number on the card Cybil had given us. She answered right away.

"Cybil Johnson."

"Mrs. Johnson, this is Detective Cataldi. We just met."

"What can I do for you, Detective?"

"I forgot to ask, where were you on the night Ms. Camwyck was killed?"

"I don't quite know. When was she killed?"

I told her the night and she didn't hesitate in answering, making me wonder if she had it planned.

"I was with Captain Cooper early in the evening, then I was at the hotel for dinner, then home. I'm certain my assistant can provide the details."

"She was with you?"

"At dinner, yes."

"And what time did you get home?"

She paused for a moment. "I'm not exactly certain, but I would guess it was around 8:30."

"Was anyone home when you got there?"

"No."

"Not your husband?"

"Detective, in case you haven't learned this from your investigation, or from the gossip around town, Rusty seldom gets home before the early hours."

"And what about you? Did you stay home all night? See anyone? Talk on the phone?"

"I'm afraid I tend to be a dull person. I poured myself a few drinks—I know this because I do it every night—then I read some before going to bed."

"And what time was that?"

She paused for a moment. "I'm not sure, but I would guess before midnight."

"And your husband wasn't home yet?"

"Not at that time, no." She sighed. "Will that be all?"

"Yes, ma'am. That will be all for now."

"Have a good day, Detective."

"Thank you, ma'am. You too."

I hung up and looked at Tip. "She's one cold bitch."

"As I said, poor Rusty."

"Yeah."

"What did she sound like?"

"She sounded real, but it was all planned. She had those answers ready way too fast. Do you remember what you did a week ago without even thinking? Not me."

"I can't remember what I did last night," Tip said.

"Yeah, but we'll still have to check with Coop, who happens to be Cybil's early evening alibi, and Cybil's admin, who had dinner with her."

"And what did Cybil do after that?"

"You didn't hear?" I said.

"I heard noise, but nothing that I could make out."

"I guess she's not as loud as Elena." I laughed, then said, "She said nothing."

"Hmm."

"Yeah, but I still don't see a woman doing this kind of murder. It's too brutal. Even for Cybil."

"I hate to say it, but I agree with you," Tip said. "We better fill Coop in."

"And check Cybil's alibi."

***

Coop picked up the intercom as she scanned the reports for the day. "Yes, Cindy."

"It's Mrs. Johnson, and she seems in a hurry."

Isn't she always. "Put her through."

"Gladys, get them dogs off my scent."

"You're reverting to your roots. Your accent and poor grammar are showing."

"Screw you. Get them off me. I mean it."

"I can't do that."

Silence, then. "Captain Cooper, I suggest you remember what you stand to lose before you commit to a course of action."

"They're detectives on a case. They'll follow it where it goes. If it—"

"I don't give a *fuck* where it goes. I can't afford to have Rusty's name dragged through the gutter because of some whore, so you better steer it on another course."

The line went dead.

Coop sipped the last of a bit of tea in her cup and removed her glasses. The frustration of dealing with Cybil wasn't worth it; sometimes she wondered why she chose this path in life.

CHAPTER 27

ACCENTS

We headed to Coop's office, eager to get whatever information she had on Barbara Camwyck. If nothing else, to see how it compared to what we discovered and what Julie dug up.

"Let me do the talking with Coop," Tip said. "I've known her longer."

"All that means is she's had more time to hate you."

"I know that, but you piss her off more."

I laughed, but as we walked down the long corridor leading to her office, I wondered if he was telling the truth. Tip lied so much it was hard to tell.

Cindy sat at her guard post across from Coop's office. She got up to greet us as we approached. "Hello, Detectives. Having a good day?"

"If I was any better I'd be you," Tip said.

"Don't you ever get tired of saying that?"

"I only say it to pretty young things."

"You're so full of it."

As Cindy made her way toward Coop's door she laughed. She enjoyed every minute of Tip's nonsense. "I told the captain you were here."

Coop was sitting behind her desk, squat and solid, like a block of stone, and staring over the rims of her glasses at a stack of papers. She didn't bother getting up to greet us. "Sit down. I'll be with you in a minute."

Tip took the seat to the left and kicked his feet up on her desk. She threw a pen at him without looking up. "Off, Denton."

I took out my notepad and looked at the summary of our talks with Rusty and Cybil, thinking about what we might have missed. After what seemed like forever, she removed her glasses and looked in our direction. "All right, gentlemen. Tell me what you found out."

Tip leaned forward, his elbows resting on the edge of her desk. "Why don't you tell us what you know first. You said you knew the victim from before."

I thought I noticed a glare in Coop's eye, but she recovered quickly. "As you probably know, I grew up in East Texas with Cybil. Barbara Camwyck was a few years behind us in school, but the town was small and we all knew each other."

"What was she like?" I asked.

Coop leaned back, running fingers through her short cropped hair as she did. "She was a little wild as a teenager, but weren't we all. The last thing I remember is she was working at a diner and dating a lawyer's son. And I heard once that she might have been pregnant, but there were no kids that I know of."

I took notes, and Tip took the opportunity to continue. "How about after she came to Houston. Did you see her much?"

Coop sat up straight. "Occasionally at a gathering with Cybil and Rusty, but aside from that, nothing."

Tip looked to me, then back to Coop.

"Were she and Cybil friends?"

"You'd have to ask Cybil that."

"Did you have dinner with Cybil on the night of the murder?"

Once again I thought she shot him a glare, but it was quick. Coop was good at covering up.

"I met her early in the evening, but I didn't have dinner with her." She narrowed her eyes so that I could barely see the blue.

"Did she say I did?"

Tip shook his head. "No, she said you met earlier. I forgot for a minute."

"Forgot my ass. Now how about you two get busy and find me a damn killer."

"We're trying." Tip stood and turned toward the door, but not before asking, "Cap, do you think Cybil could have killed her?"

"You can't be serious." Coop said.

"I *am* serious. Do you think she could?"

"Denton, get your cowboy ass out of my office, and stop wasting time on nonsense." She got up and shoved him toward the door, then gave me a nudge.

"You too, Cataldi. Get out of here and find the real murderer."

We started out the door but Coop called us back. "I know you'll be following up on this investigation. Make sure you work under the radar because Cybil's going to be watching your every move."

"And if we can't?" Tip asked.

Coop shrugged. "Then you can't. It might cost you a new captain, but what the hell. I had a different job before this one."

I patted her on the arm. "Thanks, Coop."

Tip didn't say anything as we walked back down the hall. Finally, I broke the silence.

"You did pretty good for a while, cowboy. But you just couldn't keep your mouth shut, could you."

"Fuck you."

"All right, but I ain't bending over."

Tip tried not to laugh, but he couldn't. He let out that goofy guffaw and couldn't stop. "Don't go stealing my jokes. That's what gives me charm."

"You don't have to worry. That was the first and *last* time I use one of your lines."

"Well all right then, I forgive you."

"Now all we need to do is find a murderer so Coop forgives us."

"Is that all?" Tip said. "That'll be easy now that we have a victim."

"Now what?"

"Let's go to your house so I can listen to that tape. I want to hear the mystery caller."

It didn't take long to drive to my place. I fired up the grill for burgers while Tip listened to the tape. He must have played it five or six times before he quit. We grabbed a couple of beers then sat down to eat and go over the tape together.

"I'm with you on this, Gino. Something sounds familiar about her, but nothing that I can pinpoint. I can't swear that it isn't Coop or Cybil, but I think I'd know them."

"I still think she's trying to hide an accent or something."

"I agree," Tip said. "She's not consistent."

"So let's look at this—what would the caller have to gain if she were the killer?"

Tip finished chewing and got up to get another beer. "You want another?"

"Unless you have a better idea," I said.

"I guess we could go out and troll for drug dealers. Maybe shoot one or two."

I laughed, but the hair on my neck bristled, like it did when something was wrong. *Is he baiting me? Is he the one asking Chicky about me?* "Sounds like a good idea, but I'm settled in for the night."

"Maybe another time," Tip said. "And as far as that caller and what she'd have to gain…I think I'm with you. I wasn't at first, but I can't see a reason why she'd call if she did it—unless it was to play with us. Even considering that I don't see it."

I flipped through notes from the case, and shook my head. "The problem is that every lead we have came from this woman. We haven't found a damn thing on our own."

Tip looked at me. "Somebody's yanking our dicks."

"She definitely knows *something*."

I opened up my second can of beer. "She either knows the killer or Camwyck. Or both. Either way, we have to find her."

"Phone traces produced nothing. She used a burner, probably different ones, and she turned them off after using them."

I grabbed our plates and rinsed them off in the sink. "And she hasn't called in several days. It might be she just wanted us to find out who the victim was so we could solve it ourselves, leaving her out of it."

Tip's phone rang and he punched the speaker button. "Denton."

"This is Dr. Umlang."

Tip looked over at me and whispered. "It's the vet. He's got the dog I took from Camwyck's."

"Put it on speakerphone," I said. "He's not as loud as Elena."

Tip nodded, and pressed the button for the speaker. "What's up? That dog all right?" Tip asked.

"He was dehydrated and hungry, but he'll be all right. There was no kidney damage. With a couple of days rest, and a good home, he'll be fine."

"What are you calling me for?"

"You know that Sacco doesn't stand a snowball's chance in hell of getting adopted."

"Can't do it," Tip said.

"You've got room at your place."

Tip frowned. "Aw shit, I can't. Find somebody else."

"You're probably his only shot," Umlang said.

"I'll think on it," Tip said, and hung up.

I glanced over at Tip. "What's the matter?"

"That damn dog we found in the condo. The vet wants me to take him in."

I thought that's what I heard. I figured how this would end up. "You gonna do it?"

"No way I'm taking another dog."

"How much you want to bet you'll have that dog before the week's up?"

"No fucking way."

"How much?"

He ignored me and walked outside.

"Fifty?"

"Go to hell. I'm not betting, but I'm not taking the dog either."

"What are you gonna name it?"

"He's already got a name. It was on his collar. Sacco...or something like that."

"Good name."

"Fuck you. Let's get to work."

My phone rang. "Gino."

"Detective Cataldi?"

"Who's this?"

A male voice with a hint of a Spanish accent said, "Detective Santos, DPD Homicide. I got your number from Captain Cooper."

Dallas Police Department? "What can I do for you, Detective?"

"We've got a body up here just like one of yours. Caucasian female, cut into three pieces and dumped all over town."

"Son of a bitch!" I said, and moved closer to Tip so that he could hear.

Santos filled me in on the details and I scribbled notes while he talked. Tip stood next to me, listening. "Santos, instead of me going through all we have, how about if I send you the file in the morning, and you can send us what you have."

"I'll get on it first thing," he said. "We can talk afterward."

"What was that about?" Tip asked. "I caught some of it, but not all."

"That was a detective from Dallas. It's like we figured, Tip, meaning the killer wasn't going to stop. We've got another body, but this one's in Big D."

CHAPTER 28

ANOTHER BODY

We walked out back porch, where I filled Tip in on what Santos told me about the body in Dallas as we nursed a couple of beers. Every few minutes, I wiped sweat off my head and swatted a few mosquitoes away. "I hate Texas summers."

"They *are* a bitch aren't they?"

"It got hot in Philly, but summer didn't last eight months. And we didn't have mosquitoes as big as sparrows."

"Fucking pussies." Tip gulped the last of his beer and tossed it into a can I had on the porch. "Tell me about Dallas again."

I looked at the notes from my talk with Santos. "Vic was a prostitute, a high-end one, Santos said. Her name was Patti Richards. But get this, she was almost as old as Camwyck."

"How'd they ID her? You didn't tell me they had a name."

"Prints matched a TDL record."

"This gets stranger by the minute," Tip said. "Why wasn't the killer worried about her being identified? He went to great lengths to make sure we didn't find Camwyck, and we wouldn't have if not for that rainstorm."

"And why did he bury Camwyck's head, and just dump Richards all over Dallas?"

"And he cut off Camwyck's fingers, too."

Tip set his beer on the porch railing and took out his notepad. He talked while he wrote. "Why is he spreading the body parts? Publicity? For what?"

"This is all assuming we have the same killer. It could be a copycat. Our guy tortured Camwyck before killing her. I'll be eager to see what the M.E. says about Richards."

Tip shook his head. "There are some sick sons of bitches out there."

"We'll have to wait until we look at the file to see if there's anything else."

"I hope they have more than us," Tip said.

"All we have for suspects are the mayor, his wife, and Coop. We need to generate more leads or be prepared to surrender our badges."

"We have an entire file cabinet full of leads," I said. "And they're all just as likely suspects as Rusty." I paused.

"Except of course the missing clients."

"Who's working the client list?"

"Perkins and Delgado," I said.

"Delgado's good, but we should get him some help. That's a big list."

I gulped the rest of my beer and swatted at another mosquito. "You know Delgado's my cousin."

Tip cocked his head and looked at me.

"Delgado's your cousin?"

"By marriage," I said, and drained the last sip from my can. "We also need to see if they found semen in the Dallas victim."

"Even if they did," Tip said, "she was a working girl."

"It would be nice if it matched the semen in Camwyck."

"Which reminds me," Tip said. "We've got to see if Rusty has a solid alibi for the night of Camwyck's murder. If not, we can get a warrant for a DNA test."

"I'd like to see that happen."

"Don't worry, if that dumb fuck doesn't give us an airtight alibi, I'll get one."

"How do you see this playing out with Rusty and Cybil?"

Tip shook his head. "I don't know if either one of them had anything to do with it, but something tells me there's a weasel in Rusty's henhouse. And I intend to find the son of a bitch."

"Unless you have reason to believe the weasel killed Camwyck, I'm gonna stick to the clues we have." I got up to go inside. "I'm also surrendering the porch to the insects."

We turned on the news while we reviewed our case and made plans for tomorrow. "I want to be in on any of the interviews that look promising.

Somebody has to know more about how the victim conducted business."

Tip was staring at the TV. "You hear this shit? The First Lady selected a guy from California as her drug czar."

I grabbed the remote and turned up the volume just in time to hear them repeat the guy's name. "Pete Ramirez! That pussy?"

"Jealous?" Tip asked.

"The guy's a wimp. I met him at that convention in LA last year and all he did was cry and whine about police brutality?" I poured a drink for me and one for Tip, handing him his.

"Not even a little jealous?"

I smiled. "Maybe a little."

Tip slugged the drink, nodding. "Me too. When I heard they were looking for someone to run the drug operation, some little part of me wanted that job. But I would have hated leaving Texas."

"Really? You like it here that much?"

He seemed to give it serious thought, then shook his head. "I like it all right, but that's not why. Somebody killed my mother a long time ago and the case has never been solved." He took a gulp, a long one. "I intend to find out who did it."

I didn't know what to say, wishing now I hadn't brought the subject up. "I'm sorry. I didn't know."

"That's all right. There shouldn't be secrets between partners. That's what my last partner told me."

"Was that Connie?"

"Gianelli, yeah. Damn good partner. Gutsy lady." He was silent for a few seconds, then said, "It was me fucking up that got her hurt. Almost got her killed."

I knew she'd gotten hurt on a case they were working, but this other was news to me. "You still talk to her?"

"I do, but I'm surprised she talks to me."

"Mistakes happen," I said.

Tip shook his head. "Bullshit. I fucked up. We were on a cold case. The guy who worked it originally was a piss-poor detective who was just putting time in until he retired. I knew that—and I didn't bother checking his data.

If I had, I might've caught the son of a bitch before he got to Connie." Tip got up, rinsed his glass and set it in the sink. "Enough of this reminiscing bullshit. I'll see you tomorrow."

I walked him to the door, holding it open as he went down the sidewalk, but suddenly he stopped and turned.

"Forget something?"

He walked back slowly. I could tell he had something on his mind.

"When did that woman in Dallas die?"

"A few days ago. Might have been Wednesday. The file will tell us the day, assuming the medical examiner's report is in there."

"That was the day the First Lady was in Dallas. And if I'm not mistaken, Coop was there."

I thought about what he said, and the way he said it. "Yeah, she was, but don't be going down that road. There's no way Coop did this."

"Yeah, but Cybil was there too." Tip turned and headed toward his car, then he stopped and turned. "It's something to think about. That's all I'm saying."

CHAPTER 29

CHECKING THE FACTS

All the way into town I thought about the new drug czar the First Lady had announced. I had to admit I was pissed, but I had no reason to be. There was no way I could've been chosen. I knew that, but the dreams lingered—like how people dream of winning the lottery every time they buy a ticket.

As I thought this, I realized that I was probably just thinking of anything to keep my mind from pondering on what I'd done to Rico, or more precisely, Rico's family. I didn't give a shit about Rico, but I *did* feel sorry for his wife and kids.

For the last few miles I focused on clearing my head, and by the time I arrived I was reoriented on the case.

I arrived at the station before Tip, and had coffee brewing by the time he got there. Fat Charlie had eaten his way through most of the cinnamon rolls. I figured the next time I'd hide the bag until everyone got there. I poured myself a coffee, then headed to my desk to review the Dallas file. After a quick scan, I called Santos.

"Santos, this is Cataldi down in Houston."

"Did you look at the file?"

"I went through it quickly. By the way, you should have our file by now. They sent it a few minutes ago."

"What's it look like?" Santos asked. "Same guy?"

"It might be. We've got a lot of similarities, probably too many for a coincidence, but some things are missing, too."

"What's missing? I only saw the short file on your victim before I called you."

"When you look at the whole file you'll see what I mean. The body parts on our victim were inserted into different parts of the victim. We kept that back from the public. Some of the other things that we kept quiet were also different."

"Shit," Santos said. "It could be some wacko who happened to see it in the paper and decided to do one himself."

I digested what Santos said. "If we're down to guessing, then I'm guessing you don't have much to go on."

"Nothing. Her apartment was ransacked but nothing of value was taken."

"Did you find a computer?"

"Not yet," Santos said.

"How about an address book or a list of clients."

"Nothing."

"Our victim had no cell listed to her, which we found strange, but we're still searching. We've also got the phone company pulling her home phone. We'll send you the calls as soon as we get them. Who knows, maybe we'll get lucky."

"Fat chance of that."

"Yeah," I said. "Fat chance is right. By the way, did your victim have a cell?"

"Phone company has a record of one. We're waiting on the list. I'll get it to you."

"How about a car. She have one? Did you find it?"

"She had one according to DMV records, but we haven't found it. No keys in the purse either."

I perked up at the mention of a purse.

"You found one with the body?"

"In the same dumpster as her legs."

"We didn't find a purse. She had several in her condo, but there was no way she went out dressed like she was without her purse."

"I hear you on the purse thing," Santos said, "but somebody could've lifted it from the dumpster before you got there."

"Yeah, but it's more likely the killer took it. He tried hiding our victim's identity, and he went out of his way to do it. You'll see it in the report."

I then told Santos about our anonymous caller and how that led to the ID.

"And you have no idea who the caller is?"

"No idea. And you're the only one besides me, my partner, and our captain who knows about this."

"Don't worry. I'll keep it to myself. And I'll call if we get anything else."

I hung up and went to get more coffee. As I turned the corner I heard Charlie's voice. It sounded like a whiny plea for mercy. Tip must have found the empty bag.

"I swear, Tip. I only had two," Charlie said.

"Two my ass. Two dozen is more like it. I ought to make you jog down the street to get more."

"Come on, Tip, cut it out. Besides, if you got in at a reasonable hour, there'd a been some left."

I held in the laughter and refilled my cup.

"Charlie had a point. It *is* the middle of the day."

"Fuck you, too," Tip said.

I went back to my desk, Tip showing up a minute later.

"I can't believe he ate all the rolls."

"I know you *can* believe it because you're the one who warned me about him."

Tip laughed. "I guess I did, huh."

"So where were you?"

"None of your business."

I could tell I was getting to him, but I didn't let it show. "Stop by and see that poor little doggie?"

Tip held it in for as long as he could—about five seconds—then he burst out laughing. When he stopped, I prodded him again.

"What's his name?"

"I told you, he already had a name—Sacco. And he's a good dog."

"When's he going home with you?"

"I haven't said I'd take him. I just went to check on the damn dog."

"Tomorrow night?"

He hesitated, then said, "Probably."

I didn't laugh. I figured I'd save that for another time. I *did* fill him in on my conversation with Santos, though.

"Maybe we'll get something. By the way, did we get anything from the people working on Camwyck's clients?"

"We've got three teams on it," Tip said, "And Julie's got the description of Camwyck's car out. But so far, no leads."

"We ought to get it on the news," I said.

"Our good citizens will find it sooner than we can. I mean, after all, how many blue Fords can there be out there?"

"All right, smart ass. I'll get a reporter on it."

"You gonna use Roberts?"

"We'll use somebody else for this."

We spent the rest of the morning working on Rusty's and Cybil's alibis. Rusty checked out and his alibi was unbreakable, and Cybil's alibi held good at least until eight or eight-thirty. That left a small window but it was pushing the time line. Rusty told us he got home a little before 1:00 and Cybil was already asleep. I looked over to Tip, shaking my head.

"I can't see her going home to change, going out and killing Camwyck, then butchering her and dumping her in two cans, *then* going to bury her and still getting home before 1:00."

"Be a rugged job even for a couple of men, let alone one woman. Although she is a tough son of a gun."

"That was kind of you, Tip—the son-of a gun part, I mean."

"I'm in a kind mood today."

"Sacco have anything to do with that?"

"I should've never said anything to you."

"So I guess we'll have to cut Cybil and Rusty loose as suspects," I said.

"Unless Rusty is covering for her, but I can't imagine why he would."

I stopped and looked at Tip. "What time did Rusty say he got home?"

"A little before 1:00."

"Didn't we determine the body was dumped at Starbucks after 1:00, something about an employee emptying the trash?"

"Damn," Tip said. "I think we need new suspects."

"Now you're talking," I said.

We worked the rest of the day interviewing Camwyck's "clients" but every one of them had alibis for one murder or the other. We had told Santos we'd check a few alibis for the victim in Dallas while we checked ours.

A few of the clients reluctantly told us what they paid for services, and we learned it wasn't Camwyck they were paying for, but *girls* she had working for her. Turns out Camwyck was nothing more than a high-end pimp. She charged between $500 and several thousand per night, plus expenses, which included a nice hotel room, dinner, wine, and a gift of some sort, the gift being something as simple as chocolates and flowers to one client's gift of diamond earrings.

"This lady had it made," Tip said. "I'm going to be a pimp in my next life. Or maybe a whore."

"You're a whore now," I said. "You just don't know it. Besides, at those rates, they're not called whores, they're escorts, or companions, or some such nonsense."

"A rose by any other name…"

"Damn, I'm impressed. I didn't know you read books."

"I don't. I just remember what I see on TV and repeat it."

As we debated the merits of books, which is when I discovered Tip actually *did* read—mostly mysteries and Texas history—Delgado called.

"Hey, cuz. We've got a possibility," he said. "One guy's alibi for Camwyck didn't check out, and he has no alibi for Dallas."

"Motive?"

"How about three calls from Camwyck the week before she died. And his secretary said they were on the phone a long time. She also said he was pissed-off after the last call."

"Anything else?"

"He's got no record, but we checked with a few people who know him and they say he's been moody, almost frantic, the past few weeks. It's been worse since Camwyck died."

"Why don't you let him sit today. Let him think he's okay while we gather more information. We'll pick him up tomorrow and see what we can sweat out of him."

"He'll lawyer up," Delgado said. "You know that."

"Is he married?" I asked.

Delgado nodded. "With two kids."

"He'll talk—if he wants to keep his wife out of it."

"He can hire a lawyer without her knowing."

"I'll let him know that she'll *definitely* find out. Trust me, he won't call a lawyer."

"Okay, cuz. Your call."

"Stop calling me cuz or I'll pull out the "Ribs" nickname."

"*Si, primo*," Delgado said, and laughed. "You afraid somebody's gonna find out you're nothing but a home boy?"

"We're cousins by marriage."

"Same thing where I come from. Once you're in the family, you're stuck."

Delgado was still laughing when I hung up the phone.

I filled Tip in on the new information and while we were talking Santos called, giving us an update on his end and asking a few questions about our victim also. I said goodbye to Santos, then Tip and I went through what we had.

"So we've got semen in our victim, and none in Dallas."

"But ours could have been from the night before," Tip said.

I looked through the notes from Santos.

"Her cell had six calls the day of the murder. Four in the morning, one to her neighbor, one to a local deli, the hair salon and the cable company. She got two incoming calls from an unknown number, one early afternoon and another in the evening, just before six. And it was the same number."

"I don't imagine we have an ID for that one?" Tip asked.

"No such luck. And we still have no idea where Camwyck's cell phone is. Burners are the only explanation."

"What about a family plan?"

"What?"

Tip stood and paced. "Suppose she was on someone else's plan—like Rusty's."

I scribbled a note in my tablet. "I'll get Julie to check on that first thing tomorrow. It sure would be nice if that was the case."

"What else have we got on Dallas?" Tip asked.

I looked back through the notes. "Her place was small, well-kept, paid for. No bills to speak of and a closet full of expensive clothes. She had a large-screen TV, a great stereo and—according to Santos—a great wine selection."

"I'll bet that son of a bitch sampled some, too."

"Don't complain. You got the dog."

"We still think it's the same guy?"

I nodded. "Their medical examiner said the weapons were different, but the same type. More importantly, though, the same body parts were cut off and stuffed in the same human receptacles."

"And nobody knows about that," Tip said. "We've got the same killer. Make a note to have Julie check VICAP for matches. If this guy is on the move he could be going anywhere."

CHAPTER 30

A NEW LEAD

The phone rang on Fat Charlie's desk. He looked at his watch—not even seven o'clock yet. "Hello?"

"Officer, I have someone on the line who asked for Detective Denton. He said he's calling about the pictures in the paper."

"I'll take it," Charlie said, and then, "This is Detective Charles Masterson. How can I help you?"

"I saw that picture in the paper and thought I'd better call. I was up there that night, and I saw a pickup down under the Cypress Creek bridge."

Charlie jotted notes down as the man talked. "Are you sure it was the same night?"

"No question. We had a big storm blow in that night, and I caught it on my way home."

"Can you describe the vehicle? Charlie asked.

"It was a brand new F–150 Super Crew. White, with a short bed. I remember thinking how sweet it looked and wondered why the hell someone would take a new truck down under the bridge."

"What about the time?"

"About midnight, close as I recall."

"Sir, do you mind giving me your name, so I—"

"Can't do that."

"Sir, if you're worried about your name getting out, it won't. This will remain confidential."

"Officer, I been around long enough to know there ain't much in life that's confidential. Truth of the matter is, I was up there with another woman, and there ain't no way I'm givin' my name because sure as shit stinks it'll leak and my wife will find out."

As Charlie thought about what to say, the man said, "One more thing, best as I can tell two of the numbers on the plate were six and eight."

"Six and eight? You're sure about that?"

"Can't swear to it, but I'd place a small wager."

"Sir, if—"

"Sorry, but I gotta go. Hope you catch the crazy fuck who did this."

Charlie drank three cups of coffee while waiting for Tip to get in. When he heard him, he rushed past Karl and Julie and pulled a chair up to Tip's desk. "We have a lead," he said. "A good one."

Tip looked as if he might laugh, but he didn't. "What have you got, Charlie?"

"Somebody called in off the pictures in the paper. He said he saw a pickup down under the Cypress Creek bridge on Kuykendahl on the same night as the murder. And the time fits."

Tip leaned toward Charlie. "Did he give you a description?"

Charlie looked at his notes. "He said it was a brand new F–150 Super Crew. White, with a short bed."

"What time did he see it?" Tip asked.

"About midnight, according to the caller.

He remembered because he was already late going home."

"Did you get his name and number?" Tip asked.

Charlie shrunk in the chair, almost like a scared dog. "He wouldn't give it to me, Tip. He said—"

"That's all right," Tip said. "I'm surprised we even got a call."

Charlie seemed to gain confidence. "One other thing, Tip. He gave us two numbers from the plate. He said he can't swear to it, but he's pretty sure the plate had a six and an eight."

Tip patted Charlie on the back. "You did good with this. Real good."

***

Tip looked at me and winked. "This is what we needed."

I looked at Charlie. He was all puffed up and grinning like we'd brought him a dozen bagels. "Good job, Charlie," I said. "Damn good."

"Julie, get in here," Tip said. "We have a real lead."

She walked in a moment later.

"Get the information from Charlie," Tip said, and then run the vehicle with the partial plate and print out a list. He turned to Charlie. "Help her prioritize it by age, gender, geography, anything we can think of because there are going to be a lot of those trucks in the city."

Karl had come in to see what was going on. I grabbed him by the arm. "See about getting a team up to the Cy Creek scene and have them go back over everything looking for tire tracks. We have a witness that says he saw an F–150 up there the night of the murder."

"You got it," Karl said, and headed out.

"That rain probably washed everything away," Tip said, "But you never can tell. It's worth a shot."

For the next hour or so, I helped Charlie prioritize the list of F–150 owners whose license plates contained a six or an eight, in any order. Fortunately, Texas uses a lot of letters in the plate numbers, but we still ended up with 120 that matched. While I worked on the leads, Tip filled Coop in on the new development. By the time he returned, I had a few prospects worth checking on. First up was a 2013 model that belonged to Randy Cusper, a 39-year-old registered gun activist with a plate that matched. And a record as a small-time dealer.

"Keep working the list," I said to Charlie.

"We're gonna start checking these out."

"Give the next batch to Delgado," Tip said. "Tell him to keep us posted."

Randy Cusper lived just north of the Loop, tucked into an older neighborhood that was predominantly Latino now.

We turned right on Crosstimbers, took a left a few lights down, and found Cusper living in a small ranch house off a side street. Three Latinos and a couple of dogs patrolled the street. They checked us out when we pulled up, but no doubt they knew we were cops.

Cusper's truck was parked in a short driveway next to the house. As we approached, I got my holster ready for a quick draw in case of trouble. Tip knocked on the door. I stood back a few steps and kept my eyes open on both sides of the house. A few seconds later a young teenage girl answered.

She couldn't have been more than 16 or 17.

Tip flashed the badge. "Detective Denton," he said. "I'm looking for Randy Cusper."

"What do you want him for?"

She had an attitude, but that didn't surprise me.

"We have a few questions we'd like to ask him," Tip said.

"You can ask me," she said. "My dad's in jail."

Tip shot me a quick glance, then said,

"How long has he been in jail?"

She cocked her head to the side, as if thinking, then said, "Maybe two weeks. Something like that."

"Is your mother here?" Tip said.

"Get off what you're thinking, cop. I got no mother and haven't had one all my life. I do fine by myself." She started to close the door but Tip stopped her by jamming his foot in.

"What's your father in jail for?"

"Parole violation," she said.

Tip handed her a card but he didn't even get his spiel out before the door slammed shut.

"So much for that," I said.

"That bitch has an attitude."

"I wonder why the printout didn't show the parole violation?" I said. "We better check on that in case the ungrateful one's lying."

"Not that she'd lie," Tip said. "But just in case."

We got in Tip's car and headed back toward the freeway. "Next up is Mano Perez." I said. "Married, 24-years old, and drives a 2014 model F–150."

"Where's he live?" Tip asked.

"Up on Veterans Memorial. Looks like it's just south of 1960."

Tip entered the freeway heading in that direction. "At least we won't be dealing with a smart-ass teenager this time."

It only took twenty minutes to find Mano's house. A young woman answered. She had what appeared to be a two-year-old clinging to her leg and younger child in her arms. I looked down at her belly. She was pregnant.

Tip showed his badge. She shook her head. "*No hablo ingles.*"

I stepped up next to Tip. "*¿Donde està tu marido?*"

She smiled at me. "*Está en el trabajo.*"

"*¿Donde està?*"

She fumbled with the words, trying to get her point across in English, but we eventually understood her to mean he was working at a car dealership on I-45, by the airport exit. It all became clear to Tip when he heard the name of Señor Ingle.

"*Trabaja para Señor Ingle.*" She said.

As we walked back to the car, Tip looked at me. "Did she say he worked for Ingle? If so, this is getting more interesting all the time."

"Why's that?"

"RB Ingle owns the dealership she's talking about. That opens up a whole new list of suspects."

I opened the passenger door and slid in the seat. "I guess I still don't get it."

Tip turned and looked at me. "RB and Rusty used to frequent the stripper clubs all the time."

"Used to?"

"Rumor has it that RB stopped after he married the daughter of a former police captain, but I doubt that stopped him." Tip started the engine and backed out. "Either way, though. He probably knew our victim."

"Son of a bitch."

"Yeah," Tip said. "And one of his employees has a truck that might have been seen where the body was dumped."

"I think we need to speak to Señor Perez," I said.

"Let's hope he's still there. You know the wife called to warn him."

CHAPTER 31

A COUPLE OF QUESTIONS

We parked and went inside the showroom for Ingle motors, fully expecting to find Mano gone. Tip winked at the receptionist, who flashed him a genuine smile in return. It seemed as if Tip couldn't help himself when it came to pretty women, but on the other hand, they responded to him.

He showed her his badge and leaned on the counter. "Darlin', if there's any way you can tell me where to find Mano Perez, I'd sure appreciate it."

She blushed, and then she pulled up Mano's number and paged him. Within a few seconds, she said, "He'll be right up," and then to Tip, "My name's Lisa."

"That's one of my favorite names," Tip said.

Between almost choking over his ridiculous bullshit, and wanting real information, I said to Lisa, "What does Mano do here?"

She turned to me, but her smile wasn't nearly as inviting. "He works as a supervisor in customer service."

Tip was still chatting with her when Mano showed. "Lisa, you wanted to see me?"

"These gentlemen wanted to speak with you."

I showed my badge, which drew a surprised reaction. Maybe his wife hadn't called. "Can we go someplace to talk?"

"Is something wrong? Mano said.

"Nothing wrong. We have a few questions."

He looked around and then led us to an empty office. He sat behind the desk. Tip and I sat in chairs opposite him. "Is something wrong?" Mano asked again.

"Do you know Barbara Camwyck?" Tip asked.

He scrunched his eyes up and looked at Tip, and then me. "The name is familiar, but I don't think I know her. Did she buy a car here?"

His English was very good. He spoke with only a hint of an accent. "I don't think she did," I said. "That's one of the things we're here to find out."

"Why don't you check the computer and see if she was a customer," Tip said. "It's spelled C-A-M-W-Y-C-K. First name Barbara."

He typed her name into the computer. When the file came up on the screen, recognition showed in his face. "I remember now. She brought her car in a few weeks ago to be serviced. I gave her a ride home."

I looked over at Tip, who had leaned closer to Mano. "You gave her a ride home? When was this, exactly?"

Mano checked the file and then said,

"Three weeks ago. And she picked her car up the next day."

"What kind of car?" I asked.

"A 2015 Ford Fusion," Mano said. "Blue."

"What happened when you took her home?" Tip asked.

"Nothing happened," Mano said, and became defensive. "I dropped her off outside her building and then I left."

Tip got in his face. "And what, you went back the next week to get a little something?"

"You're sick," Mano said.

"And when she wouldn't do it, you butchered her?"

"I'd never do that. I'm not like that."

"Where were you the night of the murder?"

"What murder?" he said.

"Camwyck's murder. She was the lady whose body was found in the dumpsters," Tip said.

Mano sat up straight. "*Dios mío.*" Mano blessed himself and said once again. "*Dios mío.*"

Tip and I remained silent and let him digest the information.

After a moment, Mano said, "When was the murder?"

I was hoping he had an alibi ready, but he was playing it smart, pretending not to know when she was killed. I played his game and gave him the date.

He thought and then smiled. "I was working for Mr. Ingle. He had a big party for the mayor's campaign."

Tip said, "What were you doing at the mayor's party?"

"Mr. Ingle knows I need money. I do a lot of extra things for him. I worked inside, escorting people, getting drinks, waiting on tables."

"Where did this take place?" I asked.

"At Mr. Ingle's country club where he plays golf. Raveneaux, over on Cypresswood Drive."

"What time did you start?"

"Right after work, maybe around 5:00 or 5:30. We had a lot to prepare."

"When did you leave?" Tip asked.

Mano looked to the side and rubbed his hands together. "I left the country club about 8:30 or 9:00."

"What time did you get home?" I asked.

"About 10:30."

Tip scrunched up his brow. "Why so late?"

"I drove the other workers back to their cars or to their homes. I used the company van."

"Where was your truck during the party?" I asked. "Was it with you the whole night?"

"Here," he said, and his face lit up. "I didn't even have my truck that night."

"Can your wife vouch for that?"

He shifted in his seat and fidgeted. "She wasn't home. And…she's not my wife. She's my cousin."

Tip said, "Your cousin?"

Mano shook his head. "It's not what you think. Her husband is involved with drugs in Mexico. She ran away and is hiding at my house, with me." He looked at me, then Tip. "Please, don't make trouble for her."

"What time did she get home?" I asked.

"Not until the next morning. She stayed with a friend."

Tip stood and grabbed hold of Mano's arm. "You'll have to come with us," he said. "You have the right to remain silent…"

I knew we didn't have enough to take him in, but more than likely, he didn't and I wanted a look at that truck.

Mano's eyes opened wide. "What are you doing? I didn't do anything."

I grabbed Tip's arm. "Hold on. We might not need to do all that."

Tip looked at me and winked. "The hell we don't."

I turned to Mano and said, "Maybe we can clear this up without going downtown."

"What do you need?" Mano asked.

"How about you let us check out your truck?" I said.

Mano seemed to relax. "Sure, man. Take a look. Take a drive if you want."

Tip put his cuffs away and said, "Let's see the truck."

He led us to the employee parking lot and handed us the keys. "Right there. Look all you want."

Tip got down on his back and slid partway under the truck. He checked the undercarriage and the tires. "Have you cleaned this lately?"

"Not in a few months," Mano said.

After Tip slid out from under the truck, we checked the cab, and then the back. A few pieces of lumber lay in the bed of the truck, along with an old tire and a plastic garbage bag. I climbed in the bed and moved a few things around. Back in the corner of the bed, near the driver's side, I spotted something. It was either rust or blood.

"Tip, we might have blood."

"Blood? Ain't no blood in there," Mano said.

Tip looked over the side of the truck into the bed. "Looks like blood to me," he said, and grabbed Mano's arm. "You have the right to remain silent…"

"That ain't blood!" Mano said. "It can't be blood."

CHAPTER 32

THINGS DON'T ADD UP

We took Mano for processing, and arranged for the crime scene guys to pick up and process his truck. Mano insisted he was innocent, and I felt certain he was. Regardless, we had to question him. A lot of things didn't add up about this. I had read him his rights as protection, but I didn't think we'd need it.

Once we had Mano situated in the interview room, Tip took the first shot at him.

"How did the blood get in your truck?"

Mano shook his head while staring at the table. "I don't know anything about blood."

"Have you cut yourself lately?" I asked, hoping he'd say yes.

He shook his head.

"As soon as they get the report back from the lab we'll know it's her blood." Tip let what he said sink in, then, "And once we know it's her blood, you'll go to trial and be convicted, and then they'll put a needle in your arm."

Mano looked up at Tip. "Bullshit. I want to call Señor Ingle."

"Is Mr. Ingle your legal counsel?" Tip asked.

Tip asked Mano where he was the night Richards was killed, the woman from Dallas. Mano said he was working all day and didn't get home until 8:00. If he was, that cleared him of the Dallas murder, but we didn't know for sure if they were connected. I made a note to check his alibi.

"Tell me again why you left the party so early," Tip said.

Mano sighed. Tip was getting to him. "I already told you. Mr. Ingle's assistant sent several of us home early. Once we set up there was no need for all of us."

"And you went straight home?" I asked.

Mano clenched his fists. "I *told* you. I drove the other workers home, and then I went home. I used Mr. Ingle's van."

"What's the assistant's name?" I asked.

"Reggie. I don't know his last name."

Tip and I pressed him, and repeated a lot of questions, but he wasn't changing his tune. The guy had a story and he was sticking to it.

Before long, Mano asked to use his phone call. I figured he'd lawyer-up, but he called RB Ingle, which turned out to be far worse. Mano clamped up after he spoke to RB, and within an hour a lawyer named Rengster showed up.

He was obviously paid for by RB. In no time, he arranged for Mano to be released on bail, which RB also must have sprung for.

We released the truck to Mano. The techs had already gotten what they needed. After Mano walked out with the lawyer, we went back to the office. Tip kicked his feet up on the desk. "What's your take on it, Gino? Did we let a killer walk?"

"You know we didn't," I said. "The question is who's framing him."

Tip sat up in his chair and pulled out a notepad. "What have we got so far?"

I pushed my chair to his desk and sat. "The lead called in to Charlie, the one that identified Mano's truck."

Tip wrote it down. "The guy who wouldn't leave his name."

"That's him," I said. "And whoever left the lead on the truck had to know that Mano wouldn't have an alibi for the night of the murder."

"Which means he knows him," Tip said,

"And he knew what Mano would be doing that night."

"And the big one is the blood in the back of the truck, which I'm certain is going to match Camwyck's."

"No doubt in my mind," Tip said. "The body was dumped before the rain started, and it rained way too hard that night for the blood to stay in the bed of that truck."

I thought for a minute and then said, "The blood in the back of that truck means it was probably planted sometime the next day after the rain stopped.

Which means they knew where the truck would be."

Tip stopped writing and looked over at me.

"That trail leads right back to RB Ingle."

I thought about what Tip said, and nodded. "Mano worked for Ingle. He was working for Ingle the night of the murder, and he used one of Ingle's vans to take people home."

"Which conveniently left Mano's truck accessible."

"And let's not forget that Ingle posted bail to the tune of $100,000," I said. "That's a lot of money for a low-level employee."

"That's a lot of money for *any* employee," Tip said. "Makes me wonder why he did it."

I took a sip of water and looked at Tip. "But let's not forget my mystery caller. So far she's been the source of our only good leads."

Tip nodded. "Makes me wonder where the hell she fits in. I've been thinking that ever since she called. Why is the question. Why would she call us? Why does she want us to know?"

I grabbed my notepad and phone. "I think we need to have a talk with RB Ingle."

"Remember how much fun we had chatting with Cybil?" Tip said.

I laughed. "Yeah. If you want to call that fun."

"This is gonna be worse."

CHAPTER 33

RB INGLE

Ingle probably knew we were coming to talk to him before we'd made up our minds.

A receptionist with cropped brown hair greeted us. "Good morning, gentlemen."

Tip went into his charming and flirtatious act, leaning close toward her and smiling. "Morning, darlin'. I'm Detective Denton, and that's Detective Cataldi. We're here to see RB."

"I'll see if Mr. Ingle is available," she said, but there wasn't a hint of a smile with her response.

"Looks like you're losing your charm," I whispered to Tip.

He didn't smile either.

After we waited for ten or fifteen minutes, a young man dressed in a gray suit and wearing a somber look, came out to greet us. It seemed as if no one was smiling today.

"You're here to see Mr. Ingle?" he said, without an offer to shake hands.

"We have a few questions for him," I said.

"Follow me," the young man said, and then he turned and started down a long hallway.

A maze of corridors led us to a conference room. RB Ingle sat at the head of a table that must have seated about 25 people. Without asking, the young man opened a refrigerator and set two bottles of water in front of chairs three seats away from Ingle. Rather than accept his seating arrangement, Tip sat on one side of the table—across from Ingle—and I sat opposite them.

For a moment I wondered if others were going to join us or if Ingle was afraid of catching germs from the common folk.

Tip took his seat and started right in. "Why did you bail out Mano?"

Ingle feigned confusion. "He's an employee. A good one."

I looked through my notes. "It doesn't look as if he's been with you that long, Mr. Ingle? My records show only two and half months. Do you provide bail as part of an employee's benefit package?"

Ingle laughed. "Of course not, but Mano seemed shaken up when he called. And I felt sorry for him, especially with his young wife and kids at home."

I made note of what he said. Either he didn't know she wasn't Mano's wife, or he knew and was lying.

"That's damn nice of you," Tip said. "Remind me to look you up when I retire."

"You should do that, detective. I hire a lot of retired law enforcement personnel."

"So why *did* you provide bail?" I asked again. I also began to wonder about what he mentioned regarding ex-law enforcement personnel. It made me wonder things like who he had on his payroll and in what capacity.

A cup of steaming hot coffee sat in front of Ingle. He lifted it and took a sip. "I asked around when I heard Mano was arrested. Everyone agreed that he couldn't have done such a thing." He focused his gaze on me. "I don't like it when innocent people are persecuted, especially those who can't defend themselves."

"How can you be so confident that he's innocent?" Tip asked. "He hasn't worked here that long."

"Everyone I spoke to seems to think so."

"Where were you the night of the murder?" I asked.

"As I'm sure you know by now, I was at a party in for the mayor's campaign."

I jotted down a few notes, and asked,

"What time did the party end?"

Ingle didn't hesitate. "I don't know what time the party ended, but I left shortly after midnight. I don't remember what time I arrived, but I'm sure it was no later than seven."

"Mano said he left the party about 8:00 or 8:30 and drove other employees home. Why did he leave so early?" Tip asked.

"You'll have to ask Janice. She runs the kitchen staff, and she was in charge of all help that night." He wrote her name and number on a piece of paper and handed it to Tip. "You'll have to ask her the details."

"What about Mano's truck? Tip asked, while stuffing the card in his pocket. He said he used a company van to drive the employees home."

"For that you'll have to check with Reggie," Ingle said, and then, "Reggie is my assistant, and my bodyguard."

I jotted Reggie's name down next to Janice's. From the corner of my eye, I saw Tip get up and pace.

"How well did you know Ms. Camwyck?" he asked.

Ingle cocked his head to the side and looked out the window. "I knew her. Not well, but I knew her."

"Didn't you know her from East Texas? Before you came to Houston?"

"She was younger than I was, but yes, I knew her. She was friends with Cybil."

I let Tip continue while I scribbled notes.

"I'll ask you again," Tip said. "How well did you know Barbara Camwyck?"

Ingle placed both hands on the edge of the table and pushed his chair back. "Why don't you get to the point, Detective? If you want to know if I was screwing her, the answer is no."

Tip's face twisted into one of his threatening smiles. "We have semen. If you were, we'll find out."

Ingle stood. "I have a meeting to attend. You can ask Reggie or Jonathan for anything else you need."

"Where can we find Reggie?" I asked.

Ingle leaned forward and pressed a button on the intercom. "Jonathan, have Reggie meet the detectives when they leave. They have questions for him." He looked at his watch and said, "They will be leaving in five minutes."

I raised my eyebrows. "We had a few more questions."

"I'm sure you do, detectives, but I have a meeting that I can't be late for. If you'll excuse me."

Just then the door opened and the young man who had escorted us in said, "Gentlemen, if you'll follow me, I'll introduce you to Reggie."

Jonathan led us to a small office close to the main lobby. He knocked once on the door, then opened it. A tall, muscular man stepped out from behind his desk. He had a charismatic smile, not unlike Denzel Washington, and a firm grip, similar to what I imagined Sylvester Stallone's might be.

"Reggie Grage," he said. "What can I do for you?"

After we shook hands, Reggie stepped back into a rigid stance, as if he were at attention. I made a mental note to check and see if he served in the military.

"Relax," Tip said. "We just have a few questions."

Reggie smiled but he didn't relax; he stood with his arms in front of him and his hands clasped. He appeared to be a paragon of vigilance and observation wrapped in a six-foot frame, complete with steely gaze.

Reggie had a swimmer's build, lean and wiry, and his skin was as dark as chocolate. He kept his hair cropped close and he owned a voice that couldn't be bought. A deep baritone voice that made his articulate speech sound commanding, especially with the slight hint of what I figured was a Virginia drawl.

Tip leaned forward, close to Reggie. "Why don't you tell us about the night of the mayor's party?"

"Tell you what?" Reggie asked.

"Tell us the sequence of events. Everything from when you arrived until you left."

"I drove Mr. Ingle home after work and waited for him to change clothes. That was approximately 17 hundred…approximately 5:00 PM."

I made a note: *military time.*

"And after that?" Tip asked.

"I drove Mr. Ingle to the club. We arrived before 7:32. We left at 12:24."

"You're sure about that? About the 12:24 part?"

"Positive, Detective. Mr. Ingle notified me at 12:15 and we left at 12:24. Mrs. Ingle accompanied him."

"What about Mano Perez?" I asked.

Reggie turned mechanically to face me, almost like a robot moving. "What about Mr. Perez?"

"Did you see him that night. And what time did he leave?"

"Mr. Perez left at approximately 8:30 PM. He was asked to drive several employees home."

"What was he driving?" Tip asked.

"He drove one of Mr. Ingle's vans. Mr. Perez's truck was at the office."

"What about afterward? Did Mano return?"

Reggie shook his head. "He didn't come back, or at least, I didn't notice him return. We didn't expect him, though."

"Did Mr. Ingle leave at any time during the night?" Tip asked.

"As I said, he and Mrs. Ingle left at 12:24. I drove them home, and then went home myself."

I handed Reggie my card, but before I could say anything, he did. "I know the drill, Detective. Call if I think of anything."

We left the building with nothing more than we had before. "Ingle wasn't as bad as you said," I told him.

"That's because we didn't have anything to press him with," Tip said. "If he's pressed, he pushes back hard."

"So what did you think?"

Tip clicked the key to unlock the car doors. When we got inside, he said, "I think something's fishy. I just don't know what."

"Fishy with Ingle or with Reggie the robot?"

"The robot? Why call him a robot?"

I chuckled. "As if you didn't notice. He reminded me of those characters on the Terminator movies, the ones from the future that were robots."

Tip laughed. "Okay. I'll go along with that. But no, I'm talking about Ingle. I still can't figure out why he posted bail for a low-level employee. If you knew Ingle, you'd understand. He's not the generous type."

"How about we go talk to Mano and find out?"

"Let him sit for a few days," Tip said.

"Then we'll pay him a visit."

As we drove back to the station, my mind raced. "You know what I don't like—all of our suspects have alibis."

"What I don't like is the anonymous tips about Mano's truck," Tip said. "I hate anonymous tips."

"It does make you wonder, doesn't it?"

"Makes me wonder who called," Tip said.

"I don't buy the cheating husband explanation offered by the caller either."

"Me neither," I said. "I hate coincidences. And the explanation that caller offered reeks of coincidences."

CHAPTER 34

WHERE IS MANO?

We decided to put a tail on Mano to keep an eye on him until we paid him a visit. By late afternoon, we realized how fucked we were. Mano wasn't at his house, and, when we checked, we discovered he never showed up at work. We put out an APB on his truck and alerted units on all the major freeways. If he was heading out of Texas, he could be anywhere, but if he was heading for the Mexican border, the routes were easier to monitor.

Still, we held little hope of finding him, and it brought up more questions about Ingle—like why he didn't call when Mano didn't show for work. If I had a hundred thousand dollars at risk, you can bet I'd know where the guy was at all times.

Tip and I spent the rest of the day following up on leads that went nowhere. By 7:00, I was beat and called it quits.

During the drive home, I realized I didn't want to be alone, so I went to the mall and wandered around until it closed, then I caught a late movie followed by breakfast at Denny's.

I pushed through the back door shortly after 1:00, quickly found the sofa, and flipped through channels on TV. There wasn't a damn thing on, not even with cable and two hundred channels. After searching for another minute or so, I turned the set off. As I walked into the bathroom I hit the knob on the stereo and tuned in an 80s station, medium volume, then went back and plopped on the bed. The only way I could sleep now was focusing on music.

Ever since the incident with Rico, I'd been haunted by what I'd done. Whenever I closed my eyes I saw his face, and—even worse—the look in his eyes just as I pulled the trigger. Who the hell was I to play God? As I tried not to think about it, I wondered for the millionth time about Rico's kids.

Somewhere between Bon Jovi's *Livin' On A Prayer* and *Stuck With You* by Huey Lewis, the phone rang. At first I incorporated it into a dream. Then I realized there were no phones ringing in my dream or in the songs on the radio. I bolted up, scared to death. Whoever was calling had let it ring a long time. I snatched the phone from the hook, heart racing, knowing it had to be about drugs. It seemed as if my life revolved around drugs. First the job, and now Ron. The thing I hated most now controlled my life. How ironic was that?

"Hello?"

"Cataldi, get dressed and get in here."

"Captain?"

"I'll fill you in when you get to the station. I'm calling Tip now."

I walked into the station wondering what Coop was so worked up about. When I reached the top of the stairs, I saw Tip was at his desk. "What's up?"

He shook his head. "Don't know. I've been waiting on you."

"You think it has something to do with Mano?"

"I doubt it. If it was as simple as that, she'd have told us. This is something big."

It took a few minutes to get to Coop's office, and when we entered we found Chief Renkin sitting in a chair across from her. Tip nodded to him. "John, what's going on?"

"Nothing good," he said.

I nodded to Coop. "What's up, Cap?"

Her gaze shifted to the chief. He stood to shake hands. "Cataldi, good to see you again."

Chief Renkin looked at Coop. "Show them."

She flipped her computer screen around to face us, and popped a USB drive into one of the slots. "We received this in the mail. I didn't look at it until this morning." She pressed *play* and sat back in the chair.

Within seconds the images began, starting with the door to a hotel suite opening and a woman being ushered in by what looked to be some kind of body guards.

As she entered I could see it was Camwyck.

"That's the dress," I said. "And those are the shoes we found."

Then the president came out of another room and embraced her. He nodded, and what we previously thought were simply body guards—but who were obviously secret service agents—left, closing the door behind them.

"Do we know the date when this took place?" Tip asked.

Coop shook her head. "We have an expert examining it now, but so far nothing. There were no dates embedded in the video."

I looked at her. "Are we thinking that the president had something to do with Camwyck's death?"

For a minute I thought she was going to laugh. "For goodness' sakes, no."

"Why?"

She breathed deeply and straightened herself. "I was hoping this might provide evidence that we could use to solve the crime quickly. Maybe by asking the president what he knows? You're probably not going to get to him, but you could ask his aide, or better yet, Cybil, and Bob Ingle. And if we can help it, we don't want the president exposed, so this has to stay quiet, and I mean *quiet.*"

"You're saying you want to bury this?" Tip's tone had hardened.

It took her a while to answer, but when she did I had no doubts that she had taken that time to rein in her anger. "Denton, if anyone else had said that to me..." She took a moment to gather control and then said, "I still might take off this badge and kick your ass."

"Gladys!" Renkin said.

She held up her hand. "I've got it under control, Chief. I just want him to know where I stand."

We needed to break the tension, so I moved between her and Tip. "Why don't you explain the video to us, Coop. It's tough to see from our end."

She nodded. "I want to keep the video quiet, but wanting to keep it quiet has nothing to do with protecting Tom Marsen." She shot a glare that could kill at Tip.

"If it was just him, I'd send this to the press right now." Venom had crept into her words. "But we can't risk looking like fools by releasing something that hasn't been checked for authenticity. And we have *no* idea if it has anything to do with Camwyck's murder. It could be nothing more than a guy cheating on his wife."

"Except the guy is the president," I said.

Coop gave me a one-eyed stare. "As if that's something new. Presidents have been cheating on their wives as long as there have been presidents, or close to it."

"How do you want us to handle it?" Tip asked.

"First we need to find out who sent this," Coop said. "The package came with a note apparently from one of Camwyck's acquaintances, but we haven't verified that either."

Tip held out his hand. "Let's see the note."

Coop opened a folder on her desk and handed Tip a piece of paper. "This is a copy. The original is with the lab."

I was supposed to send this to Captain Gladys Cooper in the event something happened to Barbara. If she's dead, as I suspect, you now know who did it.

A friend of Barbara's.

"Sounds pretty clear to me," Tip said.

"That's part of what I don't like," Renkin said. "It's *too* clear." He looked at Tip and then me. "Take the video and go through it. See if you can find anything to follow up on. We've got the lab going through it also."

Coop removed the drive from the computer and handed it to Tip. "Nobody can see this."

He nodded. "Understood."

"You know where this came from," I said.

"I'm assuming it to be Richards, the woman who was killed in Dallas."

Renkin nodded and looked at me. "I'm thinking the same thing, but I'd like to know for certain. See if you can verify that."

Tip snapped a salute. "We'll get right on it, John."

Renkin shook his head, but Coop looked as if she might explode at any minute. I grabbed hold of Tip and dragged him out of Coop's office before he pissed someone off. We stopped at the coffee room on the way to our desks. "This is shaping up good," I said. "Our number one framed suspect is missing, the guy who bailed him out doesn't seem to care, and now we have the president as our new prime suspect."

"Can't say it's not interesting," Tip said.

I poured two coffees and said, "Let's find a room where we can watch this with no interruptions."

Tip grinned. "You want to get a better look at her ass, don't you?"

I grabbed his arm and dragged him along. "You're disgusting."

We started the video over from the beginning. Within a few minutes we were at the point where the president started kissing Camwyck. Not long after that, Camwyck undressed herself and then him, lingering to give him pleasure.

The video progressed as I expected, with foreplay, then full oral sex and then intercourse. Tip's phone rang, and I paused the entertainment, if you could call it that.

After a minute or so, and some small talk he hung up.

"Who was that?" I said.

"Julie. Still no hits on Camwyck's car, but we'll find it. Or some good citizen will."

"How about the cell phone?"

"Not a clue. It has to be like we thought before, disposables. No other explanation."

"And she checked Rusty's 'family plan?'"

Tip nodded. "She called every number the phone company had listed, and they were all answered by ladies who checked out. Oh, yeah, nothing on VICAP either."

"So we've still got shit."

"Unless this porno flick is chock full of evidence," Tip said, "but so far it doesn't look like it."

"We need to find out when and where this video happened," I said. "She's wearing the same dress and shoes as the ones we found with the body."

"We can rule out the president as a suspect then."

"Why do you say that?"

"No woman worth her salt is going to wear the same outfit with the same guy so close together. Not a snowball's chance in hell."

"Good point," I said. "Do you think it'll stand up in court?"

"With a woman judge it will."

I pushed the play button. "Let's watch the show."

Tip leaned back in the chair. "I have my popcorn ready."

We watched the recording, pausing a few times to discuss or make note of things. It lasted a lot longer than I thought it would, cutting off abruptly at the end of the sex, but then continuing with the president mixing drinks while she walked around naked.

"This doesn't prove much except that the president had sex with a woman," Tip said.

"And that he can make love for almost an hour," I added.

Tip whistled. "Don't let that shit get out. It'll ruin it for the rest of us studs."

"Let's get serious. We've got a dead woman, remember."

"Damn!" He sat up and looked at me. "I forgot to tell you, the reports from the Dallas M.E. came in. He confirmed that Patti Richards had no semen in her and the rape kit showed nothing."

"What about the wounds?"

"Basically the same, but they were more hesitant, almost as if a different person did it."

I turned off the TV. "You think we might have a copycat?"

Tip shook his head. "I don't know how. Everything else looks identical, and we never said which parts were removed or where they were found."

I thought about what he said and something struck me. "Unless it was someone with access to the investigation?"

Tip had been on his way to the bathroom, but when I said that he stopped and turned, a strange look on his face. "Like Coop."

"Or Cybil," I said. "If Coop knew, Cybil did too."

"And she was in Dallas that night."

"So was Coop," I said.

"Fuck me."

I nodded. "Me too."

CHAPTER 35

WHAT NEXT

Houston, Texas

At the end of the day, we went to my house and sat on the front porch to chat. Tip sat in the chair and stared at the sky. We could see a ton of stars, and somehow that made for a serene moment, even after watching the video.

"What do we have?" Tip asked.

I had been with Tip long enough that I recognized his way of starting conversations about the case—'what do we have.' I figured it was as much to spark his own thoughts as mine. "All we've got is the president having sex with a woman who isn't his wife. The burning questions are who recorded the video and who sent the video?"

"And *why* was the video sent?" Tip added. "Though I'm guessing it had to be the woman in Dallas, the second victim."

I thought about what he said, which made sense. "You think Camwyck was the one who taped it?" I sat up straight, excited by the prospect. "What if she was blackmailing him…"

"And our good president didn't like that."

I gulped the last of my beer, and my stomach roiled like a shallow creek in a hurricane—to borrow one of Tip's sayings. "I don't like where this is going."

"It's worth thinking about," Tip said. "What else do we have   Cybil and Rusty,

maybe Coop— but only if you buy that she'd do this for Cybil. And don't forget the First Lady."

"You know she didn't do it."

"I'm not saying *she* did it, but she *is* the First Lady, and Washington has more hit men than the Mafia. She might have gotten pissed that her husband was screwing around and decided to take matters into her own hands."

I laughed. "That's ridiculous. Let's put that theory on the back burner, Denton."

Tip stood but gave a big sigh when he did. "You realize we never got an alibi from Coop."

"You've known her longest, remember?"

"If she fires me you'll be all alone on this case."

I stood and walked toward the door. "I'm going in. In the morning I think we need to pin down everybody's alibi for *both* nights—Houston and Dallas. Which means you better get some sleep or Coop will tear you a new ass."

"I need a new ass. Elena said it's getting flat."

"Did you tell her that hers was getting big?"

"You really *do* want a new partner, don't you? I know it's been a while, Gino, so in case you forgot, there are three things you don't *ever* tell a woman: that her ass is big; that her ass is getting bigger; or that somebody else's ass is nicer than hers—unless it's a guy, in which case you stand the chance she'll agree with you and suggest a threesome."

I looked at him, once again amazed that he'd even say such a thing, even in jest. "And just how do you know this?"

"Trial and error, but it's been mostly error."

"I have no idea how you get *any* woman, let alone one as nice as Elena."

"It's a secret."

"Go home," I said, and as he left, I closed the door.

I tried relaxing but couldn't concentrate on the book I'd been reading, so I went for a short walk enjoying the heat and humidity of a Texas night. Sometimes I hated the weather here. At other times it was like a cleansing of the soul. As I passed by a wooded area the sounds of crickets, frogs, and God knows how many insects sung their nightly chorus.

The walk relaxed me, and I lay down and went to sleep quickly after that. I dreamed of the First Lady, which led to the images of the video Coop showed us.

Something struck me as odd. I grabbed the phone and called Tip.

"What do you want?"

"I was just thinking about that video. She wasn't there just doing him, not unless she was an academy-award caliber actress; she was in love with him."

"Okay, so she was in love. What's that got to do with anything?"

"Presuming she was in love—which in itself is rare for a woman in her profession—why would she record it?"

There was a moment of silence, then Tip said, "Maybe *he* recorded it. Maybe the guy liked watching himself. Who knows. The question is, who sent it to Coop."

"I think we know who sent it, the victim from Dallas. But run with this, Tip. Suppose someone besides Camwyck planted the camera. Someone close to the president."

"It would have to be someone very close," Tip said.

"This is getting scary."

"Tell me about it," Tip said. "Sleep well."

I poured coffee for both of us, then we sat at the table. "We're going to have to tell Coop about suspecting Cybil, and the sooner we do it, the easier it'll go on us. She'll be pissed."

He nodded but didn't say anything.

"You plan on telling her today?"

"I think we should interview Cybil again."

"Before talking to Coop?"

"Yeah, before. This is bad to say, Gino, but I'm not sure I trust Coop to keep our suspicions quiet, and I don't want Cybil knowing anything before we see her."

"Why don't we tell Coop what we're doing and see if she bites? It's not going to make much difference if Cybil knows or not, and it will let us know if Coop is trustworthy."

Tip smiled. "Now *that's* an idea I like. You want to come with me when I tell her?"

"I'm game. When do you want to do it?"

He tossed the cup into the trash and stood. "How about now?"

On the way to Coop's office, Julie intercepted us. "Hey, ya'll, did Detective Santos from Dallas get hold of you?"

"Santos? What did he want?" I checked my cell and saw a missed call. *How did I miss that? Damn AT&T.*

"He said they found Patti Richards' car." She scribbled on a piece of paper and handed it to me. "Here's Santos' phone number in case you don't have it. He said he'd call later."

"Thanks," I said, then turned to Tip. "I hope there's something we can use in there."

"Which reminds me, we need to find Camwyck's car." He headed back toward his desk, talking the whole way. "Hearing about Patti's vehicle reminded me that we never found Camwyck's purse. It might be in her car. It has to be somewhere. Women don't go anywhere without a purse. I once caught Elena taking hers to the bathroom."

"Maybe she took it so you didn't go through it."

Tip laughed. "I might act stupid, but I'm not *that* dumb. You don't go through a woman's purse unless you're ready to unleash the wrath of God."

I laughed with him. "For once, he was right."

When we got to his desk he rifled through his Rolodex then gave up and called Julie.

"Will you please get me Samantha Roberts' number?"

"You mean the reporter who almost got you suspended? And by the way, Tip, when are you moving to this century. People keep phone numbers and addresses and such on their computers and phones nowadays."

"The reporter who almost got me suspended. That's the one, darlin'. She's seen the light though; now she loves me." Tip was about to hang up the phone, then said, "As far as why I'm not in *this century* as you called it, it's so I can keep people like you employed. You've got to have something to do, right?"

"You *are* a Neanderthal, Tip. Forget I asked."

Tip dialed the number and Samantha answered on the second ring. I was close enough to hear the conversation.

"Samantha Roberts."

"Hi beautiful."

"If it isn't my favorite Neanderthal."

"Don't get me excited."

"What's up, Tip?"

Tip looked around then lowered his voice to a whisper. "Remember the pictures you did?"

"Of course. You know I remember them. Why, did they get you in trouble?"

"No, but we're in a jam. I need to find the victim's car."

A long pause, then. "I noticed you tried finding it with Channel 2."

"My mistake. They aren't as good as you."

Her voice carried her smile through the phone. "You bet they're not. How do you want to handle the car search?"

"I'm leaving that up to you. Just find it."

"You'll have it in two days or less. I promise."

"I gotta go. Get it, and I'll owe you one."

After he hung up we started down the hall to Coop's office. About halfway there my phone beeped, signaling voice mail.

Goddamn AT&T. It was only an hour late. We were almost at Coop's office, so I'd have to listen to it later.

We were led into Coop's office by Cindy, who shook her head warning us of the mood we'd face once inside. Coop began her barking before the door closed.

"What do you want?"

Tip put on his best smile. "And a damn good morning to you too, Captain."

She looked as if she would bite our heads off, then surprised me by removing her glasses and setting them gently on the desk. "Okay, point taken. Good morning, Tip. You too, Cataldi."

I sat and took out my notepad. Tip did the same. "We wanted to update you on the case."

"I'm listening."

"They found Patti Richards' car."

Coop appeared confused. "Who?"

"You know, Patti Richards, the victim up in Dallas."

"Great! Any leads develop from it?"

"I don't know. Santos called and left a message but we haven't spoken to him yet."

"All right, keep me posted, and call Santos as soon as you leave here. Don't let this pot simmer. Get on it. What else have you got?"

When Tip didn't say anything, I responded. "We've got nothing from Delgado or any of the others checking local leads, and we still haven't found Camwyck's car or her cell phone. We figure she had to be using burners." I hesitated, hoping that Tip was jumping in with the Cybil information, but I could tell by the smirk on his face he was hanging me out to dry. "We thought we'd interview Cybil again."

Coop sat straight up. "What for?"

Tip leaned forward. "Because there are too many connections between Cybil and the victim, and between the victim and Rusty, and…"

"And what?"

"Between the victim and you."

She put her glasses back on and that mean face she was famous for appeared. "You're wasting time with that line of thinking. Find the real killer, and do not, I mean *do not* bother Cybil. Am I clear?"

I stood, eager to get out with my badge intact, but Tip would have nothing of it. He rested his foot on the other leg as if he'd settled in for the night.

"No problem, Captain. I had a few homeless people to interrogate anyway. I figured they might know a lot about a high-end prostitute who lives in a million-dollar condo co-signed by the mayor, who happens to be her main client, not to mention the mayor's wife, who she happened to grow up with. Oh, did I forget to mention she grew up with the president, who is on a video screwing her?"

Coop clenched her jaw and balled her fist. I felt sure that if she had high blood pressure, this kind of tension would push her over the edge. It was time for us to leave, but Tip wasn't letting it go.

"With leads like that," Tip said, "I'm sure we'll crack this case soon. Tell the chief not to worry."

"Get out of my office."

"Yes, ma'am."

Cindy blew us a kiss as we exited the office. I kept looking behind us as we hurried down the hallway in case Coop changed her mind and decided to take our badges.

I tapped Tip on the shoulder. "Where to now, my diplomatic partner?"

"I guess we go see Cybil. Those homeless people won't be back from work yet."

***

Coop jabbed her pen into the calendar and pressed down hard. What had started out as a good morning had turned to shit in a hurry. And she was in a hole that got deeper by the minute. She took a few deep breaths, calmed herself, then picked up the phone and dialed.

"Hello, this is Cybil Johnson."

"Stop with the fake voice. You have caller ID and you know damn right well who's calling."

"I was trying to be polite. What's wrong with you?"

"I'll tell you what's wrong. Tip and Gino are probably on their way to see you right now."

Cybil's voice changed to one of concern. "What for?"

"To question you about Barbara again."

"Can't you stop them? You *are* the boss aren't you?"

"I told them to back off, but they won't listen. I'd be surprised if it takes them half an hour to get there."

"I can handle myself."

Coop sighed before speaking. She didn't want to show her temper. "These are the two best detectives I've got. Don't think you can *handle* them. Just shut-up and follow advice for once in your life."

"Remember who you're addressing."

"Shut the fuck up, Cybil. I called to warn you. And if I were you, I'd get an attorney, but it's your ass, not mine."

CHAPTER 36

REPERCUSSIONS

Tip drove the speed limit all the way to Cybil's place, surprising me with his calmness.

"How do you want to handle the interview? She won't give us anything, and she'll probably lawyer up."

"We need to test her," Tip said. "Insult her. Challenge her. Just follow my lead. I know how to deal with these Texas gals."

"Cybil's not your ordinary Texas gal. There's nothing ordinary about her."

"You watch while I talk. If you see a place to jump in feel free to do it. We can't let her breathe once we get her going. We've got to keep her talking instead of thinking. Once a viper like her starts thinking she might out-think us."

"On most days that wouldn't be too difficult, Detective Denton."

"That's why I'm warning you."

Tip parked in the garage and we made our way to Cybil's office. Surprisingly we were admitted to see her with less than a ten-minute wait. Her admin led us down a hallway to a set of double doors with exquisite etched glass that looked as if it came straight from an artisan's studio. We stepped onto plush carpeting and an office furnished like a showroom. The highlight, though, was the floor to ceiling glass windows with a perfect view of the skyline.

Cybil, looking bright and vibrant as ever, made her way toward us wearing the smile she was famous for. Her eyes seemed to take everything in at once. I found myself hiding my thoughts.

"You boys care for something to drink? It's hot as a Louisiana swamp out there today."

"Would that be the Atchafalaya?" Tip said, with a hint of sarcasm.

Cybil paused then looked at the ceiling, as if to consider what he asked. "I think you're right, Detective. It's as hot as the Atchafalaya. And as humid." She let out a little chuckle, as if amused by a child, then moved toward the bar.

Tip followed her. "As for that drink, I'll have a gin and tonic, thanks."

I gave Tip a "what the hell are you doing" look, but then I said I'd have one too, even though it was *way* too early for me to be drinking. Or for *anybody* to be drinking.

Tip didn't waste time with formalities. He didn't even wait until she finished making the drinks. "Ms. Johnson, it's come to our attention that a lot of the people close to this case come from the same town in East Texas. Oddly enough it's the same town you grew up in."

Undaunted, she continued mixing the drinks without missing a beat. Her reaction convinced me that Tip had been right; Coop called and warned her.

"That town bred a lot of ambitious people." She half-turned and handed Tip his drink, then grabbed the two remaining, handing me one, and cupping her hands around the last one as if it were a life preserver. "Why don't we sit," she said, and settled into a huge plush chair covered in white fabric.

Tip took a seat across from her then pulled out his notebook. He looked down, as if reading from it. "I've got some data on that little town of yours, and you're right—that town did breed ambitious people: a president, a world-famous businessman, a police captain…and two prostitutes."

I had been watching Cybil, and I was expecting a strong reaction, but it didn't occur. Cybil flinched when Tip mentioned prostitutes, but not much. Whatever her instincts were, she smiled instead.

Tip squinted his eyes, wrinkled his brow, then acted embarrassed. "I'm sorry, that was one prostitute and a mayor's wife."

"Are you trying to insult me? My goodness, I've seen far better from the 'socially acceptable' women of our fair city."

"I'll bet you have," Tip said. "I've met a few of them at fundraisers. They frighten me."

"You, at a fundraiser? What on earth were you doing there, guarding the jewels?"

"That's good." Tip laughed, and pointed a finger at her playfully. "I like that. In fact, that was so good I'll have another drink if you don't mind."

"I don't mind at all. I love a good sport. But I'm surprised that one of Houston's finest would be drinking at this time of day. Isn't this when you should be shaking down immigrant store owners or coercing favors from the prostitutes you are *so* familiar with?" She got to the bar and looked at Tip.

"Another gin and tonic, please."

She turned to me. "Another for you?"

"I'm fine, thanks."

Cybil brought Tip his drink and settled back into her chair. She played the role of hostess to perfection, but Tip didn't let her rest. As soon as her ass hit the seat he started.

"Who would have motive to kill Barbara Camwyck?"

"How would I know? Barbara was a sweet person, perhaps a little lost, but sweet. She would do anything for her friends."

"Does that include spreading her legs?"

She shot Tip a glare to kill. "That was cruel. The woman's dead."

"Who wanted her dead?"

She pretended to think, then said, "You could start with Tom Marsen."

"Tom Marsen? The president."

"The last time I looked he was."

Tip sipped on his drink. "Why would he want to kill her?"

Cybil leaned forward. She looked as if she was about to tell us something we didn't know. "They were lovers, and that fool girl was naive enough to think he loved her."

"He didn't?"

"Come now, Detective, you've seen Mrs. Marsen. Do you think he'd trade *her* for Barbara?" Cybil stood, walked around a bit. "There is a lot I don't know in this world, but I can tell you one thing I'm certain of—Tom Marsen hasn't loved anyone but himself since he clawed his way out of his mother's womb."

I was shocked at the venom in her voice. As I thought about it I wondered why she was tainting him. Why try to push the blame to the president? She's got to know that would do no good.

"It sounds like you and the president don't get along. Jealousy?"

Cybil looked at Tip as if he were a snake about to strike. "You don't like me do you?"

"There's not a bit of truth to that…well maybe a bit, but under different circumstances I could see us getting along just fine, but I'm conducting a murder investigation, and I have questions to ask. Aside from that, I think we have a lot in common."

"Please, don't flatter yourself."

"We do, but if we ever got together there might be a struggle to see who stays on top." Tip let one of his famous, scar-tainted smiles surface, the one that both seduces and frightens women.

It seemed to work on Cybil, but perhaps in the wrong way. It acted on her like fresh meat thrown to the lions. She crossed her legs, showing a little thigh. A light shone in her eyes.

"My, my, but you *do* like to play the game, don't you?"

Tip smiled.

"What do you want to know, Detective?"

"Have you ever had sex with Tom Marsen?"

She didn't blush, but she tried to pretend she did. "My sex life is none of your business."

"How about RB Ingle?"

She laughed. "And you call yourself a detective. You don't know Bob Ingle at all, do you?"

"Why don't you tell us about him?" I said.

Cybil smiled. "Bob is an emotional mess and he has been since he was a little boy."

"He seems to have done well for himself," Tip said.

She took a sip of her drink. "He's done a lot better than you know, but it's all because of Tom Marsen. In fact every dollar and every piece of ass Bob ever had was because of Tom Marsen." She took another long drink from her glass, gave a short chuckle, and said, "For God's sake, he's still in love with Barbara, or he was before she died."

That bit of news shocked me. "Ingle was in love with Camwyck?"

Cybil looked over at me. "Say what you will about her, but she knew how to enthrall a man. Every man she ever screwed fell head over heels in love with her. Barbara Camwyck was a predator."

"Even Tom Marsen?"

A mean hard look flashed in Cybil's blue eyes. For a moment I didn't think she would answer. "Especially Tom Marsen. The difference is that he's the most disgusting kind of prey. He might be worse than a predator. Perhaps he's just a different kind."

Tip sat up straight in his chair. "Not that it would matter, since he's the president, but can you tell me what you mean by that?"

"I need a moment to think," Cybil said, and then she stood and walked in small circle before returning to her chair. She leaned back, sipped her drink, and seemed to relax. Neither of us prodded her, despite Tip having originally said to *not* give her time, and the patience paid off. After a few minutes—which seemed like an hour—she spoke. "I'm sorry for taking so long, but I wanted to find the one story that said it all about Tom."

She set her drink on a coaster, and stared at Tip, then me. "Tom always *thought* he was a ladies' man, even from high school, but he was a son of a bitch to any girl he knew. Bob Ingle was his ever-faithful friend who stuck by him. Bob could never get girls unless Tom got a girl to go out with them on a double-date. One night Tom had a date, but he told her he'd only go out with her if she found a date for Bob.

"They went to the movies, got pizza, then got a motel room. Bob paid of course. This was going to be his first time spending the night with a girl. Once they got the room, though, it became apparent that Tom intended to spend the night with both girls, and it seemed as if the girls agreed, both of them hanging on Tom like lovesick puppies."

Cybil reached over and plucked a mint from a crystal jar. She tore the wrapper off, and popped the mint into her mouth. "Bob stayed until his date was lying naked on the bed—along with Tom and his date—then he went back to his dorm. He told me later it might have been the worst night of his life."

Tip stared. "Why did Bob stay friends with him?"

Cybil thought long and hard before answering. "I think because Tom was the only friend Bob ever had."

Tip waited for her to finish. "Why would Marsen hang out with someone like Bob."

Cybil wasted no time in answering.

"Because Bob idolized him. He did everything for Tom. Did his homework, sat next to him in class so Tom could cheat on tests, and from what I hear, he got Tom through college. Later when Tom left for Houston, Bob worked on his campaigns. That's when they both started making money."

Tip didn't let her catch a breath before he threw her the next question. "Just how well did *you* know Ms. Camwyck?"

"Not as well as I thought."

"But you knew she was having an affair with the president?"

"I've already told you that."

"Did you know she had a video of their…liaison?"

"I don't believe it. She wouldn't be so stupid."

"I've got the video."

"You mean—"

"Yep, I've got it." Tip smiled. "You know that old story about getting caught in the henhouse?" He took a long swig of his drink while he waited for Cybil to digest that. "Well we have that old weasel dead to rights. And this isn't one of those fuzzy, hard to decipher videos. I can get a close-up right to the hairs on Barbara's…" He laughed. "Well, I think you know what I mean."

"I can't believe it." Cybil stood and swished her drink around as she shifted weight from side to side. I hadn't figured out yet if she did that out of nervousness or to irritate us. If it was the latter she was succeeding brilliantly.

I decided to try something out with her. "The funny thing is Barbara mentions you in the video, and from the context it seems as if you knew each other a whole lot better than you indicated."

She gulped, then stood straight. "She mentioned *my* name? I can't imagine what for." She turned and set her glass on the bar. Without looking back at us, she started up again. "What did she say?"

Her voice was tentative, lacking the bluster and command she'd put in her tone earlier. I smiled. Sure as shit we struck a nerve. "We can't release that just yet, Ms. Johnson. It's evidence in an open case."

She nodded, but seemed disappointed. "Of course."

Tip moved in close to her. He had his notepad out with a pen in hand. "You were in Dallas when the First Lady gave her speech?"

"I believe you know I was, along with thousands of other Houstonians."

"Where did you stay?"

She wrinkled her brow. "Is this necessary?"

"Yes, ma'am, it is. This is a homicide investigation."

She gave a fake laugh. "You don't think I had anything to do with Barbara's death?"

"But we're not talking about Barbara's murder. A woman was murdered in Dallas while you were there."

"Good Lord, what kind of person would do that?" She took a long slow sip of her drink and held it in her very-steady hands, then looked straight at me, without blinking. "What time was this poor soul killed?"

"About 9:45 if I remember."

She placed a finger in her mouth and pretended to chew on the nail, but I knew there was no way she would risk another trip to the salon to fix a little gnawing. She wanted us to think she were considering the question.

Cybil said, "I was busy almost all night—I do remember that—and I'll get you a list of who I was with at what times. I can have that for you no later than the day after tomorrow." That big fake smile flashed on her face again, the one that greeted every stranger she met. "Will that be soon enough?"

Tip put his notepad away and hooked the pen on his shirt pocket. "That'll do just fine." He offered his hand to say goodbye, then we were escorted out by her assistant.

***

Cybil spent some time with her assistant, assigning a few projects, then she closed the door to her office and turned the music on softly, catching the end of *Back to Stay,* an old country tune by Johnny Rodriguez. She dialed a number from her cell, got no answer, then waited for it to go to voicemail. "It's Cybil. I had a disturbing visit from two detectives. We need to talk."

She hung up, and then poured another drink. After walking around her office a few times, she took a seat in her favorite chair and continued sipping her drink. When she finished, she buried her head in her hands, and, for the first time in many years—she cried.

CHAPTER 37

EAST TEXAS TALES

We left Cybil's office and headed west, then north on I-45. I was happy to be out of that hotbox, but Tip seemed exhilarated, as if he'd popped a few pills.

"Did you see her, Gino? Guess we shook the world on that one."

"We shook it all right. And I'm afraid we're going to feel the reverberations soon."

"Do you think she'll make a call?"

"There's no doubt she'll call somebody. *Who* is the big question."

"We'll find out soon enough," Tip said, and cut across two lanes of traffic, scaring me to death.

I sneered as we passed a church and turned my head.

Tip said, "You got something against churches?"

"Let's say I'm not fond of them."

"Is this something you want to talk about?"

"What's with the questions? Are you a priest?"

"Not last time I checked, but I guess I could slip a collar on. Come to think of it, Elena might like a new fantasy; she's getting tired of me being the mailman."

When he said that, I lost my attitude and smiled. "All right, tell me how it works with her, then maybe I'll confess."

My phone rang. "It's Santos," I said to Tip, then answered the phone. "What's up, Santos?"

"I assume you got my message."

"Yeah, thanks. What did you find?"

"A patrol unit picked up a guy for speeding and when he ran the plates he saw we were looking for the car. The guy said he found the car in the parking lot of the Lincoln Hotel. He also had her cell phone, which he claims was under the passenger seat."

"Why would she leave her phone in the car?" I asked.

"Same thing I was thinking," Santos said.

"Unless she didn't leave it. Maybe she was snatched from her car and the phone fell out in the struggle."

I thought about it for a moment. "Yeah, maybe," I said. "How about witnesses? Anybody see anything?"

"I showed her picture around. None of the employees remember seeing her, but I'll send somebody back tonight after the next shift comes in. We also found a note on her calendar app on the phone. We got lucky. She's one of the few people who don't have some ridiculous password to access the phone. Anyway, all the note said was, 'Meet Magic at 9:30 at the Lincoln.'"

"That's it? Meet magic, spelled like it sounds?"

"Magic, like in a magic act."

"What do you think that means?"

"I was hoping you could tell us. You don't have anything like that on your victim?"

"I'd have sent it to you if I did," I said. I thought about telling Santos about our video but decided to keep that quiet for now. "Besides, Santos, we still haven't found our victim's car. Or her purse."

"Damn. All right, we'll send you what we've got and anything else after they finish processing. I'm waiting on the phone records now. By the way," Santos said, "the medical examiner confirmed our victim was killed quickly. The stab wounds and the cutting were done later."

"That's different. Our victim was alive when he did all that. Not the cutting, but the knife and icepick work."

"You think we have different killers?"

"I don't see how, but it's something to think about. Thanks, Santos." I hung up and filled Tip in on what he missed. "Who or what do you think this *magic* is? And why did the killer do the woman in Dallas differently? It's unusual to change a signature like that. On the other hand, if it's a professional killer, the signature might be that there is no signature. If the killer wanted our victim to suffer, why not the one in Dallas? Those kind of thoughts send me back to the theory that this is personal."

"I don't know, and we probably won't know until we figure out who wanted them dead. But I know we need to find Camwyck's car," Tip said, and took out his phone and dialed Roberts.

"Roberts."

Tip put it on speaker. "Did you find that car yet?"

"Not yet, but it won't be long."

"What makes you so confident?"

"We put a picture of the car and the license plate on the morning news, and it will run again tonight. Plus, I talked my boss into posting a reward— one thousand dollars for whoever finds the car first."

Tip laughed at that. "I knew there was a reason I liked you. I don't like you much, but I do like you a little."

"I'll call when I get something. I have to go."

Tip hung up and looked over. "That ought to get some people looking."

"I think she's right. I bet we have that car by tonight."

"Speaking of tonight, don't let me forget to call my guy at the phone company and see if he got anything."

"Call him now."

"It's too early. He said it would be late today or early tomorrow before he could get it. He doesn't have direct access, so he has to wait for the right time."

"I'll be curious to see who Cybil calls."

"Me too," Tip said. "Of course, you know we won't be able to use any of this, as it isn't exactly legal?"

"I realize that, but it will give us information."

"And that's what we need," Tip said, then he turned off the freeway, down a few side streets, and into a restaurant boasting original Texas BBQ.

"I guess it's lunchtime."

"I'm starved," Tip said.

An older woman, maybe in her sixties, greeted Tip as we entered. "Tip, how ya'll doin'?"

"Darlin', if I was any better I'd be you."

She brushed the comment aside, but her face broke into a smile like it was Christmas morning. "What'll it be today?"

"I'll have two chopped beef sandwiches all the way and an iced tea." He turned to me.

"How about you?"

"I'll go with the same, but water instead of tea."

Tip tossed some bills onto the counter, refusing to accept money from me.

"Mandy, this is my partner Gino."

Another smile popped on her face. "Nice to meet you, sweetie." She nodded to the young girl next to her. "And this here is Sharon. She's my niece."

"I should have known, pretty as she is," Tip said.

Mandy blushed again. "If you keep flirtin' with me, I'll leave Earl and move in with you."

"I'll hold my breath until that day," Tip said, then grabbed a couple of glasses for drinks.

Half the place must have said hi, or waved to Tip on our way to a table in the corner.

He stopped and talked so many times I didn't think we'd ever get to our seats. We weren't sitting down more than a minute before Sharon came with the food. We got right to the business of eating, then focused on our talk with Cybil.

"She did everything but accuse the president of killing Camwyck," I said.

"And she didn't have much to say about Ingle, other than he might have been a little shy with the ladies." Tip took a bite of his sandwich and stared out the window.

"So why would she cast blame on the president? She has to know how dumb it sounds."

"And why mention that whole thing about him in college and stealing Ingle's girl? That doesn't give RB motive to kill Camwyck." I took another bite of the sandwich and looked at Tip. "If we found the president dead, that'd be one thing, but not the girl; besides, Ingle is close friends with the president."

"Politics makes strange bedfellows," Tip said, and then, "Unless Camwyck was the girl from the double date. Remember what Cybil said—that Ingle was still in love with Camwyck."

I didn't say anything, but I looked at him with a question on my mind.

Tip devoured his sandwich and took out his notepad. "We need to learn a little more about this piece of paradise they came from."

"You know how to do that?"

"A friend of mine, Buddy, used to be a sheriff from that area. He'll know something."

"I thought you already talked to him about the case."

"I asked him to check on a few things, but we need him to dig deeper. Get to the heart of the East Texas gossip."

Tip called Buddy and told him what we needed and said we needed it now. As he finished the conversation, I finished my sandwich. "This is damn good barbecue."

"Almost as good as mine," Tip said.

"You make barbecue?"

"Any Texan worth their salt makes barbecue, but Tip Denton's *famous* barbecue might be the best."

"Famous?"

"You'll have to try it."

Mandy was passing our table. She leaned down and whispered to me. "Don't like to swell his head more than it already is, but he *does* make good barbecue."

Tip smiled, then we tossed everything in the trash and headed out.

As we were leaving he hollered back to Mandy. "Hey, darlin', next time I come here, have that suitcase packed and ready."

Mandy was still laughing when the door closed.

"Do you know *everybody*?"

"When you've been on the same streets as long as I have, you get to know a lot of people—good and bad."

A shiver ran up my spine when he said that. I wondered again if it was Tip who asked Chicky about me. I knew I should ask him about it; instead, I cleared my mind and focused on the case.

On the way back to the station, we discussed what we'd say to Coop. The last time we left her she had forbidden us to interrogate Cybil. And I was certain Coop knew by now that we'd been to see Cybil again.

We were halfway to the station when Tip's phone rang. He answered, gave me a thumbs-up about something, then repeated an address. When he hung up he turned to me with shit-eating grin. "That was Roberts. She found the car."

"Where is it?"

"In an apartment complex not far from here."

"We'll need the crime scene unit out there."

Tip was already turning the car around.

"Roberts said she already told Cooper. One's on the way."

By the time we reached the apartment complex, the crime scene guys were set up. Three satellite news trucks had already arrived, which drew a crowd of onlookers and people wanting to see their face on the nightly newscast. We double-parked, flashed our badges, and hurried over to the scene. I recognized Matt Gordon, from the CSU.

"Hey, Matt, what have you got?"

"Whoever cleaned this needs a job at the carwash."

"You got nothing?"

"I didn't say nothing. But so far, no prints, and not much of anything else, however…"

"Go on," Tip said, "or do you need a drum roll for this?"

"Denton, I see you're still the same old ass. Anyway, we found several brown hairs tucked into the back seats."

Tip looked excited. "That might help."

"Anything else?" I asked.

"Found her purse on the seat, with a note inside."

Tip perked up. "Let's see it."

"I already sent it down with the other evidence, but I know what the note said, because I found it odd:

Do you believe in MAGIC? "And *magic* was in all caps."

I looked at him. "That's all. *Do you believe in MAGIC?*"

"That's all it said. Maybe you'll find something when they process the note, but I doubt it based on how this guy cleaned up."

"But he left hairs," Tip said.

"I doubt they're his, and if they're hers that doesn't help. We've already got her DNA. They might be the killer's hair. We might have gotten lucky, but I don't think so. Anyway, I've got to go. I'll see ya'll next time."

The way he said it was so casual, like we knew there would be another murder, another butchering, another "next time."

"Yeah, we'll see you then," Tip said. "Thanks."

I turned to Tip. "'*Do you believe in magic?*' What's that mean?"

"What's the fascination with *magic*?"

"Matt said this one was in caps. I wonder if the Dallas note was. Santos didn't say."

"Call him."

I dialed Santos. He must have been sitting on the phone. I told him what we had and that we'd send it up. "How did your victim spell *magic*? Was it in caps?"

"It was spelled like a name, with just the M capitalized."

"What do you think it's about? And the riddle part, do you believe? Got any ideas, Santos?"

"Nothing, but we'll toss it around. And don't worry, I know the drill. Nobody but my partner and my captain will hear about this."

"Good. Let's keep it tight."

We stayed around until everyone finished, questioned some of the onlookers, and then assigned a unit to go door-to-door looking for witnesses. As Tip liked to say, it was a snowball's chance in hell, but it was one we had to take. We came up empty and headed back to the station.

We were almost to the station when Tip's phone started.

"Buddy, how are you?" He paused then, "I've got my partner here so I'm putting you on speaker."

"I told you I'd get back to you soon," Buddy said.

"Good thing, too. We're stuck."

"You ready for some East Texas tales, because I got a pocket full of 'em."

"I know how it is when you get started," Tip said. "Let's stick to what I asked about."

"All right, well about that one thing you mentioned, the night in the motel you mentioned, when they were in college? Tom Marsen ended up spending the night with both of them girls."

"How do you know?" Tip asked.

Buddy laughed. "You're not the only one with connections, Tip."

"I hear you," Tip said, "That's good information, but it won't do us any good. Some people might call that immoral, and others enviable, but it isn't illegal."

"I know that, Tip, but what about abortion?"

"What do you mean?"

"Supposedly one of them girls got herself a big belly after that night."

Tip and I both stared at each other. "Son of a bitch!" he said.

"There's more. The problem is most of this is based on rumors or word of mouth."

"I've come to believe in small-town rumors," Tip said.

"The people I talked to said the girl left town in a hurry. And the ones in the know back then said it was to get an abortion. And the ones really in the know said it was because Tom Marsen, our squeaky-clean president, was the father. You remember Tom Marsen—the one who rode into the White House on the anti-crime, anti-drugs, and *anti-abortion* campaign promises."

Tip looked at me and raised his eyebrows. "Do we know who the girl was?"

"Not yet. But I'm diggin'."

"Keep at it, partner. I need this."

"Don't worry, I'll get it. And then you can bring me one of those beautiful women who love you so much."

Tip laughed. "It's a deal you can count on. And while you're waitin' for me to show up, see what else you can dig up, like you said." Tip cleared his throat, then, "Buddy, I gotta tell you, this could mean trouble. We're dealing with powerful people."

"Dealt with powerful people before, besides, I got nothin' else to do. Might as well do some good."

"Well all right, partner. I'll see you at the gravesite." Tip turned off the speaker, made sure it was hung up, then cast a quick glance in my direction.

"If Tom Marsen's girlfriend had an abortion…"

"And Camwyck was blackmailing him?"

Tip nodded. "How pissed off would he be?"

"Enough to commit murder?"

"I don't know, but fifty dollars to a doughnut says that sneaky bitch Cybil had something to do with this. We need to find out what."

CHAPTER 38

FOLLOW THE MONEY

Tip headed back to the station, driving what seemed to be two hundred miles an hour half the way there, and me pissing my pants all the way.

"Tip, things are going great today so let's not press our luck. In other words, slow the *fuck* down."

He let the speedometer drift down to eighty, a speed reasonable enough to allow me to release the imaginary brake on the floor and the death grip I had on the armrest and door handle. "You're a *maniac*. I'm driving from now on."

"I'm just itchin' to see good old Captain Gladys Cooper. She knows something."

"Like what?"

"I don't know what, but you don't grow up in an East Texas town without knowing what goes on. I've had a feeling all along that Coop's been stonewalling us."

Tip parked the car and we headed inside. On our way to the coffee room, we passed Julie and asked if she had any updates.

"No updates yet, but hang on. I'll be back in a flash. I've got to give something to Captain Cooper."

"Don't tell her we're here," Tip said.

I sat at the table in the coffee room, and pulled out our notes on the case. At the top of a new page I wrote 'Do you believe in MAGIC?', then looked to Tip. "It was in caps here, but not Dallas."

He pulled up a chair and sat next to me. "What does that mean? What does any of it mean?"

"I have no idea, but it sounds familiar."

Julie was just coming around the corner. She must have heard our conversation, because she said, "If ya'll are talking about that note in the car, it's a song from the sixties."

I looked at her puzzled. "It didn't take you long to get to Coop's office."

"I told you I'd be back in a flash."

"Just how fast is a flash?" Tip asked.

Julie smiled, and her bright white teeth, coupled with purple tinted hair and rainbow fingernails, made for a unique sight in a cop station, at least for somebody not being questioned.

"A flash is quick. And as far as that song goes, I think it was from '67 or maybe '68. The Lovin' Spoonful did it."

Tip looked surprised and continued looking that way for several seconds before he said anything. "How do you know that? You weren't born yet. I don't think your mother was born then."

She giggled and went about her duties. "If you need to know anything else, you call."

"Whoa, hold up a minute." I said.

She turned around expectantly, and I said, "Can you get us the lyrics for that song. Maybe this wacko is playing a game with us. I guess you can Google it or something."

"No need to, Gino. I've got the lyrics on my computer."

Julie left, and, true to her word, she returned only a few minutes later. I didn't know if it would constitute a "flash" or not, but it was quick. We laid the printout on the desk between us and looked it over.

It talked a lot about magic, and about girls. I think freedom was mentioned, but then again the song *was* from the sixties. And I think the word *groovy* was flung around a few times…but like I said…

I read it twice, then scratched my head and read it again. "Tip, you get anything out of this?"

"Other than a hankering to go smoke some weed—no."

"So why did he leave this clue at both scenes?"

"Maybe the guy's into old hippie songs, but we don't have time to mess with it."

"We can't ignore it," I said.

"I'll tell you what we ought to do, buy about two dozen glazed doughnuts and give them to Charlie along with some hashish brownies. We let him stew for about half an hour then slip him this song and see what he makes of it."

"That's not a bad idea. He might figure it out."

"He *might* solve the mysteries of the universe, but it will only cost a few bucks, so we should do it. We'll tell Julie to put it in motion."

"I'd be worried if I thought you were serious, Tip."

"I'm sure you've been worried before," Tip said.

I shook my head. "I assume we have to go see Coop."

"Unfortunately, we do," Tip said.

As we walked past Julie's desk, Tip handed her the lyrics. "Give this to Charlie with the case files and tell him to figure it out, but *do not* give him any brownies. We might end up being sucked in by a black hole."

"And that's it?" Julie asked. "What's that about brownies? What are you talking about? And what's this about black holes?"

"Just tell him there's an endless supply of bagels with strawberry cream cheese at the end of the rainbow."

Julie shook her head as she looked at Tip. "You're about as loony as they come, Mr. Denton."

We walked into Coop's office exhibiting a confidence neither one of us felt.

"Hey, Cap, how—"

"I don't have time for your nonsense, Denton. Tell me about the car."

I decided to jump in and save Tip, because sure as the sun shines, he was going to get himself in trouble. "The car was clean except for a few hairs, which they're running. They dusted for prints and got nothing, not even hers. The victim's purse was on the seat and there was a note inside that read, 'Do you believe in MAGIC?' Magic was in caps."

Coop was good at hiding emotions, but when I said "magic" there was a slight reaction, a twitch of the lips. "Does that mean something to you?"

Coop must have known I noticed something. She shook her head. "It struck me as odd."

I didn't pursue it, but I didn't buy her explanation one bit. I glanced over at Tip and from the look on his face, and the subtle shaking of his head, he wasn't buying it either.

Cooper stared at us, one at a time, holding her glare. "I see what you two are doing, and you don't fool me. I know you went to see Cybil. I told you then, and I'm repeating it. Get another suspect. Cybil didn't do it."

I couldn't believe she kept insisting on us leaving this alone. "How are you so sure?"

"I've known her since we were kids. Cybil might be a lot of things but she's not a cold-blooded killer."

I decided to play it risky. "I noticed your reaction when I mentioned the magic note. You know something, and we're not leaving here until you tell us."

She balled her hands into fists and didn't utter a word. After a long silence, Tip spoke up and he made it sound as nice as I imagined he could. "Gladys, you can tell us what you know…or I can go see Chief Renkin."

Her eyes narrowed and her lips tightened, but then she seemed to relax. She knew that Tip and Renkin used to be partners. Things could get bad for her if it went that route.

I decided to try another angle. "Coop, we love you. If you're in trouble…I mean if you somehow got mixed up in something and you're finding it tough to get out, we can help. Please, let us help."

She rolled her eyes and sighed. "Sit down, boys," she said, then pressed the intercom button for Cindy. "Would you please bring me some tea?" She looked to us.

"Coffee?"

Tip leaned toward the intercom and hollered, "I'll have some tea, darlin'."

"Nothing for me," I said.

Coop talked to us after that. "I appreciate that offer to cover for me— which I *should* be pissed about…" She shot a threatening look, making her point. "But here's the real scoop. Stop me if I go too fast."

She filled us in on life in East Texas, mostly talking about little things— dating, dances, small-town gossip—but then she got to what we hadn't expected to hear.

"At first there were the four of them that always hung out together—Tom Marsen, Bob Ingle, Cybil Ames, and Barbara Camwyck. Then I joined the group and Cybil decided we should give ourselves a name. We argued about it for weeks, until Bob came up with an idea to use our last names. So we took the first letter of our names and scrambled them up to get—MAGIC."

"That doesn't work," I said, and tried to digest what she was admitting to.

She was already nodding. "I know, we used Gladys for me instead of Cooper because they already had Camwyck."

"And what did this elite group of yours do?" Tip asked. He was calm, displaying no reactions.

"Normal kid things. And when we did something mischievous, we'd paint MAGIC on the wall or on a street corner or a lamp post."

Tip sat up in his chair. I came close to falling out of mine.

"And you're just telling us?" I asked.

"You only told *me* about it a few minutes ago."

"I'm not talking about the MAGIC, I mean about the five of you being so tight. You didn't think that had bearing on this case?"

"I know *I* didn't do it," Coop said, "and I can't see Cybil, or Tom or Bob doing it."

"Cybil had nothing to do with it?" Tip asked.

Coop shook her head. "I can't see it."

"Are you telling me our suspect list went from you and Cybil, to the president and RB Ingle?" Tip asked.

"Don't be ridiculous."

"Who else knew about this?" I asked, following up on Tip's question, and trying to build a more reasonable list of suspects.

"I don't know. We were kids. Anybody *could* have known." She seemed to think for a minute or so, then gave up. "It has to be somebody who knew one of us from back then, or who heard about it later. *Somebody* is trying to make it look like one of us did it."

"Do you have any idea who that might be?" I asked.

Coop shook her head. "Not yet, but I'll be thinking on it."

I stood and stretched.

Tip got out of his chair, too, but he had to open his mouth. "We're thinking Ingle had something to do with this."

Coop looked at him through narrowed eyes. "Why would Bob have anything to do with it?"

"We haven't figured that out yet," Tip said.

"But you can bet we're working on it."

"Be careful where you step," Coop said. "Bob Ingle might come across like a gentleman, but he's not."

Tip started for the door. "Thanks for the warning, Cap."

"Keep me informed," she said.

Tip pointed a finger at her. "You do the same."

***

No sooner had the door closed than Coop was on the phone. Cybil answered quickly.

"We found Barbara's purse," Coop said.

"And?"

"And there was a note inside that said 'Do you believe in MAGIC?' and the MAGIC was in caps."

"And now you think I had something to do with killing Barbara?" Cybil asked.

"Did you?"

"You know who did."

"I hope you're wrong, Cybil, because this is getting out of hand." Coop squeezed her eyes closed tightly. "I'm going to have to tell Tip."

"You don't have to tell him anything."

Coop got up and made sure the door was closed tight. "I know you and Rusty don't like Tip, but he might be the best detective I have. The bottom line is that once that man gets a scent, he's like one of your daddy's old hounds; he won't let go. If you're telling me the truth and you had nothing to do with this, the sooner we tell him the better. What you did in the past is old news. Nobody will care about that."

Silence, then Cybil said, "It might not all be in the past. I think Barbara was still blackmailing people. Maybe even Tom."

"Good God! How could she be so stupid?" Coop said. "Didn't you tell her?"

"She must have figured he owed her."

"Tom wouldn't take well to being blackmailed." Coop said, and then she heard Cybil laugh.

"Gladys, old girl, you know that's more than a mouthful. Now you have your motive. If you want to sic Tip Denton on somebody, you know where to point that dog."

CHAPTER 39

BAD NEWS COMES IN THREES

We were almost to our desk when the phone guy called. Tip grabbed it and ducked into the coffee room, signaling me to follow. He turned the speaker on before he spoke.

"What's up? I thought you said tonight."

"I had a chance to check early, but I don't have much for you. She called an untraceable number in the Washington DC area."

"How long did the call last?"

"Less than two minutes. One minute thirty-two seconds to be precise."

"Thanks," Tip said. "I owe you."

My mind raced. "Who did she call?" I asked, as soon as Tip hung up the line.

"The way I see it," Tip said, "we have three possibilities—Tom Marsen, the First Lady, or a random number in the DC area."

"I wish we had more suspects," I said.

"Me too."

"Maybe we ought to pick on Coop and nail *her* ass for this. She's already broken about half the department regulations."

"I think I'd rather tackle the president," Tip said. "I arm-wrestled Coop one time."

"Did you let her win?"

Tip looked at the wall and sat silent, as if thinking. "I'm not sure."

We finished out the day documenting everything we learned and figuring out where to start in the morning. We had good reason to go back to Cybil, and if she were anybody else we'd have arrested her, but people like Cybil don't scare easily; they just call their lawyers and laugh at us. Besides, we don't have anywhere near enough evidence to go after Cybil, not even if she wasn't married to Rusty."

"I say we put pressure on Ingle."

Tip looked at me. "Maybe you don't remember what I told you before, but if we start pressuring Ingle, he's gonna push back."

"He didn't seem so tough," I said.

"He's more than tough. Don't be fooled by those stories you're hearing of him in his younger days. That boy has grown a thick skin since then, and he's a whole lot richer."

Tip grabbed a few files and stuffed them into his briefcase. "I'm taking this home to work on. You want to come over and plan this?"

"I might go see Ron."

"Tell him to hang tough," Tip said. "Tell him it can get better."

"Thanks. I'll see you tomorrow. We'll figure out the Ingle situation then."

I picked up a few burgers and fries, then stopped at the halfway house. Ron looked good; in fact, it was the first time we laughed together for a long time. He seemed to be diligent about working the program and helping others. Nothing could have made me happier. When it got to be about 9:00, I told him I had to get going.

"I still have work to do before tomorrow. We're trying to crack this case and I think we're closing in on it."

"Is that the one where the woman was cut up?"

"That's the one. Pretty brutal."

He gave me a big hug to go along with his smile. "Go get 'em, Dad. I love you."

He caught me off guard with the "I love you" but I recovered and somehow managed to come up with a response without sounding too artificial. "I love you, too, Ron. Thanks for saying that."

By nine-thirty I was home and deep into case files, trying to figure out what was going on. We had too many suspects with motive. We hadn't heard from Santos, so I thought I'd call him and see what he had.

"Did you get anything new?" I asked when he answered.

"Cataldi?"

"Yeah, it's me."

"It has been a busy day, my man. I planned on calling you in the morning, but I see you're keeping my hours. I should have known."

"What have you got?"

"We found a second cell phone and one of the numbers in her preferred list was a Houston one, registered to a…hang on a minute."

I heard what sounded like papers turning then he came back on.

"Eastex Enterprises. That mean anything to you?"

I thought I'd swallow my tongue. "It means a lot, but keep going. I'll tell you about Eastex in a minute."

"A couple of recent calls came in from none other than RB Ingle's office, which makes me wonder why one of the richest men in Texas is calling a prostitute?"

"Holy shit," I said. "When were the calls?"

"Two different calls, and both of them came in the day before she was killed."

"Holy shit," I said again.

"Yeah, and that's not all," Santos said.

"We found almost $400k in stocks and bonds in an account Patti had at another bank, plus a safe deposit box with $86,000 in cash."

"Shit! Richards and Camwyck knew what they were doing. Most of the women in that profession are junkies or at least dead broke and living in a rundown apartment in the wrong part of the city."

"You got that right," Santos said.

"Anything else?" I asked.

"Nothing else yet, but we still haven't finished going through her computer. She has a few encrypted files and our tech guy hasn't been able to crack them. I think he's bringing in an expert tomorrow."

"Encrypted files sound interesting," I said.

"Let me know if anything comes of it."

"I will. Now what about Eastex Enterprises? You said it meant something."

I thought about how much to tell him, and opted for the minimum at this point.

"Eastex Enterprises was the primary employer of our victim."

"Dios mio," Santos said.

"Don't get excited, Santos, because there's more. One of our original suspects worked for RB Ingle, and Ingle bailed him out. Now the guy is missing."

"Son of a bitch!" Santos said. "This is getting to be a mess."

"One hell of a mess," I said. "Keep me informed."

I hung up from Santos and dialed Tip's number. "Are you ready to tackle Ingle?" I asked.

"That's what we planned on. Why?"

"Santos just called. They received the report on his victim's phone. She had two calls from RB Ingle's office the day before she died. And she had Eastex Enterprises in her address list."

"Pack extra ammunition," Tip said. "We're gonna need it."

"See you in the morning," I said.

CHAPTER 40

A FEW MORE QUESTIONS

We pulled up to Ingle's building about 8:00 the next morning. I grabbed my notebook, and we went inside. The same receptionist was on duty, the one who didn't smile. A plaque on the desk identified her as Laurie Zisk. Tip winked at her and said, "Laurie darlin', you're as pretty as the morning."

She shook her head. "Detective, I've seen Lonesome Dove, and you're not the first man who's tried that line on me."

Tip scrunched up his brow and looked at her. "You mean they stole my line?"

I think she tried not to, but that last comment made her smile. "I'm guessing you're here to see Mr. Ingle."

"We had a few questions for him if he's got a minute," Tip said.

She wrote something on a card and handed it to Tip. "If you ever think up a new line, call me."

He looked at the card then winked at her again. "I just might do that," he said.

Ingle's assistant came to get us and led us to a conference room. Ingle was already there.

"What can I do for you, detectives? I don't have much time."

I shook his hand and took a seat in the chair next to his. "We have a few questions."

"About what?"

"The first one is about your employee—Mano Perez. Remember him? The one you bailed out?"

Ingle nodded. "What about him?"

"I'm sure you know by now that he's missing. Aren't you worried about your money?"

He looked at us, no emotion, and said, "I had no idea, but I'll have my people look into it. We'll find him. I guarantee that."

"Did you know Patti Richards?" Tip asked.

"Who?" Ingle asked, but he didn't seem surprised.

"Patti Richards. She was a prostitute up in Dallas."

A scowl popped on Ingle's face. "A prostitute? What would I be doing with a prostitute?"

"That's what we'd like to know," Tip said.

"You called her twice the day before she died."

"I didn't call anyone named Richards. And I sure as hell didn't call a prostitute, Detective." He stood. "Is that all? I'm a busy man."

"Where were you last Wednesday?" I asked.

"I have no idea. Why? Where were you? Do you recall?"

"We're going to need to know," I said. "You better check your calendar because it's important."

Tip jumped in. "That was the day of the First Lady's speech in Dallas."

"Oh yes. I remember now. I was in Dallas for a couple of days on business."

"Did you kill Ms. Richards?" I asked.

"What? Are you people crazy?"

"How well did you know Ms. Camwyck?" Tip asked. "Were you still sleeping with her?"

Ingle reached for the phone on the table. He pressed the intercom. "Jonathan, the detectives are ready to leave."

"We aren't done asking questions," Tip said.

"Yes, you are," Ingle said, and he stood, hands at his sides.

"What do you know about Magic?" Tip asked. "And what can you tell us about a motel room over in East Texas? The one where you and Tom Marsen spent the night with—"

Ingle kicked his chair to the side. "Get the hell out of my building. Get out and don't come back. I'll have your goddamn badges for this. I know the chief. I know the mayor." He shoved the phone off the table. "I know the *fucking* president."

"But do you know who the president was fucking?" Tip asked.

Jonathan entered and said, "Detectives…" while holding the door open.

As we exited, Tip said, "We're not done with questions."

"You're more than done, Detective. Your career is over."

Jonathan deposited us in the lobby. Tip waved to Laurie, and she smiled.

"I can't believe she gave you her phone number," I said.

"It's the wink," Tip said. "They can't resist it."

I was still laughing when we left the building. Twenty feet ahead we ran into Reggie Grage, Ingle's driver and bodyguard.

I held up my badge. "Mr. Grage, we've got a few questions for you."

He stopped, nodded his head, but didn't say a word.

"Where were you last Wednesday?" Tip asked.

Reggie's response was immediate. "I drove Mr. Ingle to Dallas."

I opened my notepad and jotted down his answer. "You didn't fly?"

"Mr. Ingle likes to drive so he can get work done. He hates to waste time."

"Where did you go in Dallas?"

"He attended several business meetings.

He went to the First Lady's speech."

We waited, but he wasn't filling in the gaps. "And?" I said.

"And what?"

"What else did you do?"

"Nothing," Reggie said.

"What about Wednesday night between 9:00 and midnight?"

"I'm not certain."

I put my notepad away in my shirt pocket and said, "Reggie, you look like a man who knows the drill. We can do this here or pick it up at the station."

He waited a moment, then he said, "Mr. Ingle would have me out in ten minutes."

"He might," I said, "but would he be happy about it?"

"I don't know."

Tip reached for his handcuffs. When he did, Reggie said, "It's true. I don't know what Mr. Ingle did on Wednesday night. I dropped him off at a club around 8:30. He said he would catch a ride back to the hotel."

I smiled. *Now we were getting somewhere.* "Which club?"

"A gentleman's club. I don't remember the name."

Tip laughed. "You mean a strip club?"

Reggie nodded.

I took out my notepad and handed it to Reggie with a pen. "Write down the address where it was. If you don't remember the exact address, give us the general area."

Reggie's phone rang. He looked at the screen and tensed up. "Yes, sir?"

I heard a voice coming through, a male voice. It sounded like Ingle. I turned and looked at the building. Ingle was staring out the window of an office on the third floor.

"I understand, sir." Reggie hung up and ripped the page from the notepad, and then handed it to me. "If you need anything else, I will need to consult my lawyer."

"That's all for now," Tip said.

As Reggie walked into the building, I turned to face Tip. "So much for that."

"I saw what he wrote—Jaguars."

"Do you know the place?"

"I've never been there. I don't fancy those kind of clubs, but I've heard of it. High class. Expensive. Just the kind of place Ingle would choose."

"Speaking of Ingle," I said, "You sure pissed him off."

"I try," Tip said, and then, "Now we need to call Santos and see what he can find out."

I dialed Santos' number, but it went straight to voicemail. "Santos, it's Cataldi. Call me."

"What now?" I said to Tip, as I opened the door to the car.

"Since RB has pretty much banned us from talking to him or his people, why don't we pay a visit to his wife."

Tip had a devious mind. "Sounds good to me," I said.

"Have you ever seen her?" Tip asked.

I shook my head.

Tip smiled. "You might want to take a cold shower first."

CHAPTER 41

MRS. PERFECT

On the way to Ingle's house, I called and left another message for Santos. He returned the call a few minutes later, just as we pulled into the long drive leading to Ingle's house. I filled him in on the connection with Ingle and told him about Jaguars.

"I'll check it out and get back to you," he said.

I hung up the phone and, as we got out of the car, Tip said. "Santos seemed more than a little familiar with Jaguars."

"I'm guessing a lot of the detectives in Dallas might be familiar with it."

"Speaking of jaguars and cougars and all that, Tip said, "do you have any rubber bands?"

I looked at him as I often did—as if he were crazy. "What the hell are you talking about?"

"Mrs. Ingle—she's an RB woman."

All I could do was shake my head. "You're going to have to explain that one to me. I have no idea what you're talking about."

Tip said. "RB. She's a *rubber band* woman. In other words, she's so goddamn sexy you'll need to put a rubber band around your dick to keep it from acting up."

I laughed. And then I laughed more. "Denton, you're one of a kind."

We followed a path along a flagstone walk, which led to a front door that belonged on a museum or a church. Tip pressed the doorbell, and within a few seconds a young Latina woman opened the door to greet us.

"*Buenos dias,*" she said. "No English."

Having been married for so long to Mary, I had picked up a decent amount of Spanish. "*Bueños dias,*" I said. "*Señora Ingle, por favor?*"

She smiled and invited us in. "*Uno momento.*"

"I'm impressed," Tip said, then he tapped me on the arm. "Would you look at this shit. This damn foyer is bigger than my living room."

I looked around. Tip usually exaggerates, but this time he didn't The foyer held two love seats, two chairs, and a large fountain in the middle with knee-high walls to sit on. Built into the back of the staircase between the two love seats was a shelf filled with books and a big selection of magazines.

Before long, the Latino woman returned and indicated we were to follow her. She led us through the house and out a sliding door to a large brick patio surrounding a pool. Mrs. Ingle was just walking up the steps to get out.

Anne Ingle had a body that…shimmered. The kind of body that took a man's mind off everything except the fact that he was a man, and it brought that home with a dangerous reminder—she's RB Ingle's wife. She had a body that stirred emotions, and feelings, and physical reactions. A body that hurt to look at, because you couldn't have it. Tip hadn't exaggerated this time— Anne Ingle was a rubber-band woman.

I closed my eyes and imagined things that would take my mind off her— car wrecks, corpses, anything that didn't stir those other emotions.

"Detectives," she said, and I opened my eyes. Fortunately, Tip picked up the slack.

"Mrs. Ingle, I'm Detective Denton, and this is Detective Cataldi. If you have a moment, we'd like to ask a few questions."

She snatched a towel from the back of a lounge chair—occupied by a little white Shih Tzu— then wiped her face and hair. I thought she would have covered herself after that, but she didn't; she tossed the towel back on the chair. As I stared at her rock-hard body and next-to-nothing bathing suit, I was torn between relief and regret. I diverted my gaze before I broke protocol.

"Mrs. Ingle," Tip said, "Were you with your husband in Dallas last Wednesday?"

"In Dallas? No, I didn't go. It was just Bob and Reggie."

"Did you talk to him while he was there?" Tip asked.

She shot Tip a questioning look. "What's this about?"

"We're looking into some things that happened while Mr. Ingle was in Dallas. That's all."

She looked at Tip, then me. "I might not be up on my criminal justice courses, but why would Houston detectives be looking into things that happened in Dallas?"

"We can't go into details, as you can imagine," I said, "but there are similarities between a case in Dallas and one we're working in Houston."

She had been standing, but now she sat in a reclining chair and crossed her long, beautiful, perfectly tanned legs. "I know what you're working on, Detective. I saw it in the paper. You can't possibly think Bob had anything to do with either of those murders."

Tip moved closer and pulled up a chair.

"We didn't say that, Mrs. Ingle. But sometimes we need to cover all angles so that we can rule out possible suspects."

She reached to the table beside her and picked up a pair of sunglasses. When she put them on, she became sexier. I didn't think that was possible, but she did. "Okay, I'll play along. You asked if we talked while he was in Dallas. Yes, we talked. In fact, we spoke quite a few times."

"Do you remember when you talked to him—which days and at which time?"

She chuckled. "If you mean, did I keep a diary of the calls—no. But I know I spoke to him the night he left, and the next morning before breakfast. Several other times, too. If it's really necessary, I'm sure we can get a record from my cell phone, or if not, from the phone company."

Tip leaned forward, getting close to her.

"Were you aware that your husband knew the woman who was murdered in Houston?"

She turned away from Tip, reaching for a drink sitting on the table. "I didn't realize that."

"He grew up with her," I said. "And he's had dealings with her since coming to Houston."

She sucked some of the drink up through a straw poking above the rim—a pink straw. "Now that you mention it, I do recall hearing something about that."

I watched her. The way she turned her head when she answered our questions. Or diverted her gaze. How she fidgeted, or grabbed her drink. I thought I'd push a little and see where it led. "Did you know your husband was having an affair?"

She placed the glass on the table, and played with the straw, moving it around in her hands. Then she took off her sunglasses and caught my gaze. "That's ridiculous. Bob would never do that to me."

"We all know he did," Tip said.

She stood in a huff, grabbed her towel and wrapped it around herself. "I think it's time you were leaving, detectives. I have nothing more to say."

Tip started to say something, but I held out my hand. "We're going, Mrs. Ingle. But us leaving won't change anything. We'll be back."

"Call beforehand. I'll want my lawyer next time." She headed for the sliding door, and I had to say the back side of her looked even better than the front.

We walked through the house, heels clicking loudly on the flagstone. Tip opened the front door and I followed. After that, we headed back to the station. Not two blocks away, my phone rang. It was Santos. "What have you got for us?"

"A lot more than I want to," he said.

Now he had my curiosity piqued. "I'm putting it on speaker so my partner can hear."

"Several of the ladies at Jaguars remember a guy fitting Ingle's description. I took along a few photos of him from the Internet, and they confirmed he was the guy. They said he was a big tipper, and there seemed to have been a few arguments over who would provide dances for him."

"Did anyone win?"

"A young lady by the name of *Sindy* spelled with an S, as in sin. But she said after her second performance, Ingle left with another woman, not an employee."

"I hope they were envious enough to get a description."

Santos laughed. "Down to the swirls in her navel. Tall, blonde, pretty, built, a half-moon tattoo on the left side of her neck. And young."

"In other words, we're fucked," Tip said from the driver's seat.

"Pretty much," Santos said. "Sure as hell that description doesn't fit our victim."

"Still, it will give us something to question Ingle about," I said.

"Don't get bored," Santos said. "Lots more fun coming."

"Spit it out," Tip said.

"Remember I told you we found her car?"

"We just talked about that, Santos. You found the note in there about Magic."

"We found something else," he said. "A small USB drive was taped under the gas pedal."

My gut started churning. "Go on."

"It had a lot of encrypted pictures, most of them of her having sex with people. We haven't gotten all of the files enhanced yet, but some of the people look familiar."

"Familiar how?"

"I recognized a few of the local councilmen and maybe some others. Of the ones I recognized, most were important men. It could have been used as a blackmail file."

"You mentioned the councilmen *and others*. Anyone else you recognize?"

"There were more references to Eastex Enterprises," he said.

"You're holding back," I said. "I asked if you recognized anyone else."

"Is this a secure line?" Santos asked.

"It's my private cell."

Santos remained quiet until I prodded him again, then he spit out the name like they say "Dracula" in the horror movies of old.

"One person in particular was very familiar—President Tom Marsen."

The reality of the situation hit me like a brick, especially after seeing the video Coop received. "What the *fuck* have we stepped into, Santos?"

"I don't even want to know, man. I was hoping you were going to tell me this was a coincidence, that the president of the *fucking* United States just happened to be getting a piece of tail from a lady who turned up dead."

"Sorry, Santos. If I don't get to sleep, neither do you. As far as Eastex Enterprises, they were the primary employer of our victim. And Rusty Johnson, Houston's mayor, owns Eastex." I paused. I felt like looking over my shoulder, or checking the locks on the doors. "And you want to know more. The mayor's wife, and our victim, *and* the president, *and* RB Ingle have been friends since birth." Before he could say anything, I continued. "And in case you were wondering, we also have a video of the president with

Barbara Camwyck. They *weren't* dancing the Fox Trot."

"*Dios mío!*"

"Yeah, no shit. *Dios mío* is right."

I thought for a minute. "I'll tell you what. Let's keep this between us and our partners. Can you keep it that way for a day or so, give us time to push a few buttons down here?"

"Consider it done. And hurry up; I like my job."

"You got it. We'll stay in touch."

I hung up and looked at Tip. He was smiling.

"Can't say we didn't catch a case this time, Gino. Two dead girls, and both of them fuckin' the president."

"All we have to do now is figure out how to solve the case while keeping our badges."

CHAPTER 42

A PRIVATE TALK

Tip's phone rang just as he entered the exit ramp to get off the freeway. He answered and began speaking. I tried to listen, but my phone rang a few seconds later.

"Cataldi."

"Detective?"

It was a woman's voice, but caller ID had been blank. "Hello?"

"Detective, you were right."

I thought I recognized her voice. "Mrs. Ingle?"

"I'm sorry. Yes, this is Anne Ingle. And you were right about the affair. I *did* know."

More silence, then, "Perhaps you should come back here so we can talk. There's a lot to discuss."

"It will take us about half an hour," I said, and hung up.

I waited for Tip to finish, trying to piece together what was being said, but he wasn't talking much, just listening. When he got off he looked to me and said,

"Shit!"

"Shit?" I said. "Is that a good *shit*, as in a lead, or a bad *shit*, as in something went wrong?"

"That was Buddy," Tip said. "Remember that story about the president and Ingle in the motel with the two girls?"

"What about it?"

"There was a rape that night."

"Are you *shitting* me?"

"It gets better," Tip said. "Buddy found the girl's brother, who seemed to be the only one in town willing to talk. As it turns out that girl's family was paid a lot of money to drop the charges and shut-up about the subject. Buddy suspected the brother didn't get to share in that good fortune, which is why he's talking, but the parents and the girl definitely got paid."

We might be finally getting somewhere on this case.

"Guess who was raped? A young girl by the name of Barbara Camwyck."

"Are you shitting me?"

"Not according to Buddy. Besides, why would her brother lie to us?"

"Son of a bitch."

"Don't fall down yet. There's more."

"What?"

"Do you remember who told us this story the first time, about the night in the motel?"

"Yeah, it was Cybil."

"Exactly, but when Cybil told the story she left out an important part— *she* was the other girl in the room with them."

"What the fuck!" I didn't know what else to say, so I said it again. "What the fuck."

I took time, trying to imagine what could make people behave like that, but all I could do was wonder. "The more I learn about that little piece of paradise in East Texas, the more I'm glad I grew up in nasty old Philadelphia."

"Funny that Cybil forgot to mention those specifics," Tip said. "Maybe we should ask her about it."

"I'm fine with that, but I don't think we should tell Coop," I said.

Tip screeched the tires as he made a fast turn. "At this point, I don't care what she thinks."

"I know what you mean, but if we go behind her back, she'll fire us, and if we trust her and she's involved with this, somebody else will fire us."

"Either way, we're fucked," Tip said.

I thought about it for a millisecond. "That's the way I see it."

"What do you want to do; it's your badge too."

It didn't take me long to decide. "I say we find whoever did this. It all starts with Cybil, but she's got an alibi."

"Her alibi is Rusty Johnson, and if he was home that early in the night I'll kiss Coop's ass."

"How do we break Cybil's alibi?"

"By breaking Rusty's alibi," Tip said.

"And how do we break the mayor's alibi?"

"We talk to some strippers."

"Count me in," I said.

"Sorry, Gino, but that's my territory. I'm afraid you'd be out of your league," Tip said, and he turned and smiled.

"No dice, Tip. Those strippers love guys like me. I'm fresh meat to them."

"That sounds fair. Let's go have fun, partner."

"Not yet," I said. "We need to go see Anne first."

He squinted and stared. "Anne? You're on a first-name basis with Mrs. Ingle now?"

I laughed. "She called while you were talking to Buddy."

"And?"

"She said she knew about the affair, and we should talk."

"Son of a bitch. This could be exciting."

I agreed. Part of me was excited about the information we might get, but a bigger part was excited about seeing her again. "I hope she hasn't changed clothes, or worse, put more on."

"I hope she took some off," Tip said, and then, "You know she stayed half naked to keep us from focusing."

"It crossed my mind, but I'm not that cynical yet."

"Bullshit," Tip said. "And you know I'm right. She wanted us thinking about her ass and feeling sorry for her."

I thought about what Tip said, and not for the first time. "If that was her plan, it worked."

"And you want to go see strippers? They'll eat you for lunch."

It didn't take long to get back to Ingle's house. When we arrived, I rang the doorbell.

The same Latina woman with the same blank expression answered and led us to Mrs. Ingle. She was sitting on a sofa in a small room off the kitchen.

She stood when we entered. "Thank you for coming back. I was rude to send you away like I did."

"Not a problem," I said.

She had changed out of her bathing suit, which both disappointed and relieved me. The positive side was that now I could focus on the case.

"You mentioned that you knew about the affair?"

"Have a seat, detectives." She gestured toward a few chairs across from where she sat.

I waited for her to speak. After a brief silence, she said, "I don't know where to start. I guess with suspicions. I suspected Bob was fooling around." She seemed to think for a moment, while twisting her hair into a bun, then said, "If I'm honest with myself, I *knew* he was fooling around but I didn't want to believe it."

She paused again, but Tip prodded her.

"What changed your mind?"

"When Bob was out of town, up in Dallas, a package arrived—overnight delivery. It had been sent from an address in Dallas, and since it was delivered to our house, I thought I should open it in case it was important." She placed her hands in her lap and shook her head slowly. "I wish I'd left that damn package alone."

Anne had my curiosity stirred. "Do you want to tell us what was inside? Was it a package or an envelope?"

Anne looked over. "I'm sorry, Detective. It was more of an envelope size. I call them all packages." Then she reached over and opened her purse—sitting next to her—and took out a folded piece of paper. She reached forward to hand it to me.

"I probably shouldn't have touched it. I know that now, but I didn't know what it was at first."

Tip put on a pair of gloves and examined the note.

I know what happened to Barbara. Don't think you can do the same to me. I have all the information Barbara had, and I want $10 million. If you do what I say, you'll never hear from us again.

"There's no signature," Tip said. "We'll have it processed, but I'm willing to bet there won't be any prints."

I looked over at Anne. She was trembling, and her hands were shaking badly. "Is that all there was in the package?"

At first, she sat still, then she shook her head. "There was a video on a USB drive."

I shot a look to Tip, then back to her. "Do you still have the video?"

She nodded. "If you don't mind closing those doors, I'll show you."

I shut the doors, then returned to the chair.

Anne was fidgeting with a computer screen. She pressed a few keys, opened the movie player, and hit the *play* button.

Within a few seconds, it was obvious that whoever had recorded this video had also recorded the one we watched of Camwyck and the president. It was a different hotel room, and Camwyck wore different clothes, but aside from that it was the same. Except this video portrayed Camwyck and Ingle.

It didn't take long for Camwyck to undress, and once she did, she waited for RB to get naked. She poured a couple of drinks, then they both sat on the bed. After they finished the first drink, Ingle pulled her to him and they kissed.

Anne spoke, but it seemed like a struggle. Her voice was filled with anger, and hurt.

"As you can see, that is Ms. Camwyck doing what she does best.'

"You don't need to sit through this," I said.

"I've watched this a dozen times…wondering what it is that is so special about her. What she *does* that makes her so desirable."

I elected not to respond. The video progressed as expected. Anne choked up when RB gave Camwyck oral sex, then, when he entered her, Anne got up and walked away from the computer.

"I'm sorry," she said. "Even though I've seen this before, I still get upset."

I stopped the video so she didn't have to endure watching it again. I couldn't imagine what she felt like. "We don't need to do this."

She didn't say anything, just sobbed. I grabbed some tissues from a table and handed them to her.

"Thank you."

I wanted to hug her, make her feel better, but I didn't even know how. If that had been Mary on the video and I were watching it…

"I think you better go," she said. She ejected the USB and handed it to me. "Keep the video. Let me know if there's anything else you need."

I looked to Tip and he nodded. I turned back to Anne and said, "We'll try to keep this low profile. If we can solve the case without bringing this up…"

She shook her head, reached into her purse and handed us business cards.

"That's my private cell number. Call me if you have questions. I need closure on this."

I put the card in my wallet. Tip slipped his into his shirt pocket. "Thanks, we will," he said.

She looked as if she wanted to go, but she hadn't moved yet. She lifted her head and studied me and then Tip, saying, "I guess what got me so upset is not why he would cheat, but why would he cheat with *her*. I mean, look at her. I *know* I'm not unattractive?"

What was I supposed to say. I *had been* looking at Camwyck, and sick as it was to say, knowing what became of her, she was damned sexy. I thought Tip might answer, but he didn't. I gulped. "No, ma'am. You're right. You are *not* unattractive; in fact, you are *very* attractive."

"But…"

"I'm sure I blushed. I felt as if I did. "Pardon me, ma'am."

"There was a "but" at the end of your sentence, Detective. You obviously didn't want to say it, but it was there."

Damn, this lady was good. I tried responding without stammering. "I'm sure your husband's actions have nothing to do with you. You are a classy woman—"

"But *she* is the kind men want to screw. Is that what you're trying to say?"

I hesitated, but decided the truth was best. "In kinder words, yes."

Her face softened, she smiled, then she headed toward the door with me admiring her the whole way. But this time I wasn't admiring her legs or her butt, just feeling sorry for her.

Before she reached the door, Tip said, "You watched the whole thing?"

She turned and looked at Tip. Her eyes closed briefly. "I don't know about the women you associate with, but in my neck of the woods if a mysterious package arrives addressed to a woman's husband and it contains a mysterious note…"

"Just checking, ma'am."

"There's no way he killed her," Anne said.

The statement took me by surprise. "Why would you say that?"

"I know my husband. He might be a son of a bitch, especially as far as being faithful goes, but he wouldn't murder Ms. Camwyck, or anyone else."

"Not even if she was blackmailing him?" Tip said.

She looked Tip in the eyes. "Do you know what Bob is worth?"

"A lot of money," Tip said.

"Almost a billion dollars," she said. "This note is asking for a few million." Anne lowered her head and shook it. "He's lost almost that much playing poker with his friends."

"Do you have any idea what the reference to Ms. Camwyck meant?" Tip asked. "Or what information the note referred to?"

"I haven't a clue," Anne said.

"Do you know who sent the package?" I asked. "Or who the 'us' in the note is?"

She walked to a desk in the library and opened the top drawer. "I saved the shipping label."

"Don't touch it!" I said, and rushed over to where she was.

"I forgot," Anne said. "That was foolish of me. But I'm afraid I've already handled it several times."

"That's all right," Tip said. "The lab might still be able to find something. There will be other prints on it anyway—the delivery men, packagers, and probably too many others to count."

"Dallas," I said, after looking at the label. "Overnight delivery the day before she died."

Anne moved closer and looked at the label. "That can't be right. This arrived long after Ms. Camwyck died."

"Not Camwyck," I said. "The woman who was killed in Dallas. She was murdered the day you received this package."

"And you think...that's ridiculous," Anne said. "Bob might lose his temper now and then, but he'd never kill anyone."

"I'm sure you're right," Tip said, "but we have to check everything."

"Does your husband know you received this package?" I asked.

She wrinkled her brow. "I'm not stupid, Detective."

I smiled. "Okay, we're going to take this and have it analyzed. If you think of anything else, call us." I put the shipping label into an evidence bag while Tip gathered the rest of the evidence.

"We'll be in touch," I said, and we headed for the door.

On the way back to the station, Tip said, "All of a sudden we have a lot of videos popping up."

"Yeah, and I don't understand why she would defend Ingle, especially after watching that video."

"Money," Tip said. "And because his son is really only her son. My guess is she'll put up with anything to stay married to that much money."

"Which makes me wonder why she showed us that video."

"I've been thinking about that myself," Tip said. "If she's convinced her husband is innocent, why give the cops evidence that incriminates him in at least one murder?"

"A lot to think about," I said. "Not the least of which is the timeline. We know Ingle called Patti Richards the day before she died."

"Which we now know is the day that package was mailed," Tip said.

"And the very next day, Ingle goes to Dallas…"

"And Patti Richards is killed," Tip said.

"Lot of damn coincidences," I said.

"A few too many for me," Tip said. "I think we need to talk to Coop and then have another talk with Ingle."

"Let's do it."

CHAPTER 43

ALIBIS

When we arrived at the station, we headed straight for Coop's office. She'd want to see the video.

"Don't forget," Tip said, "We're not going to mention Cybil."

"I didn't forget. Besides, we've got plenty to keep Coop busy."

Coop was at her desk when we entered. "You boys must have something good, if you're coming to my office without being asked or ordered."

We filled her in on what we learned from Santos, and then about our talks with RB and his bodyguard. And then Tip placed the USB drive on her desk.

Coop looked at the drive, then up at us. "Another video?"

"We haven't seen all of it," I said, "But this was delivered to RB Ingle's house and intercepted by his wife."

"That's not gonna play well," Coop said.

"What's on the video?"

"We got far enough to see RB with Camwyck, much like her rendezvous with Tom Marsen."

"Barbara always did get around," Coop said, and shook her head.

Tip brought out the evidence bag and handed the blackmail note to Coop. "This came with the video."

Coop put her glasses and held the bag up close. "I can't read it like this, and I don't want to take it out."

"No need, Captain. I remember what it says."

"Don't keep me guessing."

I recited it from memory.

I know what happened to Barbara. Don't think you can do the same to me.

I have all the information Barbara had, and I want $10 million. If you do what I say, you'll never hear from us again.

"Us?" Coop said.

"Same thing we wondered," Tip said.

Coop handed the USB and the note to Tip.

"Ask Cindy to make us a copy and then get the originals examined."

When Tip came back, Coop seemed more serious. "This doesn't look good for Bob Ingle."

"Want us to go piss him off?" Tip asked.

"We've already pissed him off," I said.

He's gonna lawyer up."

She cracked a smile. Considering her mood a moment ago, I was happy with that. "I have no doubts you could, and would, do that," Coop said, "but let's wait for our team to examine this evidence so we can see what's on this video."

Cindy came in with the copy of the flash drive and handed it to Coop.

"Time to watch the movie, boys. Get your hands out of your pockets." Coop put the drive in her computer and brought the movie up on the monitor.

It turned out to be very similar to the video we saw of Camwyck and the president, although Barbara didn't seem as animated with Ingle as she had been with Marsen. It made me wonder about her feelings toward RB.

When it was finished, Coop looked at us.

"That's it?"

"That's all we've got," I said.

She focused on the screen, then the ceiling. "I've known Bob Ingle a long time. He's an ass, and a son of a bitch, and maybe even a crook, but I can't see him killing Barbara over something like this. And I definitely can't see him killing two people, let alone dismembering them. I don't think it was him."

"That's a lot of money they were asking for," I said.

Coop pursed her lips. "Not to him it wasn't. He's been known to piss away a few million dollars for a fun weekend."

"If it wasn't about sex, why were these women killed?" I asked.

Coop pointed a finger at me. "That's exactly what you have to figure out."

She frowned and said, "How was Anne, if you bothered to notice?"

"I noticed," Tip said. "She was sexy as hell."

Gladys buried her head in her hands. "Why me, God?"

I realized we needed to salvage this situation, so I quickly said, "We *did* take our minds off her long enough to wonder why she showed us the video," I said. "She seemed convinced her husband was innocent—at least of the murders—but then she gave us evidence that incriminated him in at least one murder. Kind of strange."

Coop leaned back in her chair and folded her hands behind her head. "We've got Barbara having sex with Ingle and the president. And according to the detective in Dallas, we have Patti engaging in sex with the president." She paused for a moment then sat up straight and said, "Suppose this isn't about RB Ingle?"

The implication made me shiver. "You're talking about the president of the United States, Captain."

"I know who I'm talking about. I knew the son of a bitch when he was young." She stood and walked between us, and then she walked around us. "Earlier I said that Bob Ingle was an ass and a son of a bitch and maybe even a crook. Tom Marsen is a whole lot worse than that."

Tip moved over and sat on the edge of her desk. "You can't think the president…"

"I don't know what to think," Coop said. "But I know that if Tom had anything to do with this he'd be smart enough not to get his hands dirty, and that means Bob Ingle is probably involved even if it's only covering things up. So get your asses over there and piss him off some more, and if he tells you to talk to his lawyer, arrest him."

"Is that an order, Captain?" Tip asked.

"Damn straight it is," she said.

We drove back to Ingle's office, and I have to admit, I was excited by the prospect of clamping a set of cuffs on RB. "I can't believe Coop supported us like that."

Tip looked over at me and laughed. "I'm guessing she and Ingle didn't quite get along back in East Texas, at least that's my take on it. Every now and then old Gladys does the right thing."

"I can't wait to see how Ingle reacts. This should be fun."

We walked inside, and Tip said hi to Laurie, who looked as if she hadn't moved from her spot behind the desk in the lobby.

"Here to see Mr. Ingle," he said.

Jonathan came out to greet us and led us to the same room as before. Ingle was waiting, and no one offered us drinks. I was almost insulted.

Ingle was standing and looking impatient. "What is it, detectives? I'm busy."

"We have more questions," I said.

"I told you I was through answering questions. If you need anything you can talk to my lawyer."

"I'm afraid that answer won't do," Tip said. "We have questions about the club you visited in Dallas, and about your relationship with Ms. Camwyck."

RB grabbed a notepad from the table and wrote something on it, then handed it to Tip. "My lawyer's name and number."

"If that's the way you want to play it," Tip said. He grabbed hold of RB's arm and slapped the cuffs on him.

"What the hell are you doing?" RB said.

"Taking you downtown," I said. "You can have your lawyer meet you."

"Are you crazy? I'll have your badge. I'll—"

"You have the right to remain silent," Tip said, and then he finished the Miranda rights.

RB threatened us all the way to the car, only stopping to tell Jonathan to call his lawyer. "Tell him where they're taking me. Tell him he better be there by the time I arrive."

Ingle stopped talking long before we hit the station, and he never said a word as we led him to the interrogation room.

"You want coffee or something else to drink?" I asked.

He glared at me but said nothing.

I left him alone, with a uniformed officer at the door, and then Tip and I went to see Coop. We crossed paths on the way to her office.

"I hear we have Mr. Ingle as a guest," she said.

"News travels fast," said Tip.

"Only bad news," she said. "I've already had calls from the chief and from Cybil."

"Tell John I said to mind his own business," Tip said. "But you can handle Cybil."

Coop picked up the pace as we turned the corner toward the interview room. "Did his lawyer get here yet?"

"As of a few minutes ago he hadn't but he'll show up soon," I said.

The lawyer was in the room with Ingle when we entered. Ingle stood, his hand extended to greet Coop. "Good to see you again, Gladys."

Coop shot his lawyer a look and said, "Why don't you leave Bob and I alone for a minute."

Before the guy could object, Ingle nodded. "It's okay. Gladys and I are old friends."

Tip and I left the room along with Ingle's lawyer.

"Turn off the camera," Coop said, facing the one-way mirror.

***

Coop pulled a chair out from the table and sat across from Ingle. "Been a long time, Bob."

"If you mean other than political events and bullshit parties—yes, it has."

Coop leaned forward, her elbows resting on the table. "How about we cut the bullshit, and you tell me what the hell is going on?"

Bob looked at Coop and shook his head. "You can't believe I'd do any of this nonsense? That I'd have sex with Barbara?"

"Can't believe it?" Coop said. "I saw the goddamn video, Bob."

Ingle held her fixed for a long time. "It must have been faked, or perhaps from a long time ago."

Coop held his gaze. "That's the stupidest thing you've ever said; besides, I've known you since we were kids. You and Tom Marsen both would screw a snake if someone held it still. So don't tell me you wouldn't do Barbara Camwyck, though, for the life of me, I don't know why with the wife you have. She's gorgeous."

Ingle sat motionless and silent.

"All right, Bob. It's like I said before, let's cut the shit. I don't care who you went to bed with. I'm only interested in why these girls were killed and who did it."

"I have no idea, Gladys, and that's the truth."

Coop leaned against the back of her chair.

"It doesn't look good for you. I'm sure your lawyer will tell you that. With the videos, and with you being in Dallas and Patti getting those calls from your office the day before she was killed…"

"That's all bullshit. I didn't talk to Patti, and I didn't see her in Dallas."

Coop stood. Frustration showed on her face in the form of a furrowed brow and a scowl. "Is that it? That's all you have to tell me?"

Bob looked at her. "That's all there is to tell."

She walked toward the door and opened it, but turned back before leaving. "For old times I wish you luck. But don't expect my detectives to cut you any breaks."

Ingle clenched his fists. "Don't think you can do this to me. I'll have you guarding malls on the night shift before this is through."

"Keep talking," Coop said. "Maybe somebody will listen." And then she closed the door.

CHAPTER 44

ALIBIS

Ingle's lawyer had him out in less than an hour, a testament to how money still greased the wheels in Houston politics—and law enforcement. Before Ingle left the building Tip reminded him that we'd be chatting again real soon.

"This is only a temporary reprieve," Tip said. "Just long enough to let you fake an alibi."

"Fortunately, you won't have nearly so long," Ingle said, just before his lawyer told him to shut up.

"I believe he just threatened me," Tip said.

Coop came up to stand between Tip and me.

"Don't take it lightly. Bob Ingle has a lot of power in this city."

And it doesn't hurt that he knows the president," I said.

Coop nodded. "We opened up a can of worms," she said, and she was still nodding. "You better have your shit together, because Bob's gonna come out swinging."

Tip looked over at Gladys and said, "Have you got any more clichés you'd like to toss in the ring?"

"Screw you, Denton. You and Cataldi get your files and come to my office. We've got work to do."

Ten minutes later, Tip and I were going through the files, spread out on Coop's desk.

"I'd love to bust RB for this," Tip said, "But I don't think he did it."

"What have we got on him?" Coop asked.

"We've got him and Camwyck in the video. He was in Dallas when Roberts was killed, and calls from his office to her phone were placed twice the day before she died, though we can't connect him directly. We have the ransom note from Roberts to RB, along with *that* video. And we know that Camwyck and Ingle had a long history."

"Let's not forget that Ingle provided bail for Mano," Tip said.

"Is he still missing?" Coop asked.

"No sign of him yet," I said.

Coop adjusted her glasses and shuffled through some of our notes. "If Ingle didn't do it, who did? And why?"

I scooted my chair up closer. "Camwyck probably had dozens of people who would have liked her dead, based on the information we saw in her files. But when you add in the sex tapes it narrows the list down—Ingle, Cybil, the president…"

Coop lowered her head and stared over the rims of her glasses. "And me."

"I didn't want to point it out, but yeah. You'd be on the list, too. You knew the victim, knew the rest of the suspects, and you knew about MAGIC."

"That's all good," Coop said, "Except I didn't do it. And I can't see Cybil involved either physically or strategically. She's as big a son of a bitch as RB, but she's not a murderer either."

She looked over at Tip and then back to me. "I know you don't like Cybil. Hell, at times, I don't like her, but like I said, there's no way she had anything to do with Barbara's murder."

Tip stood and paced. "You realize where that puts us, don't you?"

Coop nodded. "Bob and Tom."

"Just to put this into perspective," I said. "That would be RB Ingle, the richest businessman in Houston, and Tom Marsen, the president of the goddamn United States."

"I don't like to think of it in that way, Gino, but it is what it is. We have two women dead and both of them were involved sexually with the president. At least one of them was involved sexually with RB Ingle. And we know there was blackmail."

"If we assume the sex tapes had something to do with them being killed," Tip said.

"Then either the president or Ingle had something to do with them being murdered."

Gladys nodded. "If one of them did, both of them did."

"The key is going to be Ingle," I said. "We've got to put pressure on him. Nail down the timelines. Break his alibis. Maybe then we can figure out who did the dirty work."

"I agree, Gino. I don't see Bob Ingle chopping up Barbara's body. He might have ordered it, but there's no way in hell he did it himself."

"How do we put pressure on him?" I asked.

"Embarrass him," Coop said. "As tough as that man is, he hates to be embarrassed. He's still got a fragile ego."

"That sounds like a job for Tip," I said. "He can piss people off without trying."

Some people were already leaving for the day by the time we arrived at Ingle's building; in fact, we ran into Tip's newfound admirer, Laurie, as she was heading home.

"Is Mr. Ingle still here?" Tip asked.

"He's here, but I don't think he'll want to see you. He came back pretty upset."

Tip smiled and then winked at Laurie. "Thanks, darlin'. And since Mr. Ingle is a possible murder suspect, I guess we'll have to upset him some more."

She tapped him on the arm and laughed. "You're a hoot, Detective."

"I've been called worse," Tip said, "but I wasn't lying about Ingle being a suspect."

Laurie narrowed her eyes and her brow wrinkled. "Are you serious?"

Tip nodded, then he leaned close and whispered, "That's not public knowledge, by the way."

"I won't say a word," Laurie whispered back, and then she walked toward the parking lot, stopping to talk to someone not twenty feet away.

I grabbed Tip's arm and dragged him inside. "You're more than a hoot," I said.

"Look over there," Tip said. "Let the rumors begin. I'm guessing half the building will know about Ingle by morning."

"I doubt it will take that long," I said.

Tip pulled his same routine with the receptionist on duty, but she wasn't quite as smitten with Tip as Laurie had been; in fact, she was downright rude. But Tip had more than one trick in his bag. He lost his smile, straightened up so he towered over her. He pulled out his badge and flashed a nasty look at her. "We're not here to hand out parking tickets. This is a murder investigation. Now get Jonathan down here, and tell him I want him here now."

That shook her up, and whatever she said to Jonathan must have lit a fire under his ass, because he showed up in about two minutes.

He exited the elevator and walked at a fast clip to greet us. "Detectives, it's good to see you again."

"We need to talk," Tip said.

"I'm afraid that is not going to happen," Jonathan said. "My lawyer has instructed me not to discuss this case with you, or anyone else."

"Your lawyer?" I said. "Would that be Mr. Rengster?"

"Yes, it is Mr. Rengster," he said. "Do you know him?" And then he smiled at us.

It wasn't really a smile; it was closer to a smirk. I hated smirks.

I moved in real close, got within inches of his face, and spoke softly. "You can hide behind Rengster for now, but once we're done with Ingle, we'll be coming for you."

Jonathan tried to maintain a calm demeanor, but his jaw and fists were clenched. He was shaken.

"See you soon," Tip said.

We couldn't go upstairs without a security card, but before leaving the building we stopped half a dozen people, asking questions that were sure to stir gossip. Even so, it didn't get interesting until we talked to Reggie.

Tip and I were exiting the Ingle building when Reggie was coming in. "Mr. Grage, we need a few minutes," I said.

Reggie stopped. "I shouldn't be talking to you."

"Said who?" Tip asked.

"Instructions from Mr. Ingle's lawyer."

"I understand why he wouldn't want you talking to us, but that doesn't mean you don't have to. You are a potential witness or accessory to a crime—a murder. You *will* be talking to us."

He glanced at the building, toward RB's office, then focused on me. "Not here. And not anywhere I'll be recognized." He shot another look toward the building. "How about after work? There's a club called Banjo's down—"

"I know where it is," Tip said. "What time?"

"It will have to be after 8:00. Mr. Ingle works late."

"Let's plan on 8:30," Tip said.

Reggie nodded, then walked inside, leaving us to gloat alone.

"You think the ice is breaking?" I asked.

"It just might be," Tip said, and we headed toward the car.

We were about twenty feet from the car, when something made me look back. RB Ingle was staring out the window of his office, and it was in our direction.

"Looks like RB's at a loss for words," I said.

Tip turned. "That's not good," he said. "If he'd have come down screaming at us and threatening us, I'd have felt a lot better." Tip shook his head. "Just staring…I don't like it."

CHAPTER 45

A NIGHT TO REMEMBER

We went back to the station and caught up on a few items before heading out to meet Reggie. Coop caught us first.

"What happened at Ingle's?" she asked.

"We just got back a little while ago," I said. "Nothing much happened."

"Whatever you did pissed him off. I've already had calls from the mayor and Renkin."

"You haven't heard from the president?" Tip asked. "I'll see if I can stir up a call from him."

"Get rest," Coop said. "I have a feeling tomorrow is going to be bad."

"How bad can it be?" I said.

"You haven't had many run-ins with RB Ingle, have you?"

Just then Fat Charlie scooted across the hall. "Charlie, did you get us anything on those lyrics yet?"

He stopped and looked our way. "Nothing yet, Gino. But I'm working on it."

"God help us," Tip said, and then, "Coop, we've got to go. We're meeting Ingle's driver. Maybe even get some evidence. If we're lucky."

"Press him," she said. "Press him hard."

We got to Banjo's a few minutes early. Reggie was already seated at a table off to the side. Tip sat to his left. I sat facing Reggie.

A waitress came by almost immediately. She was a tall Texas gal with a bounce in her step that comes with an early shift.

"What can I get ya'll?"

Tip and I ordered beer. Reggie asked for sweet tea.

"Tea? Not a drinking man?" Tip said.

"My grandmother got me started on sweet tea when I was five years old," Reggie said. "I've been drinking it ever since."

I waited for the waitress to get out of earshot, and said, "Tell me what an ex-Ranger is doing working as a bodyguard for Ingle."

"I see someone's done their homework," Reggie said.

"Enough to know you were also in the Secret Service," Tip said. "For a short time."

Reggie didn't flinch. "A *very* short time."

The perky waitress brought our orders, placed them on the table, collected our money, then quickly left. I took a sip of my beer and leaned forward.

"What happened? I know it's not easy to get in, but what did you do to get tossed out."

The muscles in Reggie's left arm tightened, but he picked up his glass and took a long swig of tea. "Personal choice," he said. "The service is not for everyone."

"How did you get hooked up with Ingle?"

"President Marsen recommended me."

I made a mental note to discuss that with Tip.

"How's the pay?" Tip asked.

Reggie pushed his tea to the side, and he folded his hands on the table in front of him. "You didn't come here to ask about my salary, or my previous jobs, so how about we cut right to it."

I finished my beer and said, "That's the way I prefer it, too. We're trying to establish where Mr. Ingle was on two separate occasions, and we hoped you could help with that."

Reggie let a few seconds pass before speaking. "I assume you're talking about the murder in Houston and the one in Dallas?"

"Exactly," I said.

"Mr. Ingle was at the party for the mayor the night the woman in Houston was killed. I think I've given you details already. We arrived early and left at 12.24."

I checked my notes, from the first time we talked with Reggie. "That's exactly the time you told us when we spoke before."

"I have a good memory for numbers," Reggie said.

"And you're sure of the time?" Tip asked.

"Positive."

"Could Ingle have gone out before then? Without you knowing?"

Reggie gave the question thought. He seemed about to shake his head, but stopped. "Maybe… but I think people would have noticed him missing."

"But it's possible," Tip said.

Reggie nodded. "Yes, possible, but not likely."

"How about Dallas?" I asked.

"As I was about to tell you the last time, I dropped him off at a club—Jaguar's. He arranged for his own ride back to the hotel."

"Does Ingle frequent clubs like that?" Tip asked.

"I can't say."

"Can't say because you don't know, or can't say because you can't say?"

"I can't say."

Reggie wasn't giving us much. I had to try something else. "What is the relationship like between Mr. Ingle and his wife?"

"You'll have to ask them about that."

"You must know something. You drive them don't you?"

Reggie signaled the waitress for a refill on his tea, and Tip ordered us another round of beers. "From what I've seen when they are together, there is no friction. She doesn't challenge him."

I thought it odd how he phrased that.

"Doesn't *challenge* him? Do you mean she is obedient?"

He smiled, but it was a quick smile, the kind that pops on and off a face in an instant. "I wouldn't use that word, but yes, that describes it well."

"Does he hit her?" Tip asked.

Reggie shook his head. "Not that I've ever seen."

I lowered my voice and leaned in close. "You've been around, Mr. Grage. In the jobs you've held, you saw a lot. What do you think? Is Ingle the kind of guy who could do this—commit murder?"

"If you mean could Mr. Ingle kill those women the way they were butchered?" Reggie looked at me, then Tip, and then he shook his head. "No. Mr. Ingle can be a son of a bitch, but in my opinion, there is no way he did this."

"Why do you say that?" I asked.

"He doesn't have the guts," Reggie said, and he didn't hesitate.

"What about Tom Marsen?" Tip said.

"No comment."

"If you had to pick—Marsen or Ingle?" Tip said.

"No comment," Reggie said, then he stood. He pulled out a $20 bill and tossed it on the table. "It's time for me to go, Detectives. If you have more questions, please contact Mr. Rengster."

Reggie left the bar, and never bothered to look back. I had a feeling we had gotten all we would out of him. I looked at Tip and then said, "You hit a nerve with the Marsen comment."

"A big nerve. Maybe we're looking at this all wrong."

"I hate to think that, but I'm afraid you might be right."

"It all starts back in East Texas," Tip said. "I think we need to dig a little deeper, see what we come up with."

"You know who to call?" I asked.

Tip tossed $20 on the table and then, almost as an afterthought, another $10. "I know who to call," he said. "I sure do." And then we headed for the door.

"You have beer at your place?" Tip asked.

"Plenty. Maybe even enough to help us figure this case out."

"Then that's where we're going," Tip said. "We need all the help we can get."

We got to my house in about half an hour, but after three beers each and another hour of dissecting the case we hadn't made any headway. We knew Camwyck was blackmailing either Ingle or the president, or both, but we weren't certain of what the blackmail was about, and both of us were convinced it was about a lot more than sex.

I gathered up our empties, dumped them in the trash bag, and went to the fridge for refills. "There's no way *anybody's* killing someone—let alone two someones—about a little sex. Not these days."

"We've already been through this, but if it's not sex, what *is* it about? What's on that video that made it worth millions of dollars?" Tip asked.

"And this whole *magic* thing," I said.

"When we add that into the picture, it has to be somebody who knew them from East Texas."

"Which brings us back to what we talked about before. I've got to get hold of Buddy and one other guy."

"Buddy? He's the one who can get you the information?"

"We can count on Buddy to dig up some gossip, but to get the real dirt I'm gonna need to pay a visit to someone else. Someone I'd rather not see."

"Who?"

"Guy's retired now. Should be in jail but he worked for all the right people, so he got a pension instead."

"Sounds like a nasty sort," I said. "And what about our mystery caller? What the hell is that about? And who is she? She's got to fit in somewhere."

"We need to figure that out sooner rather than later," Tip said. "She's got something to do with this. And don't forget we'll have that video from Santos tomorrow to analyze, the one with the Dallas victim and the president."

I downed the rest of my beer and said, "I'll tell you what I'd like to see."

"I know what you'd like to see—Mrs. RB Ingle's naked body."

I started laughing and couldn't stop. "She was damn near naked already."

"Damn near doesn't cut it," Tip said. "That last little bit covers crucial territory."

"Crucial territory? Tip, I haven't laughed this much in a long time."

"Speaking of which, don't count on me for anything tomorrow. Elena's coming over, and I told her to bring her sexiest outfit."

The phone rang, and I said, "Hang on, Tip. Let me get this."

I reached for my cell, lying on the table. "Cataldi."

"Mr. Cataldi, this is Earl Vasquez at the rehab center."

At the rehab center?

My heart nearly stopped, or at least it felt as if it did. I held up my hand for Tip to be quiet. "What's wrong, Mr. Vasquez? Is everything okay?"

A silence followed, then, "I'm afraid it's not. We've asked Ron to leave."

"What? Why? What happened?"

"Sir, I hate to be the one to tell you this, but we found drugs in his room. In his possession."

"What! Son of a bitch. That son of a bitch." My fists were clenched and

I could feel my body tightening up. "Goddamn, I'm gonna kill him."

Tip was up and pacing now, close to me.

"What's going on?" he whispered.

I shook my head. "All right. I'll be right down to get him. Keep him there."

"Yes, sir. You can count on it."

I squeezed the phone in my hand. I even considered tossing it, but fortunately found the control not to.

"What's going on?" Tip said again.

"That was the rehab. They found drugs on Ron at the center where he's house manager. He's out." I punched the wall, hard. Then I punched it again. "Mother fucker! I can't believe he did this."

My phone rang again. I punched the button. "What?"

"Dad, it's me."

I felt my skin tighten, as if veins would burst. "What the fuck did you do? How the fuck could you do this? I should—"

Tip grabbed the phone from me and pushed me aside. "Ron, this is Detective Denton, your father's partner. Are you at the center?"

"Yeah, but listen—"

"No time for that. Stay where you are. We're coming to get you."

I was reaching for the phone but Tip shoved me away again. He hung up and said,

"Let's go. We need to get there fast."

CHAPTER 46

A LOST CAUSE

"I'll drive," I said as I slammed the back door.

"Like hell," Tip said. "Get in the car and shut-up."

I cursed Ron a hundred times before we got out of the subdivision, and I hadn't even gotten started.

"Don't rush to judgment," Tip said. "We don't know what happened yet."

"Bullshit," I said. "You don't know what it's like. He's lied to me about a million times. He's a goddamn drug addict. They always lie."

"Can't argue much about the lying. But he's been doing good, or at least you said so. Let's find out what happened first."

A feeling rushed through me, calming me. It was a feeling I'd had too many times before. A feeling of trust. Wanting me to believe in my drug-addict son *just one more time.*

I fought it. I tried shaking it off. But I couldn't. I'd do what Tip said. I'd wait until I heard what Ron had to say.

Tip turned into the parking lot and pulled up to the front entrance. Ron stood outside the building, duffel bag in his hand. He had his scared look; I could tell from inside the car.

"Remember," Tip said. "Hear him out."

I did my best, grinding my teeth as I walked slowly up to see him. He set the duffel bag on the ground. For a minute I thought he wanted to hug me, but if he did he held back.

"Dad, I didn't do it. I swear."

I leveled my gaze at him, but didn't say anything for a moment while I tried to calm myself, then I said, "Tell me what happened."

He started to reach for me again, but put his hands in his pocket instead. "I swear to God, Dad. I didn't have any drugs. I'm clean. Test me."

I almost said, *You bet your ass I will,* but Tip stepped between us. He was calm. Friendly. Unlike the Tip I knew.

He held his hand out. "Tip Denton," he said. "I'm guessing you're Ron."

Ron shook his hand. "Thanks for coming, Detective."

"Just call me Tip," he said, then, "How about telling us what happened."

Ron shook his head slowly. "I'm one of the house managers. I was taking a shower about an hour ago. When I came back to the room, another house manager—a senior one—was standing there with his assistant. They said they were going to search the room, and I said, 'Go ahead.'"

Ron looked at Tip and then said, "The next thing I knew, they were holding up a couple bags of pills. I told him they weren't mine, but he wouldn't believe me."

"And nobody backed you up?" Tip asked.

"Not a soul."

"Goddamn," I said.

Tip nodded. "Gino, how about you stay with Ron. I'm gonna have a talk with the *senior* house manager." He turned to Ron. "What's his name?"

"Earl Vasquez."

Tip started inside, and I followed. "Whoa," he said. "Let me do this one alone."

"Can't do it, Tip. I need to see this guy's face when he accuses Ron."

"Okay, but let me handle it. You watch."

I nodded, and Tip led the way inside.

Vasquez was standing near the front desk, as if he'd been waiting for us. Tip flashed his badge.

"Detective Denton," he said. "You want to tell me what happened here?"

Vasquez puffed himself up a little and moved toward Tip. "We aren't pressing charges. We simply asked Ron to leave. And you're lucky for that—him being an employee and all."

He reached behind him and took a file from the nearby desk, handing it to Tip. "Incident reports are in there, as well as the signed consent to search form. All of it by the book, and as I said, we aren't pressing charges."

Tip tossed the file back on the desk. "I didn't ask if you were pressing charges, I asked what happened?"

Vasquez smiled, but it was fake. "As I said, Detective, nothing to worry about."

Tip looked around the lobby, grabbed hold of Vasquez' shirt and yanked him close. The scar on Tip's face twitched—the way it did when he got pissed. "I'm only asking one more time," he said.

Vasquez quickly broke. He led us to a small office off the left side of the lobby and closed the door after we followed him in. "We got info on where to find drugs," he said.

"What kind of information? Tip asked.

"A note left on the kitchen counter."

"Who left the note?" Tip asked.

"I don't know," Vasquez said.

"So you got an anonymous lead?" Tip asked Vasquez.

"Even if it wasn't anonymous I couldn't reveal the source."

I moved toward him, but Tip's outstretched hand stopped me. Made me think.

"You told Detective Cataldi that you found the drugs under Ron's mattress?" Tip said.

"Taped underneath it, yes."

"And you didn't suspect that someone might have planted them?"

"Why would anyone do that?" Vasquez asked. "I can think of a lot of reasons. Not the least of which is it was another drug addict who wanted to hide drugs, but not use his own mattress. Ever think of that?"

"I guess not." Earl said.

"Did you test Ron?"

"Testing wouldn't mean anything. He could have brought it in to sell."

"How much did you find?"

Vasquez looked at Tip, then over to me. "I shouldn't be telling you any of this. It's—"

"Bullshit is what it is," Tip said. "My partner is Ron's father. If you don't tell me, you have to tell him. Ron's still a minor." Tip grabbed his collar. "Or better yet, I could leave you here alone with Gino and let him ask the questions."

Vasquez opened his desk drawer and pulled out a single piece of paper tucked into a manila folder. He handed it to Gino. "As far as what I *have* to do, this should cover it. I'll file my reports in the morning. In the meantime, here is a list of three alternate facilities that Ron might consider for treatment."

"You haven't answered my questions yet," Tip said.

"And I don't intend to," Vasquez said.

"I guess that's it, then," Tip said, and he turned toward the door. Gino started through first, followed by Ron.

Tip said, "I'll meet you outside, Gino," and then he closed the door.

##

Vasquez backed up a step. "What do you want?"

Tip held out his hand, palm up. "I want your license."

"My license? What for?"

The side of Tip's face curled up into a mean look. "Give me your fucking license."

Vasquez gulped. He seemed to be having trouble swallowing. He pulled out his wallet and handed Tip the license.

Tip took a picture of it with his cell phone. "I hope RB Ingle paid you plenty of money because you're not going to be safe in this city."

"What are you talking about?" Vasquez said. "I don't know anybody named Ingle."

"That's a shame," Tip said. "Because you're not going to be able to drive to the corner store without me crawling up your ass. And one night, when it's real dark and you're on your way home…" Tip laughed. "Well shit, you never can tell what's gonna happen on nights like that."

"You're fuckin' nuts," Vasquez said.

Tip lost his smile. Then he said, "You might be right, but that won't help you." He opened the door and left.

Gino and Ron were waiting in the car. Tip got in and started it up. "Where to?"

"I don't know," Gino said. "I was thinking of checking out these other rehab centers."

"Let me see the list," Tip said.

Gino handed him the list. Tip glanced at the names. "I know two of them and they're not that good. Not sure about the third."

"Shit," Ron said.

Tip pulled out his phone. "I know a great place, but it's on the other side of town. You want me to check and see if they have any beds open?"

"I don't know," Gino said. "This ruins everything. Insurance won't cover any more time in a new facility. Not after failing that one."

Tip smacked Gino on the arm. "For a moment let's run with the possibility that *maybe* they weren't Ron's drugs."

"What the hell are you talking about?"

The tires screeched as Tip rounded a corner to get on the freeway. "Suppose this is RB's work. And don't think I'm off base here. That's the way that son of a bitch plays ball. He's nasty."

Gino's fists clenched, and then his whole body tensed. *If this was Ingle...*

The car swerved and Gino grabbed hold of the door grip, squeezing it for all he was worth. Tip took another turn onto the ramp leading to the freeway.

Pretty soon the speedometer inched past 90, but for the first time since Gino had been riding with Tip, he wasn't worried about it.

"Where are we going?" Ron asked.

It was the first time he'd spoken since he had gotten in the car. "I can't be out, Dad. I'm not ready. The house manager gig was fine, but that was because I was still there every day. I'm not ready to be out in the real world."

"I know," I said. *I know.*

"For now, we'll go to my place," Tip said.

"Ron will be safe for tonight. Nothing to tempt him there; I don't even have beer."

"That sounds like a good plan, but what the fuck am I supposed to do with him in the morning? I doubt that the insurance company is going to help with anything."

"In the morning, I'll call this other rehab and see if they'll take him in. And don't worry about money," Tip said. "They owe me a few favors."

Gino heard what Tip said, but couldn't believe it. This was more than he could ask for.

"What's the name of the place?" Ron asked.

"Into Action Recovery," Tip said. "They're down in Clear Lake."

Gino knew Tip had a lot of connections, but he wondered how good they could be if he could get Ron in on such short notice.

"They're good?"

"They're damn good," Tip said. "Run by a bunch of ex drug addicts and alcoholics. These guys know their shit. Tough, but good. Most importantly, what they do works."

Gino reached over and put his hand on Ron's shoulder. "We'll get you fixed up," he said. "That's a promise."

Tip's driving had improved. He had slowed the speed down to around seventy, which made me feel safe enough to speak. "Tip, why do you think Ingle had anything to do with this?"

"Because I don't believe in coincidences and this is just the kind of stunt he'd pull. He's got the stroke to do it too. Don't get me wrong, I'm not so sure that I'd go shoot him, but I'm not too far from that either."

Gino felt bad for Ron, and he swore to get him fixed, one way or another. *And if Ingle had anything to do with this, I'll get him fixed up, too.*

CHAPTER 47

THE PLOT THICKENS

I sat at Tip's kitchen table with Ron, drinking coffee and praying to God that Tip's instinct had been right—that this was some kind of sick setup by Ingle and not a case of Ron relapsing. I tried convincing myself of that, but experience told me not to get too optimistic.

Drug addicts always lie.

Despite what I wanted to believe, I couldn't afford to let that one truth taint my judgment.

The back door opened and Tip walked in. "They'll take him," he said. "He's got 60 days free."

The news hit me hard, in a good way. I wanted to jump up and hug Tip, but Ron was already doing that.

"Thanks, Mr. Denton," he said. "You don't know how much it means to me."

Tip smiled. "I think I do."

"How do we work this?" I asked.

"We'll pick up your car and anything Ron needs. You take him to the rehab and I'll head downtown. If Ingle did this—and I'm still betting he did—we need to put some pressure right back on him."

"How sure are you that he did this? Last night you seemed pretty sure."

"I wouldn't bet my last dick on it, but I'm confident we're following the right set of tracks."

I grinned while I rinsed out my coffee cup and then I grabbed my phone. "Who do I see at the center?"

"Ask for Tony. He's already got Ron's name."

"Sounds good," I said, and then Tip drove me to pick up my car. "I'll see you back at the station."

***

Tip was on his way in to the office when his phone rang. "Denton."

"Hello, sexy," a sultry female voice said.

"Is this Elena or one of my other admirers?"

The voice lost all resemblance of sensuality. "You'll wish it was one of them when I tell you."

"Tell me what?" Tip said.

"I have to cancel tonight."

"Cancel? What's going on?"

"Everything at once. We've got a councilman giving us trouble about the new building, one of my suppliers is playing hardball on terms regarding a shipment of scarves from Milan—after I thought we had it worked out—and to top it all off, I'm having problems with the state on sales tax issues. They're swearing that I owe thousands more, and want to inspect the books. I'm about ready to jump off a bridge."

The more Elena talked, the more suspicious Tip became. It was too much of a coincidence that she was suddenly having trouble the day after the episode with Ron. He and Gino were closing in on the killer, and now both their lives—or loved ones lives—were being torn apart. "Get me the names of everybody involved."

"I can handle this myself. I don't need the Gestapo."

"Trust me on this. Text me the councilman's name, and the supplier and whoever contacted you from the state. I'll look into it."

Concern seeped into Elena's tone, doused with a healthy dose of suspicion. "Is there something going on I should know about?"

Tip slowed down and moved into the center lane. "There might be. I'll fill you in later."

"All right. I'll text you. Call me when you can say something."

"I will. And keep that sexy outfit handy. This won't take me long to resolve."

Elena laughed. "You've got a one-track mind, Detective."

"It's your fault, darlin'. You look too damn good."

"Hurry up and solve your case," Elena said.

"I'll do it just for you," Tip said, and as he disconnected, he thanked the

Gods for Elena. Not only was she a beautiful woman, but more importantly, she understood things. If he said he couldn't tell her something, she left it at that and never asked again. There was a short time, when he partnered with Gianelli, that he thought there might have been some jealousy, but it disappeared quickly. In fact, Elena and Connie were friends now.

Tip dialed Coop to see what was going on. She answered in her pleasant voice.

"Where are you?"

"Almost there. Why?"

"Shit is hitting the fan down here. Come straight to my office when you get here. Don't even stop for coffee."

Tip checked the rearview mirror and punched the gas to switch into the left lane.

What the fuck is going on?

Charlie passed Tip, who was on his way to Coop's office.

"Morning, Tip. How's that case coming?"

"If you ever figure out the mystery of those lyrics we might catch a break," Tip said. "Get busy."

Charlie shook his head and mumbled something, but he kept walking down the hall.

"Good morning, Cindy," Tip said. "Gladys in?"

Cindy nodded and raised her eyebrows almost to her hairline. That was all Tip needed to know. "If she's in that bad a mood, you better bring both of us tea, but wait about ten minutes."

Coop was hanging up the phone when Tip walked in. "Morning, Captain."

"Good morning my ass. It's anything but a good morning." She moved a few files to the edge of her desk, looked at Tip.

"Where's Cataldi?"

"He had some personal business to take care of. He'll be here shortly. In the meantime, tell me what's got you pissed off."

"I wasn't here ten minutes before the chief called. He said the department had gotten complaints about the way some of my detectives had handled investigations. He even hinted that there was widespread corruption in our department."

"Sounds like bullshit," Tip said. "And I know where it's coming from." He thought of Ron's troubles and then Elena's. Now Coop. There was no longer even an inkling of doubt in his mind of who was behind these problems.

Coop narrowed her eyes and sat. "Pull up a seat and tell me about it."

Tip told her what happened with Ron, and then about the call from Elena. "The way I figure it," Tip said, "the only person powerful enough to pull this many strings, and do it this fast, is RB Ingle."

"And you're sure Gino's boy had nothing to do with those drugs?"

"I'm not sure," Tip said, "but I'd bet money on it. When I mentioned Ingle's name to the house manager, he recognized it, and not from the newspapers." Tip leaned forward and pushed the intercom button. "Cindy darlin', will you bring me some tea, please? And you better get a refill for Gladys also."

That drew the first smile Tip had seen from Coop since he'd arrived. "Besides," he said, "There is no way that Elena's troubles just happened to pop up now."

Coop tightened her lips, her head bobbing. "That son of a bitch is sending us a message."

"That's the way I see it," Tip said. "We hit a soft spot and triggered this."

"The question is which spot did we hit?" Coop said. "I think we're going to have to press harder to find out."

Tip walked around Coop's desk and hugged her. "I knew there was a reason I liked you, darlin'."

Coop pushed him away, but she was laughing. "You're a damn idiot, Denton. Now get the hell out of here."

When Tip got to his desk he saw a note from Julie.

See me about Mano.

He walked to her cubicle and held up the note she had left him. "What's up with Mano?"

Julie looked up from her computer. "We received a call from Laredo. They found his truck a few hundred yards off a back road just outside of town. It had been set on fire. Not much left."

"I don't imagine there's been any signs of Mano?"

She shook her head. "Not a peep."

Tip thought for a moment. "Which means he's either in Mexico or buried next to a cactus."

"I hope he's in Mexico," Julie said.

"Me too, Julie, but somehow I don't think he is."

Half an hour later a package came from Santos—the video. Tip took it to Coop and they sat down to watch it. It started off similar to the other videos, only this one starred Patti in the leading role, along with Tom Marsen.

"Looks like our president gets around," Tip said.

"He always has," Coop said. "He didn't have morals as a kid, and he still doesn't."

The door opened and Cindy came in. "There are people here from the chief's office. They are asking for files."

Coop sat up in her chair. "Which files?"

"Mostly from major crimes, but a few homicides also."

"Which homicides?" Coop's tone had taken on a dangerous edge.

"The Barajas case from last year, the Randolph killings, and the one we're working on—Ms. Camwyck."

Coop looked at Tip. "Those bastards are trying to bury this," she said, and then to Cindy, "Give them the other files, but not Camwyck. Not even copies."

Tip looked over at Coop and flashed a big grin. "Keep this up and I'll have to kiss you, Gladys."

"Try that shit and I'll break your goddamn arm."

Coop and Tip finished watching the video but saw nothing new. Coop leaned back in her chair, hands folded behind her head. "We've got three videos of either Ingle or the president screwing prostitutes who both turn up dead. And we've got blackmail demands." She braced her foot against the desk and spun her chair. "What are we missing? Sure as hell this isn't about sex."

"I agree," Tip said. "I'm still trying to figure out why Ingle would want to be with someone else when he's got Mrs. Ingle at home."

"I'm not going to get down in the gutter with you, Denton, but I do understand where you're coming from. That woman is gorgeous."

"So if it's not about sex, what *is it* about?" Tip said.

Coop got out of her chair and downed the last sip of cold tea. "That's what you and Cataldi are going to find out."

"We might ruffle a few feathers."

"I don't give a shit if you pluck them naked," Coop said. "Find out who killed those women."

"You got it," Tip said.

On the way to his car he called Gino.

"Cataldi."

"Where are you?"

"I just left the rehab. They were fantastic. Had everything ready."

"Great. I knew they would, they're a good group of guys."

"You ready for this? In the few hours you've been gone, they're busting ass on Elena and Coop. This son of a bitch is pulling out all the stops."

"Elena? Are you shitting me?"

"I'm not. I think they're trying to distract us, but more importantly, send us a message that the game just got serious."

Gino was quiet, then, "Son of a bitch, Tip. Maybe Ron really didn't do it."

"You stupid shit. I told you he didn't. I wouldn't have called in a favor if I thought he did."

"Goddamn!" Gino said. "Where are you? I'm 30 minutes from the station."

"Forget that. I'm going to see an old buddy of mine. I think you should go see Mrs. Ingle again."

"Mrs. Ingle?"

"That's right. Stop and buy a few rubber bands and maybe take a cold shower, but get over there and put on the pressure. We need her to break RB's alibi for the night of Camwyck's murder."

"On my way, partner."

CHAPTER 48

RUNNING SCARED

Tip hung up from Gino and hurried out the door, forsaking coffee. He'd been thinking of calling old George, a retired cop who knew everything that went on in the old days. When George was young he might have been in on most of it, but as he neared retirement he cleaned up and played it straight.

A quick phone call would tell Tip if it was worth the effort to go see him. He looked up George's number and dialed, letting it ring seven or eight times before someone answered.

"What the hell does somebody want?"

Recognition came instantly even after all these years. "George, is that you, you mean crotchety old bastard?"

"Who's this?"

"Tip Denton. Remember, I—"

"I remember you. The last time I saw you, you were nothing but a little fuckhead trying to push your way to the top and askin' people too many questions."

"I guess some things never change."

George laughed. "What are ya' calling me for?"

"I need information."

"IIuh. Everybody needs information. Go do the Google on it, or whatever the hell that is they do now."

"I need to know things about Rusty and the old crew."

Tip sat silent through a long pause, then George mumbled into the phone. "You know where I live?"

"I do."

"Well, I'm here, goddamnit. Come on down."

George lived in the Heights, an old section of town that used to house the white-collar types, but it deteriorated and then went on a roller coaster ride of ups and downs, shifting between high-crime district and the newest place to be. Lots of people had tried to get George to move out of there, but stubbornness and George had found each other long ago and they both seemed to like the relationship.

Tip pulled off the freeway, went down Yale Street then across 17th. He spotted George as he made the turn, sitting on the front porch, rocking.

He parked, got out and made his way up the sidewalk. "Morning, George."

Tip thought he heard a mumbled response, but he couldn't be sure. It might have been *go to hell.* "Thanks for seeing me."

"What do you need to know about Rusty?"

George wasn't one to waste time on unnecessary words. "We're working a case and the list of suspects brings us back to Rusty or his wife or their friends."

"Who's we?"

"Me and my partner, Gino Cataldi."

George reached over and took a sip of iced tea from what looked like a quart mug. It had the state of Texas image on one side and the flag on the other. "Your partner, he a Mexican?" The way he said *Mexican* pissed Tip off.

"He's Italian. What difference does it make?"

"Italian. Mexican. Same thing. Foreigners are ruining this country."

Now Tip remembered why he didn't like George, and why he hadn't been to visit him since he retired.

He didn't want to remind George that the US pretty much stole this land from the Mexicans. He didn't want to but he did, despite needing the information. Tip reminded George of that, then he called him a cranky old fuck and warned him he'd likely die alone in that rocker.

George sat and stared at Tip, probably wondering whether to tell him to fuck himself or eat shit and die. It surprised Tip when he did neither. "How far back you want to go regarding these tales about Rusty?"

"As far as your memory takes you, but I *do* have to get to work today."

George thought for a moment, as if running through a Rolodex of names in his head, then he nodded real slow, almost in rhythm with his rocking.

"There was a young cop named Edgar Harbough who used to work downtown. The man was as dirty as week-old underwear. A lot of rumors followed him around, but the one that seemed to hold the most water was that Rusty pulled Ed in and out of his back pocket as needed. And back then he was needed a lot."

"What was going on?"

George gestured to a chair beside him. "Sit. This could take a while."

Tip dragged the rocker over and sat opposite George, careful not to block his sun.

"I guess we should focus on Tom Marsen; he was the one who climbed the highest."

"How do you know so much about this?"

George stopped rocking, grabbed a cigar from the table beside him and lit it using a long match stick, the kind popular forty years ago. "I'm not going to ask if you mind, because I don't rightly care if you do."

He puffed a few times to get it started, then continued with his rocking. "Anyway, you asked how I knew about this. I was crooked as the Buffalo Bayou back then, as I'm sure you've heard. I did about everything but murder, and I can't swear I wouldn't have done that if someone offered me enough, or even if they offered me a little and I'd had a lot to drink. And back then I'd always had a lot to drink."

Tip let him stop and start at will. No sense in interrupting.

"Houston politics was a mess, and Rusty Johnson and Paul Grayson ran a nice piece of the show. They called themselves the magic act."

Tip stopped rocking and sat up attentively. "What did you say?"

"I said they called themselves the magic act," George said, and his voice cranked up a notch or two.

Tip thought for a moment, realizing it might have been Grayson, not Gladys, that represented the "G." He nodded to George. "Go on. I'm sorry."

"Rusty was a councilman and Paul Grayson was a captain on the force. They had a lot of contacts. But it wasn't until Cybil got involved that things heated up. She's the one who brought Tom Marsen and RB Ingle into it."

George stopped to sip his tea, then started right up. "Tom was a young pup, fresh in from the countryside. His rise in the political world was the result of him coming under Rusty's wing, and that was the result of Cybil coming under Rusty—if you know what I mean. It's been whispered that Rusty used a stable of young women to extract favors and commitments from supporters; some even said he resorted to blackmail."

George puffed hard on his cigar and looked at Tip. "What they didn't know was that Cybil was the brains. She knew how easy it was to get men to do things with a little sex, or even the promise of it. Combine that with a hint that it might get out, and she had herself a fistful of opportunity. She put together a bevy of sharp, witty, sexy young girls who didn't mind doing what had to be done, as long as the rewards were there. And when dealing with the clientele Rusty provided, rewards weren't the problem.

"Her first *girl* was one she knew from back in East Texas; in fact, she had me go fetch the girl and bring her here. I still remember how long her legs were, and how sassy that girl was. It took Cybil six months to train her to speak proper and learn how to talk to the kind of clients she'd have, but it paid off. This one was sweet as pecan pie."

"Do you—"

"Remember her name?" George laughed. "Like I remember my first time—Barbara Camwyck. She could send a man to heaven in ten minutes and leave him dreaming about it for weeks."

"Or years."

"What's that?"

"Nothing. I was just thinking."

"Anyway, it wasn't long before Cybil and her girls gathered enough dirt on the businessmen and politicians to give Rusty and Grayson an unbeatable edge."

"How did Marsen fit in?"

George shook his head, as if he didn't want to talk about it. "That boy was a mean one. Nasty as a cottonmouth. He rode up on Rusty's coattails, but he wasn't content to wait his turn. He convinced Barbara to seduce Clyde Bannick, who was a senator at that time. When they got what they needed, they blackmailed him."

"An affair seems like mild stuff to hold as blackmail."

George scoffed. "You're not giving that Camwyck girl the credit she deserved. She could not only suck the soul out of a man, she had a way to extract every secret he had. She could pull out a secret tucked up a man's ass for ten years. Some said she could extract things a man had forgotten about. Once she got what she came for, she reported back to Cybil."

"What did she have on Bannick that was so incriminating? Did he like young girls or something?"

"It wasn't the girls he was embarrassed of."

"Boys?" Tip asked while he sat forward to wrote notes.

George nodded. "And he liked 'em when they were too young to grow hair."

Tip scooted his chair to the side, getting it out of the sun, which was shaping up to be a typical Texas heater. He glanced at his watch as he settled back in his seat.

"I know. It's getting late and I'm getting windy. I'll wrap it up for you." He took a big puff on his cigar. "Barbara was the one who got the information, but it was Tom who decided how to use it. In this particular case, Cybil didn't want nothin' to do with it. Gotta give her credit on that. She even fought over what to do, but Tom and Barbara were set on climbing that mountain."

George pulled a match and fired up the cigar again. "I delivered the demand to Bannick. He was more than willing to pay money, but Tom wasn't satisfied. He wanted the money *and* Clyde's council seat, which meant Clyde had to step down."

George stopped rocking, and took a long sip of tea. "That night Clyde Bannick killed his wife and daughter, then himself."

George shook his head and took another long, slow drag on the cigar. "It was then that I quit, Tip. That's when I decided to go straight."

"And we elected this man president…" Tip sat back in the chair, thinking what a sad world it was, then, "What happened with Marsen?"

"With Rusty's support, and of course, Barbara's blackmail, Tom got elected to Clyde's seat. His political career was launched."

"Son of a bitch."

"He *was* that. That and a lot more. And now he's our fucking president."

Tip took a long pull on his mug. "What did Grayson get out of this? Besides money, I guess."

George looked at Tip and shook his head. "You don't know nothin', do you?"

"George—"

"I know you're itching to go, but sit back and listen for a minute."

Tip leaned back and tried to appear relaxed, but this story had him worked-up.

"Grayson had a problem with hookers. He'd been stuck on prostitutes since he worked vice. And then one of them got pregnant." George twisted his face into a scowl. "As nasty as that man was, he wouldn't abandon his daughter. He put her in an orphanage, and when he felt she was old enough, he arranged to adopt her—of course that wasn't until she was a young teenager.

Grayson wasn't much as a father though, and it wasn't long before she started running with the wrong crowds, and got pregnant." George stopped again to drink more tea. "Paul Grayson nearly had a stroke. He chased her boyfriend out of town and arranged for her to marry a proper man—although a lot of people would dispute that assessment—RB Ingle."

Tip leaned forward. "I'll be goddamned."

"I'm sure you will," George said. "But that's what happened."

Tip wrote a few notes on a pad he had in his pocket. "George—"

George got up from his rocker and limped toward the front steps. "I know. I know. You got to go now that you got your information. But that's all right. I didn't expect no more. It was nice to have someone to talk to. Now, help me down these steps so I can water the yard. I don't want it to shrivel up and die, like me." He shook hands with Tip, offering a firmer grip than Tip expected. "I appreciate you stopping by, no matter the reason."

"No problem. I'll come by again," Tip said, and as he walked toward the car he heard

George called him. "What's that?"

"I said, you were right. I *am* a cranky old fuck. But if you don't mind talking to one, come by and visit again."

Tip smiled, and called back over his shoulder. "You can count on it, old man."

"And make it before I die."

Tip waved as he got into the car. He pulled out his phone and made a note to follow up on Grayson and on Clyde Bannick. And then he put a reminder on his calendar to call George three weeks from now and come for a visit.

Nobody deserves to die alone.

CHAPTER 49

WHO ARE YOU?

I headed back to the station to pick some things up, and then went straight to Ingle's house. Tip must have felt like he could get a good lead from his friend George, or else he'd have waited and come with me just so he could get another look at Anne Ingle. Memories of her in that bathing suit popped into my mind.

I think I'd have let George wait.

I pulled up to the house and parked. The limo was in the drive. I hoped that didn't mean RB was home. I rang the bell, expecting to see the maid at any minute, but when the door opened I was greeted by Reggie.

"What can I do for you, Detective?"

"I'm here to see Mrs. Ingle."

He stepped aside, and I walked in.

"Come with me," Reggie said.

I followed him, joined by Ingle's dog as we passed the dining room on our way to the study. Mrs. Ingle sat on the sofa reading a magazine. The dog jumped up on the cushion next to her. It wasn't much bigger than a basketball, not like Tip's dogs.

I reached to shake her hand but she remained seated and offered no handshake. *So much for my dreams of her being an irresistible warrior and wanting to ravish me.* "Detective Cataldi, what brings you back here?"

"I have a few more questions."

She nodded to Reggie, who left the room and closed the door.

"Mr. Ingle isn't here?" I said, looking around as I did.

"He's working, but he sent Reggie by in case I needed anything." She was petting the dog, but stopped to reach for a glass of water. "You said you have questions?"

"We need to clarify some things on the night of Ms. Camwyck's murder. I thought you could help with that."

The dog nudged her arm and her drink spilled. She jumped up. "Fluffy! Look what you've done."

She brushed off her skirt, then went to the door and opened it. "Manuela, please bring a towel."

The maid came running, and from the expression on her face, I wondered what the reprisals were for not rushing.

"Fluffy spilled my drink," Anne said.

Manuela handed her towel, and then hurried to the sofa and began wiping it dry, then patting Anne's clothing dry.

Before leaving, Manuela scooped the dog up in her arms. "You come with me, bad dog."

Anne took a seat at the other end of the sofa—the dry end—and flashed me what I perceived to be a fake smile. "Sorry about that, Detective. If you've ever owned a dog, I'm sure you understand."

"I don't own dogs, but my partner has several, so yes, I do understand."

I waited a few seconds then said, "What can you tell me about the night of the murder?"

She leaned against the back cushion, crossing her legs as she did. "If I remember, we got to the club about 7:32. Shortly after midnight, Reggie informed me we'd be leaving. We left at 12:24, if memory serves me right."

I wrote down what she told me. "And Mr. Ingle was there all night?"

"As you know there were a lot of people who attended. I can't vouch for Bob's whereabouts every minute, but I did bump into him now and then."

"You have a pretty good memory, Mrs. Ingle—recalling what time you left down to the minute. Saying 12:24 is rather odd. Most people would just say 12:25, you know, round it up."

She chuckled. "I spent too many years in an orphanage run by Catholic nuns. They have a way of drilling things into your head."

My own memories from Catholic school brought a smile to my face. "Tell me about it." I was about to say something else when the sound of her yelling *"Fluffy! Look what you've done,"* came to mind.

Fluffy.

And what she just said about the orphanage…it reminded me of what the mystery caller said that night on the phone, about the fire, and going upstairs and down the long hall. And about the girl never saying it was her sister, and of the shoes she couldn't replace for a week.

And of a dog named *Fluffy*.

Suddenly Anne's accent seemed *very* familiar. I narrowed my eyes and looked at her from a different perspective.

Could she *be the caller?* As ludicrous as it sounded for RB Ingle's wife to be the caller, I had to give it a shot. "Do you still like expensive shoes?"

She had been in the process of situating herself on the sofa, but when I said that, she whipped her head around. She quickly recomposed, but not before a flicker of surprise registered on her face. She blushed, then lowered her head. "Detective, I'm sure a lot of people like expensive shoes. Just what are you implying?"

There was no way I could stop now. She didn't get that look on her face for nothing. "I'm not implying anything. I asked if you still liked expensive shoes."

She cocked her head to the side, just a little, and stared at me from a different angle. "As in…"

"As in Ferragamo shoes. As in the story you told me about the fire at the orphanage and your dog at that time—who was also named Fluffy. I'm assuming you named this one after in honor of the one you had in the orphanage."

For the longest time she sat still, then she nodded. "When did you figure it out?"

"When you mentioned the orphanage. Combined with Fluffy it struck a chord.

She smiled, but it looked as if it were a fake smile, too quick, almost as if she was angry at herself. "I *knew* it was wrong as soon as I said it." She moved to sit in a chair and folded her hands in her lap. "It seems we have a *lot* to discuss."

"A whole lot," I said. "I think I'll take that drink now."

"I don't remember offering you one."

"You didn't but I'll take it anyway."

She got up and fixed drinks then took her seat in the chair.

I sat, dumbfounded, wondering where to start.

Did I hear right? Did she admit to being the mystery caller?

"Ask away," she said. "I'll answer your questions."

Her revelation was so unexpected that I didn't know where to start, so I opened my mouth and let words fall out. "Why did you call *me*?"

"I discovered you were on the case. From what I'd heard you seemed…honest, so I chose you."

I tasted my drink, then took another sip before I got the nerve to continue. "How did you know about Ms. Camwyck?"

She took a long swig—enough to tell me she'd had more than a few drinks in her day—then she stared at the wall before turning to face me. "My husband was having an affair with her, as you know. I knew too. It had been going on for a long time."

I gulped. I couldn't help it, but I did. "How did you find out about it…the affair, I mean."

She hesitated again, thinking before speaking. I would do well to learn that trait. "I knew about many of his affairs, but when I saw the pictures in the paper, I…" She got up and fixed another drink.

"Another for you?"

"No thanks."

She walked back, handed me a drink I hadn't asked for, and sat in her chair, leaning forward. "When I saw that picture in the paper I panicked. At first I didn't know what to do. I was horrified. Then I felt a great rush of anger…then I felt pity—for her." She shook her head. "That poor woman. What someone did to her."

I waited a reasonable amount of time, at least I thought it was, then continued with my questions. "And you recognized her from the picture in the papers? The one in the Chronicle?"

She nodded. "As soon as I saw it."

"Did you say anything to your husband? About the affair, I mean?"

She rested both hands on her knees, wrapped around the glass. "His relationship with Barbara Camwyck had been going on far longer than I care to think about. From what I've learned, it started before we were married, and it never stopped."

"And all this time you've said nothing?" I realized how stupid it was of me to say that, but not until after the words left my mouth.

She narrowed her eyes, but then they softened, almost as if she forgave me. "I hope your marriage was a good one, Detective—yes, I know your wife passed—and that you never experienced the pain I've been through. But if it wasn't, or if you have someone close to you that has been through this…then you'd know. After a while, *saying* something does nothing but agitate the situation."

Her hands were shaking. For a moment I was afraid the glass she gripped might break. "I felt infuriated…then hurt, then jealous…" She looked down at her knees, then back at me. "Eventually I believe it grew into guilt. Somehow, Bob's indiscretions caused *me* to feel guilty. How that happened I don't know, but happen it did. Soon, I was less than a woman. I was nothing but a rich man's mute wife."

I thought I saw a tear in her eye. I wanted to hold her and tell her it wasn't her fault, that she didn't deserve this…but I sat there, silent. I no longer saw her as a sexy woman, or an object of desire, or even as a rich businessman's wife—she was a person in need, and I wanted to comfort her.

I took a deep breath, trying to figure out how to ask the next question. "How did you know about the dress…and the shoes?"

She stared at her glass, as if it could provide the answers, then she looked at me. "She was at a party for Rusty the night before. She wore a blue dress and Ferragamo shoes."

"That was the night before she was killed."

"I know," Anne said. "I do remember she left early. Perhaps she met someone, or maybe Bob asked her to leave. I wouldn't be surprised if she didn't meet one of her clients there and then leave."

I jotted down notes. "I have to ask, Mrs. Ingle, was your husband at the event the *entire* night? Do you recall him leaving at *any* time?"

"Do you mean at the club, or the private party the night before?"

"The club. The night Ms. Camwyck was killed."

She took a moment, perhaps to gather her thoughts. "As much as I'd like to say he slipped out…to my knowledge he didn't."

"Do you know of anyone who would have wanted to harm Ms. Camwyck?"

Her eyes took on a hard glare. "Do you mean besides my husband?"

I tried a fake smile, but I knew it didn't work. "Yes, ma'am. Besides him."

"I hope your notebook is empty." Her face seemed to harden and her voice dropped. "Let's start with Cybil and Rusty Johnson. I'm sure you're familiar with them."

I nodded while I wrote.

"Add Randy Beaucamp to the list."

She must have seen the look on my face, because she immediately expounded on her statement.

"Randy is one of the biggest campaign donors to Texas politicians."

"Why would Randy have a motive?"

"I'm surprised at you, Detective. Ms. Camwyck was one of the biggest cogs in that political wheel *ya'll* call the good old boys network."

She had switched to the accent she used when she called me, and I had to admit it was pretty damn good, if a bit exaggerated for this occasion.

Anne downed the rest of her drink, but still clutched the glass in both hands. She seemed to be a broken woman. When she spoke again, it was with a new resolve.

"Barbara Camwyck had more ambition than anyone I know, with the exception of Bob and Tom Marsen. She worked for Tom when he was a senator; she worked for Rusty; and she worked for anyone else who could pay her fee—including my husband. In the end though, she proved to be a master at extracting secrets from the men she bedded. She made herself rich from those secrets, and she made Rusty and Cybil powerful. Eventually she built a business out of providing young girls to powerful men." Anne stood and paced a moment. "Didn't you wonder how she earned that condominium?"

I slipped into detective mode before I realized. "And *you* didn't have a motive?"

Anne smiled. "I'm flattered, Detective, in a way. Insulted in another. But I *was* at the event all night. And I was in Houston when the woman in Dallas was killed. I have any number of people who are able to vouch for my whereabouts, and as to motive, other than her having sex with my husband, I had no reason to murder Ms. Camwyck or the other woman." She sighed.

"And while that is deplorable, it certainly is no reason to kill someone."

Her tone sounded like a teacher admonishing a student. I'm sure I blushed. "I had to ask," was all I managed to give as an apology. "Who else might be suspects, or should I say, have a motive."

"Ralph Duerr, Billy Watkins, Emerson Dodds…" She walked to the bar but just got water. "There are too many to list. You can add any male who has been in Houston politics for the past 20 years and you'd have a starting point. That list, of course, includes my husband."

That was the third time she mentioned her husband had motive. I made sure to put that in my notes. "And the mayor and his wife. You mentioned them first…any reason?"

"If you mean other than the fact that Rusty had been sleeping with Barbara since she was seventeen…"

"Son of a bitch!"

"Precisely my point. Barbara was a person who used whatever information she had to get what she wanted. How would it look if Houston's mayor was involved with a teenager?" She lifted her head toward the ceiling, as if thinking. "I believe they call them hebephiles, at least according to Google."

"Excuse me, ma'am."

"I'm sorry. I was ranting. A hebephile is one who is attracted to adolescents. Rusty Johnson falls squarely into that category. From what Bob told me, Rusty preys on them."

"So you think the mayor could have done this?"

"I don't know what to think. I only know that this investigation threatens to expose a lot of people, including my husband, as adulterers. By itself that would be embarrassing, but not catastrophic; however, it also threatens to expose them as potential conspirators in blackmail operations and political corruption." She raised her eyes to the ceiling again, this time with a sigh. "I believe you can figure the rest out, Detective."

I scribbled a few more notes, then pressed her with the question that had been bugging me since the first time she called. "Why were you so interested in the time of death?"

I expected a stalling tactic, something to give her time to compose herself and come up with a response. But she answered right away—almost too fast.

"I had to know the time of death so I could be certain that RB wasn't involved." She paused and took a deep breath. "After I was certain it couldn't have been him, I gave you the clues."

That took me by surprise, but it made sense. "If you recognized Camwyck, surely your husband did." I put it out there and waited for her to respond.

"I can't speak for RB," she said. "Or for Cybil, or Rusty, or any of the others who must have recognized her—including your captain. All I can tell you is that the relationship between all of them was fragile at best. Considering what went on in those days—with the blackmail and prostitution—there is little wonder they didn't come forward. Who wants to be associated with a prostitute?"

She was right. Knowing what I do now, there was no way any of those people were going to admit an association with a dead prostitute.

I looked into her eyes, stared at her lips, and risked a quick glance to those legs, bestowed upon her by a god or goddess. I had a rotten feeling in my gut telling me something was wrong, but I couldn't put my finger on it and I didn't trust myself to reason it out. Not with her so close to me. I decided to play this out and see where it went. After a deep breath, I did my best to hold her stare then stabilized my voice.

"How would you continue with the investigation if you were me?"

Anne thought for a moment, then as she started to answer there was a knock at the door.

"Come in."

Reggie Grage poked his head in and spoke in a voice that seemed just loud enough to reach us but probably not five steps beyond. "We need to be going. Mr. Ingle called and I have to pick him up early."

She looked at her watch and nodded. "I'll be one minute."

Grage closed the door and exited.

I stood, not knowing what to anticipate.

"I have to leave, but we can continue this whenever you want. Just call me."

As I stepped toward the door, she called me back.

"Can we keep this private? This talk?"

This was an interesting twist. "Why?"

She looked to the door, as if checking to see it was still closed. "As you have probably gathered, my husband isn't the man the public thinks he is. In fact, he's…" She shook her head. "Never mind. Forgive me for asking. I know you have a job to do."

She started for the door and I grabbed her arm. "Has he hit you?"

"For God's sake, no." She said it, but I didn't believe it. Not even a little bit She had a look of fear in her eyes when I mentioned it.

"I can keep it quiet," I said. "At least for now."

She closed her eyes and sighed. Then she took my hand in hers and whispered, "Thank you."

Reggie was waiting to escort me out. As we walked through the house, I said, "Are you going to tell Ingle I was here?"

"No," he said, and then he opened the front door.

As I walked to my car, a lot of thoughts popped into my mind. The first was wondering if Reggie really was a robot, but more importantly, I had to figure out what was going on with Mrs. Anne Ingle. If she was telling the truth, I felt sorry for her.

If she's lying…we still have a lot to figure out.

I got into the car and started it, then drove off. A few blocks away, I pulled to the side of the road. Something had been bugging me and I wanted to check it out. I opened the notebook to the page where Tip and I had questioned Reggie. He said Ingle got there at 7:32 and left at 12:24. A rush of adrenaline raced through me.

I knew it!

The times Reggie gave us were identical to the answers Anne gave—down to the minute. *Nobody* is that good on memory, not without a reason.

CHAPTER 50

CATCHING UP

As I drove home, I thought a lot about the Camwyck investigation, and my visit with Anne Ingle, which put a new twist to a strange case. I dialed Tip's number.

"Hey, partner. Where are you?"

"Just left Ingle's house."

"Did you remember to take off the rubber band?"

Tip could always make me laugh. "I didn't need to use it, asshole. But there is a hell of a lot to talk about."

"I got a big list myself," Tip said. "Come up to my house and we'll mull things over."

"I'll need directions."

"Directions? You were just here last night."

"I know, but my mind was elsewhere."

Tip texted the address, which I plugged into the phone's GPS. "I'll be there in half an hour," I said.

"Bring beer," Tip said and hung up.

I parked in the driveway and walked up to Tip's back door without a single bark or growl to alert him I was there. Before I could knock, Tip opened the door and grabbed one of the six packs from my hand. "Come on in, partner."

I looked over to see his Australian Shepherd sitting on the sofa. She fixed me with a hard glare and a growl, but didn't bother moving.

"That's Flash, in case you don't remember. Pay her no mind."

"Where's Sacco?" I asked.

"He's in the kitchen, under the table."

When I walked in, Sacco looked up and wagged his tail. "I hope you're not counting on these dogs for protection," I said. "Flash growled, but Sacco hasn't moved."

Tip laughed. "Flash wasn't growling; that was a smile."

I put the beer in the fridge and took a seat at the table. "Who's going first?" I said.

"Might as well be you," Tip said, and popped the top on his beer.

I gave him a sideways look. "That beer is still hot. I just put them in."

Tip shrugged. "I don't mind if the beer doesn't."

"Whatever suits you," I said. "By the way, I found out who the mystery caller is."

"What?"

"Anne Ingle," I said.

"Bullshit."

I shook my head. "I'm serious. We were talking and she said something that made me suspicious. I asked her, and she admitted it."

"Son of a bitch!" Tip said. "What the hell?"

"That's not all. She gave us a whole new list of suspects." I opened my notepad and flipped to the page. "Ralph Duerr, Billy Watkins, Emerson Dodds, Randy Beaucamp. Those names mean anything to you?"

Tip took a quick sip of his beer. "Some of the biggest names in Houston politics, or should I say political fundraising."

"Hold on to your ass because the rest of the list gets better. Rusty and Cybil Johnson, Bob Ingle, and Tom Marsen."

"That *is* interesting. I know we were already looking at them as potential suspects, but when someone else—especially someone close to the case— gives you the same information, it carries more weight. My big question is still the same though—*why.*"

"Hold onto your ass. I'm getting to that." I opened the fridge and grabbed one of those disgustingly hot beers. "I was as confused as you, but Anne said Camwyck and all the rest of them were involved with blackmail for political favors. I know that blackmail isn't a definitive reason for murdering someone, but it's a lot closer than sex."

I looked over at Tip. He was nodding his head.

"I'm convinced this isn't about sex," I said. "This is about criminal operations and blackmail."

"It all fits, Gino. Old George told me the same kind of tales, but even worse."

"What could be worse?"

"You haven't been around long enough to remember this, but back in the day, Clyde Bannick was a big name in town. He was a US Senator and he ran Houston's politics with an iron grip. Then one day he up and killed his wife and daughter, and then killed himself. No one knew why."

"Hold on," I said, and downed the rest of my beer, then got refills for both of us.

"I'm guessing George filled in details on the 'why' part."

"Blackmail," Tip said. "Camwyck had him dead to rights on molesting little boys. They threatened to go public with it."

"Goddamn!"

"According to George, that's what pushed Rusty and Tom Marsen to the top in this city."

I let the information run through my mind for a minute, and then said, "We've got a 1,000-piece puzzle and we still have a lot to put together."

"I'm not even half done," Tip said, and then he told me about Captain Grayson and the "Magic Act" and about Grayson's daughter—now known as Anne Ingle.

I tried digesting all of this information, but it was a lot to take in. "Do you think Anne has anything to do with the murder?"

Tip downed the beer and crushed the empty can in his hand. "We've got a lot to figure out tonight. And we need to do it fast because RB is putting the heat on everyone."

CHAPTER 51

THE CLUES ADD UP

Tip brought out his charts and made a few notes—quite a few notes—then he stepped back and stared at the chart.

"Looks different now," I said. "As far as suspects go, we have RB Ingle, Tom Marsen, and a file cabinet full of Camwyck's former clients who had a reason to want her out of the picture."

Tip grabbed another beer. "And let's not forget Mano—who disappeared somewhere near the Mexican border."

Tip put an asterisk next to Ingle's name as suspect number one. "We know Ingle was being blackmailed by Camwyck and, after she died, by Richards. The question is why were they blackmailing him. And why now?"

"Exactly. If she'd been having sex with Ingle for all this time, what changed?"

"Which leads me back to our theory that these killings aren't about sex," Tip said.

I got up and looked over the files on the table, but nothing new jumped out at me. "It has to be the blackmail operation Camwyck had going on. But that still makes me wonder why she waited until now to do something about it?"

I thought about it for a minute and then grabbed the marker and drew a line connecting Ingle and Marsen. "Here's why," I said. "Because Tom Marsen just got elected, and a blackmail operation would be more than embarrassing to our new president."

"Goddamn," Tip said, "I believe you stepped in some sweet-smelling shit. Ingle and Marsen have been friends forever. I'm guessing that if the president asked Ingle to do something—or have it done—Ingle would do it."

"And if we move into the *have-it-done* territory, I would put Reggie the Robot right at the top of the list."

"What do we know about Reggie?" Tip asked, leaning against the table.

"We know he's an ex-Ranger and he worked for the Secret Service for a short while. And we also know that Marsen recommended Reggie for the job with Ingle."

Tip flipped through his notes. "Do we have alibis for Reggie on the murders?"

"He was at the event for Rusty the night of Camwyck's murder, and he was in Dallas when Richards bought it." I looked through my own notes. "As far as I can tell, we don't have an alibi for Reggie when he was in Dallas. We only asked about Ingle. But Reggie could have done Richards."

"That leaves the night of Camwyck's murder," Tip said. "We questioned a lot of people about where Mano was that night, and we asked about Ingle. But we never established an alibi for Reggie."

I flipped through my notes to find the page when we questioned Reggie about Mano.

"Okay, check this out. These are Reggie's answers about Mano.

"I asked him about Mano and said, 'Did you see him leave?' Reggie responded with, 'Mr. Perez left at approximately 8:30 PM. He was asked to drive several employees home.'

"Then you asked, 'What was he driving?'"

"And Reggie said, 'He drove one of Mr. Ingle's vans. Mr. Perez's truck was at the office.'"

"When I asked if Mano returned, Reggie said, 'He didn't come back. We didn't expect him.'"

Tip thought for a moment then said, "Reggie never said he saw Mano leave. But if Reggie *was* there at 8:30, it would still be possible for him to kill Camwyck and finish the night by taking Ingle home."

I shook my head. "I can't see how. Not and dump the bodies, too."

"You want some pretzels?" Tip asked, and then he grabbed a bag from the pantry and brought it to the table. "As far as dumping the bodies, that could fit into the timeline.

Let's assume Reggie left right after Mano did, around 8:30. He goes to…wherever, and kills Camwyck, dismembers her, and then he cleans up."

I could see where Tip was going. "So Reggie picks up Ingle at 12:24—according to him—drives him home and then goes back to get the body and dump it."

Tip looked my way and smiled. "Reggie could have done it, but if he did, it had to be on orders from RB Ingle or Tom Marsen."

"Or both," I said, and then took a swig of beer and munched on a pretzel while I gave this consideration. "You got any plans on how to deal with this? We've already brought the wrath of God down on us for messing with Ingle. What the hell would happen if we involved Marsen?"

Tip downed his beer and crushed the can. "We let somebody they can't control do it—the press." Tip laughed and picked up his phone.

"You calling Roberts?" I said.

"Let's see if she's got enough balls," Tip said.

CHAPTER 52

THE PRESSURE IS ON

My phone rang while I was in my kitchen making coffee. It was Coop. "Captain, what's up?"

"Did you and Denton have anything to do with the morning headlines?"

I hadn't seen the paper yet, but I knew what she was referring to. "And if we did?"

Coop laughed. "Then for once I wouldn't be pissed off."

"In that case, blame us. But we all might be in trouble if this backfires."

"I'll worry about that," Coop said. "You and Denton see me when you get in."

I hung up the phone and checked the *Chronicle*. Roberts had done her job.

RB Ingle questioned about murder of prostitute.

I called Tip. "You see the paper?"

"Not yet."

"Roberts has balls. I'll give her that."

"Did she do us good?" Tip asked.

"Front page headlines. *RB Ingle questioned about murder of prostitute.* She didn't hold back."

Laughter came through the phone. "I guess we better get to the station. Shit is going to hit the fan now."

I put the phone on speaker and poured another cup of coffee. "I need to stop by Ingle's house first."

"What for?"

"I was looking through my notes last night and I realized she never answered me about why she called the murder in." When Tip didn't respond,

I went on. "Think about it, Tip. She could have shut her mouth and we might never have had anything. So why the hell did she call in the clues about the dress and shoes?"

"It's something to think about," Tip said. "You want me to come to Ingle's house with you?"

"I can handle it. I made a connection last time."

Tip laughed. "Connection my ass. I think your rubber band slipped. You better take two this time."

"You better watch out or I'll tell Elena about your perverted ways."

"She's the one who taught me," Tip said.

"Okay, asshole. I'll see you at the station later."

***

I pulled up to Ingle's house and went through the ritual with the maid. She showed me to the study and offered coffee, but I passed. Anne showed up a few minutes later.

"Good morning, Detective. What brings you back?"

I stood and shook her hand. "As I was reviewing my notes, one thing popped up. I don't know why you called me."

"I think you asked that last time," she said.

I shook my head. "I asked why you called *me* last time. In other words, why me and not Detective Denton or someone else. What I want to know is why you called *anyone*."

She folded her hands in her lap and lowered her head. "I see."

She sat there for a moment, then slowly lifted her head. "I told you I felt sorry for Ms. Camwyck, and I did. What I didn't tell you is *why*."

The maid brought coffee for Anne, and asked me again if I wanted some. "Thanks, I think I will."

She poured me a cup and then left, closing the double doors behind her. I looked to Anne and she continued.

"Not many people know this, but my mother was a prostitute."

I tried to hide my emotions, but I didn't do it well. I felt my eyebrows raise, and I leaned forward—like an old hen waiting for gossip. Anne must have noticed.

"My father kept it a secret. He told everyone my mother ran off, but the truth remained—she was a whore. He was so embarrassed that he put me in an orphanage. My mother tried getting me out but he wouldn't approve of it. Shortly afterward, she died a junkie's death. Years later, after the orphanage couldn't place me anywhere, my father took me in."

She stood, walking slowly across the Oriental rug, onto the hardwood floor, and back. All the while she sipped her coffee.

"It was then that I met Bob Ingle and the rest of my father's *friends*. Bob wasn't a nice man either. Not him, or the president, or Rusty, or any of them. But I had a home, and I was being taken care of. I felt safe, not wondering every day if someone might come adopt me or if I'd be stuck in the orphanage forever, destined to become a nun.

"When I was barely old enough, I became pregnant. The father was a young boy from school, and we were convinced we had fallen deeply in love. We wanted to marry, but my father wouldn't hear of it. It would shame his reputation, he said. So my father married me off to Bob Ingle to cover up the pregnancy." She paused to sip her coffee, and stared right through me. "I still remember what he said, Detective—the exact words. He said, 'I'll be damned if I'll have another whore in this family.' What he said broke my heart. He attacked my mother and me both." Anne used a tissue to swipe a tear. "After my wedding, I never saw him again, not until his funeral."

Anne shook her head, then she shook it again. "I'm sure the wedding was some sort of deal between my father and Bob, but if it was they were good enough not to tell me. Bob pretended as if he loved me—for a while. I quickly learned why. Bob Ingle was thrilled to have a young girl to screw anytime he wanted, and it made it better that I was pretty enough and trained enough, for him to be able to take me out in public. It was the perfect arrangement for Bob. As for me...I was young and stupid. I thought that Bob might actually love me."

My heart bled for this woman. I wanted to say something because I know this had to be painful to tell. "Despite what problems there might have been, it sounds like he did a lot of good for you."

She spun on her heels and shot me a glare. "The only good thing Bob Ingle ever did in his life was take care of my son. For that, I'm eternally grateful. For the rest, he can rot in hell."

My head was spinning. Tip had told me about her being the former captain's daughter, but I didn't know anything about the rest of the story, and I'm guessing Tip didn't either. I finished taking notes then turned to Anne. "So you called because you felt sorry for Barbara Camwyck?"

"Because I felt sorry for her. Because, being Catholic, I despised the thought of her not being buried properly. But most of all because I had to know beyond a shadow of a doubt that Bob had nothing to do with it. I couldn't live the rest of my life with a man who could do…what was done to her."

I waited a moment, then asked the question I'd been wanting to since she started telling me her story. "Are you convinced he had nothing to do with it?"

She gave a thin smile. "Yes, Detective. I am. My husband is a lot of things, but I'm convinced he's not a murderer."

I stood, thanked her, and then she walked me to the door. "Have a good day, Mrs. Ingle."

"You too," she said.

I got in the car and headed for the station. It was time to get Tip and raise some hell with somebody, and I suspected Ingle was on the list since we couldn't go after the president. I called Tip but it went to voicemail. "On my way in, partner. Got a few juicy details to share."

As I turned the corner, I saw Ingle's limo heading in my direction. I turned my head slightly and put the phone to my left ear as if I was talking. It wouldn't be good if Ingle knew I'd been to his house.

CHAPTER 53

9-1-1

I met Tip at the station, and we headed to Coop's office. On the way, I filled him in on my talk with Anne.

"It sounds like the Ingles have a happy home," he said.

"I feel sorry for her," I said.

Coop was standing at Cindy's desk when we turned the corner. Tip raised his voice, and said, "Gino, forget about being such a nice guy. You need to practice being a son of a bitch like Gladys."

She didn't flinch. "I heard your loud mouth, Denton. But if I was half the son of a bitch you pretend I am, you'd be in deep shit."

Coop grabbed a folder from Cindy and turned to face us. "The phone hasn't stopped all morning. Ingle must have been calling people since he got up."

"Who's pressing the hardest?" I asked.

"Rusty's been the worst, but that's not surprising considering what he stands to lose. But I'm getting pressure from the chief, Cybil, the councilman, and quite a few business leaders."

"Damn," Tip said. "Sounds like we stirred the pot with that article in the paper."

"Like you wouldn't believe," Coop said. "I even had a call from the senator."

"The senator! What makes him think he can stick his nose into our case?" I said.

Coop walked into her office and took a seat in one of the guest chairs. "Tom Marsen pulled those strings," she said. "I'm sure of it."

Tip plopped into the chair next to Gladys.

"Don't tell me we're holding off on this."

She shook her head. "Not one damn bit. In fact, I want you to gather every bit of evidence you've got, put it all in order, and bring it to me. I'm taking it to the DA. I want to make sure we're good before moving on this one." She balled her fist and slammed it on the desk. "If that son of a bitch thinks he can run roughshod over me…"

I took the seat across from Tip. "We'll get him. Don't worry about that."

"The question isn't getting him, it's making something stick," Tip said.

"I want Ingle in prison," Coop said. "I know it's a long shot, but we're not going to stop trying."

I filled Coop in on my visit with Mrs. Ingle this morning. "She's convinced that her husband didn't have anything to do with the murders. I wouldn't go that far, but I agree with her that I don't think he did it himself. At least not alone."

Coop nodded. "He might not have done the deed, but he had something to do with it. I'd bet money on that." She looked at me, then Tip. "Either of you have a good suspect?"

Tip stood and stretched. "We think it might have been Ingle's driver/bodyguard."

"Do you really think he's a suspect, or is this just bullshit?"

"I don't know, Captain, but he's our best shot right now. Besides, something's going on. Both victims were blackmailing Ingle, so even if RB isn't involved in the murders, he's guilty."

Coop narrowed her eyes. "And you're betting on the bodyguard. Why?"

"He's a former Ranger and he knows the president; in fact, Marsen is the one who got him the job with Ingle."

"That cinches it as far as I'm concerned," Coop said. "If Tom Marsen arranged his job it was for a reason." She stood and went behind her desk, making a note on her calendar. "Get your files in order and then go question the bodyguard. Let's see what develops."

Tip headed for the door. "Hold onto your ass, Gladys. Before the day's over there might be a lot of people after it."

We left Coop's office and went to work, scrutinizing all of the information in the files and double checking to make sure we had made no mistakes.

"We should pay another visit to Cybil," I said. "She knows a lot more than she's told us and since she knows Ingle from the old days there's bound to be information we need; it's tucked away somewhere."

"I agree, but the problem is going to be convincing her to share," Tip said.

"We'll have to find a way to persuade her," I said.

Tip and I dug in to compile the facts. We were almost finished when the phone rang. I picked it up. "Cataldi."

"We have a 9-1-1 call at Ingle's house. Shots fired. Get moving!"

"Holy shit. We're on it." I hung up and looked to Tip. "That was Coop. There was a 9-1-1 call at Ingle's house. Shots fired."

He grabbed his phone and keys and we headed out.

When we arrived at the house there was an ambulance in the driveway and two patrol cars parked in front, not to mention a gallery of onlookers gawking from behind the line the uniformed officers had set up.

As we walked toward the house, one of the techs from the medical examiner's office was exiting the house.

"Is Ben here?" I asked, and then, "What's it look like?"

"Ben's inside. Two cold, two warm."

Two cold, two warm. I ran it through my mind a dozen times in a few seconds, but the only way it played out was murder suicide. Ingle and Anne were dead, and Reggie and the maid were alive.

Tip picked up the pace. He greeted the uniform at the door and then we went inside. I heard crying as soon as we entered the lobby. When I looked to the left, I saw Anne sitting in a chair, her face buried in her hands, crying. Now I was really puzzled.

Who the hell got killed?

Tip and I went to her.

"Mrs. Ingle, are you all right?" I asked.

She looked up at us, but she was still crying. The left side of her face was bruised and her nose was bleeding, possibly broken.

I knelt beside her. "Are you all right?"

She nodded, slowly. "He's gone. I had to do it." She sobbed. "I thought he was going to kill me."

I looked up at Tip, surprised. *If Ingle was gone…* "Who's gone?" I asked.

"Bob. I shot him."

Tip tapped me on the shoulder and leaned down to whisper, "I'm going to have a look."

"Mrs. Ingle," I said, "Would you like something to drink? Can I get you anything?"

She shook her head.

Just then the ambulance tech came over. "We need to get you to the hospital, ma'am."

I stood and got out of his way. Another tech was coming in the door pushing a gurney.

"We'll talk later," I said, and they wheeled her out.

I found Tip standing next to Ben Marsh, the M.E., who was examining a body on the floor. It was Reggie. "What the hell is going on?" I said.

Tip gestured down the hall. "Ingle's down there. Looks like he tried breaking into the bedroom. She must have shot him when he broke through."

"Then who shot Reggie?"

"We'll know soon enough," Ben said.

"This is a hell of a way to wrap up a case," I said.

Tip nodded. "I'll take it. It's another marble in the box."

I had no idea what he was talking about, and I didn't want to ask now. "We're going to need to question her at the hospital. I don't want too much time to go by." I looked around. "And where's the maid?"

"I sent her out back," Tip said. "Let's go chat with her now."

We walked out the back door. The maid was sitting on the edge of a chair near the center of the pool, rosary beads clutched in her hand.

I extended my hand. "Señora, are you all right? Are you hurt?"

She shook her head but didn't look at us.

Tip pulled up a chair and sat next to her.

"Can you tell us what happened?"

She looked at Tip, then up at me. "Señor Ingle yelling at señora. He say she tell papers about him. She yell back, then he yell louder."

"Where were you?" Tip asked.

She pointed to the study. "Cleaning, but when yelling start, I left. Went to room." She moved one bead up on the rosary. "I don't like when they yell."

I made a note to ask her later if they yelled often, but I wasn't comfortable enough with my limited knowledge of Spanish to ask myself. "What happened next?"

"I closed door on room so I don't hear fighting, but then I hear gun." Manuela shook, blessed herself, then ran her fingers over the rosary beads.

I jotted this down in my notebook. "You heard a gunshot? How many?"

She took her hand off the rosary and used her fingers to count, as if recalling the scene. "I hear one, then two, then one more."

"How much time between the shots?" Tip asked. She looked confused, and Tip repeated the question. "How much time?"

"*No se.* Maybe one minute before two shots. Then maybe one minute again."

"Are you sure?" Tip asked. "A minute is a long time during an emergency. Could it have been less?"

She shook her head. "I think one minute."

"Okay. Then what."

"I stay in room until policia come."

"You didn't call anyone?"

She lowered her head and stared into her lap. "I was afraid."

I didn't know if she meant afraid of the situation or afraid of being found out by immigration, but that didn't matter. "We talk later," I said, then attempted it in Spanish, hoping it was close enough for her to understand. "*Hablaremos más tarde.*"

She nodded. "Si, señor."

I finished making notes, handed her my card, then Tip and I went back inside.

Ben Marsh had moved to examining Ingle's corpse.

"Are we good to come down the hallway, Ben?" Tip asked.

"Not yet."

"Have you figured this out yet?" I asked Ben.

He looked up at me. "Ingle was shot twice. The other one once, close range."

"And there's a slug in the wall," a tech said, and pointed to the wall above where Reggie lay.

"Looks like a missed shot," Tip said.

"I think we need to pay a visit to Mrs. Ingle," I said. "Coop's going to want answers."

CHAPTER 54

THE QUESTIONS NEVER STOP

The ambulance had taken her to Methodist Hospital, the crown jewel of the Texas Medical Center. Traffic had come to a near stop and I could tell Tip was getting impatient—he hated being stuck.

"I'm parking in the first garage we see," Tip said. "We can walk the rest of the way."

"Might be a long walk," I said. "This is the largest medical center in the world."

"No shit?"

"It's true. More than 100,000 people work here."

"You're just full of useless information, aren't you?"

"I should have known you'd have no interest," I said.

Tip turned into a parking garage and started up the ramp. "If I need heart surgery, I'll call you for details."

We found a parking spot on the sixth level, and we made our way to Methodist. When we entered the lobby, Tip whistled softly.

"This looks like a damn hotel," he said.

"And a five-star hotel at that."

After taking a minute or two to look around, we headed up to see Mrs. Ingle. We stopped at the nurses' station before going in.

I showed my badge. "We're here to see Mrs. Ingle."

"Room 1248," she said, and pointed it out for us.

Mrs. Ingle was sitting up in bed, talking on the phone. Her nose was bandaged and a huge bruise covered the left side of her face. When she turned, I noticed her left wrist and forearm were also badly bruised.

She looked at us and held up her index finger, indicating she'd only be a moment.

"Yes, Christopher. Send someone to get him and bring him home now. Make sure to tell him I'm all right. And don't tell him about Bob. Not yet. All right. Thank you."

She set the phone on the nightstand and pressed the button to raise the bed. "I'm trying to get my son home before he hears about this. He's away at boarding school." Anne shook her head. "My God, I don't want him finding out from someone else or reading about it in the news."

"That wouldn't be good," I said, and then, "How are you feeling?"

"Better, thank you. But I still can't believe it happened. It's just…"

Tip pulled a chair from the side and took a seat. I got my notebook.

"If you feel up to it, can you tell us what happened?" Tip said.

"I don't feel up to it, but I know it needs to be done." She reached for a cup of water on the table and took a sip from a long orange straw. She looked over at me. "Not long after you left, Bob came home. I thought it strange that he was coming home at that hour, but as soon as I saw him I knew something was wrong."

"Why do you say that?" Tip asked.

"He slammed the front door, and then he glared at me and yelled very loud. He said, 'Who the hell did you talk to?' When I didn't answer, he shook his fist and said, 'I asked you a question. Who the fuck did you talk to?'"

I wrote what she said, and made note that she seemed frightened while repeating the story—she trembled and her voice cracked. I looked over at Tip, but he wasn't taking notes. He had his *understanding* look on, and he was focused on her.

"What happened next?" he asked.

"I told him I didn't do anything. Then he grabbed my arm and twisted it. It hurt." She adjusted the sling the hospital had fitted to her arm, then said, "I tried hitting him but he twisted harder, and then he punched me in the face."

She closed her eyes and shook her head, barely moving it. "I tried holding him off, but he was crazy. I'd never seen him like this. I told him if he didn't stop I'd tell the reporters about him and Tom blackmailing people." Anne rested her head back against the pillow. "That was a mistake. He got this look on his face, and then he hit me again—real hard." She reached for her nose, touching lightly. "I almost passed out. I kicked him and tried breaking free—that's when he punched me and broke my nose."

"Who was in the house?" Tip asked.

"Just me and Manuela, the maid. I remember she was in the study and she ran out when Bob started yelling. She hates yelling."

"Where was Reggie?" Tip asked.

"I guess he was in the car. Bob probably told him to stay there." Anne looked at Tip.

For a minute I thought she was going to cry. "Reggie came in after Bob broke my nose. He must have heard me scream."

"What happened then?"

"He yelled at Bob to stop." Anne lowered her head. "Thank God he did. It's what allowed me to break free. I ran to the bedroom."

Tip just looked at her, waiting.

"I heard yelling between Bob and Reggie, and what sounded like physical fighting. Then I heard a gunshot. A few seconds later, I heard another one."

Tip sat up and leaned forward. "How much time was there between the shots?"

She took time to think. "I don't know. Maybe ten seconds? I'm not sure."

"Ten seconds? Think about that. Ten seconds is a long time."

She took her time, then said, "No, I think it was about ten seconds."

"What then?" Tip asked.

"I went for the phone in the bedroom. I was going to call 9-1-1, but then I heard him at the door trying to get in. I didn't know what to do. I was scared he was going to kill me, so I got his gun from the nightstand and yelled as loud as I could. 'I'm calling the police.'"

A few tears welled in her eyes. "I thought that might stop him but it didn't. He continued banging the door. It looked as if it was about to break, so I dialed 9-1-1, and told them he was trying to kill me."

She shook her head. "He must have heard me, because he pounded harder on the door. I yelled at him and told him I had his gun. The next thing I knew he kicked in the door." She shivered and more tears fell. "That's when I shot him. God forgive me, but I had to."

"Did he have a gun in his hand at that time?" Tip asked.

She looked from one of us to the other. "I don't know. Maybe…but I don't know." Anne grabbed a tissue from the table and wiped her eyes. "Right after that, the police arrived. I guess 9-1-1 sent them."

"And Reggie?" Tip asked.

"He was in the hall, lying on the floor. Blood was everywhere. I think I even stepped in it."

Tip stood up and moved the chair back where it was. "Mrs. Ingle, that's all we've got for now, but we might have more questions later. I'm sorry for your loss."

She nodded. "I'll be here tonight," she said. "After that, I'll be at the Four Seasons. I'm not staying in that house."

"I understand," I said. "We'll keep you informed."

I waited until we were far enough down the hall so that no one could hear, and then said, "What do you think?"

"I'm not sure," Tip said. "But it seems like she's telling the truth." Tip turned toward me. "Did you see what that son of a bitch did to her? I can't stand a man who hits a woman. He's lucky she did him in."

"Which reminds me of the first day we met her," I said. "I don't know if you noticed, but she had a couple of bruises on her thighs and one on her back. I wondered back then what they were from."

"I remember," Tip said, "But I was too busy looking at other parts of her body. Now I feel bad about that."

"The one thing that puzzles me is the gunshots," I said. "It doesn't match what the maid told us."

We exited the building and started toward the parking garage. "Let's wait until we talk to Ben," Tip said. "We'll see what he has to say."

CHAPTER 55

GUNSHOTS

Coop called while we were driving. "See me immediately," she said. "Don't even stop for coffee."

Julie was ahead of us in the hall, almost racing toward Coop's office. She only walked fast when she was nervous.

"What's up, Jules?" I said.

She turned to look at us, but didn't stop. "Captain Cooper wants to see me, and she sounded upset."

Tip laughed. "Don't worry, darlin'. You'll have us to protect you."

She slowed, waiting for us to catch up.

"You're going to see her, too?"

"She might have half the department in her office," I said. "In case you haven't heard, Bob Ingle is dead."

"That explains why she's upset," Julie said. "But why does she want to see me?"

"We'll find out soon enough," Tip said.

The door to Coop's office opened and she stepped into the hall. "About time you got here. Tell Cindy what you want to drink because it's gonna be a long day."

"Tea for me," Tip said.

"Coffee for me," Julie said. "Cream and sugar."

Before I could say anything, Cindy said, "I know how you like it, Gino."

Chief Renkin was sitting in the chair next to Coop's desk. The frown on his face looked as if it had been etched in there. He nodded to Tip and me, but then he stood when Julie walked in. Renkin was about a foot taller than Julie, and probably twice her weight. She should have been intimidated just by his size, but she wasn't; I think Coop scared her more.

"Good to see you again," Renkin said, and shook her hand.

"Thanks, Chief. Good to see you too."

Coop sat on the edge of her desk and looked at Julie. "We're putting you in charge of a research team to finish going through all of the files associated with these cases."

Julie raised her brows. "Captain, I—"

Coop waved her hand, stopping Julie. "We need to make sure nothing is out of place on this. We'll be under scrutiny from everyone, including the mayor who was a friend of Bob's." Coop looked at Renkin and sighed. "Not to mention the president."

Julie shrunk back. "Maybe you should give this to someone else?"

"We're giving it to you, along with a couple of assistants. Go through all of the records from Camwyck's files and Ingle's. Document everything. You're familiar with our procedures; if *anything* looks out of place, tell Gino or Tip."

Julie had been writing notes. She stopped and looked up at Coop. "Is that all, Captain?"

"That's all. Get the files then see Joyce Huang for whatever help you need sorting this out. Time is critical on this, Julie. I'm counting on you."

Julie started for the door. "I'll get on it right away."

"You can wait for your coffee or tea," Renkin said.

"No thanks. I'm fine."

Tip pulled up a chair that had been sitting against the back wall and offered it to Renkin. "Have a seat, John. What's going on? You here to meddle in my investigation?"

Renkin leaned forward. "I'm here to stress the importance of how we handle the remainder of this investigation—no matter how little or how much that happens to be."

"What the hell is that supposed to mean?" Tip said. "Are you questioning what we've done?"

"I'm not questioning anything. I'm stating facts. We've got a grisly murder that still isn't solved, and now the only real suspect is dead. It's not going to look good."

"I think we can make a good case for Ingle being guilty," I said.

"And that's why I want this to be clean—I mean *clean*. There's nothing more that Tom Marsen would like than to see our reputation smeared."

Coop nodded. "You got that right. It would be just like Tom."

"Now tell us about the scene at the house."

We filled them in on what we saw, the maid's account of what happened, and Mrs. Ingle's account.

"This is a damn mess," Renkin said. "How's Mrs. Ingle?"

"A little shook up," I said, "She took a good beating."

"What's your take?" Coop asked Gino.

"Not sure yet," Tip said. "We'll see after we listen to the 9-1-1 call and get the report from Ben."

Coop slid off the desk and went to her computer. "The Chief already got us the recording of the call. Listen up and take notes."

9-1-1. What is your emergency?

He's trying to kill me.

Stay calm, ma'am. Where are you now?

I'm in the bedroom, but he's at the door. Please send someone. Now!

(Pounding on door heard in background.)

Who's trying to kill you?

My husband. Hurry! Please hurry.

Where is he now, ma'am?

I'm calling 9-1-1.

(More pounding on door.)

Stay out! I've got a gun!

Ma'am, someone should be there any minute. Stay calm. Can you lock yourself in another room?

(Sound of door breaking.)

No!

(Sound of two shots.)

Oh my God. My God, I shot him.

(Line goes dead.)

Coop looked up at me and Tip. "What do you think?"

"Play it again," I said.

We listened to the recording again, and then a third time.

I was shaking my head when we finished. "Sounds legit. It's pretty much what she told us happened."

Tip nodded.

"So things look pretty good?" Renkin asked.

"Everything except the order of the gunshots," I said.

Coop said, "Tell me about the gunshots."

"They don't add up," Tip said. "Mrs. Ingle's version and the maid's contradict each other."

"Son of a bitch," Coop said, and smacked her hand on the desk.

I stood. "We'll have to wait until we hear from Ben. His findings might explain a lot more."

CHAPTER 56

AUTOPSY

We worked at our desks, analyzing notes and, in our spare time, we helped Julie get set up, making sure she had all the files and documents she needed. She seemed nervous.

"Suppose I mess up?"

"Don't worry," I said. "Just go through everything extra carefully."

Tip tapped Julie on the shoulder. "Like Gino said, don't worry. This is nothing that we don't do every day. Coop just wants it extra clean."

Julie smiled. "Thanks."

We stayed where we were, doing paperwork almost all day. Around 3:00, the doctor from Methodist called with the report on Anne. It was pretty much as we expected. Broken nose, left side of face bruised from what appeared to be multiple punches, left arm bruising was from someone squeezing and twisting.

I filled Tip in on what he said. Tip called Ben. "You got anything for us yet?"

"Damn you're impatient," Ben said. "I'll call in about half an hour. I'm wrapping a few things up."

True to his word, Ben called back, but it was more like an hour later.

"I've got Gino with me. I'm putting it on speaker. What have you got?"

"Not everything yet, so take it all with that in mind."

"Go on," Tip said.

"Ingle was like you saw—two shots to the chest at close range. He had gunshot residue on his chest—where he was shot—but also on his hands, which for now, I'm assuming to be the shot fired into the wall and the one in Mr. Grage's heart."

"Does the angle of shots work out? Anything look weird?"

"Preliminary analysis looks consistent with what we know, but as I said before, we're not finished."

"But if you were going to call it?" Tip asked.

"If I were asked to make a call now…I'd say the wife shot Ingle, twice with the gun she showed the police, and before that, Ingle shot Grage with the gun he had in his hand. It looks as if there might have been a struggle for Ingle's gun, and during the struggle one shot went into the wall. The next one hit Grage."

"What makes you think the shootings went down that way?" I asked.

"Both Grage and Ingle have gunshot residue consistent with that theory. And there is a bruise on the left side of Ingle's face that would appear to be from Mr. Grage's right fist."

"That's all good, Ben, but that doesn't fit our theory," Tip said. "The maid said she heard one shot, then two, then one more. If it went down like you said, she would have heard 2 shots followed by 2 more."

A short silence then Ben said, "So now you're siding with a maid over the medical examiner?"

"I'll tell you who I side with later," Tip said. "Just dig some more and see what you come up with. Something's not right about all this."

Tip hung up. He didn't have to say anything. I knew what was coming—a long night of working this case.

"What are you cooking?" I asked.

"Nothing. We'll pick something up. I'm in the mood for some egg rolls from Jack in the Box. And maybe some stuffed jalapeños."

I shook my head. "How is it that your arteries aren't clogged?"

Tip grabbed the files and put them in a briefcase. "Let's go, Gino. I'm hungry already."

We went to the lot, and I said, "While you're driving, think about how a wimp like Ingle wins a struggle with Grage."

"I'll have the answer by the time you get to my house. By the way, what do you want to eat?"

"Jalapeños is fine by me. Order me two packs."

"No egg rolls?" Tip asked.

"Just the jalapeños," I said, and headed toward where I'd parked the car.

It was one of the few days when Tip and I drove separate cars, and I was relieved we had.

I started up the freeway thinking about the case, but before I drove five miles I was thinking of Ron, wondering how he was doing. I desperately wanted to call him, but he wasn't allowed to talk to family yet. Instead, I called Anne, hoping it would take my mind off the worry of drugs.

"Mrs. Ingle, this is Detective Cataldi."

"Hello, Detective. How nice of you to call."

"It's not quite a social call, ma'am. I had a few more questions."

"Of course. How silly of me," she said. I could almost hear her embarrassment. "What can I do for you?"

"I'd like you to think of how much time passed between when you first heard your husband and Mr. Grage struggling and when the gunshot sounded. Take your time."

"I don't know. Perhaps five or ten seconds."

"Five or ten seconds?" I asked.

"My mind is a little fuzzy, but I think that's right. I can't be certain, Detective. I was scared out of my mind. It seemed like an hour, but if you pressured me for specifics, I'd say five or ten seconds."

I waited a moment, then asked, "And how much time between the first and second shot?"

"Like I told Detective Denton this morning—about ten seconds."

"You're sure about that?" I asked. "It couldn't have been five seconds or fifteen?"

She didn't answer right away, then she said, "Definitely not five. And not as long as fifteen. I just timed it myself on the phone, and besides, I do a lot of ab crunches where I hold the position for ten seconds. I'm accustomed to that length of time. I think it was very close to ten seconds, Detective."

"Thank you, Mrs. Ingle. I'm sorry to have troubled you again."

I hung up the phone and her words bounced around in my head. If she was right, Reggie and Ingle fought for about five or ten seconds, and then a shot went off—presumably the one that hit the wall. Then they fought for about ten more seconds before Ingle shot Reggie in the heart.

Not a snowball's chance in hell. There's no way RB Ingle would wrestle a gun away from Reggie the Robot.

CHAPTER 57

BROKEN PUZZLES

Tip was home, sitting on the side porch, when I pulled into the driveway. "Damn you're slow, partner. If you hadn't gotten here soon I was gonna eat your egg rolls."

He tossed me a bag when I reached the porch. "Jalapeños?" I asked.

"Got you both in case you changed your mind. I simply can't believe that anyone could not like Jack in the Box egg rolls."

I took a seat next to Tip and reached in for an egg roll. "I called Mrs. Ingle on the way up."

"And?"

"And she didn't change her story—not even a little bit. That bothered me some. But what bothered me more was thinking about the fight between Reggie and Mr. Ingle."

Tip downed the last of his egg rolls and gulped the rest of his beer. "No way Ingle should have come out ahead if he fought Reggie, an ex-Ranger and Secret Service agent. I guess it *could* happen in an alternate universe, and since Ingle had a gun, maybe it did. Still, I'm with you. The scenario bothers me."

"I don't care if Ingle had a howitzer, I don't believe he'd have gotten the better of Reggie."

My phone rang. Caller ID showed it was Coop. "I'm putting you on speaker, Captain. Tip's here."

"I saw the preliminary from Ben," Coop said. "Can we wrap this case up tomorrow?"

"We're close," I said. "But we'd like to see the final report from Ben, and go over a few more things."

"What kind of things?" Coop had her irritated voice going.

Tip leaned close to the phone. "A few questions we haven't figured out yet. Shouldn't be anything to worry about, but like you said, you want all the details accounted for on this one."

"Hurry up. I've already gotten a call from Rusty. I expect if we don't deliver a report soon I'll get a call from Tom, or one of his henchmen in Washington."

"Damn Yankees!" Tip said. That made Coop laugh.

I hung up and set the phone on the porch railing and dug into the cheese jalapeños. "Not much better than this."

Tip leaned back in his rocker. "Seems to be a lot of pressure to put this case to bed. You'd think that Ingle's friends would want us to find out everything. Clear his name and such."

"By his friends I assume you mean the mayor and the president?"

"Of course, if we believe the gossip we've been hearing from old George and others, Ingle's friends have the most to lose." Tip shifted in the chair and looked over at me.

"Which makes me wonder again about why Camwyck was killed."

I got up and headed for the kitchen. "If we're doing this, I need more beer."

"Get the chips out of the pantry," Tip said. "We might as well take this inside."

He grabbed a sheet of poster board and a marker from the living room, and brought it out to where he kept his charts. Across the top he wrote Camwyck's name, followed by Ingle's and the President.

"Okay, what do we know?"

"It's simple," I said. Camwyck knew Ingle and the President; she had sex with both of them; she blackmailed them; and she aborted a child that belonged to one of them."

Tip drew a new chart on the poster board.

"Tell me again what our theory was for why she waited so long to blackmail Ingle."

Camwyck	Ingle	Pres
Friends with	✓	✓
Had sex with	✓	✓
Was blackmailing	✓	?
Abortion—whose kid?	?	?

"I believe we agreed that due to Tom Marsen's recent election as president, it was a good time for Camwyck to blackmail them. In other words, she had them by the balls."

Tip reached for his beer, and took a swig.

"Even if it was Ingle she was blackmailing, he had to go along or risk embarrassing the President."

"If we assume she was after the President, what was she using for blackmail?"

"Either the abortion or the previous blackmailing she had done with them. Remember what old George told us about that senator." Tip scribbled another note and looked back at me. "It really doesn't matter who she was blackmailing and with what.

"If we're right—and it's not about sex—then anything it *is* about would hurt the president."

"And that would set Ingle off," I said, then, "How about Richards?"

"Different, but similar," Tip said, and drew another chart.

Richards	Ingle	Pres
Friends with	?	?
Had sex with	✓	✓
Was blackmailing	✓	?
Abortion	X	X

I looked at the chart. "Richards was only blackmailing Ingle because Camwyck died. At least it looked that way. And how do we know she didn't have an abortion? Why'd you write that down?"

"Because the M.E. would have reported it if she had," Tip said.

I looked at Tip, then flipped through the file on Camwyck, which was sitting on the end table next to me. "I don't remember seeing an abortion listed for Camwyck. How do we know she had one?"

"George told me. Remember?"

"We better check on that," I said. "Gladys wants all details checked."

Tip grabbed his phone and punched in a number.

"Ben, this is Tip.

"Yeah, I know it's after hours. Did Camwyck have an abortion?

"You're sure? Go check."

"Did she?" I asked.

Tip shrugged, then Ben must have gotten back on the phone.

"She did? And you're sure? Okay, thanks," Tip said. "Looks like George was right. She had an abortion."

I went to the bathroom and returned to the chair, trying to pick up where I'd left off. "If this is about an abortion, or even if it's about blackmail operations they'd run, why didn't Ingle just pay her the money?"

Tip munched on a handful of chips. "I have no idea why. A few million bucks is a piss hole in the snow to Ingle. He wouldn't have missed it."

"Maybe he was worried it wouldn't stop at one payment," I said. "Or maybe this wasn't the first time?"

"Let's go back to suspects for Camwyck," Tip said. "No matter how much we want to pin the murder on Ingle, he doesn't look good for it. We can put him with no alibi in the vicinity of where Richards was killed, but it would be hell to prove he slipped out of Rusty's fundraiser to kill Camwyck and get back in time for a 12:30 drive home."

Sacco, came over and sat next to me. I reached down to pet him. "Remember, Reggie could have done Camwyck. In fact, Reggie could have done Richards, too."

"But why would he?" Tip asked.

"We know he came *recommended* by Marsen. Maybe the President sent Reggie to take care of business."

"Are you listening to yourself?" Tip said.

"You're saying the President ordered a hit on these women?"

I looked at Tip, and then at the chart. Then I shook my head. "I have no fucking idea what I'm saying. All I know is something's not right, and it hasn't been right since we got this case."

"When we look at the players involved, there's one thing in common—they all knew each other. Tom Marsen, Bob Ingle, Cybil, Camwyck, even Coop."

"I hear what you're saying, Tip. All the pieces fit, and yet, somehow they don't. Sort of like a broken puzzle."

"You're right. That's exactly what it is—a broken puzzle." Tip got up and paced. "We need to take this back to the Piney Woods. That's where it all started."

"Sounds like we're taking a road trip tomorrow," I said. "If we're driving to East Texas, I'm behind the wheel."

Tip headed for the fridge. "Pick me up early."

"See you at six," I said.

CHAPTER 58

THE MAYOR'S WIFE

The next morning, I pulled into Tip's driveway a few minutes before six. I half expected him to be sleeping, but he was sitting on the sidewalk waiting.

"Thought you'd be early," he said, and got in the car.

"Directions?"

"I've been thinking about this all night. It might be good if we pay Cybil another visit. She's got to know something."

I put the car in reverse and backed out into his circular drive. "No question she knows something, but the way I see it, it'll be a cold day in hell before she tells us."

"Probably," Tip said. "But it's worth a shot."

"She won't be in her office this early. You got anything in mind for the next few hours?"

"I was thinking we'd be on our way to East Texas," Tip said. "But I'd prefer we see Cybil first. Since she's not in yet, I was thinking breakfast."

We stopped at our favorite spot, and while I thought we'd be wasting time, we actually accomplished something. We determined once and for all—at least in our minds—that Ingle couldn't have killed Camwyck and Richards. Not without help. We had come to this conclusion earlier, but today we confirmed it.

"That leaves our prime suspect as Reggie Grage," Tip said.

"The problem is, he's dead."

Tip signaled the waitress. "Hey, darlin', can you get me another order of sausage, please?"

"And more coffee," I said. "Please?"

Tip smiled. "Damn we're polite."

We finished stuffing our faces, filled our guts with coffee, and then finished a slow commute down a traffic-jammed freeway to Cybil's office.

I parked in the garage, then we headed into the lobby.

"May I help you?" a young girl at the desk asked.

Tip leaned close and gave her his best smile. "Darlin', if you could tell Cybil that Detectives Denton and Cataldi are here to see her, I'd surely appreciate it."

"Of course, Detective. Have a seat," she said, and showed a wide row of white teeth.

"I'll be right here, Darlin'. Don't forget me now."

She blushed. "Would you like something to drink? I've got fresh coffee."

"I'll take you up on that. Cream and sugar, please."

"I'll be right back," she said, and disappeared through a door behind her station.

Tip turned and stood beside me. "I wonder if Cybil breeds pretty young things like her, or just has a damn good recruiter to hire them for her."

I didn't acknowledge his speculation, but in either case, I had to admit *somebody* was doing a good job. A minute later, the sweet thing from the front desk returned with our coffees, but before we could even sip it, Cybil came out.

"What can I do for you?"

"Is there someplace we can talk privately?" I asked.

"This way," she said, and walked down a long corridor, her ass pushing each side of a tight skirt, threatening to break through at any moment. Cybil was still a looker for her age.

About ten yards down a long hall she opened a door and stepped aside. "Did you boys enjoy the show?"

I blushed.

Tip smiled. "I did," he said. "Thanks. It would have been nicer if the hallway was longer though." He brushed past her and took the nearest seat.

Cybil closed the door behind us. "I hope there was a reason why we needed to speak privately."

"Where were you when Patti Richards was killed?" Tip asked.

"Who?"

"Patti Richards, the woman who was murdered in Dallas shortly after Barbara was killed."

Cybil looked at Tip as if he'd lost his mind, and I have to admit, I was thinking along those lines myself. "I have no idea."

"Did you know Richards?"

Cybil made her way to the bar, grabbed a glass, and mixed a drink. She looked in my direction. "One for you, Detective?"

"Not now, thanks. My liver thinks it's a little early to start with the booze."

"Mine too, but I pay it no mind." She turned to Tip. "Where were we?"

"Did you know her?" Tip asked. "Richards, I mean."

"I don't believe I did."

"Funny. She had your name in her address book. Your maiden name."

Cybil paced while she drank.

"Patti Richards. Let me think. Richards…Was that a married name?"

"I think you know it wasn't. She was a prostitute."

Cybil's eyebrows reached for the ceiling. "Oh my."

"You seem to know a lot of prostitutes."

Cybil stopped and held Tip fixed with a hard look.

"What are you implying?"

"I'm just stating it straight out. You seem to know a lot of prostitutes. From what I've heard you used to run a ring of blackmailing whores to get dirt on politicians." Tip set his glass on the end table and cocked his head. "How's that for speaking plainly?"

She slammed her glass on the bar top, splashing the drink. "I think you should leave."

"Fine, but if I walk out that door without any answers, everything I know about the old days is going to hit the papers."

Cybil shot Tip a look that I'm sure had made big men cower. It made me want to hide in a corner. "If you slander us, I'll—"

"No need to go on," Tip said. "I know all of the things you'll do, but the fact remains that Rusty has an election to win, and if this hits the papers, we both know he won't win."

"Nobody would *dare* print garbage like that."

When Cybil said that, Roberts came to mind. She'd have the balls. As I thought that, I realized that it just *might* get printed.

"If you're arrested, they will," Tip said. He pulled out his handcuffs and approached her. "In case you're wondering, these aren't for fun and games, Ms. Johnson."

She half-laughed and took a few steps back. "You can't be serious."

"Turn around, ma'am. You are under arrest for the murder of Patti Richards."

When Tip said that, I almost lost it. I knew he was crazy, but I didn't imagine he'd carry things this far.

Tip and I walked her back down the hall in cuffs. When we exited into the front office, Cybil looked to her left and said, "Amy, get Ben Sanders. Tell him I've been taken to the police station. And call my husband."

Tip led her out the front office door leading into the walkway leading to the garage. Cybil turned and hollered before the double doors closed, "And tell Rusty he better get his ass there fast!"

Tip removed the cuffs before we got in the car.

"Not worried about me overpowering you?" Cybil said.

"That was just for show," Tip said. "But the rest is real."

It didn't take long to drive to the station from Cybil's office, but during that short drive she used every curse word I knew at least a dozen or more times, and 90% of them were directed at Tip. She threatened him and all of his living, and, dead relatives, and swore a curse upon all future offspring.

When I reached the parking lot, Tip said,

"Pull over, Gino."

"Where?"

"Any empty spot."

"I knew this was bullshit," Cybil said. "But you're still going to suffer for it."

Tip turned around in his seat, facing Cybil.

"This is bullshit. I'll grant you that, but just so you know what you're facing—we have your hair on Patti Richards' body and your name in her address book. Your maiden name. And you were in Dallas at the time Richards was killed."

I watched Cybil closely, looking for reactions. The way she raised her brows and then narrowed them made me think this was news to her. She could have been faking it, but I didn't think she was.

"That's absurd," she said.

"I think so too," Tip said, "But Ingle and Camwyck are both dead, and that doesn't leave us with a lot of suspects. Besides you, there's our captain and the president." Tip paused, and said, "See how it looks? Someone is going out of their way to make it seem like you had something to do with this."

"This is *bullshit!*" Cybil said again.

"I agree," Tip said. "So we can continue this *bullshit,* or you can tell me what I need to know."

"What do you think I know?"

"Why was Camwyck killed?"

Cybil shrugged, then looked at me. "Are you recording this?"

"No, ma'am."

She took a moment, then breathed in deeply. "I don't know who killed Barbara, or why. But my guess is she fell in love with the fool, and by *fool* I mean Tom Marsen. She always was a sucker for him, even after he raped her." Cybil shook her head. "She must have done something to really piss him off."

"You're saying the president—"

"Killed her?" Cybil shook her head. "I know he didn't do it himself— he'd never dream of getting his hands dirty—but he'd have no problem getting somebody else to do it. That's the special kind of son of a bitch that our president is."

Tip shot her a look. "You're trying to convince us that the president had her killed?"

"Who else?"

"Why?" I asked.

Cybil shrugged again. "Barbara was a damn fool. It's only speculation, but I guess she was blackmailing Tom for things he did in the old days."

"Blackmailing the president sounds pretty stupid," I said.

"If you knew Barbara, you'd understand. She wasn't the kind of person who gave up on anything. And once she got her hooks into someone, she never gave up." Cybil shook her head. "*Never.*"

"That's good to know," I said, "But what would have gotten her killed?"

"I don't know. It must have been something from the old days. Maybe having to do with her abortion. Tom wouldn't like it if that got out."

"We tried digging into that," Tip said.

"People back in your home town are pretty tight lipped, especially when it comes to anything dealing with the president."

I remained silent. Tip's line of shit didn't stop at flirting, it seemed. We'd never talked to anyone about Marsen.

"No surprise there," Cybil said. "You'll have to find out where she went afterward. Get a record of that procedure and you'll have something to discuss with Tom."

"Where did she go?" Tip asked. "I mean after the procedure."

"All I know is that Barbara left town after she got pregnant. I left shortly after that and came to Houston. About a year later, she called me and said she was looking for work." Cybil hit the button to roll down the window, and breathed in fresh air. Since it was a personal car and not a patrol car, she could do that. "I told Barbara if she was willing to do whatever it took to get ahead, then I had work for her. I gave her the number for an old cop named George—"

"I know him," Tip said.

"Good. If he's still alive he can probably tell you where he picked her up."

Cybil looked at Tip, then me. "I told you all I know. It's your turn to deliver, and by deliver I mean keeping things quiet. We can't afford this kind of publicity during Rusty's campaign."

"I'm not promising anything," Tip said.

"I've got something to trade."

"I can't imagine *anything* that you have to interest me."

A smirk popped on Cybil's face. "How about your mother's killer?"

Tip turned in the seat, his face white, and blank.

"I know you've been on that case a long time," she said.

"You don't know shit about my mother's case."

"Can we work something out?"

"What do you know?" Tip asked, but then he shook his head. "I can't, and I wouldn't even if I could. But if you know something about who killed her…really know something…"

She reached over the seat and patted his shoulder. "Screw you, Denton. I hope you never find him."

Tip's hands balled into fists. He looked like he wanted to hit her, but then he turned and faced forward. "Gino, I'm going inside. Take her back and get her ready for processing, will you?" He slammed the door when he got out.

***

Tip wondered about what Cybil said as he walked into the station and up the steps. How did she even know about his mother? Who told her? Why? And the worst thought of all—did she really know something? Or was she bluffing?

Charlie met Tip at the top of the stairs.

"Coop wants to see you."

In a couple of minutes, Tip was sitting in Coop's office. "You wanted to see me?"

"I heard about Cybil. What the hell is going on?"

Tip didn't answer right away. When he did it was with some hesitation. "I was hoping we'd get information from her."

"What kind of information? Isn't this case wrapped up?"

Tip leaned forward, resting his hands on Coop's desk. "You know this case isn't over. Ingle's dead, and his bodyguard is dead. But nothing adds up, Gladys, and you damn well know it doesn't."

She let out a grunt of some sort. It sounded like disgust. "Close the case, Denton.

Rusty is putting pressure on the chief, and he's pressing me."

Tip slammed his hand on the desk. "I'm not closing a case because some damn politician wants it closed. That makes me more suspicious than anything. I may not follow all the rules, but I'm not bending over for anybody. This case is getting solved, and it's getting solved the right way."

Coop leaned back in her chair. "Don't tell me about suspicions. I've been getting pressure on this case since it started, which is why I told you to lay off Cybil to begin with."

"Why didn't you tell us you were under pressure?"

Coop laughed. "And if I did? Would you have quit? Besides, I mentioned it more than once. What the hell did you want, a billboard with a plea for help?"

"Coop, you know me by now. I would have done what I had to do. Nothing less."

"Just like you and Gino *didn't* go to Cybil's when I told you to lay off."

Tip gazed into her eyes, refusing to back down. "Kind of. I thought we had to do it."

"And you didn't care that I instructed you not to?"

"Not really."

"That's what I thought." Coop removed her glasses and set them on her desk. "There's a lot more to this job than catching bad guys. When you're at my desk, it's all about bullshit and politics."

Coop shook her head. "I admire what you're doing, but let's stop dreaming. You know nothing good will come of you embarrassing the mayor."

"I know," Tip said, "But we might put enough pressure on Cybil to get some answers."

"More dreams."

"Maybe so," Tip said, "But we've got to try something. I'm not closing this case with what we have. We owe it to Camwyck and Roberts to find the real killer. If it's Ingle, fine. If it isn't, let's find out who it is."

Coop stood and paced. "Fair enough. Push Cybil, push anyone you need to, as long as you know it will be a rough ride."

Tip smiled, and stood. "You got it, Captain. Thanks."

"Sit down, Denton."

She stared at him. "I've been straight with you, now tell me what's going on with Gino."

Tip knew this day was coming. Now he had to do something. "Nothing."

She sat back in her chair again. "More bullshit." She stared at him for a long time, head cocked, eyes narrowed. "You wouldn't lie to me, would you?"

"Not unless you were in bed with me."

For a moment Coop looked as if she might get pissed, but then she laughed. "You are a *pain* in the ass, but for some reason I like you."

"Thanks, Cap. I kind of like me too."

"Get the hell out of here. And make sure you do everything right with Cybil. Her lawyers will be looking for loopholes."

"I'll keep you posted," he said, and moved toward the door.

"You realize if you don't get me info on Gino, someone else will."

"Nothing to get," Tip said.

"We'll see. Go finish this case. It's driving me crazy."

"One for the records. That's for sure."

"An awful lot went on in that town where we came from," Coop said. "I guess it's like Cybil said—that place bred a lot of ambitious people."

"A lot goes on in all towns, and all houses, we just don't know about it until it comes out."

"You getting philosophical?"

"Yep, that's me. And you better be careful, Coop; now that I know all it takes to be captain is bullshit, I might be after your job. I can do bullshit pretty good."

Coop laughed. "Get the hell out of here."

CHAPTER 59

THE PINEY WOODS

I got back to the station and found Tip at his desk. Papers from the case file were spread all over. "What's up, partner? Looking for something new?"

"New *or* old," he said. "Just looking for something. By the way, are we going to see that ex-cop you know?"

"You mean George? No sense in driving over there," Tip said. "We'll give him a call."

Tip put the phone on speaker. After about six rings, George picked up. "Yeah?"

"George, it's Tip Denton."

"I'm listening."

"The last time I was over, you mentioned that Cybil had you pick up Barbara Camwyck from over in East Texas and bring her to Houston."

"I remember," George said.

"Do you remember where?"

"Lumberton," George said. "Little town north of Beaumont. She was waiting for me outside of an HEB grocery store."

"That's a pretty good memory for something that happened so long ago," Tip said.

"Like I told you before, that woman had an effect on me, even from that first day. She was standing in front of HEB and she looked like she'd been crying. When I got out of the car she quickly wiped her tears. I tried being nice to the kid. Back then I wasn't a very nice person, but this girl got to me. I said to her, 'You all right, kid?' And she looked up at me and said 'Fuck off, old man.'"

George's laugh came through the speaker loudly.

"That one sentence cured me of bein' nice," George said.

"What happened after?" Tip asked.

"She didn't say jack shit all the way to Houston. I dropped her off and that was that."

"George, you've been a big help. I appreciate it."

"Stop by and visit sometime," George said. "You know where I live."

"I will," Tip said, and then he hung up.

Tip called Julie on the intercom. "We need to dig into employment records, tax filings, anything you can find on Barbara Camwyck from back when she was in East Texas. She was in Lumberton for a while. I believe it was about 18 years ago, and she might have worked at the HEB grocery store."

"I'll get right on it," Julie said.

"Hurry up. We're on our way there now."

When I heard Tip say that I jumped at the opportunity. "I'm driving," I said, and headed for the door.

"It's about time we got going," Tip said. "We've been planning this trip since last night."

"We're on the way now, after all of your bullshit." I drove east on I-10. Tip talked nonstop, jumping from discussing the case to talking about his dogs. I spent half the time nodding and saying "uh-huh", when I wasn't thinking or worrying about Ron and wondering how he was making out at the new rehab center.

Worry seemed to have found a permanent place in me since the first time I caught Ron with drugs, and that brought up another sore subject—my mother. The only insightful thing she ever said in her life was when she told me that 'A parent never stops worrying from the moment their first child is born.' I know I'd said it before, but this one stuck with me. For once, she had been right.

Tip's phone rang as I passed a sign announcing the exit for Winnie, Texas, a town that looked big enough to support a couple of gas stations, but only because of the freeway.

"Hello, darlin'," he said.

He didn't need the speaker on; Julie had a pretty big voice.

"I couldn't find income tax records, but I did find a report of social security wages paid by Dairy Queen, on Route 96 in Lumberton."

"When was it?" Tip asked.

"That's the thing. She only worked there about three months."

"And you didn't find anything else? No utility bills? Or phone records? Hospital records?"

"Nothing," Julie said, "But I'll keep digging."

"All right, let us know," Tip said.

"Three months?" I said. "Doesn't sound right."

"Not for a young girl who went off to have an abortion," Tip said. "What was she living on?"

I tried to come up with an explanation. "If we assume Marsen paid for the abortion, he might have given her money to live on, too."

"Maybe she was boarding with someone," Tip said. "I imagine it wouldn't be hard to find a room to rent in a small town."

"Maybe so," I said.

A little less than an hour later we arrived in Lumberton. It wasn't difficult to find the HEB that George had mentioned, and the Dairy Queen was only a short walk away.

I showed my badge to one of the cashiers and asked to speak to the manager. A tall string bean-thin man came out a moment later. He looked to be about fifty.

"I'm Brent Hegl," he said. "How can I help?"

Tip said, "We're investigating a case and need to know if you remember a young girl named Barbara Camwyck. She worked here about 18 years ago." Tip produced a picture of Barbara Camwyck that dated back about ten years, which was the closest we had to when she lived in Lumberton.

Hegl looked, then held the picture up and brought it closer. "I was here back then, but I can't place her."

"Do you have records we could look at?" I asked.

"Everything's computerized," he said. "It's a project we've worked on for years. Come back with me," he said.

We followed him to a small office in the back of the store, and before long he located the records we needed, personnel and payroll records from that time.

He thumbed through a few files, then said, "She only worked here for three months."

"We know that," Tip said. "Do you have an address where she lived? Or a name she might have listed for someone to contact in case of emergency?"

"There's an address listed here," Hegl said, then he reached for a notepad and wrote it down. "It's not far from here. A small ranch house on the corner. Back in that time, Mrs. Zelker owned it, but she's gone. Her son lives there now."

Otto Zelker was working on his lawn when we pulled up. He had grass stuck on his arms from sweating, and he was breathing heavily. I told him what we wanted after showing him my badge.

"I remember her," he said. "Not a very pleasant girl, but pretty."

"Did she live here long?" I asked.

Otto shook his head. "Couldn't have been more than a few months. She rented a room from my mother and she helped out around the house. She was good with the garden, too."

"But she was only here a few months?" Tip said.

Zelker nodded. "No more than three. After that, she left. I remember my mother being upset because the girl didn't even tell my mother she was leaving. She left enough money on the table to pay her rent through the month, but nothing else. Not even a note."

We pressed to see if he knew anything else, but he didn't. And he had no clues who else in town might be able to help.

We checked in with local law enforcement before leaving, telling them why we were here asking questions, and also to see if they had any information.

After that, we talked to an old-timer who was clerking as a part-time job. He said he'd been there 30 years. He didn't recall Camwyck, and when he checked, he had no records for her. After a few more dead ends, we got back on the road to Houston.

"Struck out there," Tip said. "And we're back to where we started. Why the hell would Ingle kill her for a couple of million? And why would Marsen risk killing her for any reason? He's the goddamn president."

Things had been stirring in my mind since Julie had called with the employment records. Suddenly it clicked. "Suppose it was a lot more than a couple of million?"

"What are you talking about?" Tip asked.

I smiled. "Suppose she didn't get an abortion, and there's a seventeen-year-old kid running around East Texas who looks like the president? Or Ingle."

Tip cracked one of his smiles. "Then I believe we'd have what we call a Texas conundrum."

"A what?"

"A Texas conundrum," Tip said.

"How's that different than a normal conundrum?"

"It's the same thing, but bigger."

I shook my head. "Either way, it's big blackmail. If it's Marsen's kid, we're looking at a president with an illegitimate kid. And if it's Ingle's kid we've got a *whole lot* of money involved."

"That would explain the missing nine or ten months between Camwyck disappearing and her working at the Dairy Queen." Tip pulled out his phone and dialed. "Julie, we need you to go over everything in the Camwyck files. I mean *everything*. Get more help if you need it, but check financials, phone records, bank accounts, taxes, properties she owns…all of it."

"What are we looking for?" Julie asked. "I'm already doing that."

"Then do it harder," Tip said. His voice was loud and gruff. "Look for a kid," Tip said. "But I'll take anything that looks out of place."

He hung up and said, "We need to find out where Camwyck was for nine months."

"The hell with Camwyck," I said. "We need to find the kid."

"I thought Ben said she had an abortion," Tip said.

"Could have been after the fact," I said. "She could have had a kid, then later gotten pregnant again and had an abortion."

"I guess so," Tip said.

CHAPTER 60

A MISSING CHILD

I decided to take a different route back to Houston, opting for highway 105 instead of the freeway. It would take longer this way, but the drive was more pleasant.

"What I can't figure out," Tip said, "is why they killed Camwyck. I know we've been through this before, but hear me out because the kid makes a difference."

"I'm listening. But don't forget the kid is speculation. We don't know if there *is* a kid."

Tip turned slightly in his seat so he was facing me while I drove. "Forget *if*. I'm convinced she didn't get an abortion—at least not at that time. We know from Ben she had one, but it could have been later as we've already said. So let's assume the kid belongs to Marsen. If that's true, we've got a president who is going to be damned embarrassed by his past indiscretions, but presidents have survived worse. Hell, he wasn't even married then."

"Suppose Camwyck was saying it was rape and the child was the result of rape?" I asked.

"It would be her word against his. And I'm sure Ingle would come to his defense, and probably Cybil, too. Camwyck wouldn't stand a chance."

I agreed with Tip on that. "Okay, what's your next point?"

"We assume the kid belonged to Ingle. Why would he care? Certainly he wouldn't care enough to kill her." Tip looked at me and I saw the question written on his face.

"Why not? It would cost him a fortune. Half of *his* fortune."

"That's my point," Tip said, and then he smiled. "He has no kids, so why would he care who gets it when he's gone?"

For a moment, Tip remained quiet, giving me time to think. Then I saw what he was getting at. "But who stands to lose at least half, if not all of his fortune if a real, live heir pops onto the scene?"

Tip smacked his hand on the dashboard. "Goddamn right! *Mrs.* Ingle. She could end up losing a few hundred million or more. It would depend on what kind of terms they agreed to in a pre-nup."

"If she has one," I said.

"I'd bet my last dick she signed a pre-nup, but knowing RB Ingle, his lawyers would have made certain it was all in his favor, and at the time of the marriage, she was in no position to argue."

I glanced over at Tip. "How many dicks do you have?"

"Just one, but if I had more than one, I'd bet my last one on that gamble. That's saying something."

"Tip, I'm starting to worry about you."

He laughed. "You have to admit, the theory about Mrs. Ingle is sound. She's the one with everything to lose."

I gave it more thought. "Do you really think anybody would worry about losing a few million, or even a few hundred million, when they'd have so much anyway?"

After Tip stopped laughing, he said, "You better join the real world, partner. The people that worry the most about money are the ones who have it all."

"Maybe we should pay another visit to the recently widowed Mrs. Ingle."

"We've got nothing better to do," Tip said. "Besides, I think she said she'd be staying at the Four Seasons. I love their menu."

"If we're going downtown, we need a new route. Pull up a map."

Tip looked at me and said, "A map? What do you need a map for? You've got me in the car."

"Spit out some directions then."

"Not too far up the road you'll hit Highway 146. Take a left. When you get to Liberty, take a right on Highway 90 and follow that into Houston."

We were about thirty minutes outside of the city when Coop called. Tip answered.

"Yes, dear?"

"An update would be nice," Coop said. "Are we closing this case?"

"Not yet."

A long pause followed. "Tell me what not yet means, and it better be damn convincing. Your friend, Chief Renkin, is waiting on my call. And he's not happy."

"Tell John to sit tight. We've got issues, Captain. Something's not right, but we'll fill you in when we get there."

"Where are you? And what's not right?"

"Sweet little Mrs. Ingle isn't right," Tip said. "We're on our way to see her."

"Denton, you better not cause trouble. That woman still has a lot of influence and with the sympathy she'll draw from having her husband killed…"

"I know all about it. Let us do our job. You handle Renkin."

"Goddamnit," Coop said. "Goddamnit." And then she hung up.

We called ahead to the Four Seasons, and made an appointment to see Mrs. Ingle. Tip told her to expect us around five, and we didn't miss the mark by much, pulling into the parking garage at 5:10. We rode the elevator to her suite, and were shown in by the maid who worked at the Ingle house.

She nodded, smiled, and led us to the sitting area, where Mrs. Ingle sat on a sofa, nursing a cup of tea. The bruises on her face looked worse than when she was in the hospital.

"Like a drink?" she asked. "Or coffee, tea?"

"Water for me," I said. Tip opted for tea.

"Be right back," the maid said.

Ingle waited until we were seated, then asked, "What brings you to see me?"

"We had a few follow-up questions," I said, and pulled out my notepad.

She set her drink on the end table, folded her hands on her lap, and smiled. "Go on, Detective."

I flipped back to the notes I took at her house. "We are confused about the order of the gunshots. You said you heard yelling between Mr. Ingle and Mr. Grage, followed by a gunshot, and then a few seconds later, another shot."

"Yes, that's right," she said.

"How much time was there between the shots?" Tip asked.

"About ten seconds, if I remember. Why? Is it important?"

The maid brought the water and tea, and turned to leave. "Hang on, ma'am," I said. "I have a question for you also."

She turned back to face me, but her face tightened up, and she turned to Mrs. Ingle.

"¿Si?"

"Can you tell me about the gunshots that day at the house? What you heard?"

She clasped her hands together, her right thumb rubbing the back of her left thumb, like she was counting rosary beads. "Heard yelling. Then gun. I cover head with a pillow, then another gun fire." She glanced over at Mrs. Ingle after she finished.

Tip looked to me, then up at the maid.

"How long between the first and second shot?"

Again, she looked at Ingle. There was a brief pause, then she said, "Don't know. Maybe…ten seconds." A quick smile appeared on her face when she said it.

I pretended to look through my notes, but I didn't need to refer to them. It wasn't what she'd told us that day at the house.

"Ma'am, you told us before that there was a shot, then about one minute later, two more shots. Then after another minute, a final shot." I closed the notepad and looked up at her. She wouldn't look me in the eyes.

I then did my best to translate what I'd said into Spanish.

"No. Was confused. Very upset."

Tip stood and looked down at her. "It's pretty difficult to confuse a timeline so different."

The backs of her fingers turned white from squeezing. She was stressing. "Don't know. Like I said."

Mrs. Ingle got up from the sofa, walked over and gave the maid a hug. "It's okay, Manuela. I know you're still upset. We all are."

She looked at Mrs. Ingle. "I can go now?"

"Of course you can. And don't forget we have guests coming tonight."

"Si, Señora," she said, and quickly exited the room.

"We weren't done asking questions," I said.

Mrs. Ingle took her seat again. "I'm sure any questions you have can wait for another day. You can see she's upset."

"I noticed," Tip said. "Mrs. Ingle, remind me why you called us in the first place."

"I don't know what you mean," she said.

"When you called Detective Cataldi and told him about the dress. Why did you do it?"

"I believe I already answered that, Detective." She looked at the clock on the wall and said, "Now, if you'll excuse me. I have guests to prepare for." She walked to the door and opened it. "Good day, gentlemen."

We reluctantly followed her to the door, and then, as we waited for the elevator, I said, "I've never been thrown out of a place so politely."

"Or such a nice place," Tip said. "I think we struck a nerve."

"We certainly did with the maid. Funny how her story changed."

"Damn funny."

I pressed the button again, knowing it did no good, but I did it anyway. "Mrs. Ingle's story didn't change, though."

"Not a single bit," Tip said. "Despite all the stress she's been through."

The elevator opened, and a guy with two small kids got out. I stepped inside, pressed the button for the lobby, and said to Tip, "We need to dig deeper. A *lot* deeper."

I was about to open my car door when the phone rang. It was Julie.

"What's up, Jules?"

"I hope ya'll are on your way back here, because I think I've got something."

"We're on our way," I said.

CHAPTER 61

THINGS DON'T ADD UP

"**W**hy didn't you ask Julie what she found?" Tip said.

"We're ten minutes away, for Christ's sake. Have patience."

Tip dialed the phone. "Patience, my ass."

The phone rang a half a dozen times then went to voicemail. "This is Tip. Call me, damn it."

I laughed. "You *are* an impatient son of a bitch."

I parked the car a few minutes later, purposefully taking extra time to find a spot. After listening to Tip's moaning, we went inside. We had barely started up the stairs when Tip started calling out Julie's name. By the time we got to the top of the steps, she was waiting with a folder in her hand.

"What is it?" Tip asked.

Julie handed him the file. "It's gonna take some explaining. Your desk or mine?"

"Mine," Tip said.

Julie arranged some papers on the desk, most of them printouts of spreadsheets and a folder with receipts inside. "We started going through everything Camwyck had," Julie said. "Nothing seemed out of place. In fact, her books were meticulous, almost like a CPA's. At one point, Jeremy said, 'What a deal this woman had— huge consulting contract and health insurance to boot.'"

I looked up at Julie, trying to grasp the significance.

"I didn't catch it at first," she said, "but a few minutes later, when I was going through the files for a second time, I ran across a reference to United Health. It was a $1,500 recurring payment from her bank account. I looked over to Jeremy and said, 'Didn't you say she had health insurance at work?' Jeremy flipped through a file, and said, 'Full coverage.'"

Julie stopped and looked at me and Tip. "You see what I'm getting at? She was covered at work but we have checks every month made out to United Health."

"So who's United Health?" Tip asked, "And try to keep the explanation to less than an hour."

Julie frowned. "Cut it out, Tip. I don't know who they are yet. There isn't a policy number referenced, and I called United Healthcare, but they didn't have a policy in Camwyck's name."

"What about the bank?" I asked.

"I caught them before they left for the day, and was able to talk them into helping us." Julie turned to Tip and gave him a smirk. "They weren't going to help initially, citing confidentiality, but when I explained the situation, and that Ms. Camwyck was the 'dumpster lady', they agreed to cooperate." Julie smiled, obviously exuberant. "Are you ready for this?"

"Hurry up," Tip said.

"These payments have been going on for 17 years! And for the same amount each month. Insurance policies woulnd't stay the same for 17 years."

A jolt of excitement ran through me. "Tell me you have an address."

She handed me a piece of paper, with a name and address.

Joshua Camphurst
1723 North 10th Street
Orange, TX 77630

"Tip, looks like we're heading to East Texas. Again."

"It's too late now," Tip said. "Pick me up in the morning."

I got to Tip's house by 6:00, and by 8:15 we were turning onto North 10th Street in Orange. The house, an old green clapboard bungalow style, sat on the corner with a good-sized yard—maybe a quarter of an acre. A front porch spanned the width of the house, white pillars sitting atop brick supports. It looked like it might have been around a while, maybe 40 or 50 years, but it had been kept in good shape.

I parked on the street and Tip and I went up and knocked on the door. A man who appeared to be mid 40s answered, wearing blue coveralls and a white T-shirt. He stared out at us through a screen door that appeared to be wearing a coat of new paint.

Tip flashed his badge. "Detectives Denton and Cataldi," he said. "Have you got a few minutes to talk?"

"About what?" Respect for the law wasn't deep in those words.

"About Barbara Camwyck," Tip said. "She's dead."

He might have tried denying everything—might have—but when Tip said 'She's dead', the man's expression told it all. He knew Camwyck, and he *didn't* know she'd been killed.

He looked behind him, then stepped out onto the porch. "Let's walk," he said, and started strolling toward the street.

"You say she's dead? How'd that happen?"

"Murdered," I said. "Bad."

He turned to me. "Not that one in Houston? The one in the dumpster?"

I nodded. Didn't need to say anything else.

"Damn shame is what that is. She was a good woman."

I shot Tip a glance then focused on the man. This was the first person we'd met who had a decent thought about her. Whatever else Camwyck had been, she was obviously a complicated woman. "We know she was sending you money each month. For a long time."

"You showed your badge but I wasn't payin' much attention. Badges are pretty much alike. What department you from?"

"Not the IRS, if that's what concerns you," Tip said.

He shrugged. "It crossed my mind. By the way," he said. "I'm Joshua Camphurst."

"Tell us about the money Ms. Camwyck has been sending you," I said.

He shoved his hands in his pockets, and his gait slowed. His drawl seemed to come out more, too. "There's a girl back there in the house who doesn't know anything. I'd like to keep it that way if I could."

I looked at Tip. He shrugged. "We'll see what we can do," I said.

Joshua's next words carried a little pain.

"Barbara's her mother—I guess *was* her mother. But the girl doesn't know. She thinks her mother died—which is true enough now—but I been tellin' her that lie all her life. She thought my wife was her mother, and she died ten years ago." He bent and grabbed a pebble from the sidewalk. "I'm not a church-goin' man, but I don't take much to lying to little girls. Still, it had to be done. It was best for the girl, and Barbara wanted it that way."

He walked a short way without saying anything. Then Tip said, "What happened with Camwyck?"

"My wife worked as a nurse for a doctor. Barbara came in one day lookin' for an abortion. She was either too young or too stupid to know you don't find butcher docs in a place like Orange. Betty—that was my wife—talked her into comin' home for supper."

Joshua sighed. "I still remember that night. We had a brisket with mashed potatoes and asparagus." He picked up another pebble and tossed it into the street. "Anyway, before two days passed my wife convinced Barbara to deliver that baby and let us raise it. We didn't have no kids at the time, and Betty had failed with two pregnancies."

The sounds of laughter, and giggling, came from behind us. I saw three teenage girls running out of the house, chasing after one another. The man smiled. "The tall gangly one is Barbara."

"I thought your wife—"

"We tried for years with no luck. After we got Barbara, my wife's troubles disappeared. Had two more one after the other. Would've had another if not for some damn drunk who plowed into her."

"You been raising them yourself?" I asked.

"Had help from my mother until she passed about three years ago. And my sister used to lend a hand, but she moved to Oklahoma two years ago. Been just me for the past couple of years." He looked at me for a long time. I swear his eyes spoke to me. "They think they're sisters," he said.

"They won't find out from us," I said. "I can't imagine how much work three girls are."

"They're worth it." He looked at Tip and then me. "Tell me why you're here and what's gonna happen."

"Do you know who her biological father is?" I asked.

He pursed his lips and shook his head. "Never asked."

Tip sighed. "We're gonna wrap this up and see about keeping it quiet. If we have to do anything, we'll call you first." He handed the guy two cards.

"Keep one and write your number on the other so I'll have it."

We walked back to the car, and the man started toward the house. "I need a picture." I said. "Stand by the girls and I'll make it a family thing."

"Hey, girls. Friends of mine want a family picture. Get on over here."

The girls lined up next to him, laughing and chattering, and I took a few close-ups with my phone. Barbara was far taller than the other two, almost six inches taller. "All right. See you later."

We got in the car and headed back to Houston.

I called Julie first thing. "Julie, I need you to patch me through to Coop, but before you do, know that you're a genius."

"It helped?" she asked.

"We found Camwyck's daughter."

"That's fantastic, Gino. Thanks so much for letting me know."

"Now put me through to Coop."

Coop answered quickly. "Give me the good news first, Cataldi."

"Today all we have is good news. We found Camwyck's daughter."

"I'll be damned." Coop said. "She never told anybody."

"That's a tough woman to go 17 years and not tell anybody," I said.

"I'm gonna shove this information up the mayor's ass," Coop said. "Now what?"

"We're still a long way from closing this case," Tip shouted from the passenger seat. "We can put the pieces together about what might have happened, and now we have motivation, but it's a far cry from proving anything."

"I hear you," Coop said. "But there has to be evidence somewhere. Camwyck was a meticulous person. For the biggest score of her career she wouldn't suddenly slack off."

I had to agree with Coop's idea. "You're saying she had a backup plan?"

"Damn straight. We're going to tear up her life, her files, her condo…" she stopped for a moment. "We're going to tear up Ingle's also. Somewhere there is a piece of evidence that ties all this together."

"We'll find it," I said.

"Hurry up, because the chief is going to be all over my ass."

"Damn, but I'd like to see that," Tip said.

I thought I heard Coop laugh, but then she said, "Denton, it's a damn good thing you're not here or I'd be all over yours."

"I'm gonna tell Elena what you said, Cap. But in the meantime, get a team to Camwyck's condo, and one to Ingle's office, and another one to his house. We'll join the one at the house."

I hung up and looked at Tip. "You think we'll find anything?"

"If not, we'll have to bluff," he said.

CHAPTER 62

WHERE'S THE EVIDENCE?

Four hours of searching turned up nothing at Camwyck's condo, and so far we hadn't fared any better at Ingle's office or his house. A representative from the legal department dogged the crime scene unit's every move at the office; meanwhile, Mrs. Ingle paid a visit to the house and did her best to interfere with our search. One of her lawyers—Paul Jackson—stayed by her side.

"Make sure everything goes back in place, Detectives. I wouldn't want Mr. Jackson to have to file a suit against the department."

"Keep her out of the way," Tip said to Jackson, and gave him a slight shove. "And make sure she doesn't touch anything."

I followed Tip into Ingle's bedroom. "I just got off the phone with Santos. They've been going through everything at Richards' place, but no luck."

Tip punched the wall. "Where the hell did she put it?"

"Put what?" I said. "We don't know what we're looking for, or if there even is anything."

"You know what pisses me off?" Tip said. "Camwyck and Roberto were brutally murdered, Mano is missing, Ingle and Reggie are dead—and we can't prove a *goddamn* thing."

"I'm not ready to admit that she's smarter than us," I said. "Not yet."

"It doesn't much matter if you're ready to admit it," Tip said. "So far she's beaten us at every turn."

I heard Coop's voice coming from the hallway. She walked in a moment later.

"Anything?" she asked.

"He was just talking about how Mrs. Ingle outsmarted us," Tip said, pointing at me.

"So we've got nothing?" Coop said.

"I don't want to say it, Coop, but you're right. We've got nothing. On the contrary, we found more evidence that backs up *her* claims, but I don't believe a word of it."

"What kind of evidence?" Coop asked.

"Doctor visits," Tip said. "The kind that show bruising on her legs and back consistent with domestic abuse. Her lawyer eagerly provided them, of course. They would make her sympathetic as hell to a jury."

Coop signaled for the tech taking pictures to leave, then she closed the door. "Are we damn sure she's guilty? I sure as hell can't afford the negative press this is going to bring if we're wrong about her."

"Knowing who we're dealing with," Tip said, "it's the only thing that makes sense as far as motive goes. And we've still got conflicting reports on the gunshots the day her husband and Reggie Grage were killed."

"What about that?" Coop asked. "Could it have been confused reporting on Ingle's or the maid's part?"

"It could have been," I said. "Except that now the maid's story is *exactly* like Mrs. Ingle's."

Coop narrowed her eyes and nodded, too. "Interesting," she said. "But we're going to need a lot more than theory. It'll take old fashioned evidence to put this case to rest."

"Captain—"

Coop pointed a finger at me. "Before you start talking, Gino, let me remind you how many lawyers her money can buy."

"We're open to ideas on where to go with this," I said. "As Tip would say, 'we're plumb out.'"

Coop looked around the bedroom. "Hell of a place she's got. I'd hate to see her keep it."

"Which is what's going to happen if we don't come up with something," Tip said.

Coop pulled out her phone and dialed a number from her favorites' list. She pointed a finger at Tip and me. "Not a word."

I recognized the person's voice as soon as I heard her answer.

"What the hell do you want, Gladys?"

"I don't have time for any nonsense," Coop said. "If you want to keep Rusty out of the news, you better help me figure out what was going on with Barbara."

"I have no idea what—"

"Bullshit!" Coop said. "You know as well as I do that Barbara would have had a backup plan. Which reminds me—did you know she had a daughter?"

"What?"

"Seventeen years ago, or thereabouts."

Silence, then, "That girl sure was tight lipped."

Coop cracked her knuckles. "We're running out of time, Cybil."

"What's going on? I thought you had Bob or Tom pegged for these killings?"

"We're coming at it from a different angle now." Coop lowered her voice and said,

"We think Barbara was blackmailing Anne."

"The daughter is Bob's?" Cybil asked.

"We're guessing it is. His fortune would be one hell of a motive. Even part of it."

Another pause followed. I could almost see Cybil pacing her office, drink in hand, although I couldn't hear the ice cubes swirling in the glass.

"Let's be clear on this, Gladys. If I help you, Rusty and I stay out of the news."

"I can't promise that," Coop said.

"Good luck on your case."

Coop looked up at Tip, then over to me. She raised her brow in a question.

I mouthed, "Okay by me."

Tip seemed to be fighting internal demons, biting his lip and twisting his head, but after a moment, he nodded.

"All right," Coop said. "You've got a deal."

"As you said, Barbara always had a backup plan." Her voice got softer. "What most people didn't know is that she liked to keep things hidden where no one would expect it."

"Don't play games with me."

"Pay attention," Cybil said, enunciating each syllable. "Barbara used to be involved with one of the owners of a small hotel chain. She hid the blackmail material in a safe at the hotel. No one questioned her keeping the safe because she made regular use of their suites. She did the same with the CEO of a local bank, keeping a safe deposit box with videos of them together."

"I don't see how that helps us," Coop said.

"Look in his office, his house, his car dealerships, everything he owns," Cybil said. "Barbara hid it somewhere. I guarantee you."

Coop stood. "We'll let you know if we find anything."

"Remember what you promised, Gladys."

Coop hung up and we walked her to the front door.

"Think hard, gentlemen. Where haven't we looked?"

"We'll stay on it," Tip said. "Something's bound to turn up. By the way, what kind of deal did you make with the devil?"

"Nothing more than we would have done anyway. I told her we'd keep her involvement and Rusty's name out of the paper. Or at least that's what I implied."

Tip nodded. "All right. I can live with that."

Near the end of the day, we ran into Mrs. Ingle again near the foyer. Her lawyer whispered something to her and then he left. "Call if you need me."

"I'd have thought you'd be afraid to be left without counsel," Tip said.

The smile that popped on her face deserved to be smacked off. "Not when dealing with the likes of you." She turned and started to leave.

"One thing I'm curious about," I said. "How did you get Reggie to go along with you?"

Anne stopped, looked at me and smiled again. "I'm not sure what you're talking about, but if I had to guess I'd say it was as simple as anything dealing with a man. Assuming you had a suspect who looked as good as I do…let's just say she could get a man to do anything she wanted. *Anything.*"

Tip's face tightened and his scar twitched. "Sweetheart, you give yourself too much credit. I wouldn't screw you with my worst enemy's dick."

"What a fortunate coincidence," Anne said. "I wouldn't let you."

I couldn't believe this was the same woman. She had me fooled when we first met, I'll say that, of course I was a little distracted. Maybe Tip was right. Maybe she used her body purposefully to throw me off guard. "I see the grieving's over now. And the abused victim act, too."

Anne looked at her watch then at me. "How much longer will you be here?"

"As long as it takes," Tip said.

Anne put her phone to her ear when she walked away. We watched her go, but this time it was with contempt. I wasn't ogling over her ass. A few minutes later Coop called.

"Anything?" she asked.

"Nothing new," I said.

"Wrap it up and get back here."

"Wrap it up? We're not done."

"Gino, I said wrap it up. Renkin just had a call from the White House. The goddamn White House."

"Son of a bitch," I said, then hung up the phone and said it again. "Son of a goddamn bitch."

"I presume that's our cue to leave," Tip said.

"Direct from DC."

We rounded up the rest of the team, and took everything that might still bear fruit with us. *Everything* included laptops, tablets, iPhones, and files from the desk in his home office.

Once we got it all loaded into a couple of police vans, Tip and I got in the car. I glanced back to the house before leaving. Anne Ingle was in her car, staring out the window, and I swear she had a smirk on her face.

Damn, I hate that woman.

CHAPTER 63

WRAPPING IT UP

Coop wasn't in a good mood, and I can't say I blamed her. She was catching shit from all angles: the papers, the chief, the mayor, and Cybil. If forced to choose, I'd have to put Cybil near the top of the worst-offenders list. Of course that might have been my bias. I wasn't that fond of Cybil.

"I was hoping you'd come back with something solid," Coop said, from behind her big oaken desk.

"I was hoping so too," Tip said, "But we struck out all around. I hate to say it but Mrs. Ingle kicked our asses."

"What kind of circumstantial do we have?" Coop asked.

"Not enough to make a charge, unless Ben turns something up." I said. "The *only* thing is the inconsistency between Ingle's report of the gunshots and her maid's version. And now the maid has changed her story."

"Bullshit on changing stories," Coop said. "Break it. Get that maid by herself and break that damn story. Tell her to give us the truth or we'll ship her ass back to wherever she's from."

"It's still not enough," Tip said. "It would be a grieving widow/battered wife's word against her maid's word."

Coop tilted her head to the side. "I'm just thinking. If the maid *is* in the country illegally, as we suspect, that could play in our favor."

"Maybe in New Jersey it would," I said, "But in Texas?"

"You're probably right," Coop said. "Got anything else?"

I considered what had happened recently, then said, "She knew about the crime scene—if we take her anonymous calls as insider knowledge."

Coop chewed on her finger nail. "We might need to play that up. I don't know if it will get us anywhere, but it could be worth a shot." Just then, her phone rang on the desk. She pressed the intercom. "Who is it?"

"It's the chief," Cindy said.

"Tell him I'll call back," Coop said, and then she turned back to us. "That was the chief, in case you're deaf and didn't hear. Within minutes the mayor, or God forbid, Cybil will be calling. If I don't do something quickly, President Marsen's office will call." She glared from one of us to the other. "Do you understand what I'm saying?"

"Yes, sir," Tip said. "We're leaving to break the maid's story now."

"Is she staying at the Ingle's house?"

"Not now," I said. "She's with her daughter until this is all finished."

"Good. That's a start," Coop said. "Hurry up."

It didn't take much to break the maid's story—not after Tip threatened her with deportation. We had her repeat what she *really* heard and it aligned nicely with what she told us the day of the shooting.

I waited for her to calm down some, then asked, "We know Mrs. Ingle had you lie, but tell us why. Why did Mrs. Ingle ask you to lie? *¿Por que?*"

"She wants to be done," Manuela said. She fidgeted with her hands, as if searching for the right words. "You know, *enterrarla.*"

"I understand," I said. "*Enterrarla.* Funeral."

"You're going to have to testify in court," Tip said. "And you have to tell the truth."

She smiled. "*Si, señor.* I understand. I watch TV."

We left feeling as if we had accomplished something, but both of us knew Manuela's testimony wouldn't amount to much.

Without evidence to support her, we'd still have nothing. About a mile before getting to the station, Ben called.

Tip picked up and said, "I'm putting you on speaker so Gino can hear. And please tell me it's good news."

"That all depends on whether you're an optimist or not."

"I don't like the sounds of it, but tell me anyway."

"Most everything checks out the way Mrs. Ingle explained it," Ben said.

"Shit!"

"Hold on, Tip. I said *most* of it. There are a few inconsistencies with blood splatter, and maybe a question about gunshot residue, although it could just as easily be explained away as occurring during a struggle."

"Tell me what's wrong with the scene," Tip said.

"Mrs. Ingle had blood on her face that belonged to Reggie Grage. Of course that could be explained by her stooping down to examine him, which she said she did."

"What else?"

"Reggie Grage had blood on him from Mr. Ingle. I see it as the likely result of blood splatter from him being nearby when Ingle was shot, but in a court of law the defense could easily find an expert who would swear it was blood splattered from when Grage and Ingle fought."

"We only have her version of them fighting," Tip said.

"Not quite. Ingle's face has bruises consistent with a fist fight." Ben said.

"Remember, these *are* inconsistencies, but nothing to build a case on."

"Do we have enough to prove anything?" Tip asked.

"Right now you don't even have enough to *bluff* anything. Not with the kind of lawyers she'll hire."

"All right," Tip said. "I appreciate the call. Keep us up to date."

He hung up and looked over. "We're fucked."

"Sounds like it," I said. "Inconsistencies and maybes aren't winning a case like this."

I took my time driving back to the station, not in the mood to hear Coop after we told her the news. Before we went inside, I turned to Tip and said, "You have any ideas?"

"Not yet," he said.

Charlie met us at the top of the stairs. "Captain Cooper wants to see you."

"Of course she does," Tip said, and damn near growled at him. "Did you figure out those song lyrics yet? You better get your ass to work."

"You know I didn't, Tip. And I don't think there's anything to figure out either."

Charlie went back to his office while we slowly walked to Coop's office and discussed how to delay her from shutting the case down, but we hadn't found a solution, and now we were standing in front of her door.

"Go on in," Cindy said.

We walked into Coop's office. A guy in a suit was sitting in a chair pulled up from the wall, and across from her was the man from Orange and Camwyck's daughter.

"I believe you know Joshua Camphurst" Coop said.

He stood and extended his hand to shake. "In case you don't recall, I'm Joshua Camphurst and this beautiful young girl is my daughter, Barbara."

As I reached to shake, Barbara cleared her throat.

Joshua laughed and gestured toward Barbara. "That noise coming out of her ain't some wild animal caught in her throat, it's her signal that I called her *young girl* again instead of *young woman*. I guess by all rights she is a young woman, but I don't want her to grow up."

Barbara stood, glared at her father, then flashed us a smile and shook hands. "Dad told me everything," she said.

The other man didn't bother standing. "Jonathan Karber," he said. "I'm Mr. Wiggins' legal counsel."

As I was wondering what Wiggins needed a lawyer for, Coop said, "Find a seat. This is interesting."

A monitor sat on Coop's desk. The lawyer reached over and inserted a USB drive. "This was sent to Mr. Wiggins. We don't know who sent it."

I looked at Wiggins. "Did you have this when we were there? Why didn't you tell us?"

He shrugged and looked at the lawyer. "I've had it for a long time, but before you came, I didn't know she had passed. When I heard, I remembered her instructions."

The lawyer spoke up. "The instructions were clear, Detective. In the event of Mrs. Camwyck's death he was to contact a lawyer. The letter listed three choices. I was one of them."

Tip gestured to the monitor. "What's on the drive?"

Karber leaned over and hit 'enter' on the keyboard, kicking off a video. A woman's face appeared on the screen.

"My name is Barbara Camwyck. If you're watching this, I'm dead. But this video will help you catch the ones who did this to me. Make sure they don't get away."

The video showed Camwyck adjusting her hair in what looked to be the rearview mirror of a car. Afterward, she applied lipstick, then said, "You are about to watch a video of my meeting with Mrs. Anne Ingle, wife of Bob Ingle. Make no mistake about the nature of this—I am blackmailing her for $7 million. I could have asked for more, but $7 million was enough for me, and the Ingles will barely miss it. If I'm not successful in this venture, they will kill me. Either Mrs. Ingle or Bob, or both of them. I'm sure you'll figure it out."

She smiled, adjusted her blouse, then said, "Okay, I'm going in now."

The rest of the video showed a meeting between Camwyck and Anne Ingle, the obviously hidden camera focused on Anne but with audio from both of them. It was pretty damn incriminating—it showed Camwyck demanding $7 million for her silence, and Ingle agreeing to the terms.

When the meeting was over, Camwyck returned to her car. She had one last statement.

"If you're wondering why I did it this way…why I didn't just let my daughter take her inheritance…it was because I didn't want her growing up in that sick world with Bob Ingle and his friends. But I wanted her to have enough money to help her through life." She closed her eyes and sighed. "I owed her that much."

The lawyer removed the USB. "I hope that's enough for you to charge her," he said.

"Combined with what else we have, it might do it," Tip said. "It's sure as hell enough to arrest her."

"What are you waiting for?" Coop said. "Go put cuffs on that peacock."

Tip shot off a salute. "Yes, ma'am. But first I need a copy of that video."

I turned young Barbara. "I'm sorry about your mother," I said, "But I'm happy it will work out for you DNA will prove you're Ingle's daughter and that should release big money to you."

After we got the copy of the video, we left the office, and had to restrain ourselves to keep from racing down the hall. I couldn't wait to nail that son of a bitch.

CHAPTER 64

CLOSING THE CASE

I didn't drive Tip Denton speed to Ingle's house, but I pushed harder on the pedal than I normally do. We got to Ingle's hotel room in less than 20 minutes.

She seemed surprised to see us.

"More questions?"

"Just a few," Tip said.

"You're not getting away with this," I said. "We've got enough to convict you now."

She laughed. "You have nothing."

"And you want to know the best part?" I said. "You won't get to keep any of the money. When you're convicted all of the money goes to his daughter."

She scrunched her eyebrows. "Bob doesn't have a daughter."

"We know he does," I said.

"What do you *detectives* think you have?"

"You knew about the blackmail that Camwyck had going on. We've got inconsistencies with the blood splatter—and trust me, the medical examiner will work that out. We have an inconsistency with the sequence of the gunshots as reported by you and your maid." I waited for her smile, then I said. "And by the way, your maid—ex-maid—is going to testify that you coerced her into changing her story."

"And don't forget we have you as the anonymous caller who knew too much about the crime scene," Tip said.

She smirked. "I'll say it again. What you have is nothing, detectives. Absolutely nothing."

Tip smiled. He'd been waiting for this. "Do you have a computer here, Mrs. Ingle?"

She wrinkled her brow and looked at him as if he had asked if she had water. "Of course I do. Why?"

"I'd like to show you something," Tip said.

She led us to a laptop sitting on the desk.

Tip inserted the USB drive in the side, and when it came up, he pressed the *play* button.

"My name is Barbara Camwyck. If you're watching this, I'm dead. But this video will help you catch the ones who did this to me. Make sure they don't get away.

"You are about to watch a video of my meeting with Mrs. Anne Ingle, wife of Bob Ingle. Make no mistake about the nature of this—I am blackmailing her for $7 million. I could have asked for more, but $7 million was enough for me, and the Ingles will barely miss it. If I'm not successful in this venture, they will kill me. Either Mrs. Ingle or Bob, or both of them. I'm sure you'll figure it out."

By the time the video finished playing, Anne's face had turned ash gray.

"You can't use that."

I took hold of her arm and then put the cuffs on her, being careful not to be too rough. I didn't want accusations about mistreatment to surface.

"What are you doing? You can't arrest me."

"I believe we can," I said.

"I want to call my lawyer," she said.

"You can do that from the station," Tip said. "In the meantime, enjoy our company. I'm sure you'll find us preferable to your cellmates in prison."

"I'll say it again, you can't arrest me."

Tip tightened the cuffs. "Say it all you want, but you're under arrest for the murder of Robert Ingle, Reginald Chase, Barbara Camwyck, and Patti Richards."

"You're insane!"

"That could be. In fact, some people swear to it, but you're still under arrest. Let's go."

Tip read Ingle her Miranda rights, then put her in a patrol car he had waiting outside and sent her to the station.

"You think it will stick?" I asked.

"By the time Ben gets done with his evidence, and when the jurors see the video, they'll convict her. Any video that starts out with 'If you're watching this, I'm dead.', is going to have impact."

"I guess we closed up another one," I said.

"Like hell!", said Tip. "Julie broke this case. Without her finding the daughter, we'd still be playing with our dicks."

Either way, we better hurry and enjoy the respite. I'm sure we'll have another killer to catch before long."

"Probably," Tip said. "But for now, let's just put another marble in the slot, and count it as a win."

"Sounds good to me," I said, and got in the car.

CHAPTER 65

CONFESSIONS AND RESIGNATIONS

I helped Tip finish the paperwork, then left the station with mixed emotions. The Ingle case had been the one of the toughest cases of my life, a roller coaster of emotions that tore me up and still hadn't stopped. Add Ron's drug problems to the mix, and it was a wonder I wasn't in rehab with him. Which reminded me I had to call. I dialed and got an answer right away.

"Hey, Dad. Are you back?"

Relief settled in when I heard his enthusiastic voice. Despite my optimism, there was an ever-present fear that he might slip up and fall back into drugs. "I'm back. I got in a couple of hours ago, but had to go to the station. We were closing that case."

"The gruesome one, with the chopped up body?"

"Yeah, that one. It's over."

"I've got good news, too."

I brightened up. "Tell me."

"They talked to me today about staying here at the center, but training to be a house manager, like before."

I felt the weight leave my body. "That's great. I couldn't be happier. This is a new start for you, son."

"That's what I like most about it. I can help other people and get a chance to make a real difference in someone's life."

"Seems like we both have something to celebrate. Why don't we go to dinner?"

"I can't tonight, but tomorrow would be great."

"It's a deal. I'll take off early and pick you up after lunch. We'll make a day of it."

"Perfect. And Dad, I know you don't like it, but maybe we can go to church together and say a prayer for Mom."

I teared up. "I'd like that. I really would."

"Okay, see you tomorrow."

I felt so good after talking with him that I took back roads home, taking time to enjoy the change of pace. I kept going over our conversation. As I contemplated what he said about me not liking church I realized I might have been depriving him of more than my love since his mother died. She had always taken him to church on Sundays. That stopped when she died.

I passed a church, St. Edwards, and wondered if it was fate. I checked my mirror, did a quick U-turn, and headed back. As fortune would have it, today was Tuesday and they had confessions starting at six-thirty. I looked at my watch—only half an hour to go. Redemption was right around the corner.

What the hell. My new life has to start somewhere.

For twenty minutes I flip-flopped between wanting to run out of there and go home, then back to figuring out how to confess so many years of sin. Right at six-thirty a priest entered one of the confessionals. Nobody was in line, so I mustered the courage and walked through those curtains of death. It felt like I was walking into hell.

In the few seconds it took for the priest to slide the confessional door open, my palms started sweating, my feet and legs twitched, and my gut ached. I felt like a little kid again, the same one who was afraid to tell the priest about the lies I'd told and the times I disobeyed my parents.

The sins I had to confess now were a little worse. I prayed that the good father had not made dinner plans. He might be late.

The priest said something, which I missed. It was my turn now. Despite how long it had been since I'd been in a confessional, the proper words came right back to me. "Forgive me, Father, for I have sinned. It has been…twenty-seven years since my last confession."

"You must have something big to tell, my son."

I almost laughed. At least the guy had a sense of humor, though I was about to put that to the test. "It's big, Father. I'm not going to bother with the little stuff; the only one that's really important is that I killed someone. Actually three people."

After I said it, I sighed so loud that I know he heard.

A silent period followed before he spoke. "When you did this were you defending yourself, or your family, or—"

"No, Father. This was cold-blooded murder."

There was a long hesitation, longer than before. "Why did you do this?"

"I'm a cop. And these were drug dealers. They killed my partner and God knows how many other people. I'm not making excuses. I know it was wrong, it's just…I don't know."

"Why are you here?"

It was my turn to be silent, then, "I don't know."

That statement led to a conversation that lasted a half an hour or more. We got into far more than I intended to about my feelings on the church and religion in general but, I have to admit, when I came out of there and knelt in that pew to start my penance I felt a thousand pounds lighter. I felt like a good person. A *clean* one.

I thanked God for giving me the strength to come here, then I said a few of the prayers the priest gave me for penance. The rest I'd have to do on the installment plan. This wasn't a "three Hail Mary's and two Our Father's" type penance.

I was oddly calm on the drive home even though I faced an even tougher decision. The priest told me for complete absolution I'd have to turn myself in. That meant turning in the badge, the gun, and probably my life, just when I was getting it back. *Was it worth it?* That's what I had to decide.

I picked up a burger near the house, then made coffee to help me mull this over. When my eyes closed for sleep I was still undecided.

I took a shower in the morning, packed my gun and badge, and put them in a box before heading to the station. I planned to see Coop and bring this era of my life to an end. Surprisingly, I felt a serenity that I hadn't known in…forever.

As I drove down I-45 the phone rang. It was Tip. I ignored it, but a few minutes later it rang again. I let it ring, and focused on how I would tell Coop. Then I heard sirens blaring behind me. I looked in the rearview mirror and saw it was Tip. I was still laughing when I pulled to the shoulder of the freeway. The phone rang again just as he pulled in behind me.

"What the hell do you want, Tip?"

"Let's get something to eat," he said.

Before I could say no, he started in on me.

"There's a Cracker Barrel about two exits south of here. Let's go."

We grabbed a table near the back, got coffee, and ordered breakfast from a waitress named Marcy. Tip always looked at their name tags, and he never seemed to forget a name. He was usually chipper in the morning, but seemed more so today.

"What're you in such a good mood about?" I asked.

"We closed our case. It's a new day. What's not to like about it? We got a bad person off the street," Tip said.

"Not us," I said. "We didn't do shit." I downed my coffee and signaled for more. "All we've ended up with were two dead prostitutes, a dead businessman, and his bodyguard."

Tip looked out the window for a few seconds, then he turned to me. "I'm not saying Anne didn't do wrong, but we both know Camwyck and Richards were doing a lot more than spreading their legs. I don't give two shits about that part, but the blackmail and—"

"She didn't have the right to decide," I said.

"You blame her? After what they did to so many people?"

I poured creamer into my coffee and set the cup down hard. Then I picked up the water and took a sip.

"Well?" Tip asked.

"I don't know."

"What would *you* do faced with the same situation?"

The waitress brought our food. "Anything else?"

"Not now," Tip said, "But keep checking on him, Marcy. He's a needy man."

She laughed and headed to another table.

"Well?" Tip asked again.

"I'd do…something. Find some way to bring them to justice."

Tip bit into his bagel. When he finished chewing, he said, "I talked to Chicky."

I tried not to show emotions, but I know I gulped, and I'm sure my expression showed my surprise. "What's Chicky got to do with anything?"

"He's got nothing to do with *this* case, but you know what I'm talking about."

I looked to the side, signaled Marcy for more coffee.

She returned with a smile on her face. "I guess you're thirsty today. Or do you just need waking up?"

I smiled back at her. "Waking up is more like it."

"Where's your gun?" Tip asked, after she left.

"In the car."

"What's it doing in the car?"

Tip had a way of pressing me that I didn't like. "I left it in the fuckin' car. Okay?"

"Leaving a gun in a car is a dangerous thing to do. But getting back to our discussion, who's to say what's wrong?"

"People can't play God. Anne was wrong."

"I wasn't talking about her," Tip said, and gave me one of his hard looks.

I braced my palms against the table and pushed back a little. It was time to cut through the shit. "Are you talking about Rico?"

Tip pushed his plate aside and leaned he elbows on the edge of the table. "We both know Rico was guilty. Didn't need a jury for that."

I said nothing, so Tip did. "You know how many people Rico killed?"

"It doesn't matter, Tip, and you know it." I looked out the window so I didn't have to face him.

Tip looked up when another waitress walked by. "Hey, darlin', can you ask Marcy to get me some hot tea please?"

"I'll get it," she said. "Be right back."

Tip looked me square in the eyes. "You said it doesn't matter. What doesn't matter?"

"People can't take the law into their own hands," I said.

"Gino, I'm sure there's an argument in there somewhere, and I know you like to argue, but I'm too damn tired for it. I don't know what you had planned with your gun in the car, but I'm guessing your badge is there too. So here's what you're gonna do." He leaned partway across the table, got real close, and then he whispered. "You're gonna get in your car and put your goddamn gun back where it belongs, and then we're gonna go catch us some bad guys."

What Tip said felt good, but I was determined to do what I had to do. "I can't do it, Tip."

"You *can* do it. And you're gonna do it, or I'll kick your ass."

The waitress brought Tip his tea and hurried off. I was grateful for the interruption, as it gave me time to think. I wasn't sure what game Tip was playing, or *if* he was playing, but I decided to go along with it. "You're okay with this?"

"I'm never okay with breaking the law, but Rico's where he belongs. And I'm gonna need help finding the Ranger—in case you forgot, that's the son of a bitch who killed my mother." The left side of his face wrinkled up and he smiled. "And you can bet your last dick I'm gonna' get him."

"My last dick?" I smiled. "If you're that sure about things, I might have to go along with you."

We both laughed, but I stopped before I wanted to. "Tip, I'm going to see Coop. I'm gonna' tell her what happened."

Tip shook his head. "Don't do it."

I stood and tossed a twenty on the table. "I've got to. I'll let you know how it goes—if she doesn't put me in cuffs."

Tip stuffed the money in my shirt pocket and threw two twenties on the table. "Call me," he said, and we walked out of there.

It didn't take me long to get to the station, but I thought about turning around a dozen times, and I sat in the car for ten minutes after parking. Finally, I mustered the balls to do what had to be done, and I got out, walked in, and headed to Coop's office.

"Good morning, Cindy."

"You here to see the captain?"

"If she's in."

"I think she's busy, but—"

"It's really important, Cindy. If you can get me a few minutes."

She glanced at the box in my hand, and must have noticed the lack of a gun on my hip. She looked at the calendar on her desk and smiled. "Okay. We can do that." She got on the intercom and announced me, then indicated I should go in.

Coop was reading the paper when I entered, her glasses perilously close to the end of her nose. "Good morning, Gino. What problem do you bring me?"

"A big problem, Captain." I placed the box on her desk, took out the badge and gun and set them in front of her, then I sat down.

She looked at me with her mean glare. "What the *hell* do you think you're doing?"

"I'd like to spend time with my son. Maybe I can make some things up to him."

"That's a nice plan, and a wonderful idea. Take a week off. Hell, take two weeks off, but then get your ass back here and solve some cases."

I shook my head. "I'm done with it, Captain. I've made up my mind."

"You can't leave me with that lunatic partner of yours without a leash."

I laughed, feeling her pain. "You'll find somebody else."

She was silent for a minute, then pushed the gun and badge aside and tossed the box onto the floor. "Now tell me the real reason for this nonsense."

I breathed deeply, chewed on the inside of my lip, squeezed the chair, then found all the courage I could and looked into her eyes, those same eyes that had meted out justice for a lot of years. "Coop, when I'm done talking you're not gonna like me. I've done some terrible things in my life. Things I'm not—"

She held up her hands. "Hold on, Cataldi. Before you say anything else, does this have anything to do with Rico Moreno?"

I stared back at her, stunned, and nodded.

"Then shut-up. Do you hear me, shut *the hell* up. Now!"

I sat and said nothing.

She got up and paced. "We are the fourth biggest city in the country. We need every good cop we can find. I'm not about to let one of my best get away. So, if you think you can still follow orders…*never* bring up the name of Rico Moreno again."

I got that good, clean feeling in me again. "Why are you doing this?"

She looked at me with the softest eyes I'd ever seen. I didn't know her eyes could even show that emotion. "Forget the fact that Rico Moreno was a drug-dealing, scum-sucking son of a bitch. Forget the fact that his drugs killed God knows how many people and ruined thousands of lives. And forget that he would have continued for a long time because we couldn't bring him in."

Coop walked over and gave me a hug. "I'm doing this because one time a cop thought I was in trouble and he offered to help."

I hugged her back. "Thanks, Gladys."

"Now, more orders. Take two weeks off, have a good time with your son, figure out what you need to do to get straight, then, if you still want to be a cop, get your ass back here and help me control Tip Denton. That cowboy gives me ulcers."

I couldn't control the grin. "Yes, ma'am. Is that all?"

"No. Don't *ever* call me Gladys again."

I kissed her on the cheek. "You're the best, Coop. I owe you big time."

"Tell Ron I said hi."

"I will, and I'll see you in two weeks."

CHAPTER 66

GRAVES AND REUNIONS

Never had I felt better in my life, and certainly not since before Mary died. It was a feeling that I wanted to wake up with every day. I vowed to never do anything that would compromise that. I drove slowly on my way to pick up Ron, appreciating life in general and the mild day we were having in particular. He was ready when I pulled up, and I could tell before he even got in the car he was in a great mood.

"Hey, Dad." He reached over and gave me a hug, then buckled his seat belt. This was definitely not the kid who went into rehab a few months ago.

"Where to first?"

"I thought we'd go to Mom's grave. I need to show her I'm all right now." That choked me up. "I'm sure she knows."

"Me too," he said. "But I still want to show her."

We stopped and got her favorite flowers—white and peach roses—then drove to the cemetery. I set the flowers in front of her headstone. We knelt and said a few prayers.

Then I spoke to her. "Mary, you know I don't like to express myself in front of other people, not even family. I never could with anyone but you, and even that was tough. But I'm here to try, like you always asked. Ron's with me." I stopped, trying not to cry. "We've both been hurting, baby. Real bad. Ron got in trouble for a while." I reached over and put my arm around his shoulder. "But he came back better than ever. It was you who did it for him. You somehow left enough love in this nasty world to keep him going. Heck, you might have even left enough for us to share and help each other out. I hope you did."

Ron knelt and blessed himself. "Hey, Mom. It's me. It's been a long time since I've been here sober. But you can count on me now. I'm all right and I'm planning on staying that way." He grabbed my hand and squeezed it. "And what Dad said, about you leaving enough love for both of us—you did. And don't worry, I'll take care of this old fart."

I closed my eyes and said a final prayer, then I felt Ron hug me. I heard, and felt, him crying. "I love you, Dad."

"I love you too, Ron. More than you know."

We said our goodbyes to Mary, promising to be back at Christmas.

"Toss the keys, old timer. I'm driving," Ron said.

"Where are we going?"

"I'm taking you to dinner."

"I'm game. Let's go."

As we exited the cemetery, I felt peace for the first time in a long, long while.

Thanks, God.

<<<<>>>

If you enjoyed this book (and I don't know how you wouldn't), check out my other books at all online retailers.

You Can Also Sign Up for the Mailing List to Get Free Offers and Special Deals.

http://eepurl.com/kS-IX

Authors live and die on recommendations and reviews, so if you liked the book, please tell someone about it. And if you have a spare moment, I'd love for you to post a review on Amazon or Goodreads, or Apple or B&N.

If you want to keep up with all of the books, go to my website.

http://www.giacomogiammatteo.com/

OTHER BOOKS COMING SOON

Fiction

Promises Kept—The Story of Number Two (A Novella) (being proofread)

Lisa Benz was brilliant, street smart, and full of potential. She could have had any job she wanted, but she decided to join the police force. She didn't join to carry on a family tradition, or to fulfill a lifelong dream. She didn't join to impress anyone or make her mark on society.

She joined for one reason only—a promise she made to a young girl.

For those of you who read Necessary Decisions, this is a novella about Number Two.

A Promise of Vengeance (Fantasy)

My first fantasy, and the first book in a four-book series—the Rules of Vengeance. (Three are already written and the fourth is being outlined.)

Murder Is Invisible ### (going through editing)

Frankie and Nicky are back.

Non-Fiction

- No Mistakes Grammar, Volume I, Misused Words. (being proofread)
- No Mistakes Grammar, Volume II, Misused Words for Business (being proofread)
- No Mistakes Grammar, Volume III, More Misused Words. (being proofread)
- No Mistakes Writing, Writing Shortcuts (being proofread)
- Uneducated—Thirty-Seven People Who Redefined the Definition of Education (being proofread)

- Whiskers and Bear—Volume I of the Life on the Farm Series (sent to editor)

Children's Books

- No Mistakes Grammar for Kids, Volume I—Much and Many (Sent to editor)
- No Mistakes Grammar for Kids, Volume II—Lie and Lay (Sent to editor)
- No Mistakes Grammar for Kids, Volume III—Then and Than (Sent to editor)
- Shinobi Goes to School—Life on the Farm for kids. (working on illustrations)

Get on the mailing list and you'll be sure to be notified of release dates and sales. Mailing list

ACKNOWLEDGMENTS

It's been a long time since I published a book, and even a longer time since I wrote one. Early last year, I had 2 heart attacks and 2 stokes which left me damn near dead. I couldn't move—literally.

I was communicating with people by blinking my eyes to indicate yes or no. Later I progressed to a letter chart. I couldn't eat, and had to survive on nourishment through a tube peg.

That was all before a few phenomenal people offered their help. Mithu and Tran, my physical and occupational therapist, worked relentlessly to improve my condition. And also Faustin and Chelsea who worked just as hard to make me improve.

As a result, I am now talking (not as good as before, but talking), and using a walker to get around (not far, but after four months in the hospital I couldn't even use the wheelchair), and most importantly, typing. The typing is slow, but it's improving.

I, of course, have my magnificent wife to thank also, but fortunately I get to tell her that all the time. For Tran and Mithu (and the people who assisted her, Faustin and Chelsea) I give my eternal gratitude.

For my wife, Mikki, I give my eternal love.

About the Author

Giacomo (Jim) Giammatteo is a headhunter and has done retained searches in the medical device/ diagnostics & biotech/pharma industries for 30 years. He successfully completed more than 500 assignments, and he evaluated, edited, and wrote thousands of résumés. Giacomo has also interviewed and done reference checks on more than 1,000 candidates.

As if that wasn't enough to put him into a small room with padded walls, Giacomo is also a bestselling author of several mystery/suspense novels, including: Murder Takes Time, Murder Has Consequences, and Murder Takes Patience in the Friendship & Honor series; and A Bullet For Carlos, Finding Family, and A Bullet From Dominic in the Blood Flows South series. Other fiction includes Necessary Decisions, Old Wounds, and Promises Kept (coming soon), in the Redemption Series.

His non-fiction work includes No Mistakes Resumes, Book I of No Mistakes Careers, as well as book II—No Mistakes Interviews.

He has also written the No Mistakes Grammar Series, No Mistakes Writing, No Mistakes Publishing, No Mistakes Grammar for Kids, and How to Select a Self-publishing Service, Uneducated, and the Life on the Farm Series for both kids and adults. Giacomo's first fantasy series—the Rules of Vengeance—is coming soon.

In his spare time, Giacomo and his wife run an animal sanctuary with 45 loving "friends."

www.ingramcontent.com/pod-product-compliance
Lightning Source LLC
Chambersburg PA
CBHW032202180726
48284CB00001B/154